Holiday Vibes

Over The Top Love Book Two

Sarah Brenton

Contents

Content Note

While my books are not centered on trauma, traumatic events sometimes inform a character's past. In the case of Holiday Vibes, Nic's parents died (off-page) in a car crash about a decade before the events of the book. There is also an on-page concussion and a overnight hospital stay, and as always, explicit sex and strong language. For more information, please visit www.sarahbrento n.com/books. Please take care of yourself. xx

To everyone who feels like they're never enough.

Chapter One

Jessie

December Nineteenth

"I'm a candy cane slut and it's my time to shine," I whisper as I hit the end of the family group chat. There's no mention, no suggestion, no hint *he's* going to be here.

From my rental car parked at the end of the long drive, my parents' craftsman-style house is beautiful, glowing like a Thomas Kinkade painting in the silvery-blue world of moonlit snow. Vintage lights are strung along the windows. Smaller lights twinkle through the bare branches of a couple of trees. And inside a warm welcome awaits me, along with hot chocolate laced with Bailey's, topped with whipped cream, and I want it bad.

Dominic Fontana won't be here losing at a board game or helping my mom in the kitchen or someone would have said something in the group chat. He hasn't been here for the last four Christmases, so why should this year be different?

Except he's my twin brother's best friend, and he's recently divorced, so where else would he be, with no other family to claim him? There's a high chance Mr. Big Sexy Movie Star *is* inside and I don't want to see him again. Ever.

Cold is creeping into my rental. I'm not going to scour the last four weeks of the family group chat for clues again, though I'm tempted. No, I'm going to march inside and spend the next two weeks enjoying my favorite time of year with the people I love, because no way in hell is Nic here.

As soon as I get out of my rental car.

Which I'm totally going to do. Any second now.

Oh, god, I'm stalling hard.

This is annoying. It's been five years since the last time I saw Nic and while I'm still a hot mess, I don't *look* like a hot mess. Tonight, I'm armored with my impractical but sexy-as-hell boots and my favorite lipstick in "heartless red". Battle-ready.

And honestly, apart from potential death by humiliation, a little low-intensity warfare would hardly ruin two weeks of booze and food. He's probably not even here, and I'm freezing my ass off for nothing.

The pull of a hot drink wins. I climb out of my car, retrieve my suitcase from the back—with a grunt because I've overpacked it—and start up the driveway.

In the dark, with only the lights of the house, I don't see the patch of ice.

One foot shoots forward, and the other follows. Pain blossoms across the side of my ass and for the first time in months, I'm on my back with my feet in the air, and not under the circumstances I prefer.

I scramble to my knees and scan the windows in case someone saw my fall. Mercifully, there are no witnesses.

Grabbing my suitcase, I slowly climb to my feet, wobbling, sliding each foot forward inch by inch until I can reach the other side of the ice. My ass hurts, but since no one saw me fall, I'm going to pretend this never happened. Because I'm an adult and my shit is together.

The effort it takes to lug my suitcase up the first step nearly puts me back on my ass. I've packed everything I need to ensure I won't look like a swamp hag at any point over the next two weeks. I'm not repeating the mistakes I made five years ago. I've also crammed this beast with gifts and vibrators.

Those have nothing to do with Nic. I do graphic design and social media for a family-owned sex toy company called Sploosh! and as a perk, I get more freebies than I can use, which I happily off-load onto various family members.

Okay, I also packed half a dozen of my favorites, in case I need them. Again, nothing to do with Nic and everything to do with a sudden and unfortunate lack of men worth my time.

A couple more heaves and grunts, and I make it up to the wreath-laden door. The warm smell of apple, cinnamon, and cloves engulfs me when I push it open and I suck it into my lungs, sighing in contentment. My mother's kitchen is the birthplace of good aromas, but something about the holidays makes everything deeper. Better.

My mother is none other than the legendary Celia Foley, an on-air institution who single-handedly launched the Home Cooking Channel with the first of her many successful cooking shows. If food is her first calling, Christmas is her second and her ability to make the magic of the season last beyond childhood is nothing short of miraculous. Never mind that our family only steps foot in church for funerals or weddings, this is our holiday. It is food and drink and family.

'Family' sometimes being loosely defined.

I listen to the voices and laughter floating above the soft holiday music. I don't hear Nic and I'm pretty sure I can identify all the jackets in the foyer as belonging to various family members here for game night. Everything is reassuringly the same as it is every holiday, from the banister ringed in deep green garland to the massive wreath with gold and red baubles hanging on the wall.

He's not here. All that worry, for nothing.

I let out a huge sigh of relief, and when I draw my next breath, everything smells more Christmassy, more magical. I feel joyful and triumphant.

I leave my coat and scarf on a hook, abandoning my suitcase by the stairs, and head down the hallway to say a quick hello on my way to the booze.

My father is in his favorite chair by the fire, his nose in a book, oblivious to the noisy room around him. My sister Amanda, who's ten years older than me, is playing Scrabble with her gorgeous wife Hazel, my cousin Lauren, and Aunt Kimberly. A group of kids go down in a tangle of limbs at a game of Twister and a roar goes up from the dining room, where a card game is in progress.

Lauren sees me first, squealing even though we saw each other two days ago. We work together at Sploosh! and spend a lot of time hanging out and gossiping about family dramas—namely our cousin Ashley, who never comes to Christmas and has gotten herself on a reality TV show. I used to babysit Lauren when she was little. Now she babysits me when we go clubbing, so I don't make bad choices. It's the circle of life, the young taking care of the old. Nature is beautiful like that.

Games are momentarily forgotten as I'm swallowed into a sea of hugs, everyone talking without waiting for anyone else. The commotion manages to pull my father from his book long enough for a quick kiss on the cheek as he asks me about the drive.

My twin's voice rises above the din, loud and booming, from the direction of the kitchen. To find Timbo, follow the noise.

I haven't seen him since before the accident. The one that nearly killed him and cost him his career as a stunt performer. The one my family didn't tell me about for days after it happened because they didn't want to 'ruin' my holiday in Italy.

That accident.

I offered to fly out to LA to look after him, but he didn't need me or even want me there. Then he didn't come home for Thanksgiving, spending it in California with some girlfriend.

Which, okay, it hurt. A lot. I get it, we aren't that close anymore. We haven't been close since we were fourteen and Nic moved in across the street, replacing me as Timothy's best friend. But Timothy's accident scared the hell out of me, and I want us to get back to how things used to be. This holiday—the two weeks out of the year my entire family gets together under one roof—is the perfect opportunity. Nic's absence is going to make this easier.

Extricating myself from everyone, I head toward the kitchen and the sound of Timothy's voice. Doesn't matter what story he's telling—they're all the same. Huge explosions. Massive jumps. Impressive falls. Timbo the handsome stuntman, no fears. Certain death. A hot doctor or nurse if this is about one of the times he broke something or needed stitches.

I round the doorway into the kitchen and slam hard into someone headed out.

Dominic Fontana grabs my arms, stopping me from falling as my holiday cheer goes up like a Yule Log.

"You."

I might have growled that.

He stares at me with those damned silver-gray eyes of his. They're cold and aloof because he's cold and aloof. His lips press together in displeasure, and same, buddy.

He hasn't changed. His long dark lashes are proof the universe is an asshole, as are those cheekbones. Hair a shade lighter than black sets off the silvery undertones of his flawless porcelain skin and his resting dick face manages to come across as a broody smolder.

He's ruined pretty men for me.

"Jessie," he says in a rumble, barely moving those lips.

He glares, and I glare back. It's a battle of the wills I'm not losing.

Timothy coughs. Nic looks first, so I win.

My brother points up.

Nic and I look up.

Oh, hell no.

Mistletoe.

We shove at each other in our haste to escape and once again, I end up on my ass.

"Fuckstick," I mutter, getting to my feet, but Nic's long gone.

My brother is smirking at me. I'm about to march over and give him hell when my mother, kitchen goddess, queen of cookbooks and TV shows alike, sails out of the butler's pantry, crushing me into a hug that's three parts cinnamon, one part Dior.

She pulls back and squeezes my arms. "You made it. I was starting to worry."

"Mom, take the mistletoe down. Please."

"Oh, sweetie." Her light brown eyes search my face first, then look about the kitchen, noticing the sudden absence. Her smile widens. "Nic wouldn't kiss you?"

Neither mistletoe nor spinning bottles could make that happen.

Timothy snorts. "Jessie wishes he would."

My stomach swoops. "I do not."

He shrugs and knocks back his beer, which is more maddening than if he'd tried to argue with me.

My mother laughs on her way back to the butler's pantry. "Maybe next time, hon."

"I'll kill him. Bludgeon him to death with a dildo from the factory reject pile." No way am I wasting a perfectly good sex toy on him.

Timothy wraps me in a bone-crushing hug of muscle and cable-knit sweater until I shove him away, reaching to muss his shaggy honey-blonde hair because that stupid head injury nearly took him away from me. A second later, I'm in a headlock.

He has seventeen minutes on me, several inches, and probably seventy pounds. I haven't stood a chance against him since puberty. I slap my hand twice on the counter in surrender, squealing at him to let me go.

Releasing me, he laughs. "Whatever, J."

Timothy never figured out the protective brother role. He'd laugh his ass off if Nic had kissed me. Or he'd make gagging noises. Hopefully, he'd question Nic's state of mind. Or...

Wait, why am I thinking about this?

I elbow my twin. Hard. "What's *he* doing here, anyway? Shouldn't he be off celebrating his divorce by screwing his way through another modeling agency?" I can't judge him because glass houses and all. Except I'm not pulling men hot enough to have a career in modeling, which is wildly unfair. And I haven't had a hookup in months. So I will be judging him. Respectfully.

Timothy laughs. "He's gone through them all."

I grumble under my breath and my brother gives me an obnoxious smile, letting me know he's going to enjoy every minute of my suffering.

And I'm going to have to take it if I'm going to fix my relationship with my twin.

"Be nice," he says mildly. "He's had a rough year."

My first *be nice*. Hell, I should turn this holiday into a drinking game—drink every time someone tells me to *be nice* to Nic. Two drinks if they bring up sleeping with models like that defines a 'rough year.'

Nic is the favorite of everyone in this family, except for me. If they only loved him for being a moderating influence on Timothy—which I used to be—I might be okay with it. But they side with Nic, seem to enjoy his company more than mine, and shower him with attention.

The thing is, Nic hates me as much as I hate him, but no one else sees it. No one tells him to *be nice.* He can insult me and say things that hurt me, and no one blinks. We've never gotten along, and after the shitshow five years ago, we never will.

But, I need these two weeks to fix things with my twin.

"I'll try," I mutter. I'll pretend Nic is somewhere else. Far, far away. The moon, perhaps.

A horde thunders into the kitchen, kids clamoring about pie and ice cream, saving me from what would no doubt be a lecture from my brother on the merits of Nic Fontana. The kids gather around the island, jostling for the best barstools, while the adults file into the room, talking and laughing. Hazel catches Amanda in the doorway for a quick kiss under the mistletoe.

My mother catches the direction of my gaze in passing and stops, pointing. "It stays up."

She would never take it down anyway. The sheer delight she takes in other people's terror at getting caught beneath it is the reason it's there. With only family around tonight, I'm safe, but at the wild Christmas Eve Folly, with my mother's infamous punch flowing, and Nic lurking...

He walks back in on cue, through the dining room to avoid the mistletoe.

My face is on fire, and he hasn't even looked my way. I need a drink.

There's always mulled wine in a slow cooker over the holiday, mugs on the counter. My mug is bright pink, the words *Blow Me, I'm Hot* printed across it. Everyone has a unique mug, from my mother's *Boss B*tch* to Timbo's Christmas T. rex. Nic's *Festive as F*ck* mug is on the counter, pulled from the back of a shelf after four years of gathering dust.

My skin prickles as a phantom breath whispers across the nape of my neck. I can't see him, but I know he's watching me. He always does, trying to unnerve me. It's not going to work.

By the time my mug is full and I turn to glare at him, he's no longer looking at me. His shoulders are tense though. I hate the way his shirt pulls tight on his chest when he reaches back to rub the base of his skull as he pretends to listen to Lauren and Timothy. It's obvious he's pretending. He's a shitty actor.

I take a big drink and spit the wine back into the mug, along with ten thousand incinerated taste buds. *Dammit.*

Nic, of course, saw that. He raises one perfectly thick eyebrow as if to say *good move, genius*. With a hell of a lot more care, I take a sip, extending my middle finger in his direction. He pretends not to notice and looks away.

Two weeks. Why didn't anyone tell me? I could've booked a hotel. In another state.

Okay, that's exactly why no one told me and there wasn't a single mention of Nic in the family group chat.

There's a small chance Nic had similar thoughts. I elbow my way into a spot along the island next to Amanda, accepting the slice of apple blackberry pie from my mother before leaning close to my sister. "Is *he* staying here?"

"Yes." Amanda looks at me pointedly while she sips mulled wine from a floral *This Might Be Wine* mug. The mug is massive but true—it's always wine. "Be nice."

Oh, hey. *Be nice* number two.

"*Here* here?" I prompt. "In this house *here*?"

Amanda rolls her eyes, tucking a strand of light brown hair that's fallen free from her messy mom bun behind her ear. "Yeah. The kids all think it's cool."

I scoff. "The kids also eat their boogers."

"Not since they were three." She protests, but amusement turns up the corners of her mouth.

"Their uncle was a goddamn stunt performer. Why don't they find Timbo cool?" Kids who eat boogers are possibly the only people who would mistake my twin for cool.

Amanda laughs. "They do."

Timothy's talking animatedly at the other end of the island. He's only this excitable when he's about to blow something up. Or leap off the roof. Or jump a car on a snowboard while another car tows him down the street. And he can't do those things anymore.

Early retirement isn't killing him yet. In fact, he looks good. Genuinely happy.

Totally not suspicious at all.

I take a bite of the pie, forgetting about my obnoxious brother and his dick of a best friend. Even on my poor scalded tongue, it's perfect, the pastry buttery and light, the fruit tart and sweet.

My little involuntary moan at the deliciousness of what will be the first of many, many good things stuffed in my mouth over the holidays goes unnoticed by everyone.

Except for Nic, apparently. His eyes are wide and the faintest hint of a blush creeps up his neck.

He scowls at the *'what?'* look I shoot him, tugging at the collar of his expensive shirt before going back to his pie.

Timothy drops a massive paw on Nic's shoulder, whispering in his ear. Whatever he says deepens Nic's scowl.

I smirk.

Until Timothy passes behind me, his voice close to my ear. "I saw that."

Saw what? A glare? Plenty more where that came from.

And yet...watching all my boisterous family talking and laughing, I have to admit Nic's reserved silence adds something to the chaos. A quiet sturdiness in a sea of noise and motion. Now that he's back, I feel how much it had been missing.

Not by me, to be clear. I enjoyed the unbalanced, unhinged pandemonium, and I'll hold my grudge against Nic forever.

Chapter Two

Nic

"Bullshit."

Through some miracle, I bite back my sigh as I pick up the pile of cards on the table. Every goddamn time. How is Jessie doing this? That smug turn of her full red lips has made itself at home under my skin.

It's been five years since I've seen her, but I haven't forgotten the special brand of hell that is being under the same roof as Jessica Foley. She's effervescent, chatting and laughing, but the moment her gaze lands on me, she looks two seconds from violence.

She's never liked me.

The day I moved in, Timothy marched into my parents' house with the movers and declared himself my new best friend. We walked down to the small lake behind his family's house, and Jessie was there, sitting with her back against a tree, a sketchbook in hand. Timothy ignored her, so I ignored her—but I watched her when he wasn't looking. Anytime she caught me, she scowled and went back to her sketches, but there was something before the scowl. Curiosity.

I suppose I was curious too. I'm still fascinated by her. The constant shifts of her expressive face put nearly every thought on display. Worse, she's pretty—dark brows over creamy skin that regularly blushes a deep pink. Long, thick auburn waves caught up in a loose braid. Lush mouth. Her amber eyes shift in color, like a glass of whiskey held in front of a fire. She's captivating.

I stretch my feet under the table, bumping into someone. Jessie, from the sudden look of disgust on her face and the rapidity with which she withdraws her feet. Her whiskey-fire eyes accuse me of purposefully attempting to play footsie with her. I ignore her.

At least she didn't stab my foot with the stiletto on those fuckers. Everyone else is in socks or slippers, but she has to keep the uncomfortable-looking-but-sexy-as-hell boots on.

I'd hoped to sink into the familiarity of a Foley Christmas after four long, lonely years, but everything's different. The only thing that hasn't changed is Jessie's hostility. Not exactly the comfort I'm after.

Timothy's waxing poetically about his girlfriend when before he'd be practically levitating with excitement regaling everyone with a story about jumping an exploding bridge or something ridiculous. Amanda and Hazel have enough energy to be the most cutthroat players at the table, now that Evie's six and Liam ten, and both put themselves to bed an hour ago. Celia's relaxing and watching the card game from her perch on William's ottoman, not rushing around the kitchen. Every so often, she comments on the game.

And I'm losing my mind. I want to undo the dark auburn braid loosely draped over Jessie's shoulder, wrap her hair around my fist, and pull her head back so I can steal a kiss under the mistletoe.

What the hell is wrong with me?

Not that I haven't been attracted to her over the years. Her tits caused me to fail tenth-grade English and I've come so close to kissing that fucking look off her face more times than she could ever know. Self-preservation and a desire to keep my place in her family have always held me back, but tonight I want to strike that match and watch it all burn.

I'm losing it.

Jessie's lush lips press tight as she catches me staring at her again. I hold her gaze long enough to bring an angry flush to her creamy skin. I've won, but I've also lost because now I'm picturing her naked with a full body blush, her eyes closed, a little moan escaping—

Hazel nudges me. It's my turn.

Shit. What number are we on?

Seven, Hazel mouths with a smirk.

"Two sevens." I slap my cards on the pile, my voice a growl from the uncomfortable direction of my thoughts.

"Bullshit." Jessie. Again. The instant my cards hit the table.

I flip the two sevens over and raise one eyebrow at her.

She swears under her breath, angrily picking up the pile.

Serves her right.

Amanda wins the game. Jessie's scorched-earth tactics destroyed both our chances.

Finally, it's the last round of drinks, the final chance to snag a piece of pie for the lucky few who make it to the kitchen in time. Timothy catches my eye and winks.

Shit. It's time.

"Listen up, people." Timothy booms from his spot near the fireplace. The room instantly quiets. It always does for him. The man is enigmatic, able to pull anyone along for the ride. Which is why I'm here and not hiding on a white sand beach.

Timothy cornered me a few months ago, begging me to come home for Christmas. "It's important to me," he'd said. "I want you there when I tell everyone."

What could I say to that?

I'd tried to say no, but he wasn't having it.

"I need you." He'd insisted. "You're a red cape, I'm a matador. Jessie's a bull."

"So, you want her to rip me to shreds instead of you?"

"Precisely."

I didn't need the reminder she doesn't like me, but I was surprised that it hurt. And in the end, I agreed to come home, because as much as I'd rather be anywhere else right now, I love this family, and I've missed them. I want to be here for this and for Timothy, the way he's been here for me.

And I owe it to him. He was injured on set doing a stunt I couldn't get right. My best friend, the man I love like a brother, nearly died because of me. I will do anything for him. Even take the brunt of Jessie's feelings.

He's grinning now, enjoying every second he keeps us waiting. When the anticipation reaches a peak, he claps his hands together. "Mina and I are getting married."

Everyone cheers except Jessie. Her jaw hangs open, her eyes wide. "Is this a joke?"

The room goes silent, everyone turning to Jessie. Her eyes are wide and shocked like she can't believe she said that aloud. Stunned out of her own filter. She's panicking, and when Jessie panics she either runs or doubles down.

"No joke," Timothy says mildly.

She doesn't run. She crosses her arms over her chest. "You've done a lot of stupid shit, Timbo, but marrying a woman you barely know?"

It comes from a place of love, but Jessie's nothing like Timothy. She sees a disaster waiting to happen where he sees happily ever after.

"They've known each other for five years." I remind her, my tone soft. Jessie's glare morphs to hurt.

"Five *years*?" Her brows are drawn together and oh no.

She didn't know?

Shit.

Timothy didn't tell anyone in his family about Mina before his accident out of some ridiculous fear of jinxing himself. But after the accident? His parents met her. Amanda, Hazel, and the kids have met her over video chats. They know the story. So what did he tell Jessie?

Seeing the hurt on her face, I can guess.

He told her nothing beyond that he'd been seeing someone for the last few months. Nothing about Mina caring for him after his accident, living with him. Nothing to indicate this was a serious relationship.

Everyone is still staring at Jessie and her hurt is slowly shifting back to anger as her expression hardens.

I touch Jessie's arm, but lightly so she doesn't stab my sock-clad foot with her murder boot. "You'll like her. Mina's good for him."

Jessie's eyes flare, fire through whiskey. "Are *you* seriously advocating marriage? The man who cheated on his lingerie model ex-wife?"

Timothy was wrong. I'm not a red cape he can use to distract her. He doesn't have the slightest bit of control. Jessie's a storm and he wants me here because I'm a bigger lightning rod than he is.

I've had a lot of practice taking her anger and I can do it better than Timothy. And if she can stay mad at me—which she will because I'm nearby and still breathing—it will keep her and Timothy from fighting all holiday.

My toes curl in at the thought of her stomping my foot for this, but I clear my throat anyway. "This is about your brother," I say in a low voice. "Don't ruin his moment." *Wait until everyone goes home*, I try to tell her with my eyes. *Then murder him.*

I won't be coming to his rescue if she corners him later.

Jessie's face flushes crimson, but instead of firing an insult at me, she presses her lips together.

Shit, if she cries...

"Congratulations baby brother," Amanda says loudly, pulling Timothy into a hug and stealing the spotlight off Jessie. "When's the big day?"

Timothy grins. "Friday. Mina's flying in tomorrow."

What?

Celia's shocked *"Timothy Alexander Foley"* fills the space before the room erupts.

Jessie pushes past me, throwing just enough elbow for me to know it's intentional.

Timothy's riding the high of the chaos he caused, assuring everyone all the arrangements have been made, all anyone has to do is show up. I have to wait for my turn with him while he's mobbed by aunts and uncles and cousins.

Five years ago, that was me. I announced my engagement to Addison and got swamped by slightly more subdued Foleys, but unlike Timothy, I'd been nervous. I hadn't wanted to announce it.

Jessie had looked stunned, similar to tonight.

I shove that memory aside and step up to Timothy, leaning in close. "You should've told Jessie."

Timothy nods like he agrees, which is frustrating as hell. He glances around the room, but Jessie's gone. "Can you make sure she's all right?"

"No." I walk off as he's accosted by his mom.

Jessie won't want to see me. She won't get any comfort from my presence or my words—if I had any to say beyond 'I'm sorry your brother is a real dickhead sometimes.'

I stick around long enough to drink one toast to Timothy and Mina. Considering how my marriage spun out, publicly crashing and burning, I'd rather not be a cloud hanging over his good news anyway. I give Celia a quick peck on the cheek and bid everyone good night. The congratulatory slap on Timothy's back turns into an awkwardly long bear hug, and by the time I escape, I'm wrung out.

Addison dragged me through the tabloids, feeding them gossip about my supposed infidelities while she was busy screwing around. Her betrayal and the subsequent divorce took a toll on me. I'm not ready for a wedding—even Timothy's.

It's not all Addison's fault, if I'm being honest. While I've made bank by doing the Warwick films, those movies are a success despite me, not because of me. I'm sick of critics panning me and late-night comedians joking about my "smolder" being one step below a Derek Zoolander "Blue Steel" look.

I'm currently "taking a break," my publicist citing my divorce and a need for privacy and time to "find myself."

I haven't found shit. I have a career I stumbled into, a house I didn't choose, and people to tell me what to do nearly every hour of the day. I should be grateful—most people who go to LA never make it big and I did it with no talent beyond a camera-ready face—but instead, I'm restless.

At least I have the Foleys. They've always made me feel welcome and loved. Except Jessie.

A massive hard-shelled suitcase sits at the bottom of the stairs. Bright pink and plastered in faded stickers—snark and butterflies—it has to be Jessie's. Since she's having a shit night and it's only going to get worse when Celia or Amanda corner her, I grab the handle and lug it up the stairs.

I'm in pretty good shape from the Warwick movies but Christ this suitcase is heavy. What the hell did she pack in it? Free weights? Is something inside *vibrating*?

A balcony overlooks the great room, and I pause for a moment when I reach the top. There's still noise and bustle below, most of it coming from Timothy.

Cousins, aunts, and uncles mill about and it's all cozy. Homey. My parents' house was empty and dull. They were always busy, always traveling, always chasing success. Pushing me to be like them. I didn't have brothers or sisters to help shoulder the burden. It all came down to me.

I escaped to the Foley house so often that Celia gave me a key and the spare room on the first floor. After the accident that took my parents when I was twenty-four, it became the only place I thought of as home. Being under this roof again feels like a warm hug. It's safe, comforting, and accepting. I need this, not some tropical getaway where I know no one and everyone thinks they know me. I'm glad Timothy talked me into coming home, even if it means facing Jessie.

Leaving the suitcase in front of her door, I head down the hall to Timothy's old room. He claimed the first-floor guest bedroom this year, citing more privacy since Mina's coming tomorrow. She'd changed her flight to attend some fashion event with a designer friend. Probably a good thing, considering the scene with Jessie.

I've never spent much time upstairs. Timothy wasn't the kind of guy who wanted to hang out in his room when he had the whole world outside to explore. I could probably count on one hand the number of times I've been up here.

It's large and comfortable, done up in a creamy shade that sets off the dark wood of the exposed rafters, accented in deep greens. Celia's redecorated since he moved out and nothing of his remains, but the watercolor of the lake hanging over the bed is Jessie's. I don't need to look for her signature. I remember her painting it the summer before we graduated from high school. She accosted me with a paintbrush when I wandered too close. I grabbed her wrist and her eyes went wide, her breath catching. Naturally, I ran away.

Her room is next door to Timothy's, and I've only been in there one time.

Which I'm not going to think about. That wasn't the worst night of my life, but it wasn't far off.

I leave my clothes in a heap on the floor, climbing into bed naked. My hands slip under the cool pillows and I stare at the ceiling, unable to close my eyes.

Unable to kick Jessie out of my head. The only thing that chases away the hurt in her eyes is thinking about her lips closing over that bite of pie. The shape of her breasts under her soft-looking sweater.

It's been too long since I've gotten laid. That's my problem. I stopped trying to screw my way out of how my divorce made me feel, and now I can't stop thinking about how Jessie's red, red lips would look wrapped around my cock.

Beautiful. That's how they'd look.

I reach under the covers and give myself a half-assed stroke. It's electric. I tighten my fist. I haven't fantasized about Jessie since we were teenagers and she was one of a too-large and constantly rotating cast. It doesn't mean anything if in my head I'm peeling her sweater off, licking and sucking on her tits before diving between her legs. Making her beg. Watching her drop to her knees in front of me.

Imagining her hot wet mouth sliding up and down my cock instead of my hand is going to get her out of my system and make the next thirteen days tolerable.

God, she'd be good too. Her lipstick smeared on me, her amber eyes hungry…

I shoot my load in record time, all over my stomach, because I'm too caught up in the image. When the sensation finally ebbs, I let out a shuddering breath and stare blankly at the ceiling for a solid minute.

Shit. That was wrong in so many ways, but wow, was it good.

I reach for the nightstand with my clean hand.

No tissues.

Groaning, I drop back onto the mattress. With Celia insisting on doing my laundry, I can hardly clean myself off with a sock, like some teenager.

A quick shower will do. The bathroom is an en suite, thank god. I get out of bed, walking quickly, cupping the mess on my stomach in case it drips onto the carpet.

I swing the door open, and...fuck.

It's a Jack and Jill bathroom.

Jessie's standing at the sink in her pajamas, toothbrush hanging out of her mouth as she turns, her wide eyes taking me in—all of me, and the state of my stomach—before she turns and bends to spit into the sink. Her shorts ride up higher over her round ass.

My face is on fire. There's no retreating, no showing weakness or she'll win. I flick the shower on and will her to leave.

When I look back, she's leaning against the vanity, amber eyes amused as they drop to my cock. Her head tilts, her eyebrows arching in a silent *Huh, how disappointing*.

My cock isn't the rumored fifteen inches some corners of the internet claim based on a fuzzy image from a movie and I don't look like I do on screen. My muscle definition has faded and I'm not dehydrated to make the veins in my body pop. She's not the first woman I've disappointed by being real.

But Jessie's nipples are hardening through her shirt and a light blush is creeping up her chest.

Maybe...she's not disappointed.

"You're a mess," she says with a *tsk*.

Her lips are stripped of that red, but her smirk is a reminder of the mess I made of them in my imagination, and Christ, suddenly my cock is preparing for round two.

"Lock the goddamn door." The shower is steaming, so I step in, turning my back to her.

"If I knew you were in Timothy's room jerking off, I would have."

I glare at her over my shoulder, but she's turned to rummage through the arsenal of beauty products that have overtaken the vanity. She's not leaving. God, why is she not leaving?

It's a minute before I hear it. She's humming a melody and the moment I recognize it my blood goes cold and my returning arousal dies.

It's a song from *Summer Camp*, a massive box office flop my ex-agent strong-armed me into. I was twenty-two playing the part of a fifteen-year-old in a musical when I could neither sing nor dance. Not even the rest of the cast could redeem that train wreck.

Jessie knows I hate that movie.

I tip my head back in the water, closing my eyes, and resolving to stay in here until she leaves.

There's a tap on the glass.

"I'm sorry," Jessie says with a wince, standing right next to the shower. At least she hasn't pressed her face to the glass.

I'm about to nod, to accept her apology so she'll go away when I notice her hands. Both index fingers pointing down.

"For your dick not living up to the hype." She finishes.

My jaw clenches and it takes everything in me to act like I'm not pissed. "Get out."

Jessie smiles, waves, and saunters away in her short little pajama shorts.

I am in so much trouble.

CHAPTER THREE

Nic

DECEMBER TWENTIETH

MY HEAD IS THICK in the morning, last night's embarrassing encounter with Jessie front and center, refusing to budge even after a predawn three-mile jog in the bracing cold. I dreamed about her last night. All night. We did things that heat my face and distract me enough that the patch of ice at the end of the driveway nearly takes me out on my way back into the house. I shower on autopilot—locking the door—and dress before heading to the kitchen.

"Good morning." Celia chirps, pressing a cup of coffee into my hands.

It's Cookie Day. She's up early to make hundreds of Christmas cookies to give to friends and family. Bags of flour and sugar line one countertop. Butter. Eggs. Everything she'll need for this marathon effort.

"I'll help," I say, heading toward the stack of mixing bowls. I've always spent the better part of Cookie Day helping out. Or I did when I used to come home every year.

Celia steers me toward a stool instead. "Sit. Drink your coffee. Let's talk."

I got in only a few hours before Jessie, so Celia hasn't had the chance to grill me about my feelings. She tried a few times when she was in LA following Timothy's injury, but I managed to escape thanks to early casting calls and her willingness to accept my flimsy excuses.

That willingness is gone. Celia's light brown eyes hold mine until I look away.

"I'm sorry it didn't work out with Addison," she says quietly.

I shrug, because I know she didn't like Addison, and if I'm being honest with myself, in retrospect, I'm glad Addison's out of my life.

"It wasn't your fault," Celia says, her hand coming over the top of mine for a moment.

That's...not entirely true. I tried to be the man Addison wanted me to be. I took her to the hottest parties and the best restaurants, and introduced her to the right people. I played the part of a doting husband in public, and when I begged her for quiet nights at home, she pouted.

I was a disappointment to her after a few months of marriage. Eventually, she became a disappointment to me. I hit my limit; she hit hers. Told me I was worth less than the Warwick action figure.

A lump of fucking plastic.

The reason we made it four years when one should've been enough was down to busy schedules and decent sex. And ignoring the obvious—neither of us wanted each other. We also didn't want to be alone.

Celia drifts back to her bowl and picks up a wooden spoon. "The tabloids are the worst, anything to sell a story. We know you never cheated."

She has firsthand experience with that. There was an incident not long after I moved next door. I don't remember what it was about, but whatever she did to manage it insulated the entire family and her home. Paparazzi never come into her ungated neighborhood. Even for me.

"Jessie knows it too," Celia says. "Last night—"

'Last night' and 'Jessie' conjures a very different memory and I don't want to talk about this. At all. Ever.

Luck is on my side. My phone buzzes in my pocket. "My agent," I say in an apologetic tone, getting to my feet. Thank god for business trips. If my agent were in LA, she'd still be in bed, unable to save me from this conversation. Not that I'm looking forward to the one Denise and I are about to have, but at least it won't involve Jessie.

Celia sighs, dismissing me with a nod. I grab my jacket and head back outside.

Denise is a good person and a great agent, especially considering what little talent I give her to work with. She should be getting ready for the holidays, not trying to save my career. "Did you read the script?" she asks, moving straight from greetings into business.

I take a deep breath. "Yeah."

The studio is shaking things up, bringing in a new director for the next Warwick film, and the new script is a beast. There's talk about hiring an acting coach for me and Denise is concerned they'll break my contract to recast the role.

"And?" she prompts.

And I'm not good enough. I've already signed on to do this movie and it's going to be a disaster. Worse than *Summer Camp*.

The tune Jessie hummed at me last night comes back, along with her smirk. Everything else gets dragged in behind it until I can't think straight.

"I don't want to do it," I say before I can stop myself.

Shit. *Shit*. Those little words have bounced around my head for months and now they're out there. I can't take them back. What is wrong with me? Most actors would kill for this opportunity.

The silence on the other end of the call makes the simple act of breathing into the cold air absurdly loud. I run a hand over my jaw, momentarily blocking the fog of my exhale. What if I quit?

I'd regret it like I regret every decision I've ever made.

Finally, there's a sigh on the line. "Are you sure? The acting coach might help."

Doubtful. All I'll ever be good at is taking off my shirt and staring moodily into the distance. The problem is, I don't care. I don't want to do it anymore.

I don't love the long hours repeating lines or the early mornings in makeup and wardrobe. The thought of eating nothing but baked chicken breast and working out eight hours a day makes me want to break out in hives. Being around Timothy made it all okay, but he's moving back here.

My eyes land on the house across the street. Someone else lives there now, filling it with warmer memories, I hope. My parents were pissed the day I dropped the future they'd lined up for me to follow Timothy to LA.

Had they lived to see me starring in a massive superhero franchise, maybe they would've come around. If a dream or a passion had taken me to LA, it might have reconciled us. They respected ambition. The problem was I didn't have any.

Nothing's changed. I sigh and turn away. Since I brought all this up, I might as well ask the big question. "What happens if I don't want to act anymore?"

Silence again. She has to be adding up the income she'll lose.

I'd be, except I inherited a fortune from my parents and I've earned more from the Warwick movies than I could hope to spend. And Celia forced Addison to sign a prenup, so I didn't lose anything in the divorce outside of my pride and sense of self-worth, or what was left after four years of marriage.

Denise clears her throat. "What do you want to do instead? Write? Direct? Produce?"

"I don't know." I don't think I want to do any of those things. I take one last glance at my parents' old house before I turn my back on it. They'd be disappointed. Hell, I'm disappointed. I have a life most people would love and I waste it moping around and feeling sorry for myself.

"Take the next two weeks and think about what you want, okay?" Denise says softly. "I'll help you in any way I can, but you need to decide."

That's the problem.

"One more thing. Have you completed your submission for the Hollywood Art Show and Auction? Angie asked me to remind you."

Shit. I haven't started. I've attended the auction for the last five years but this is the first time I've been asked to contribute beyond a monetary donation. A handful of celebrities create some kind of art—usually a painting—for people with money to bid on. There's also a showing of art loaned for the night by the rich and famous, dinner, and speeches. It's one of the more entertaining events and the money raised funds art programs across the city.

My submission is due December twenty-eighth. I should've finished it and had my assistant Angie send it in already. "I'll get on it."

Denise makes me swear I'll give some thought to what I want to do about my career and the Warwick movie. The call ends with us wishing each other happy holidays.

I jog up the steps and into the foyer, trying to shake off my mood and the cold, tossing my jacket over the banister before heading into the kitchen and making a beeline for my coffee.

Jessie's up, sitting at the table, doodling on an iPad. She's wearing flowy ribbed pants today and the softest-looking sweater, all in creamy shades. Her hair is in an artfully messy pile on top of her head. I want to find whatever pin is holding it together and pull it out. Leave her undone and flustered because that's how she's making me feel.

Our eyes meet. She looks away but I still catch the mournful look in those deep amber eyes. Celia must have said something to her about last night. I doubt Timothy got a scolding over keeping Jessie in the dark—everyone accepts that he's a wild card—but even if someone scolded him, it would roll off his back.

Nothing rolls off Jessie's back. Ever.

I grab my coffee and stick it into the microwave. The seconds tick slowly by. Celia mixes some dough, softly singing a Christmas song. My back is to Jessie, but I'm uncomfortably aware of her stylus moving over the screen.

She's not drawing me again. She wouldn't.

What if she draws me naked and covered in cum?

The ding of the microwave makes me jump.

Jessie won't draw me naked in front of her mom. I'm pretty sure.

I pull my coffee out, sighing as the warmth from the mug seeps into my cold fingers. Leaning against the counter, I watch Celia bake and Jessie draw and suddenly it feels like the last few years never happened. Except everything inside me is different. Out of place.

Celia pauses behind Jessie. "Ooh, pretty. Print that and I'll put it on the fridge next to your brother's head CT and your sister's family Christmas portrait."

I glance at the fridge to see the portrait. It's a family of four inflatable T. rexes in massive, hideous Christmas sweaters. Cute. I wonder if there's one sitting in the pile of mail Angie left on my kitchen table. Amanda and Hazel always sent me one, but Addison would take it down and stuff it in a drawer, preferring a clean aesthetic unmarred by family or life.

After I won the house in the divorce settlement, I bought hundreds of magnets and plastered them all over my fridge. The rest of the house still looks like Addison's, but I've reclaimed the kitchen. When I get home, I'll hang Amanda's family Christmas portrait.

"Thanks, Mom," Jessie says with a little laugh.

Celia squeezes her shoulder. "You're the Salvador Dali of dicks."

I choke on my coffee and they both turn to look at me. "Went down wrong." I wheeze. *Dicks?*

Jessie's eyes, no longer sad, linger on me after Celia looks away. "It's not a miserable, limp dick draped over a branch. Try again." She says it to her mom, but it feels like a dig at me and my face heats thinking about last night's encounter.

"Monet?" Celia guesses, walking to the sink.

"No, but that would be lovely. Want me to print one to hang in your bathroom?"

"What if you paint me something instead?"

Jessie stiffens, the tips of her ears going red as she bends her head over the iPad, mumbling some excuse.

The silence that follows is uncomfortable. It's like Jessie has sprouted spikes and her mom doesn't want to venture too close. I don't blame her. I think I'll keep my distance too.

Celia puts me to work rolling out some gingerbread. After a while, I relax. Losing myself in the process of baking always soothes me. Or maybe it's the scent of warm cinnamon and spice in the air as Celia pulls trays of cookies out of the oven. Last night drops away. I forget the conversation with my agent. Even Jessie's presence fades into the background—though never completely.

The gentle but earthy tones of this kitchen, the aromas of food, and Celia's warmth have been a soft hug anytime I've needed it. When I'd come over as a kid, sulking over a report card full of Bs and Cs and the inevitable grounding when my parents came home, she would sit me down with a simple task, like peeling potatoes or kneading dough. My parents didn't have time to cook, let alone teach me, so it was a novelty. Celia never got mad or upset over any mistake

I made. A small laugh with a 'here, I'll show you' was the closest thing to a scold I'd ever gotten from her, and she was always quick to praise.

I think she needed those days as badly as I did. With her husband always busy or with his nose in a book, Amanda away from home, and Timothy and Jessie uninterested in cooking and baking, I think she was lonely too.

Retreating to my kitchen has become my stress response. Every time a movie flops or a critic ridicules me, I spend hours baking. It's not the same as being here though.

"Back in a few minutes, kids." Celia announces, untying her apron and leaving it over the back of a chair.

Jessie ignores me. I should let it go, but I can't forget about her Dali dick comment, so I brush the flour off my hands and walk over to sneak a look.

Jesus. She is drawing dicks. A sketch of a penis, complete with hairy balls, stands proud amid a city skyline straight from the '80s.

"You need a new hobby," I tell her.

She adds curly hair to one of the balls. "It's for work."

I snort. "That's not going to make it into the Louvre."

Jessie taps the screen. The dick disappears, replaced by a sleek sex toy. "I work for a sex toy company, asshole."

Sex toys.

This might be my nightmare. I don't want to think about Jessie and sex toys. I don't want to picture her lying alone in her bed, her cheeks flushed, her lips parted in pleasure.

I retreat to the safety of the island and Celia's old-fashioned cookie cutters and clear my throat. "So I need to make some art for this charity auction, and—"

"I'm not doing your homework for you, Nic," she says dryly.

Dammit. "Got any old paints I could use?"

She shrugs. "I don't know. Ask Mom."

She doesn't know? Jessie always has paints somewhere, brushes too. And those notebooks full of paper thick enough to handle her watercolors.

She refused to paint something for her mom a few minutes ago. I'd expect her to refuse to help me out of spite, but to turn down her mom?

It clicks together in my head. "You don't paint anymore."

"I don't have time," she says in a haughty tone.

"Too busy testing out the vibrators?" Dammit, why did I say that?

Jessie turns around and smirks at me. "I'm locking the door, Nic. You'll never know."

A timer saves me and I turn to take a tray of cookies out and put another in. Hopefully, the heat of the oven will explain my suddenly red face. Explaining my thickening cock is going to be impossible.

Thankfully, she's silent while I cut out gingerbread people and snowflakes. We've just exchanged more words in two minutes than we have in ten years. It's unsettling. I'm gathering the scraps of dough when she pushes her chair back, turning to face me, brows furrowed with worry.

"What's Mina like?"

I stare at her for a moment, surprised she's asking me. "She's careful. Kind. Understanding," I say, lightly kneading the dough back together. I want to add scary as fuck, but that's not going to help anything. "She doesn't put up with bullshit. Especially Timothy's. They're good together."

Jessie bites her lip. I want to bite it.

"You don't think this is weird?" she asks after a moment.

I reach for the rolling pin, refusing to look at her. "Have you met your brother?"

"Weird for him." She amends.

I close my eyes for a moment. I am a lightning rod. I don't want to be a lightning rod.

When I open my eyes, I keep them on my dough. I can't see the hurt in her eyes again because I'll want to make it go away and I'll only make it worse. "Let it go, Jessie. He loves her and you don't want to do this with him. Not at Christmas, not before his wedding."

I'm concentrating on rolling the dough evenly when she gets to her feet with a huff and walks out, the tread of her socks angry but muffled on the hardwood floors.

Chapter Four

Jessie

Technically speaking, I'm not supposed to be working over the holidays, but Nic's words in the kitchen have me wound up and I need the outlet. An hour later and I have an entire new Valentine's Day campaign for our top three bestselling products and I'm still irritated.

Who cares if Nic thinks I'm a bad person?

Not me.

He went downstairs with Timothy twenty minutes ago and I hate that I noticed.

My boss's number flicks across my phone screen. Like she can sense I'm working when I shouldn't be. After a quick check to make sure my niece and nephew aren't in the room, I accept the call with a bright and cheery "Merry Dickmas!"

My dad doesn't look up from his book.

There's a long moment of silence before my boss cracks up. "I hope the season brings you bountiful blessings," she says finally.

"Me too," I say with a dramatic sigh, throwing myself across the couch. "It's been a while since I've had my stocking stuffed." Stupid sex drought.

Elle laughs. "Well, I have a Christmas present for you. I had a little get-together at my place last night, just a few close friends—"

No such thing exists for Elle. She crammed at least one hundred people into her swanky apartment.

"—and Gretchen Torres from Midnights admired your sketch—"

"Doodle." I correct, but my blood goes cold at the mention of Midnights. It's a small but prestigious art gallery. I never submitted my paintings to them, but when Gretchen Torres was at Torres and Strauss, she rejected three, politely informing me I lacked that special something they were looking for in a watercolor.

Elle carries on, ignoring my interruption. "—of the hand clench, so I showed her last week's sketch."

Shit.

"You showed it to her." A gallery owner who knows her shit about art, and Elle showed her my fucking gel pen doodle. Could this week get any worse?

If I don't doodle through meetings, I get bored and clock out. Elle provides me with paper and various types of pens. Last week, in glittery neon pink and purple, I doodled a woman's face, contorted with pleasure. It felt appropriate for a meeting about the launch of a new line of clitoral stimulators. Elle wanted it, so I gave it to her instead of dropping it into the recycling on my way out of the room.

"She wants to talk to you about commissioning a few pieces. But in a medium other than gel pen. I mentioned you're skilled with watercolors and she was intrigued."

"No." I can't hold in the groan.

"I told her I'd speak to you first, give you a chance to think about it, see if you had the time."

"I'm not doing it," I say, then lob the only thing I can think of at her to change the subject. "Timothy's getting married."

Elle lets out a delighted squeal. "I'm so happy for him!"

Timothy and Elle dated for a few years, and when I needed a job, he called her up. They've always been on good terms, so I'm not surprised she's excited.

Elle doesn't get a chance to quiz me—one of her kids urgently needs her so she ends the call asking me to think about the commission.

I already have and my answer is no.

This holiday is not going how I planned.

Last night, though—that was a gift. The image of Nic's horror-struck face is going to stay with me forever.

So is the image of his body.

Life's not fair. Even covered in spunk with a flagging erection he's the hottest man I've ever seen naked.

It would be a lie to say I didn't spend a sizable portion of last night and this morning thinking about that dick—and the thing between his legs.

Which makes me want to squirt lemon juice in my eyes and book an appointment with a therapist because Nic Fontana should not be having this effect on me.

This new problem with Nic will go away the longer I'm around him—his personality guarantees my body's foolish attraction will wither and die—but this thing with my brother isn't going anywhere.

I need to apologize. I was an asshole last night. He's leaving soon to pick up his fiancée from the airport. I won't get another chance like this.

With a sigh, I drop my tablet and stylus on the coffee table and head downstairs.

When Timothy landed his first major job, he had our parents' basement finished as a gift—a man cave for our father, who seldom sets foot in it. But our parents kept it, I suspect because it keeps Timothy out of trouble whenever he visits.

Nic spots me first, going rigid, cue stick in hand.

"I need to talk to Timothy," I say pointedly.

The look Nic exchanges with my brother gets right under my skin. They have this whole separate language they developed as boys. Like Timothy and I had when we were little but different. This one is closed off to me.

Nic turns to put his cue stick away. "I should get back to the kitchen."

We watch him disappear up the stairs, and when Timothy turns my way, his smile is gone.

I lean against the pool table, fingers smoothing over the felt edge. "I'm sorry I ruined your announcement last night."

"You didn't ruin it," he says, taking a quick shot and knocking a couple of striped balls into a pocket.

I watch as he lines up another shot and sinks a few more balls. "You never told me about her," I say. He's my twin. He's been in love for five years and I didn't have a clue.

Timothy gives me a look, but it's in that language he shares with Nic and I don't know what it means. "Do you tell me about your unrequited crushes?" he asks.

"I don't have any."

"Okay, liar. Let's pretend, for a minute, you have this huge crush on *someone*. You're not telling anyone about this crush because what if they laugh at you or they think you're shooting for the stars? What if talking jinxes it? What if everyone has watched you pretend you don't have this crush—how do you tell them?" He gives me a pointed look I don't understand.

"I don't have a crush on anyone, so..." I motion for him to get on with it.

Timothy taps his cue stick on the table a couple of times. Holding still was never easy for him. "So let's say this person suddenly has feelings for you. Am I getting the first call the next day while he's still snoring in your bed?"

I sigh because it is impossible to get through to him when he latches onto some train of thought like this. Might as well ride it to the end and see where he's taking me. "If we're going to make up fictional people, my crush doesn't snore."

"Oh, he snores," he says with glee. "Talks in his sleep too. Have fun with that, by the way."

I can't connect these dots—Sherlock Holmes couldn't connect these dots. "We both know you snore. I don't understand what you're getting at. Does Mina talk in her sleep?"

"No," he says quickly, the excitement rolling off him. "But Nic does."

Ah. That's what he's getting at. "I do not have a crush on Nic." I grab Nic's cue stick. I need to hit something.

Timothy gives me a maddening little shrug. "Would you tell me? If you did?"

I line up my shot. "I. Do. Not. Have. A. Crush. On. That. Asshole." I grit out, shooting the stick forward. I knock a few balls around, none of which find a pocket. My face feels hot. To think I came down here to *apologize*.

My brother puts a hand to his chest and gasps. "I never accused you of having a crush on Nic." He leans across the pool table toward me, eyes wide. *"Do you have a crush on Nic?"*

"For fuck's sake." I drop the cue stick, spin on my heels, and head for the stairs while Timothy laughs.

"I love her." He calls after me. "I was scared. Didn't want to tell anyone because I was afraid I never had a chance. When we got together…I couldn't believe my luck. It didn't feel real—this amazing woman loves me as much as I love her."

I stop on the bottom step and turn.

"I'm sorry I didn't tell you about her, Jessie, but I was afraid you wouldn't trust it. You wouldn't give her a chance."

I cross my arms. "I would've given her a chance."

He raises an eyebrow.

Goddammit, he's right. I would've found a million small things to pick at, afraid he'd get hurt. Timothy has a huge heart, and he gives it away too easily, too carelessly.

"Okay, fine. Maybe I'm a little cynical." I've always been that way, but having my heart broken five years ago cemented it.

"A little bit," he says, holding up his thumb and index finger. The distance between them starts small but grows until Timothy shrugs and holds both hands wide apart. "Just a little."

I glare.

"You'll like her, I promise."

I really, really hope I do. "She can't be too bad if she's marrying you. Delusional, maybe. Masochistic, definitely."

He laughs. "Thanks. Now get over here, I haven't kicked your ass yet."

Grumbling, I stomp back to my cue stick because I want quality time with this dipshit. "Fine."

Timothy sinks another ball. He's going to kick my ass and I'm going to deal with it because I've missed him.

He clears his throat. "So Nic—"

Why have I missed my brother? "No Nic."

Timothy sends another ball into a corner pocket before asking, "What did he do? And don't give me some long list of tiny grievances. I want one big thing that Nic's done or said to hurt you."

He ruined painting for me, but that one hurts too much. I choose the next one down on my list. "Do you remember Camden?"

Timothy's puzzled frown is fake. "Camden, New Jersey?"

"Adams, dumbass. From five years ago."

"The boyfriend who was supposed to propose to you?" He becomes engrossed in his next shot. Not at all suspicious.

I lean over the table. "Yeah. The one who broke up with me after spending Thanksgiving Day hanging out with you and Nic." In truth, the breakup was more mutual—but Camden brought it up first so he can bear the burden.

Things were getting serious between us. We'd been talking about moving in together and he'd asked me questions about what kind of ring I'd like, so I brought him home to meet the family. Foolishly, I left him with Nic and Timothy while I went to bed early. It was good for him to bond with my brother, right?

Wrong.

Nic woke me up in the middle of the night, drunk as hell and wanting to talk, which was so unlike Nic I let him in my room. He didn't talk though. He stood swaying on his feet and staring sometimes at me, sometimes at the wall. The look on his face was something between befuddled and terrified.

"What do you want?" I finally asked, irritated he woke me up for this.

He sat on my bed, looked at me with those damned eyes of his, and said quietly, "Don't marry him."

It made something in my chest ache. Something I hadn't realized was there. I didn't like it.

Then the asshole climbed into my bed, wrapped his arms around my plush cuddly unicorn Roxy, and passed out cold. When I tried to wake him, he grabbed my arm and tried to tug me into bed, murmuring at me to stop hitting him and go to sleep.

Yeah, no.

I had to go find my boyfriend/soon-to-be-fiancé, drag his drunk ass out of the basement, and set us up to sleep on different couches because I was pissed. My mood didn't improve when Camden got sick in the night, and I begrudgingly let him on my couch so I could make sure he didn't aspirate vomit in his sleep.

Timothy knows Nic ended up in my room and Camden and I slept on the couch, but I can't bring myself to tell him what Nic said to me. He'll read too much into it. I tell him Camden's version.

"Nic shit-talked me. Told Camden all this bad stuff. That's why he ended it." I don't know the specifics of their conversation, but lord knows Nic witnessed me at my lowest often enough. And whatever he said to Camden stuck.

"Or he broke up with you because he was a loser named after a city in New Jersey." Timothy unhelpfully suggests.

My heartbreak over Camden, while acutely painful at the time, was misguided. He wasn't worth it and I'm glad the relationship ended, even if the timing was shitty.

Because the next time I saw Nic, at Christmas five years ago, he announced his engagement to a beautiful lingerie model named Addison Kincaid, while I was an unwashed mess on my third day in a cow onesie, trying to find the end of my heartbreak in the one-two punch of sugar and booze.

Embarrassing enough, but Addison's parents are big in the art scene out west. My mother, showing her around, pointed out one of my watercolors hanging in the great room. It was an orchid—the one that looks like a naked man—and I'd given it to my mother for her birthday. I'd worked damn hard on that painting. I thought it was quite good.

Addison glanced at it and rolled her perfect blue eyes. To my mother, she proclaimed it "nice" but to Nic, she'd called it simplistic, boring, and tacky. Overhearing that brought back every failed attempt I'd made at getting my art into galleries. All the rejections, all the comments that I had the technical skills but lacked a certain something they couldn't articulate.

In a quiet tone, his arm tightening around her waist, Nic agreed with his fiancée, murmuring she was right. She was the expert.

Something inside broke. I couldn't pick up a paintbrush without hearing her words and the words of hundreds of galleries, of the professors in my art program at college. I was mediocre at best and wasting my time.

I packed up all my paints and canvases, my easels and everything, stuffing it all into my Fuck It Closet, where unwanted things go to die.

I was good at painting. The problem—the reason I couldn't get into galleries or appeal to someone like Addison—is that there's nothing special about my art.

Just like my life. I'm not successful like Amanda, not fun like Timothy. I'm a short-tempered grudge-holding bitch who fears rejection and lives on spite. So yes, Nic is the asshole, and when he asked me to paint his stupid charity donation? I could've drowned the man in eggnog. The little slights and shit from our childhood don't matter anymore, but this wound still bleeds.

Timothy's watching me take my little spin down memory lane, waiting with a quiet patience he doesn't possess. If this is Mina's influence, she's good for him.

"I want to give you a heads-up," he says in a low voice, glancing toward the stairs. "Nic got you something nice for Christmas this year."

I haven't gotten him anything. I didn't expect him after his Thanksgiving Day no-show. Traditionally we give each other mean-spirited gifts, the rest of the family shakes their collective heads at us, and the day goes on.

Maybe he'd appreciate a Soul Breaker clitoral stimulator in cerulean blue. I have an extra in my suitcase, still in the box. I could throw a note on it. 'Nic, give this to the next Mrs. Fontana so she has something to do while you're out screwing around.'

Except I'm not stupid. Nic wasn't the one screwing around. It was Addison. It was always Addison. Nic was too oblivious to see that in her.

"I didn't get anything for Nic," I finally say, "since I didn't know he'd be here." Yet another thing Timothy didn't tell me.

"Get him something nice. He's had a shitty year. No more two-inch crocheted penis cozies, okay?"

"I worked hard on that." I protest. I didn't. I half-assed it while watching The Bachelor during my brief period of getting really into, then really out of, crocheting. One of the many hobbies I've abandoned over the years. Painting is the only thing I've ever truly loved, which explains why I stuck with it in the face of constant rejection. Until Nic and Addison, anyway.

"Fine." Timothy waves it off. "Get him some nipple clamps, I don't care. But I need you to do me a favor," he says. The exaggerated wince on his face lets me know I'm not going to like this. "Can you organize something for the bachelorette party?"

"Timbo!"

"Please?" he clasps his hands together and falls dramatically onto his knees. "You're the queen of girly games and shit."

I slap my hand over my forehead. "It was one game of pass the parcel!" Who needs music when you can stick an app-controlled vibrator in a wrapping paper ball full of gag gifts?

"I'll never forget Great-Aunt Glenda's face." He laughs then clasps his hands together, giving me puppy dog eyes. "Please? It would be a good chance to get to know your future sister-in-law."

I head toward the stairs, hating that he's right. Getting to know her is important if I'm going to bridge the distance between me and my brother. "Does she like drinking games?"

"Of course." Timothy follows me up the stairs, steps around me into the kitchen, and randomly smacks the back of Nic's head because boys are weird I guess.

I stop in the doorway. "Mom, do you know where the Ping-Pong balls are? I need them all. Some spray paint too." Time to get started on the games.

Nic glances up from folding a kitchen towel in half. "Making more dicks?"

I give him the sweetest smile in my arsenal. "It's been a long time since I've seen an adequate one. I...I guess I'm afraid I'll forget what one looks like."

He *blushes*.

Victory is mine.

"Spray paint is in the garage." My mom pauses, oven mitts on her hips, brow furrowed. "I'm not sure about the Ping-Pong balls."

"Those are in the attic," Timothy says, slipping a shortbread into the pocket of his sweats. "I'd get them, but I have to go to the airport. Pick up the wifey. Find some quiet back road so I can have my way with her in the back seat. Nic can help you find some balls."

The attic is a graveyard for my watercolors. I'm not going up there.

"Hey, Jessie," Timothy says, giving Nic a not-so-gentle push toward me. "Mistletoe."

I do the smart thing and run.

CHAPTER FIVE

Jessie

I SIGH INTO MY hot chocolate and stare at the unbroken snow out the dining room window. Big flakes drift down, slowly accumulating on the shrubbery. Even the weather is half-assing it today.

The house has gone quiet, emptied of the noisiest people. Amanda and Hazel took the kids to visit some friends, Timothy's at the airport awaiting his bride-to-be, and Nic must have gotten lost looking for his balls.

Or the Ping-Pong balls Timothy volunteered him to find.

What if Mina thinks my games are dumb? I need this to work. I need her to like me.

"Jessie, honey. Are you all right?" My mother is deftly slinging tray after tray of cookies in an endless cycle, filling the entire island and most of the table with fresh-baked deliciousness.

"Fine, Mom." My offer to help her with Cookie Day was politely turned down. Nic gets to help. He always does. Baking isn't my thing, but it always annoys me how easily he fits into my family when I don't.

My Bailey's-laced hot chocolate and all the cookies surrounding me are a good consolation prize. Thank god my cream-colored pants are soft and stretchy. After being introduced to Addison Kincaid while wearing a cow onesie, I stopped wearing pajamas all day at my parents' house. My goal is the intersection of hot and comfortable and this outfit is exactly that. Cozy but polished.

My mother taps me on the shoulder. "Come make the mulled wine."

"Wow," I say, leaping from my chair at the opportunity. "You're trusting me to make the mulled wine?"

My mother follows me into the butler's pantry. She pulls out a couple of bottles and stuffs them into my arms, piling on some spices, a couple of oranges, and lemons. "That'll do it."

I edge my way back to the sole patch of kitchen counter not already claimed, nodding as she rattles off directions while she prepares another batch of cookies for the oven.

Not like mulled wine is hard.

I open the bottle before I remember I need the slow cooker. My orange rolls toward the edge of the counter and I reach for it, bumping the bottle of wine. It teeters for a second before falling forward with a clunk, unleashing a red tsunami over the countertop, splashing my clothes, and spilling onto the floor.

"Goddammit!" Panic grabs hold as I pluck at the cream-colored sweater, my favorite pants. Ruined.

My mother is on me with a kitchen towel, dabbing at the wine stain before turning her attention to the floor. "Go strip in the laundry. There's some vinegar on the shelf—soak it, rub some liquid laundry detergent on it, and put it in the wash. Grab a coat from the mudroom. Go, quick."

Grumbling curses, I dash across the hall, into the mudroom, and through to the laundry. The washing machine and dryer are both going, filling the room with warmth, noise, and the smell of fabric softener.

Both the sweater and the pants are probably stained beyond saving but I love them so I'm willing to try. I strip to my underwear and spread my clothes out over the washing machine, frantically scanning the nearby shelves for some vinegar.

Something brushes against my foot and I jump, choking on my scream.

A Ping-Pong ball?

There's a ton of them, rolling across the floor toward me, bouncing into corners.

What the ever-loving fuck?

A basket lies on its side in front of sock-clad feet. I follow the dark jeans up to the charcoal Henley, up again to Nic's wide eyes. I didn't hear him come in or drop the basket over the noise of the washing machine's spin cycle.

Our stare-off ends when he bends to grab the basket. Pink creeps over his cheeks.

Fine, he's embarrassed. I'm not. I'm not naked and covered in spunk, so I'm already winning. Except now I'm picturing him naked, wondering what a full hard-on might look like on the still impressive semi I'd seen the other night. Dammit.

I turn back to the shelf. There's no vinegar in here. Detergent it is. I grab it and pour some onto my clothes. My body is already prickling with awareness as he moves closer, picking up the Ping-Pong balls.

He's probably ticking off my flaws. I'm incredibly average—and happy about it—and he sleeps with models.

"Festive." Nic's strangled voice is barely audible above the noise and suddenly I can feel him looking at me. That prickling sensation is a full-on tingle now.

"It's Christmas." I snap. And Nic Fontana should not be having an impact on the red plaid panties he's mocking, but I can't deny the rumble of his voice has me wet as hell.

I need to get my head checked.

I scrub at the stain harder, making my boobs jiggle. Dammit. Well, maybe that will scare him away—my bra is covered in tiny candy canes and he's a Grinch. He'll run out of the room, terrified. My totally average tits will be the hero of the day. I'll buy them something nice. Lacy. Black. Something some other hot guy will appreciate if I ever manage to get laid again.

Nic crawls closer, still gathering the Ping-Pong balls. The closer he gets, the more charged the air feels. What is it about a hot man on his knees? Especially this man? God, the thought of him kneeling at my feet, begging...

Gritting my teeth, I rub my stained clothes harder and faster.

I'm losing it. I'm probably giving off desperately horny vibes.

Nic's voice cuts through the noise in my head. "You're hopeful."

I glance down at him, fully prepared to give him a quick kick in the ass, but the expression on his face stops me. He's crouched next to me, his eyes hooded, staring at a spot on my panties, a smug little smirk on his face.

Fire surges up to my cheeks, down into my stomach. Maybe I'll kick him after all. My fingers trace the mistletoe embellishment on my panties. I'd snickered when I bought them, but they seem pretty stupid now. Soaked, because my body is inexplicably revolting against my brain.

Hopeful.

I finally shrug, leaning against the dryer, and looking down at him. "Season for miracles. Going to give me a little kiss, Nic?"

That should be enough to get rid of him—except he isn't moving. He's staring at my panties with an intensity that burns my skin.

"Jessie."

The way my name carries off his lips—a warning on a breath—causes the temperature to jump a good ten degrees. Goose bumps pebble my arms.

"Nic." That *is not* my voice, a desperate whimper where I'd meant to sound annoyed.

He drops a Ping-Pong ball, slowly bringing his hand up, toward me. There's more than enough time, as the Ping-Pong ball bounce gets smaller and smaller, for me to step away from him. To push his hand aside or tell him no.

I'm frozen in place, betrayed by the ache in my body as his fingers lightly brush over the mistletoe embroidery. His touch sparks a flash of desire in my core, cinching my lungs tight. Before I have time to process *Nic Fontana is touching my panties*, he stands up, lifting me onto the dryer. He grips the machine on either side of my legs, his eyes darkening as he brings his nose inches away from mine.

My mouth opens but...nothing. I can't find the appropriate words—or the inappropriate ones—for the situation. He smells too good, like home. Leather, wood, and fire from the great room, cinnamon, cardamom, pink pepper from my mother's spice rack, and something more. Something rougher. Uniquely him. All layered over the smell of clean linens.

I lick my lips, his eyes following the movement of my tongue. Urges, so many unacceptable things I want to do to him, like run my fingers over the planes of his jaw or kiss the hollow at the base of his throat. Trace my finger along the tiny scar near his left eyebrow. I gave him that scar when Timothy's homemade zip line snapped and Nic broke my fall and I've never touched it, which somehow seems wrong all of a sudden.

Mostly, I want to grab his stupid Henley and haul him onto me.

I fight every last urge, but focusing on the hum of the dryer beneath me instead is a big mistake. A big, big, vibrating mistake.

"I'm going to give you that kiss." His voice is quiet, but something ripples through the threatening tone, an undercurrent of excitement running down my spine in response. "But if you tell me to stop, I'll stop."

The rumble of the dryer under me, the hunger in his gaze…I shouldn't want this. Maybe that's why I do. A taste of the forbidden. The man I can't stand most in the world touching me. My breath catches. Oh yeah, I want that.

His lips quirk like he's enjoying every minute of rendering me speechless. "Are you listening?"

If you tell me to stop. The ache between my legs deepens in anticipation. "Don't stop."

He raises an eyebrow. "We walk out of here and it never happened. Okay?"

I nod. That goes without saying.

The delicious drag of his hands against my legs as he eases my panties off has my heart thumping in my ears. When he pushes my knees apart, when the cooler air hits my exposed skin and he crouches down, my heart doubles its efforts. It stops altogether when he kisses my inner thigh, his breath hitching as he gazes at me.

Oh, god. The longing in his eyes might undo me—it steals me away from the gentle hum of the dryer, from the stroke of his hands, from everything else, making me wonder if this is something more.

No.

This is nothing. A brief pause in our decades-long cold war. A single moment of shared bliss to break the boredom of the day. That's all.

His grip on my thighs tightens and his breath returns to my skin, rough. Fast.

I tremble as he pushes my thighs open wider, holding me in place. Just looking.

Fuck, I wish this wasn't half as hot as it is.

He finally tears his gaze away and meets my eyes.

Jesus Christ.

He could melt the camera on a movie set with this look.

I'm wound so tight that the moment the heat of his mouth touches me I nearly fall off the dryer. His tongue circles my entrance, the tip pushing, teasing, before slowly sliding up to flick over my clit. Warm, slick, and firm, capturing my breath as his metallic eyes continue to hold me.

It's too much. I close my eyes, tipping my head back. The swirl of his tongue, the softness of his lips, the gentle suction—I melt into the sensation, gripping the edge of the machine for dear life.

He shifts from leisurely to something desperate and all thought drains from my head, every cell in my body straining for his tongue as he loosens his grip to allow my hips to rock. And rock they do.

I'm already close, so close.

A cross between a groan and a growl buzzes from his mouth, the sensation making me moan. I open my eyes and look down at him. He's still watching me, his eyes hungry, and that's all it takes.

The noise of the dryer swallows my soft cry as I come apart in a million bright, crackling sparks. Nic doesn't let up, changing the pressure from his tongue, those embers bubbling to life, sustained by his mouth, coaxed along until I finally burn out with a whimper, my body going slack.

I float, a lazy snowflake slowly coming down. The softly rumbling dryer and his uneven breath against my thigh leave me feeling safe, unable to process anything beyond the full sense of satisfaction.

Wow.

Nic stands, his hands coming to rest beside mine, his hips between my thighs. His eyes are still hooded, his gaze hot.

I brush my thumb over that tiny scar. The one they always airbrush away. "You still owe me a mistletoe kiss." Yesterday, earlier today...two kisses, technically. That blissed-out feeling has loosened my tongue. "I bet I taste good on you." I want to taste him too—the erection straining against his jeans has to be painful. Watching those gray eyes when I take him in my mouth...*that* is going to be fun.

In a blink, his hand cups the back of my head, his lips surprisingly soft against mine as his tongue demands admittance, sliding slowly over my lips. I don't hesitate to let him in, my arousal sparking anew. I fist the front of his shirt, pulling him tight against me, the shock of his jeans against my over-sensitive clit making me gasp into his mouth.

It changes everything.

Nic jerks away but my grip is tight and I fall forward. He pushes me back, but the ache in my body over the loss of contact sends me tumbling on the inside.

He takes a deep, ragged breath and draws himself up, adjusting his pants. His face shifts from unrestrained hunger back into cold reserve, dousing the heat between my legs, and without a word he slips out of the room.

I slide down from the dryer, my orgasm-fogged brain trying to figure out what the hell just happened and coming up blank.

Well, not completely blank. "Asshole," I mutter after him, bending to pick up my panties.

CHAPTER SIX

Jessie

IT TAKES ME HALF an hour to get my shit together. To give up on ever getting the stains out of my clothes. To pick up all the damned Ping-Pong balls. To sneak upstairs and change into leggings and an oversized sweater big enough to hide in.

To go from sated to shame to rage.

I want to strangle Nic with my mistletoe panties.

The nerve of that asshole, working me up only to send me reeling. And over what? A kiss?

It's fine. I'll avoid him. For two whole goddamned weeks in the same house. Can't get arrested for murder if our paths don't cross. Since it's Cookie Day, Nic should be in the kitchen with my mom, so I veer into the great room and—

Nic's sprawled on one of the sofas, book in hand, staring out the window.

His gaze flicks my way, immediately dropping to his forgotten book, a hint of scarlet creeping up from the Henley I'd wrapped my hands in half an hour ago.

My mistletoe panties are in the hamper, but I don't need them to commit murder. I take one step toward him but freeze at the sound of a page turning.

Shit. My father.

Will he look up from his book and notice if I smother Nic with a throw pillow?

Maybe.

A strategic retreat is necessary. If I'm going into hiding for the rest of the afternoon, I need supplies. As many cookies as I can steal before my mom looks up and *knows* what Nic and I did in the laundry room.

My mother has her back to me when I sneak into the kitchen. Snowball-shaped cookies, coated in powdered sugar, are the first edible thing my eyes land on. The closest to the door. I creep in and stuff one in my mouth.

Hmm. Pecans. These will do. I grab a handful.

My mother doesn't glance up from the sink where she's washing a mixing bowl. "Did you get the stain out, honey?"

My favorite pants...*too soon, Mom. Too soon.*

"Jessie?" She finally glances over her shoulder, frowning.

I shake my head and back out of the kitchen with my horde of cookies before she can see *I recently climaxed on Dominic Fontana's face* is stamped across my own.

God, I can't believe we did that. Nic doesn't like me, I don't like him, and people don't perform oral sex on people they hate, so what the hell happened? Why does it feel...inevitable?

I reach the bottom of the steps, pausing long enough to stuff another cookie in my mouth when the front door flies open.

For one heart-stopping moment, I think it's Nic and he'll rush through the door and take me right here on the stairs while I enjoy my cookies. *What is wrong with me?*

Instead, Timothy's staring at me and I'm pretty sure my eyes have gone cartoon-character wide. I've got one round powdered sugar-covered ball sticking out of my mouth, my hands cradling another four cookies like I'll fight him to the death over them.

I might, actually. They're really good.

"Oh. My. God." Timothy pulls his hat off, tossing it on the floor, a massive smile on his face. "What the hell have you been doing?"

Before I can juggle the cookies into one hand to pull the one from my mouth, he cups his hand to his mouth and shouts. "Nic!"

Oh god. Timothy *knows* something happened between us.

I'd rather choke on this damn cookie and die than admit I hooked up with Nic to Timothy.

A pretty, dark-haired woman in an adorable jacket steps into the house next to Timothy.

Shit.

Mina.

Can this day get any worse?

Nic walks out of the great room, the smile falling off his face when Timothy points at me. Nic's eyes sweep over me and he shrugs at Timothy, giving him a *She's your sister, I don't know what the hell is wrong with her* look as he moves forward to greet Mina warmly.

Sure, *this* is his only ever Oscar-worthy performance.

I cough, inadvertently sucking powdered sugar and cookie crumbs into my lungs as my brother continues to stare at me, while Nic asks Mina about her flight.

My death on these stairs is going to be as slow and as awkwardly painful as possible. Tears burn in my eyes and I can't stop coughing. I shoot Timothy a look that hopefully communicates *help me, I'm dying, you loser* rather than *your best friend, who I hate, ate me out and I'm dying of embarrassment. And also cookie.*

The three of them stand there, staring at me—Timothy grinning, Mina smiling politely, and Nic looking like he wants me to disappear through the floor—while I stare back in horror.

Mina breaks the silence. "You must be Jessie."

Her wide smile is beautiful. If it weren't for the tears streaming from my eyes or the fact that I can't breathe, I'd admit Timothy's punching well above his weight getting this woman to agree to marry him. Instead, I cough, splutter, and finally bolt for the kitchen and a glass of water.

Timothy's laughter chases me down the hall.

"What—?" My mother glances up with a frown as I drop the cookies into the garbage, spitting out what's left in my mouth with zero grace before snagging my mug and filling it with water.

Timothy, Mina, and Nic aren't far behind. Timothy pushes Nic away from the mistletoe-baited doorway before planting a massive kiss on a surprised but laughing Mina.

Ugh, if I hadn't just dry-heaved a cookie into the garbage, my brother's noisy kissing would make me vomit. My coughing subsides, but my eyes are still watering. I grab a cloth and wipe the powdered sugar off my hands and mouth, heading back to the table.

I walk smack into Nic, who came around the long way since Timothy and Mina are still in the doorway. He grabs my arms, steadies me, and walks away. Like he can't get away from me fast enough.

Whatever. Half an hour ago, his face was all up in my pussy.

I dust powdered sugar off my sweater, trying to collect myself. I need to force Nic out of my mind so I can meet my soon-to-be sister-in-law with a tiny shred of dignity intact.

My mother catches Mina up in a hug when Timothy finally releases her. My father waits for his turn. They met her after Timothy's accident. Amanda, Hazel, and the kids come thundering in from the front door, and everything descends into chaos.

Turns out, everyone has already met Mina. Except me.

Okay, that stings, but I still see Timothy's point. He's absolutely wrong, but I know the things I've said to him, trying to convince him I was fine after Camden. The things I've said about love and relationships. I'm not that cynical, but it's easier to be cynical than to admit it hurts that I can't make a relationship last.

Timothy and I haven't been close enough as adults for the trust between us to overcome my bullshit. I have a lot of work to do.

It starts now. Here. With Mina.

Mina wraps me into a tight hug when we're formally introduced, signaling her openness to get to know me. I mirror her enthusiasm and try not to think about Nic, whose eyes I feel on my back.

Cookie Day is officially on pause as my mother hands out hot chocolate and coffee, ushering everyone into the great room as they talk about the wedding.

My eyes snag on Nic. His attractiveness has always been eclipsed by the fact that he's a giant asshole, but something changed in the laundry room. I can't ignore the tug I feel toward him. He's rearranged my DNA with that muff dive and a part of him melded with a part of me. Like a bad sci-fi horror flick that's going to end with some kind of Chestburster. Or a Clitburster.

I want him again.

This is inconvenient. Terrifying, if I think about it, so I'm not going to think about it.

His eyes snap to mine and I look away, the press of my thighs alerting me to my arousal.

Okay, not thinking about it isn't going to work. The way he watched me as he went down on me is haunting me, the pure lust keeping me on a simmer. That's what my problem is—I'm desperately horny, and it's making me reckless. I want to drop to my knees, rip his pants open, and take him in my mouth.

Dammit, now I'm staring at his crotch because I can see the outline of his dick. Is he half hard? I should look away, but I don't. My motives are pure. This has everything to do with getting another orgasm and nothing to do with the man who could be giving it to me.

An elbow catches me in the ribs and I jump. Hazel, the owner of the elbow, gives me an imploring look.

Oh no.

Everyone is staring at me and I was staring at Nic's crotch and I'm not sure if that's better or worse than everyone thinking I'm a sulky, bitchy little sister who doesn't want her brother to be happy.

Nic clears his throat, giving Timothy a look. It could say a hundred different things from *Help her* to *Ugh, your sister is the worst*. I can't tell, but I don't need to. It's always that last one.

"Excuse me." My voice sounds small and scratchy, stiffly formal to my ears. I bolt from the room before anyone can see me tear up.

In the safety of my room, I sprawl across my bed, smothering my frustrated groan in the soft pillows.

I've messed up. Again. Worse, Nic's moved into my head and is living his best naked life rent-free. I hate his pretty face.

Nic doesn't matter, and what happened between us is a distraction from what does. How am I supposed to fix things with my brother? He's going to be pissed at me again and I can't tell him it's Nic's dick's fault.

My childish resentment might have opened up the fissure between us when we were fourteen, and maybe it grew naturally over the years, but I want Timothy to come to me when shit happens in his life. I don't want to find out he's been in the hospital days after an accident, or find out he's been in love for years a couple days before he marries. I don't want him to keep things from me because he's afraid I'll rain on his parade.

There's a tentative knock on my door and I sit up, doing a quick shimmy to plump up my tits because my thoughts immediately fly to Nic.

Except it won't be him. He doesn't give a shit about me. He was bored and horny and I was there. It doesn't hurt, I'm just disappointed because I'm more bored and horny than he is and I have a suitcase full of sex toys. I want him despite not needing him, and that puts me at a disadvantage.

I pluck at my bra, undoing the work of the shimmy. Jesus, I need to get my shit together. "Come in."

The door pushes open slowly. Mina sticks her head in. "I brought wine," she says, holding up a bottle.

"Oh, thank god, I need a drink." I dab at my eyes and sniffle. "I'm sorry, today's been—"

Mina kicks the door shut and drops onto the bed next to me. "It's okay," she says, carefully pouring the wine. "Nic explained everything."

My eye twitches. Forget the possibility of more orgasms. Murder's back on the table.

"He can be such an ass." She hands me a glass and pours her own. "Starting shit with you over caroling. I bet you sing better than he does, anyway."

Nic covered for me?

I touch my glass to hers, relief and every single event of the day tempting me to down this glass in one long gulp. Self-control wins, and I take a small sip. Bawdy Caroling is tomorrow, so Mina's going to find out how wrong she is about my singing abilities, but I'm glad Nic threw himself under the bus for me. It's the least he could do since he's impervious to buses.

Mina takes a drink of her wine as she glances around my room. "That's pretty," she says, motioning to the watercolor hanging on the wall above the bed. It's from my flower era, a bunch of pink dahlias.

"Thanks," I say awkwardly—I have no idea if she knows I painted it but I have to assume Timothy told her more about me than he's told me about her, in the guise of preparing her to meet everyone.

Then again, it's Timothy, so who the fuck knows?

Mina's expression softens. "I'm sorry he sprung this on you the way he did. I'm not going to justify his decisions, but I wanted to meet you earlier. He wants us to be close, and I'd like that too."

"So would I," I say.

Mina's eyes fall on my open suitcase, and the sex toys scattered everywhere. "Timothy said you work for a sex toy company." She grins. "The overtime must be awful."

I laugh. "Surprisingly hazardous occupation. What do you do?"

"I design and produce eco-friendly underwear."

Her company is called Wild Things. I haven't heard of it, but Mina pulls out her phone and shows me some of her products. They look really good.

There's a bit of an awkward lull after we've talked a bit about undergarments, and a smile slowly spreads wide across Mina's face. "So how's Nic?"

I cough. Hard. There's something about the look in her eyes that is anything but innocent. "Bit of cookie, still stuck." I croak out the lie and drain my glass.

Mina laughs. "Is he all silent and broody here too?"

Cunnilingus has me paranoid—she's being snarky, not insinuating anything. "I mistake him for a houseplant all the time," I say.

That smile of hers is sly. "A cactus."

"Because he's a prick." I add with a grin.

"I think we're going to get along just fine," Mina says, refilling our wine. "I've got some shopping to do tomorrow before the wedding. Want to come?"

Shit. I need to. My Folly dress isn't fit for a wedding—even Timothy's.

"Sounds good." I need to find a Christmas present for Mina too. And Nic. I might get him something nice this year since he gave me a hell of an orgasm.

Okay, he's taking up too much space in my head. It's time to make sure I'm taking equal square footage in his. I shouldn't have to suffer alone. It's Christmas.

Chapter Seven

Nic

Sitting through the chaos of another family game night is surreal when scarcely six hours ago I was licking Jessie's pussy.

What the hell was I thinking? She taunts me over a kiss so I dive between her legs?

The moment I saw her standing there in her underwear, I should've fled. Staying to pick up the Ping-Pong balls when she looked so irritated was a mistake. Talking to her was a mistake. Going down on her was a mistake. Escaping the moment I realized what we'd done? Not a mistake, but a regret. It could've been her mouth giving me much-needed release instead of my hand.

Why do I keep doing this to myself? Going down on Jessie was another bad decision in a string of bad decisions and I hate how I still taste her on my lips, how little echoes of the sweet sounds she made play on a loop in my head. The way she ground herself against my mouth scrambled my brain and I still haven't recovered.

"Muff. Twelve points." Jessie lines up her tiles on the Scrabble board, her grin a challenge, her eyes betraying us to anyone who looks her way.

My face flushes warm. I take a swig from my beer to buy some cover while Jessie's older sister Amanda considers her options, blissfully ignorant of the conversation Jessie's eyes are having with me.

Hazel is calling out moves to the kids playing Twister. Timothy is noisily losing a game of cribbage to his father, much to Mina's delight. Celia's in the kitchen, putting the finishing touches on dessert.

In a room full of people, Jessie and I might as well be alone.

Thank god the seismic shift between us has gone unnoticed. I have no idea what any of the Foleys would think about us hooking up, and I never want to find out. I don't want to lose the closest thing I have to family because I couldn't keep my hormones in check.

Jessie hasn't told anyone. I don't think she will, not when she can torture me.

"Your turn." Amanda nudges me.

The letters on the tiles in front of me might as well be Greek. I toss an *er* on the end of Amanda's 'cheat.' "Cheater, twelve points."

"Apt." Jessie proclaims, plucking her beer up.

Instead of defending myself, I rest my elbow on the table, my chin in my hand, and stare at her.

She copies my posture, meeting me with a stare of her own. The Christmas tree lights, the candles, the fire, all come together to dance in her whiskey eyes. As good as the view from between her legs was, watching the supernova in her eyes as she comes would be better.

Her lips quirk, like she knows I want more.

A smile finally breaks across her face. "I can go all night, Nic."

The tone in her voice has my jeans feeling a lot more restrictive. It doesn't matter what I want. I'm done with her. I raise an eyebrow because I'm not done with this stare-off.

"Jesus Christ, you two," Amanda mutters under her breath, arranging her tiles. "Take your turn, Jessie, or forfeit."

Jessie wrinkles her nose, attention dropping to her tiles. I hate that I find her adorable.

I look away and my eyes lock with Timothy's. His head tilts slightly, his lips press flat, and his eyes bore into mine. His 'you and I gotta talk' look.

For two awful seconds, I hold his stare before the Christmas tree catches my eye and I look away, pretending I'm seeing it for the first time.

Has Timothy figured out something happened between me and Jessie? Shit, he might only suspect something's up and I don't want anything I say or do to confirm it.

I force myself to focus on the tree and count my breathing. In for four, hold for four, out for four. The massive tree is lit up and beautifully decorated in green, red, and gold baubles. Garlands are artfully draped over branches. Red velvet bows are carefully positioned. Everything is traditional with informal elegance.

The tree Addison put in our house last year was like something out of a horror movie. Silvery gray and dripping with red glass ornaments, every one sharp enough to cut.

Does Jessie put up a tree in her apartment? If she does, it probably features handcrafted tampon ornaments and an assortment of dicks, or maybe—

"I finally got an orgasm." Jessie announces cheerfully.

I jerk back around, nearly knocking over my beer. She smirks, pointing at the board.

"Seven points, since the G is a blank tile. Not exactly a ten." Her eyebrows rise innocently, apologetically.

The fuck it wasn't a ten.

"A ten is impossible." Amanda, the resident Scrabble master, corrects. She's too busy trying to find a game-winner in her tiles to notice the edge in Jessie's voice or the blush that has my face hot. "The most points you could get for 'orgasm' would be nine unless you were on a double or triple letter or word square, which you aren't."

Timothy's laugh cuts across the room and every muscle in my body clenches. Amanda might be oblivious, but if Timothy caught any of that...

I need this game to be over. Now.

Celia saves the day, calling everyone into the kitchen for Irish coffee and cannoli, ending the games. In my haste to get away from Jessie, I end up right next to Timothy. He slings an arm around my shoulder, preventing me from escaping. "Get your ass kicked at Scrabble?"

"Every time." The only person in this house who can beat Amanda is her father William, but I'm pretty sure the only person who loses as often as I do is

Jessie.

We grab our coffees and a couple of cannoli and find a spot around the massive island—now cleared from Cookie Day.

"Look." Timothy nudges me. Jessie and Mina are laughing over something at the other end. "Mina's won Jessie over already. Looks like I might not need you to be that red cape after all."

If any of this were funny, I'd laugh. I'm definitely a red cape now. Or a lightning rod. Whatever I am, after what happened in the laundry room, I have her attention.

Timothy turns away to answer a question, and as if she'd heard, Jessie looks up and our eyes meet. She's the actual devil, raising the cannoli to her lips as she listens to Mina's story. The way she leisurely licks the creamy filling gets right under my skin, as intended.

"Dude. Did you growl?" Timothy turns back to me with a laugh.

"My stomach." I shrug it off, reaching for my second cannoli. "Still hungry, I guess." I'm not. I've eaten so many damn cookies today. Not one tasted as good as Jessie.

Timothy's grinning at me. I don't like it, but I put on my best blank face and try to keep my attention on the conversation around me and not on how good it would feel to have Jessie lap at me like she does the cannoli.

My hopes of escaping to bed early when Amanda and Hazel and the kids do are dashed as Timothy hands me a glass of whiskey and drags me to the table. Jessie, at least, says good night and disappears, leaving the room less suffocating.

Mina whispers something in Timothy's ear that makes him smile, then kisses him and says good night. William's already snuck out and is probably reading in his chair by the fire, and with a smug, satisfied smile on her face, Celia hangs her kitchen towel, warning us not to stay up too late.

And I'm alone with Timothy.

"You okay?" he asks, leaning back in the chair, legs stretched out in front of himself.

"Yeah, fine."

"You sure? You're a bit...squirrely since I went to get Mina. What's up?"

"Nothing."

"Is it Jessie?"

"No." I say it way too quickly, way too loudly. My face goes warm, so I grab my glass and take a long drink to hide.

"Dude." Timothy sighs, and here it is. He's about to tell me he knows. I tip my glass back, ignoring the burn down my throat because this is it. The consequences of my bad decision.

My glass isn't quite empty when I set it down. Timothy raises his and takes a long, drawn out drink. I swear he does this on purpose.

He sets his glass down, staring at it. "She doesn't show it, but she's sensitive. You can't give her shit about her singing voice the night before Bawdy Caroling, or she won't go all out. We've got to win this."

Relief—and the straight shot of more alcohol to my system—makes me slump in my chair. He bought that story I told him to explain away Jessie's freak-out.

I need to finish off my drink so I can escape before he figures out what really happened.

Timothy looks back up at me. "She was staring so hard at your dick, I thought your pants would catch fire."

I choke and Timothy bursts into laughter.

I'd noticed she'd been staring, but Timothy noticing? Not good.

"Maybe she hoped it'd fall off." I suggest.

Actually, that was probably it, and she's been messing with me all night because she's upset she got caught.

"Didn't work." I add, glancing at my groin and getting to my feet with a half-hearted shrug. "I'm going to bed."

"Sit down," Timothy says sharply, all laughter gone. "We need to talk."

Shit. He doesn't get serious often. "I'll apologize about the caroling in the morning." I'm clinging to my lie until he proves he knows what happened in the laundry room.

"This isn't that. What did you say to Camden?"

I sink back into my seat. Images of a clean-cut, averagely handsome man float up from where I've buried all the shitty memories. "How am I supposed to remember what I said five years ago to some guy I met once? Besides, you were there the whole time."

"Not the whole time," he says in a quiet tone. "I went to bed. You two stayed up drinking."

"I don't remember." It's not entirely a lie. My memories are booze-soaked. I kept Camden drinking with me because the thought of him going upstairs made me ill. Camden brought Jessie up. I told him...

I groan. Pretty sure I told him I'd ruin their marriage. Not my finest moment, but I was drunk enough to think that I could. That Jessie was somehow mine, even though I'd been seeing Addison.

Timothy grips the rim of his glass, turning it slowly. "He broke up with her when they got back to New York."

I found out a week before Christmas. Jessie was miserable when I saw her, and that misery rubbed off on me. "People break up."

"He had a ring. He planned to ask her to marry him."

The cannoli and Timothy's whiskey roil around in my stomach, along with all the damn cookies, because I know that too. Camden told me.

"You said something to him, didn't you?"

The only thing I regretted was going to Jessie's room. Asking her not to marry him. Believing she understood what I meant when I had no fucking clue myself. Falling asleep and waking alone in her bed.

The whole night was an embarrassment.

"If he wanted to marry her, he wouldn't have broken up with her," I say, getting to my feet and walking over to the sink for a glass of water. I should feel guilty, but Jessie's dislike of me wasn't a secret, and neither was my indifference to her. She chose him—they were cuddled together on a couch in the morning—so he should've stayed.

Can I call myself indifferent anymore?

Timothy is silent, but I feel his eyes on me as I slowly drink the water. It doesn't help my stomach, but it buys me time. When I turn around, he waits me out. I should say good night and walk away from this conversation, but he'll follow me upstairs. I settle on something to appease him. "Camden wasn't good enough for her."

It works. He brightens. "I agree. I'm glad you broke them up."

"Hey, I was drunk. *If* I played a role—"

"You played a role." He grins. "Pity Jessie didn't return the favor and break you and Addison up at Christmas."

Christ. She almost did, though she didn't mean to.

Addison's parents are influential in the art scene in California, handing down a fair amount of pretentious snobbery to their daughter. So when Addison turned to me with some snarky commentary on one of Jessie's paintings, I'd pulled my fiancée close. "Right. You're such an expert."

I'd kept my tone quiet and mild, but Addison took it for the dig it was. Her brief stint as a gallerist in one of her parents' galleries had been an unmitigated disaster. The fight we'd had later that night was epic. Hushed voices and more hurtful words.

I doubted. Thought about ending the engagement. After a long solo walk in the snowy dark, I'd come back to the quiet house, crushed. I needed to marry Addison. I wanted to settle down. And Addison pushed me. She believed in me.

Fucking lies. Addison only believed in herself and wanted me to open as many doors for her career switch into film as possible.

Last I heard, she was dating some producer. I've no doubt she'll be cast as some eye candy in a film soon. Maybe she'll even find some success. As long as I never have to work with her, I don't care.

"I wish Jessie had broken us up." I admit. "Or any one of you had. Addison was a mistake."

Timothy just nods. "What did you get Jessie for Christmas?"

I couldn't bring myself to get her something mean-spirited this year. Maybe because I can't forget how sad she was five years ago.

"An Eric Kouame bag and the framed front page of the Sexiest Men in America cover. Which I'm on this year, by the way." I'd fallen to number two the last few years thanks to Gabriel Sinclair, but I'm back on top.

He laughs. "Okay, but Eric is sort of like a business partner and I'm betting you had him pick it out."

"I didn't."

Timothy has been involved in helping a couple of young designers expand their brands back in LA and when he asked, I opened my bank account to him. I'd hardly call myself a business partner.

He smirks. "Okay, so Angie did."

Guilt bites me as I nod. My assistant did my Christmas shopping like she has the last four years. The framed magazine was my idea, but Angie was the one to do it.

"Well, Jessie will love the bag and hate the framed magazine, so give her both. But you need to get her something else. Something you pick out. Lucky for you, we're going shopping in the morning."

I stare at him in horror. "Are you kidding? This close to Christmas?"

"Embrace the chaos, Nic. Plus, we need to make sure your suit fits and the measurements the wardrobe people gave me haven't changed."

So much for a quiet morning. "So, what am I supposed to give her?"

His grin widens. "What do you *want* to give her?"

What I want to give her—more orgasms—isn't happening, and I glare at Timothy's suggestion.

"Give her something nice." He pushes to his feet. "It's past time you two made an effort to get along. Why don't you go up to her room and apologize for the caroling thing?"

"She's probably asleep." I'm buzzed from an evening of alcohol. Bad decisions are likely, so I'm not going anywhere near Jessie tonight.

"Wake her up," he says. "Get on your knees."

Bad choice of words. Now I'm thinking about dropping to my knees and lifting her leg over my shoulder. Getting another taste of her. "No way. She'll murder me."

Seems she's going to be my cause of death no matter what.

Chapter Eight

Nic

December Twenty-first

Timothy drags me outside at the ass crack of dawn to shovel the two inches of snow that fell overnight. I'm clearly here as his audience, as he leans against his shovel, going on and on about Mina and getting married while I do all the work. His excitement is palpable, but I can't relate. I didn't feel this way before my wedding. All I felt was a vague unease and a desire to get it over with. Another sign it was a mistake.

"Remind me to pick up some road salt," Timothy says after I slip on the damn ice again. He marks the spot with a small reindeer he 'borrows' from the neighbor's lawn. It's his only contribution, yet he still claps me on the shoulder after we put the shovels away, thanking me for the help.

I bite back a retort about doing all the work myself because the exercise has me feeling better.

We stomp the snow off our boots and head inside, shedding jackets and hats and gloves, giving each other shit like always.

"I'm going to go warm up the best way," Timothy says with a wink, heading to the door of the guest bedroom. "Be ready to go by nine." He opens the door and pauses. "Nine thirty."

I don't point out Mina won't be happy when his cold hands wake her up—Timothy thrives off the thrill.

Maybe I don't have someone to warm my body, but at least a cup of coffee is uncomplicated.

Celia intercepts me on my way to the coffeepot, phone pressed to her ear as she grabs my fingers. "Cold. Perfect." She shoves a bowl into my hands and pushes me toward the island. "Rub that in for me, will you, honey?"

Amanda glances up from her book with a smirk. All the Foley kids can cook—every one of them learned from the best—but Celia working in her kitchen with any or all of her kids is like oil and water. Timothy's a distracted mess, too busy talking. Amanda vies for control, insisting on exact measurements and getting frustrated with her mother's intuitive style. Jessie spends more time sampling the food or looking at her phone than actually helping.

I set the bowl of flour and shredded frozen butter on the island and head to the sink to wash my hands—with cold water.

"I get it, really I do." Celia rolls her eyes at the phone as we pass each other on my way back to the counter. "No, the concept is more about simple recipes, twists on old traditions, not about fancy—" Celia disappears into the butler's pantry, her voice growing muffled.

"Rough puff for some appetizer." Amanda answers, though I hadn't asked. After a moment, she sets her mug down. "What was up with you and Jessie yesterday?"

"Same bullshit, different day." With some luck, Amanda will drop it before thoughts of Jessie warm up my body and melt the butter.

She snickers and goes back to her book. I get to work, quickly rubbing the butter into the flour with my fingertips. Celia comes back into the room, still talking on the phone, and eventually sets a measuring cup of water and vinegar next to me.

"Yes, Jessie's in town for the holiday," she says into her phone. "Oh? You catered a function for her boss...Oh, well...her brother's wedding is in a couple of days, why don't you come as her date?"

Her conversation has my full attention now. I add the water and lightly mix the dough until it comes together, ears perked. It won't be the first time Celia has set Jessie up, usually without warning.

Most times, the guy doesn't stand a chance. One look, one half a conversation, and Jessie taps out. Sometimes...well, sometimes she hits it off with the guy. It never lasts. Camden was the only one who stuck. Jessie's always been a casual dater, moving on quickly. I wonder what it was about him that made her stick around.

Knowing Jessie, she'd say it was his dick.

But do I really know her anymore?

It's been five years since we've been under the same roof. She could've dated someone for four of those years and I would never have known. She might be looking for something serious.

It's weird no one in her family ever offers me any insight into her personal life. Then again, maybe it's strange I never ask.

Wrapping the dough tightly in cling wrap, I stick it in the fridge, behind another batch of dough. Going down on her once doesn't give me any claim on her attention or company, but...I don't like Jessie getting set up.

At long last, I fill my mug with coffee, returning to lean against the island, concentrating on the warmth spreading through my fingers and the effort to keep my face neutral.

Maybe I should ask to be set up with someone too. Anything to take my mind off Jessie.

Celia's eyes land on me and light up. "I'll email you the details," she says into the phone. "I've got to go." She glances down to end the call and when she looks up, there's a wolfish smile on her face. "Nic."

I freeze, coffee at my lips, my brain screaming to drop the mug and run.

Celia turns to Amanda. "The kitchen looks good on him, don't you think? Sexy."

Amanda snorts. "Mom. Settle down."

She rolls her eyes. "The flour on those forearms, a little on the stomach. That dark, broody scowl. He'd be a fantastic cohost."

"No," I say, taking a sip of coffee. Did she put Bailey's on her cereal this morning? I'd be an awful cohost.

Celia grins. "He's Nigella. Oozes kitchen sex appeal."

Amanda wrinkles her nose but turns to me, apologetic. "She's gone full cougar. Run."

I laugh. Celia says a lot of stuff, but she's never given off cougar vibes.

"Here." She hands Amanda her phone. "Take a video of us."

I straighten as she comes around the island. "You know this will have to go through my team before you throw it online."

Celia ignores that, her eyebrows knitting together as she tousles my hair. "Undo that button on your Henley," she says, dipping into the butler's pantry. After sharing a brief shrug with Amanda, I do as instructed and pop the button. Celia comes back with Jessie's frilly purple unicorn apron, tossing it over my head.

"Do I look like Nigella?" I ask Amanda, holding my arms out.

"Put a sultry look on your face, talk about chocolate with a husky voice like it's sex, and you're golden." Amanda advises.

I tug at the apron, suddenly self-conscious. No one would want to watch me cohost a cooking show. Unless I was clad in leather and glaring at predetermined fixed points on set.

Celia drops the rested rough puff dough and more frozen shredded butter on the island. "I need a sexy cohost for a show we're developing. We've been looking at some of these young hotshot chefs—"

"The Colton Craigs of the world." Amanda interjects.

Prick. I accept the rolling pin from Celia. Colton Craig's face could benefit from a good, solid thwack of a rolling pin. Five years ago, he hit it off with Jessie at the Christmas Eve Folly. The last time I saw her before this holiday, she was walking upstairs with him.

Celia nods at Amanda as she continues, "—but they're all about ego. We want to go more in an 'everyday, sustainable, ethically-sourced, and affordable' direction. Big flavors, smaller budget, shopping by season, traditional skills, et cetera. But chemistry. We need it to come through, especially for a younger audience. Unfortunately, these young bucks are all a bunch of inaccessible hipsters who think they should call the shots on my project. The assholes."

I laugh, offering her the rolling pin. "Do you need to hit something? Make a graham cracker crust for a cheesecake?" Pulverize Colton Craig's face so I don't have to?

She laughs, pushing it back at me. "Shut up and roll. Anyway, I'm wondering if we should consider a new direction."

"Huh." Amanda smiles, phone in hand, presumably recording as I roll out the dough. "Warwick's bulging muscles as he rolls out rough puff in a frilly apron with a sexy look on his face. I can see the appeal."

She's overestimating my appeal. I place the first portion of butter on the lower two-thirds of the rectangle I rolled out, folding it in thirds before turning it. Roll, fold, turn. More butter. Roll, fold, turn.

Celia keeps talking, asking me questions, a dry run for her show that makes thinking about anything other than what I'm doing impossible. Eventually, I relax into the easy banter. She's grinning when she takes the dough from me and places it in the freezer.

I am too.

"I'll talk to the higher-ups," she says. "Show them the video if I have to, and see what they think about ditching the trendy chef in favor of a sexy celebrity to pair with the smoking hot, far more accomplished—and experienced—lady chef." Celia fluffs her hair, giving me an exaggerated wink.

I cross my arms and lean against the island. "I do have a job, you know." As much as I don't like it, I already know I won't leave it. Not for an uncertain future on a show that probably won't make it past the first season.

Celia throws a dishcloth at me. "It doesn't have to be you. We could take some muscle-head from a reality show. Or some former professional athlete. Or we could make it a guest spot. But, honey"—she pauses to rest her hand lightly on my arm for a few seconds—"you know I'd welcome you into any of my kitchens, anytime."

"Video looks pretty good." Amanda gets to her feet. "Mind if I show Hazel? She can give it a light edit."

Celia nods and Amanda slips out of the kitchen to find her wife.

Editing won't save me from coming across as wooden and boring. It's one thing to get panned for playing a fictional character. Another to get roasted for being myself.

Celia takes my mug and refills it. "Are you going to be all right in LA without Timothy?"

I accept the mug and take a drink. "Yup." If my voice comes out tight, it's because the coffee is too hot, not because I don't want to return to a place where I have no real friends beyond my personal trainer. And I'm not sure I can count a man who makes me do a million burpees as a friend.

She fills her mug, adding cream and a spoonful of sugar. "Come on, let's sit before we clean up. I have to admit, I'm surprised you've stuck it out in LA. Timothy always wanted to be a stunt performer, but acting never seemed like something you'd want to do."

It wasn't. I tripped into it and the money was good and somehow I kept getting roles. My whole career is a series of fortunate mistakes. "You think I should've stuck with modeling?"

She takes a sip, considering. "You know, Jessie still has a magazine page from a cologne ad hidden away in her home office in New York. Don't tell her I told you, I'm not supposed to know. It's under her hot firefighter calendar."

Interesting. I force a laugh. "Are you sure it's not on a dartboard?"

She smiles. "She's altered it."

Of course.

"Seriously though. Are you happy?"

"This past year has been hell," I say. It's true, but not the whole truth.

Celia clucks her tongue. "Even before that, honey. You went to LA because Timothy did, not because you wanted to."

I shift in my seat, uncomfortable at being so transparent. "Someone needed to keep an eye on him." I joke. Not that I did a good job of that. He was injured doing a stunt I couldn't get right. I could have lost my best friend because I struggle with moderately complicated choreography. The way he was on set that day, slurring his words, angry and confused after hitting his head...I shudder at the memory.

Celia reaches over and takes my hand. "It's not your job to look after him. It never has been."

The truth is, Timothy looked after me more than I did him, and it was easy to get caught in his enthusiasm. To chase his dream with him while accepting whatever came my way. Maybe if I hadn't found success things would've been different. I'd have come home.

"What would you do?" she asks me quietly. "If you could do anything."

"Am I that irredeemably bad at acting?"

"Yes." Jessie answers as she walks into the room, heading straight for the coffee.

I don't respond. I'd like to ignore her, but every step she takes makes her short black sweater dress lift half an inch up her thigh and my brain goes where it doesn't belong. I'd give anything to find out what kind of Christmas underwear she's wearing today. Candy canes? Gingerbread men? If we were alone, I'd step behind her, pull her thick hair back, put my lips to her ear, and ask.

Thank god we're not alone.

"Ignore her," Celia says to me, patting my hand and turning to Jessie. "You have a date for the wedding."

Jessie glances sharply over her shoulder at us. "Me?"

"Yes, you."

When Jessie turns her suspicious amber eyes on me, I shake my head. She turns back to her coffee, but not before I catch the look on her face. Relief.

I'm so broken that even though I expect it from her, it still hurts.

She doesn't ask who her date is. She snags a Danish and walks quickly under the mistletoe and out of the kitchen.

Celia turns back to me. "Do you want to keep acting?"

The reprieve Jessie brought me with her coffee run is over. "I don't know. What do you think I should do?"

"That's up to you, sweetie," she says softly. It's the response I expected, but I'm disappointed anyway. "You're always welcome here if you want to take some time to think about what you want."

That, right there, is the biggest reason I need to stop thinking about Jessie. I'm welcome now. If things went sour, her family would take her side. Or maybe they'd remain neutral, but I would never feel comfortable here.

"Thanks," I say to Celia, then change the subject. "Got any pretty chef-friends that would like to be my date to the wedding?"

She takes a sip of her coffee. "Yeah, honey. I know plenty."

Chapter Nine

Nic

Timothy and Mina stroll into the kitchen at nine thirty-five, smiles on their faces. "Let's go!" he calls out, grabbing a couple of Danishes. "Jessie!"

Shit. So much for avoiding her.

Five minutes later Jessie and I are crammed into the back seat of Timothy's truck. Fiancée beats longer legs when it comes to shotgun, unfortunately for me. The truck has an extended cab, but it's not that big, and every bump or turn sends my elbow or knee onto Jessie's side. She defends her territory, elbowing me back like we're children, knocking her knee against mine. It's hard not to stare at that stretch of leg between her knee-high boots and the hem of her dress. Yesterday I had my hands on those thighs. My mouth on her smooth skin.

Maybe, as long as I avoid being alone with her, I can pay her back for tormenting me with Scrabble and cannoli and this too-short sweater dress.

"God, do you have to man-spread?" Jessie whines, pushing me away after I allow Timothy's turn to dump me on her.

I slide closer, pressing my leg against hers and bumping her with my shoulder, just to be an ass. "Where the hell am I supposed to put my arms and legs?"

"I'd like to file a complaint with your personal trainer," she mutters, shoving me again. "No one needs to be this big."

There's nothing in her tone to suggest this is a compliment, but it's the closest she's ever come to giving me one. So I take it. "Thank you. Now scoot over."

Jessie doesn't hesitate. She scoots over—closer. Pushing herself against me.

She smells so good, like blackberries and cinnamon, I want to bury my face in her neck and breathe her in. My hand is on her knee before I think it through, pulling her closer.

In the front seat, I catch a glimpse of Mina nudging Timothy's leg. His eyes flick to us in the rearview mirror.

I shift my hand and shove Jessie's legs away from me, using my shoulder to push her back onto her seat.

Too late. Timothy's grinning.

Jessie notices we're being watched and turns, angling herself away from me.

The truck barely stops and I'm out of the back, gulping in air that doesn't smell like her. The four of us gather on the sidewalk as Timothy looks at his phone.

"In two hours, we meet for lunch at Ginger and Jasmine," Timothy says. "Don't be late, we have to get back in time for caroling. We are not losing to the Stuarts on my watch."

Mina and Jessie link arms and walk down the street. For a moment we stand there, watching.

"You checking out my future wife or my sister?" Timothy finally asks, his tone vaguely threatening before he loses it to a laugh. "Come on."

The three-piece suit fits perfectly and best of all, it's understated in a dark charcoal color. Hearing Timothy had taken care of everything for the wedding had me nervous, but I guess I should've counted on Mina to tamp down some of his wilder impulses.

"So, what are you going to get Jessie?" Timothy asks as we walk back down the busy street after hanging the suits in the back seat of the truck. With my beanie pulled low and my scarf pulled up against the cold, no one gives me a second glance, which is nice for a change.

I shrug, but then spot a craft store and duck inside.

He follows me in, frowning. "What are we doing here?"

When I went into the attic for the Ping-Pong balls, I found Jessie's old paintings. Hundreds of them on canvases and in art books. I looked at all of them, following the years as she honed her skill. Paintings of her mother in the kitchen, Timothy laughing, and her father with a book. A few of me, with Timothy, or in the kitchen with Celia, or by myself staring off into the distance. Paintings of flowers, landscapes, trees, and the lake.

Judging by the most recent dates on the paintings in the attic, she stopped five years ago.

Maybe it's unrelated to Addison's comment. It could have nothing to do with me at all, but something tells me it does.

I stop in the middle of an aisle full of watercolors. "Jessie doesn't paint anymore."

Timothy crosses his arms. "So?"

"Would she start again?"

"If you bought her paints?" He shrugs. "She can buy herself paints and hasn't, so I'm going to guess no. Come on, there's a jewelry shop down the road."

I'm not buying her jewelry. It's impersonal. And she doesn't wear any. The first Christmas after we met, I got her a necklace because I thought that was what girls liked—a rookie teenage mistake. Jessie was unimpressed and probably dropped it in the trash. "She might have overheard Addison's critique of one of her paintings."

Timothy straightens. "Addison shat all over one of my sister's paintings?"

"I'll give Jessie the paints with an apology. Would that work?"

"Dude," he says with a long sigh, "you can't apologize to the world because Addison is a dick."

I shrug.

His eyes narrow. "Is there more to this story?"

Another shrug.

Timothy thinks about it for a moment and grabs a basket from the end of the aisle. "Okay, yes, this is going to be great. Apologize before Jessie opens the gift so she doesn't smash a canvas over your head."

That's a good idea.

I can't remember what brands Jessie liked. She seemed to have a few of everything, so that's what I get her. Timothy grabs some canvases.

There's a Watercolors for Beginners pack and I toss that in too.

"Be nice." Timothy scolds, pulling it out.

"That's for me." I snatch it from him and drop it back in my basket. "I'm doing the Hollywood Art Show and Auction."

"You are?" He blinks twice, then laughs. "Oh, that's too good. Jessie can give you a lesson."

I shake my head. She wouldn't, but also, I need to avoid any situation where Jessie and I could be left alone together if I don't want to end up back between her legs.

Half an hour later, as the clerk, who's at least eighty, rings up everything at glacial speed, Timothy elbows me. "I know, by the way."

"Know what?" When he doesn't answer, I look his way. His grin is trouble. "Know what?" I demand again, the blood in my veins turning to ice.

"That you're a *closeted* art collector."

Fuck.

I've never told anyone. Never showed it to anyone.

"Did she give it to you?" He appears genuinely curious.

"Why were you snooping in my closets?" I shoot back.

Timothy laughs. "So that's a no."

I shove my hands in my pockets. "She threw it in the trash, okay?"

He stares at me in wonder. "You took it out of the trash. After you yelled at her."

I clench my jaw and look away. It was a private moment. No one was supposed to be there. It was two weeks after the car crash that took my parents. I was in their empty house trying to come to terms with the reality that they were never coming home and I'd never get a chance to make things right with them.

Jessie found me crying on the stairs. She came up to me, slow and silent. When I didn't acknowledge her, she sat with me. Her presence was comforting. She didn't fling empty sympathies at me, or try to soothe me with empty words or say she understood. She put her arm around me and we sat without speaking. I felt safe.

A few days later, I walked into the Foley kitchen, where Jessie was painting by the window. We were alone, and since she'd comforted me, I decided to show my interest in her art.

I wasn't ready to be confronted with my face, pinched with grief, tears streaming from my eyes. She'd captured my pain from a private moment and put it on canvas for anyone to see. Hurt and angry, I'd lashed out. Insulted her, her artistic abilities, everything. Yelled loud enough to bring the rest of the Foleys into the kitchen. Timothy had to drag me away.

Later, when I'd cooled down, I'd gone over to apologize. I found the canvas sitting out in the trash. Even though I hated it, I couldn't leave it, so I picked it up and brought it to LA, hiding it from prying eyes deep in my closet.

For a couple of years, I refused to touch it. Then one day near the anniversary of my parents' deaths, I took it out.

It looked different. The grief was still present, but there was a strength in it that I hadn't noticed the night I'd yelled at her. I stared at it for hours, and for a while, I felt like I had with her on the stairs, the only time she'd put her arm around me. I was safe. Jessie had taken all the emotion that was too big for me and released it through her brush.

Addison never found it, thank god. That would've been a shitshow. She became paranoid about Jessie after our fight over Jessie's other painting. I told myself that was why I didn't press the issue when Addison wanted to spend Christmas in Paris or St. Barts—having Addison around Jessie or any of her family brought out Addison's nasty side and I didn't want to deal with the inevitable fights. Mostly, I was too ashamed of the woman I chose to marry to share her with my favorite people.

The clerk finally finishes and I hand over my credit card. Most of the stuff I arrange to have shipped to Jessie's apartment, but I leave with a bag of paints, brushes, and canvases, something for her to open on Christmas Day.

"One more stop," Timothy says as we exit the shop. "We need fuel for Bawdy Carols."

To the liquor store, it is.

Chapter Ten

Jessie

I shiver, bouncing while Mina carefully arranges the garment bag in the back seat of Timothy's truck. The guys have already hung their suits and Nic and I are going to be forced to cuddle in the crowded back seat, which shouldn't make my stomach dip and swoop, but it does.

I blame Nic. The intensity of his silvery stare from between my legs in the laundry room has me fixated. I don't understand what happened between us and chalking it up to a chance encounter between two bored and horny people feels like I'm missing something. We've been alone heaps of times over the years and he's never once offered to go down on me. Why now?

If I can't stop thinking about it, then I'm not going to let Nic forget. I'm dressed to remind him he's been between these thighs and he's not welcome back, but the cold biting at my exposed legs has me regretting not wearing leggings or tights. Sometimes spite is shortsighted.

It's been fun shopping with Mina though. She knows the best shops, and she quickly found me a dress. Shoes too. She didn't pressure me to buy something *nice* for Nic. I did anyway because excellence in cunnilingus should be rewarded.

"We're early," Mina says, slamming the truck door. "But let's go to lunch. I'm freezing my tits off and I need them to hold up my dress."

We take off at a brisk pace, arms linked. The street is lined with trendy shops and wreath-ringed streetlights, last-minute shoppers rushing along, arms bulging with bags.

"What do you want to do for the bachelorette party?" I ask.

"Let's drink and play silly games. Lexi and Charlotte—my high school friends—like to keep things simple too. How many people fit in the massive hot tub outside your parents' room?"

That was another Timothy present, but one that gets some use—my mother and her friends frequently hit it after yoga. Often with a few bottles of wine. "We'll fit." The damn thing holds ten. Twelve if people are willing to get friendly.

Mina laughs. "You know Timothy will crash our party."

Yeah. Likely involving nudity.

We push into the trendy Asian fusion restaurant. Good smells and warmth wrap around me. I shed my coat, hat, and scarf, sinking into the soft, high-backed leather booth with a contented sigh. The closest thing to post-orgasmic bliss has to be walking from the freezing cold into a cozy place. I let the satisfaction roll through me as I snag the drink menu.

We order our drinks and Mina orders a couple of shots. When the waitress leaves, Mina leans over the table, her voice dropping. "What's up with you and Nic?"

"Nothing." My heart kicks up a gear and I pretend to skim the menu even though I already know what I want. "We don't like each other."

"I can see that. Except for the whole thing where you're always looking at each other."

"Scowling," I say, slapping the menu onto the table. "Because hate."

"More like eye-fucking." She grins. "Because pants-feelings."

My spine snaps straight. "I am not eye-fucking Dominic Fontana!"

Mina motions for me to settle down when the tables nearest us shoot me a look, but she's barely keeping her laugh contained.

"Stop it." I point a finger at her. "There is nothing but mutual dislike between us."

She's still laughing. "And a strong desire to bone."

The waitress drops off our drinks and I grab my beer, taking a gulp. If Mina is anything like Timothy, continuing to argue with her will convince her she's right. I have to ignore her and she'll get bored.

Turns out Mina is nothing like my brother.

"You'll have to play nice with Nic," she says after a few minutes of silence, sitting back in the booth, looking smug. "You're walking down the aisle with him."

I stare at her, waiting for her to tell me she's joking.

She's not. "I want you to be my maid of honor. Surprise!" She does jazz hands.

This explains the dress she shoved at me, insisting it was The Dress. It was so pretty that I hadn't given a second thought to how suspiciously quickly we'd found it. It's an odd mix of sexy and demure, with a lace cold shoulder bodice and a satin skirt that hits just below my knees. The pale gold color works well with my skin tone and dark auburn hair. Mina's bridesmaid game is top-notch. But the maid of honor?

"Um, but..." How do I politely point out we've only known each other for twenty-four hours?

"Charlotte and Lexi have been my friends since high school, and while I love them, I am not choosing between them. Also, they're both a bit intimidated by Nic. The whole celebrity thing. It's for their comfort, as well."

It's more than the celebrity thing. Nic's so pretty that to stand next to him, even in a beautiful dress with professionally styled hair and makeup, is to fade into the background. I'm used to it, at least. "We'll murder each other. Ruin your wedding."

Mina shrugs. Does she seriously not care if we ruin her day?

I shake my head. "You're out of your mind."

"I *am* marrying your brother." She tips her beer at me before taking a drink.

I'm going to have to touch Nic. Take his arm. Dance with him. Pose for photos with him. How can I make it through all that? I'm going to be a distracted, confused mess of sexual frustration and irritation within ten minutes.

"Nic's not going to be able to keep his eyes off you." Mina winks, pushing one of the shots she ordered to me. "Lots of dark corners in the venue, by the way."

"He wishes," I mutter. Except he doesn't. He didn't stick around in the laundry room, he hasn't asked for more or tried for anything. He clearly regrets what happened and that hurts.

I turn the shot glass in my hand. The drink is a delicate pink, pale as a cherry blossom. The color my cheeks might be if I had feelings for Nic, instead of the scarlet or crimson they're turning. Humiliation and rejection have an uglier palette.

Mina must pick up on my lack of enthusiasm because she changes the topic. "I want to embroider something floral for my spring release, but I can't draw anything beyond a simple daisy. You painted those gorgeous flowers in your room—any ideas?"

Mina's already pulling a pocket-sized sketchbook and a pen out of her hand-bag, pushing them across the table to me. I don't have any ideas, but Mina's too invested in telling me her struggles over a pumpkin spice latte to let me get a word in. I pick up the sketchbook and rifle through it. Dozens of tidy sketches dot the sheets before I find a blank page.

It's just a doodle. It doesn't matter if she doesn't like it.

"What kind of flower do you want?" I ask, picking up the pen.

She shrugs. "I've done daisies and tulips. I tried to do a cherry blossom once, but it didn't look right."

I sketch a couple of cherry blossoms as Mina tells me about her embroidery machine and how it works, what sort of designs work best for the small size she needs. I do a few other flowers, too, irises, lilacs, wisteria, as she talks.

"These are really good," she says after I hand the sketch pad and pen back. "This one would make a beautiful screen print." She points to the wisteria.

Huh. It would be cute on a canvas bag or a T-shirt. Guess I never thought about putting any of my doodles on clothes. I still can't believe anyone would want them, let alone my boss Elle or a gallerist like Gretchen Torres.

There's an email from Elle sitting unopened in my inbox with the subject line: Commission for Gretchen Torres. It's probably a reminder or Gretchen's contact information, but I can't bring myself to look in case it was all a mistake and Gretchen liked some other piece of actual art Elle has on her walls.

Mina stares at the designs, a thoughtful look on her face, before she glances up at me. "Would you consider doing some designs like this a few times a year for me? I'll pay and credit you."

I'm already shaking my head. "They're doodles, nothing special. You should hire a professional."

"You are."

"I photoshop vibrators. It's not the same."

Timothy saves the day as he launches himself into the booth, kissing Mina like it's been years instead of hours and putting an end to the conversation.

Nic's standing next to me, hat pulled low, scarf still covering the lower half of his face, sunglasses still on. "Scoot," he says in a quiet voice.

I slide deeper into the booth and Nic drops in next to me.

Timothy and Mina are whispering. I should say something to Nic, but he's staring at his phone, so I don't.

Something brushes my leg and I'm ready to shove him out of the booth, but I glance down first.

He sets a small box on my lap. Booze-filled fancy chocolates. My phone buzzes.

> For the ride home. Put them in your hand-bag—they'll melt in my pocket.

UNKNOWN NUMBER

> How do you have my number?

ME

> I don't know. I've always had it.

UNKNOWN NUMBER

I slip the chocolates into my handbag because I'm keeping them. I might let Nic have one if he keeps his thick thighs on his side of the truck.

The waitress takes our order and Timothy sheds his outer layers and takes charge of the conversation. Something about a house they're looking at.

"Are you going to eat lunch with your scarf wrapped around your face?" I finally ask Nic because it's driving me nuts that he's still all bundled up. No wonder he was worried about melting the chocolates.

He unwraps it without a word, setting it in the space between us.

I keep my mouth shut for five minutes. I don't know why his discomfort is pissing me off, but it is. "Aren't you hot?" I ask him, interrupting my brother.

"Sexiest Man in America." Timothy chirps, raising his beer. Nic, with no expression whatsoever on his face, raises his bottle to tap Timothy's.

I'm proud of myself when I don't gag. "You're going to get heatstroke."

"It's his disguise," Timothy stage whispers.

I roll my eyes. "A smile would work better. Throw in a laugh, no one will recognize you."

Nic turns to face me, pulling his sunglasses off so I get the full effect of his glare.

I circle my finger around his face. "Not a smile. Try again."

His lips twitch before his hand covers them and he rubs his jaw to hide it.

"Jessica Foley," my brother says in mock wonder. "I think you made Dominic Fontana smile."

The sunglasses snap back in place and Nic glances around the restaurant. "Timothy. Shut up."

This is ridiculous. "Get up."

Nic doesn't so I give his arm a push and finally he slides out of the booth. I slip past him and motion for him to take my place.

"Yeah," Timothy says with a laugh as I sit in Nic's spot. "That's gonna hide him. Like an elephant behind a parking meter."

Given the high back of the booth and our location toward the back of the restaurant, and our side with our backs to the door, only a couple of tables now have a clear view of Nic.

Thank you, he mouths to me as he slips his coat off a few minutes into Timothy's next tangent. I tip my head in a slight acknowledgment.

No one recognizes Nic during lunch—or if they do, they don't care enough to gawk.

Timothy and Mina carry on the conversation. Nic manages to contribute a few grunts. I barely speak, but Mina lets me doodle in her sketchbook. I'm so engrossed in Christmas doodles that I don't notice Timothy and Mina ditching us while Nic pays the bill.

Fine. I need to get something for Mina anyway. I tuck her sketchbook into my bag and follow Nic. Walking out into the bitingly fresh air jolts me awake. "Meet you at the truck," I say to him before taking advantage of a break in traffic to dart across the street. I duck into a quirky housewares shop, the scent of cinnamon candles and the victory of my escape bringing a smile to my face as I skip over to the table full of snarky Christmas mugs.

Ten seconds later there's a tug on my coat sleeve and I drop the mug. The clatter hides my gasp of surprise.

Irritation sharpens Nic's voice. "Don't do that again. I was almost hit by a car."

He followed me. Into traffic? He's exaggerating. I make a dismissive noise as I inspect the dropped mug—not broken. "You can toss those things around like toys, right?"

A heavy sigh is his response, as if my quip gave him a headache. I put the mug down, reaching for another. "You can wait outside. This won't take long."

"Getting rid of *Blow Me—I'm Hot*?"

"Never." I turn to find him a hell of a lot closer to me than expected. The smart-ass in me wants to point out that he did blow me, but I'm too afraid he'll say I'm not hot and I have no comebacks for that. "I'm getting one for Mina. Early present."

"Good idea." Nic reaches across me to pick up a mug. I have to fight the urge to breathe in his leather and spice scent. He makes it worse by not moving away once he has the mug, his breath near my ear as he speaks. "Thoughtful of you, considering a few days ago you didn't like her."

"It wasn't about her." I keep my eyes on the mugs, heat creeping up my neck. "I don't—"

"Excuse me, are you...?"

We both jump, spinning around. I'd forgotten we were out in public, caught up in my annoyance with him. Nic's hat is stuffed in his coat pocket, his scarf loose and away from his face.

"He is!" A smaller voice, a kid. A family of five stands there, gaping at Nic. Starstruck.

The scowl melts off Nic's face, replaced with an easy smile and softer, engaging eyes. His entire body loosens in a way I've never seen before. He's not relaxed. He's not even...Nic.

Huh. He's acting.

This is weird, so I slip back as the family eagerly peppers him with questions and gushes at him. The two teenagers correctly determine I'm no one famous, but the parents don't look as sure, their eyes flickering to me from time to time.

Phones come out. It's selfie time and everyone gets a turn.

I go back to looking at mugs, but my focus is on Nic's laugh and easy banter. I think I prefer silent and surly Nic.

"Can we get a photo of you and your...girlfriend?"

I snort, clapping a hand over my mouth.

Some of the goodwill disappears from Nic's face as he adjusts his scarf. "She's a family friend. Let's not."

Is he too embarrassed to be photographed in public with me? Afraid people will think we're dating? I know I'm no Addison, but ouch.

That's probably what he wants, isn't it? Another Addison, but more faithful.

"He's a great Warwick, isn't he?" the father asks me. They're still looking at me like they're trying to place me. The longer we stay here the higher the chance they realize I look a little like my mother.

Nic's eyes meet mine.

I grin. "I liked him best in *Summer Camp*."

Nic slips back into himself for a second, his eyes hardening. He's all but scowling at me when one of the teenagers asks about the next Warwick movie.

He reaches for that persona, but it fails and it's just Nic standing there, staring and looking lost, unable to talk.

Shit. Did I break him? I told the truth. That stupid movie with bad singing and ridiculous dancing is my favorite. It's the one movie where he didn't play someone too powerful, too enigmatic, and too perfect.

Nic's eyes land on me again and drop to the floor before he answers the kid. "I don't know if I'll do it."

Stunned silence.

What the actual hell?

I narrow my eyes at him, but he won't look at me.

The family bursts out with "Oh, no, you have to," "No one can play Warwick like you," and "We love you in those movies." On and on, in a rising cacophony that's sure to attract more attention. The corner of the store we're in isn't busy—just a few older people stopping to give us confused looks—but it won't take long, with the busy street outside, for us to get overwhelmed here.

Nic smiles, laughs uncomfortably, and tries to pass it off as a joke.

Shit. He's lost his ability to be Nic Fontana, Hollywood star. We need to leave—now—because I have no idea if he can handle a stampede of Warwick fans.

My eyes land on the perfect mug. *Tinsel Tits*, with tinsel wrapped around the text. "Found it!" I say, snagging the mug before turning to the family. "Sorry, we have to go. It was nice meeting you."

Nic echoes me, and I drag him to the front of the store. "Go wait by the truck." I snatch his hat, shoving it down over his dark hair. To be safe, I wrap the scarf around his face. Tightly.

He tugs the scarf down and ignores my instructions. Screw it. If more fans crawl out of the kitchenware, he can scare them off with that scowl.

There's no line and a minute later, we make our escape onto the streets.

Nic pulls me out of the way of pedestrians, holding my arm and keeping me close.

"*Summer Camp?* Really?" His eyes flash. "Do you always have to come at me swinging like that? It fucking hurts, Jessie."

He doesn't give me a chance to reply before he releases me and stalks off.

I want to shout after him that he's hurt me too, but a deep breath and the interruption of my phone cost me the moment.

> Get your asses to the truck, if we lose this year I
> swear—

TIMOTHY

Nic's already in the truck when I climb in. He refuses to look at me. Fine. I get it. He hated *Summer Camp*, even skipping the premiere, according to the tabloids. I'd always assumed he'd been embarrassed by the role, but he admitted it hurt. I struck a nerve.

We've caused enough damage to each other over the years that he can't understand my answer was honest. It's like we don't know how to stop. Maybe we can't and this is just who we are.

I don't know why that depresses me, but it does. I want...I don't know. A truce.

I reach over, poking him in the thigh. He turns to me, wary. I mouth the word *sorry* and pull the chocolates out of my handbag, offering them to him. After a tense few seconds, he inclines his head slightly, takes one out of the box with silent precision so Timothy doesn't realize we have food in his truck, and goes back to looking out the window.

Chapter Eleven

Jessie

The moment we walk through the door, Timothy throws the house into an uproar, bellowing that if we're not ready to roll in forty minutes, we'll face his wrath. Nic bolts up the stairs to his room, so I dip into the kitchen to help my mother with the booze. When he comes downstairs, I go upstairs to change into jeans, a thermal, and my warmest sweater. Not that I'm avoiding him...I'm just trying to not be around him.

It's chaos as we all gather in the entry, scrambling to don hats, scarves, and mittens. Timothy attempts to run us through some vocal warm-ups as my mother hands out flasks. My brother takes the lead, marching down the driveway, pinching a plastic candy cane from a neighbor's yard and swinging it like a parade marshal.

"Watch the ice!" Timothy points the candy cane at the patch of ice that took me out on my arrival. The plastic reindeer that had been marking the spot is gone, back in the same neighbor's yard Timothy stole the candy cane from. No doubt my mother will be bringing over a massive box of Christmas cookies later to smooth things over.

Ten-year-old Liam is a step behind Timothy, mimicking every move, and my brother pauses to 'borrow' another candy cane, bestowing it upon our nephew with ridiculous solemnity.

Evie is struggling to catch up, so Nic scoops her up and settles her on his shoulders before falling into step with our fearless leaders.

The rest of us trail behind, my parents commenting on new neighbors or new decorations; Amanda, Hazel, Mina, and I take up the rear, drinking and laughing.

"What, exactly, are we doing?" Mina asks, flipping Timothy off when he bellows at us to hurry up.

"Something I ask myself every year." Amanda takes a swig from her flask.

Hazel slips her arm through her wife's. "I don't know how this all started, but every December twenty-first, we get drunk and walk to the Gullivers' house, where they'll judge us as we engage in a battle of dirty carols against the Stuart family. Amanda and I then spend the next few months trying to get the kids to forget the lyrics."

"We always win," I add. "Because swearing children are adorable."

"And Mrs. Gulliver thinks Timothy has a phenomenal ass, which he never fails to twerk on up to her." Hazel grins, tipping her flask back. A ruddy glow is already spreading across her cheeks and she cuddles closer to Amanda.

Timothy stops in front of a house that appears to have vomited every Christmas decoration ever made in a haphazard fashion that screams the kids did it. Except the Gulliver kids are teenagers, so two reindeer are screwing and baby Jesus is stuck in the basketball hoop. The whole family is bundled up in lawn chairs lining the end of the driveway, waiting for the show, hot drinks in hand, and piles of snowballs in buckets for the losers.

Greetings are called out and when the Stuart family shows up wearing tacky hats covered in Christmas lights, Timothy pulls us all into a huddle, demanding we down the contents of our flasks immediately for maximum drunkenness as he hands each of us a copy of the songs we're doing.

It's chaotic, off-key, and wonderful. Timothy leads us through our three songs swinging his massive candy cane like a drunken conductor as we take turns with the Stuarts to serenade our neighbors. Mrs. Gulliver gets her lap dance, too, and this year Mr. Gulliver tips a bucket of snow over them.

Standing at the edge of the group, I snap a few photos with my phone. Liam and Evie, singing their little hearts out, eyes alight from all the naughty words they get to use this one time. Amanda and Hazel, arms around each other, belting out a song about balls. My mother getting way too into it with her dancing while my father's deep voice carries the day on a song about hos. Mina claps along, laughing so hard she has tears in her eyes.

And Nic, his cheeks pink from the cold, Evie still perched on his shoulders and banging on his head like a drum. He's relaxed. He doesn't have to be the man he pretended to be with his fans earlier. Everyone here knew him before he became a big deal, and no one is going to ask invasive questions about his divorce or who he's dating, or what he's working on next. He's just Nic. Timothy's scrawny best friend who grew up.

And goddammit he grew up.

The late sun bathes his face in soft lighting, making his gray eyes sparkle. My breath catches at the pure joy in the laughter of a man who so often keeps everything buttoned up tight. He's beautiful like this.

Maybe it's the cold, or the camaraderie of this silly tradition, or the booze from my now-empty flask, but dammit, for a minute, I wish this side of him was mine—that I could make him smile and laugh instead of scowl.

When it's all over, Timothy and Ian—leader of the Stuarts—step forward, prepared to accept their fate while the Gullivers toss snowballs in the air, smirking as they consult among themselves. After a suitable amount of ass-kissing and insults, the snowballs are lobbed at the Stuarts as we are proclaimed the winners.

Nic's face lights up. Our eyes meet and instead of the smile falling from his face like it so often does, it widens and I find myself smiling back.

Timothy whoops, grabbing Mina and spinning her like he's won the lottery. Maybe he has. He races off down the road, Mina yelling at him to set her down. Soon they're out of sight. Our group fractures more as Amanda, Hazel, and the kids take the long way home to look at Christmas lights now that dusk is upon us. My parents stop to chat with a neighbor who comes outside.

Everything is falling into place for Timothy. Amanda has her perfect family. I didn't think I'd be the last, but here I am, walking home alone from Bawdy Carols.

It's been five years since my last and only serious boyfriend. It's bleak out there—the idea of trying to find someone serious is laughable. I had to kiss a lot of frogs to find Camden and he turned out to be a toad.

Snow crunches on the street behind me. I spin around, uncertain if I'll be facing a snowball ambush or a serial killer.

Nic's walking a few feet back, hands stuffed into the pockets of his expensive wool coat, the tips of his ears and nose pink in the lavender twilight, his eyes on the ground—until they fly up to me, widening in surprise.

"Sorry. I didn't mean to follow you." He freezes and looks around, a frown tugging his brows down. "Everyone left. Can I walk you back?"

Guess I'm not the only one alone. I wait for him to join me, and we walk on in silence. Nic looks at the lights on the houses. I commit the deep lilac of dusk on snow to memory. The wanting usually passes, but it's always surprising that after all this time, after all the shit, I long to pick up my brushes and watch my watercolors bloom.

Maybe I need to get over myself and paint. Embrace my mediocrity.

Occasionally Nic's arm brushes mine, intruding more and more on my musings on colors until I can no longer ignore him by my side. His problems appear to be at least as big as my own, and frankly, I'd rather think about them. He doesn't want to do the next Warwick movie. Is he unhappy?

"You don't have to keep acting." I blurt out, startling him. Myself too.

He scowls. "Why wouldn't I?"

The snap in his question almost brings a *fuck off* to my lips, but I remember how he unraveled in front of his fans and push past the urge. I shrug. "I don't know."

He eyes me as we walk. Trying to figure out if I'm genuine or about to kneecap him. I hate that it's like this with us. We can't even have a civil conversation.

"I don't know either." His voice is quiet as we continue slowly down the street, our hands in our pockets.

"Do you love it?" I ask, genuinely curious. I always assumed he loved the lifestyle that came with it. Namely, beautiful women.

Nic stops in front of a house with Christmas lights blinking over the shrubbery, and I stand next to him, arm to arm. His answer is a deep breath, the plume of steam as he slowly blows it out hanging between us. "I get letters, Jessie. Kids, teenagers. Parents. They're undergoing treatments at a hospital for something awful like cancer, dealing with stress from bullying, or whatever. How watching these movies helped them through a dark time. And I remember how hard it was for me after my parents died. Timothy would put on a movie and for a few hours, it all went away."

I grab his arm. "They can turn on any movie. Watch any other actor play any other role. It doesn't have to be you if you aren't happy."

His brow furrows as he turns to face me. For a long moment, he stares at me. "Are you trying to cheer me up by telling me I'm not special?"

I squeeze his arm and let go. "One hundred percent, yes."

A smile cracks his lips, a huff of a laugh escaping. "I can always count on you for perspective on my own insignificance, can't I?"

"Isn't that what we do for each other?"

His smile drops. "What?"

"You know," I say, feeling a little like I'm on thin ice. "We take each other's egos down a peg or two."

"Jessie, I—"

A snowball to the back of the shoulders cuts him off. The next one catches me as I turn, nailing me in the face—thankfully one of Evie's softer throws—and I don't wait around to get hit again. I take off down the street.

Timothy and Mina jump into the melee, drawing fire from the kids and Amanda and Hazel, allowing me to escape down a cul-de-sac. The snow pushed into the middle by the plows has been turned into a fort by the neighborhood kids, so I scramble up and jump in. The four walls are uneven but high enough that I can tug my jacket over my ass and sit, perfectly concealed.

Nic leaps over the wall, landing in the middle and crouching. It's so like a scene out of one of his Warwick movies that I snicker.

"They all turned on your parents," he says, sitting next to me. "I don't think anyone saw us. How's your face?" His gloved fingers tentatively grip my chin, tilting my head as his eyes sweep over me. "Meh."

"Asshole," I grumble, batting his hand away.

His laugh is soft under his breath. Shifting, he peers over the rim of the wall again, then leans over to whisper against my ear. "Liam's at the end of the street. We might be stuck here a while."

Great. The cold is already seeping through my jeans.

We sit shoulder to shoulder and I hate to admit it but Nic's warmth is nice. I shift, digging into my pocket, pulling out my flask, and bringing it to my lips before I remember it's empty. I pocket it in disgust. Next year, I need two.

Nic nudges me, handing his flask over.

The whiskey burns on the way down, warming me from the inside. I lick my lips and hold the flask out to Nic. When he doesn't take it, I turn to him and—oh.

His eyes are heated, focused on my mouth. Smug satisfaction wraps around me, warming me more than the whiskey. When he realizes I've caught him, he takes the flask and tilts it back and it's my turn to appreciate the way his lower lip curves around the opening, the bob of his Adam's apple as he swallows. His eyes hold mine spellbound as he lowers the flask. In the deep blue of our frozen hiding place, they look almost black. Fathomless, like they'll swallow me whole.

He leans into me to pocket the flask, and suddenly we're close, exchanging the same breath of whiskey-scented air.

It happens in slow motion in the fading light, the cold of the snow fort giving way to the warmth of his lips as I kiss him, the gentle touch of his tongue as he kisses me back. The snow around us muffles the world outside, muffles the rustle of gloves on jackets as we pull each other closer, this soft moment between us sparking into a blaze.

He shoves me away with a gasp. "Jessie, stop."

Hurt expands through my chest with every breath I draw, anger warming my face. I don't know why this keeps happening to us. "Make up your fucking mind."

"Jessie, it's not—" He reaches for me and I slap his hand away.

"Don't touch me." I pull my scarf tight because tears are already stinging my eyes. If I don't get out of this snow fort in the next ten seconds, I'll be ugly crying, which pisses me off because Nic isn't worth a single goddamn tear.

"We can't—"

"I don't want to," I whisper, standing directly into an onslaught of snowballs. I immediately drop back down.

Nic stares at me, eyes wide, as I wipe snow out of my face and shake it out of my hair.

He laughs.

"Oh, fuck this," I mutter. I'd rather get slaughtered than make my last stand in this fort with him, so I run for it, leaving him to his fate.

Chapter Twelve

Nic

December Twenty-second

"Looks like the Picasso of Peens has entered her blue phase," William says, taking a sip of his coffee as he stares out the dining room window the next morning.

My blood turns to ice and I glance up, expecting everyone to know, to be looking at me, watching for my reaction. Instead, William's still looking out at the snow-covered lawn. Celia's cooking the waffles I mixed up.

Jessie's sitting at the table. Even with her back to me, I can feel her anger.

Most people build snowmen. Jessie builds snow dicks. I have no idea how she turned the enormous balls flanking it blue, but I know she built it sometime before the sun came up, and I know it's for me.

I've replayed that moment in the snow fort a hundred times. I don't know if I kissed her first or if she kissed me. With how quickly it escalated and how abruptly I ended it...I can't blame her for being pissed. This thing between us is a problem and she can make a hundred snow dicks and glare at me all she wants. I'm still going to ignore until it goes away.

I pick up my coffee, blow on it, and set it down again. Still too hot.

"I'm guessing I'm out of blue food coloring." Celia looks out the kitchen window with a grin. "Impressive though. Suppose our Picasso needs to get some D?"

"Mother!" Amanda gasps, walking into the kitchen and quickly trying to earmuff Evie, who races to the window.

"Looks like it." William cedes the window to Evie, mussing her hair. He passes me on his way out of the kitchen, clapping a hand on my shoulder and chuckling as he goes by.

His nose is nearly always in a book. No way has he noticed anything between me and Jessie.

Or has he?

"Breakfast is ready." Celia adds the final waffle to the tray keeping warm in the oven.

"What is that?" Evie asks, tugging on Amanda's sleeve while pointing out the window. "Is that a D? What's a D?"

Amanda sighs, defeated. "It's a penis."

Evie's button nose wrinkles. "Why? Penis starts with a *P*."

"There's another word for a penis that starts with a *D*, and it's a word you don't get to say. Your auntie is a perv. She's going to stop making snow d—penises."

Jessie gets up, and the moment she heads my way, I look at my phone.

"It's vaginas from now until Christmas," she announces.

I snicker and out of the corner of my eye, I catch her glaring at me as she gives the whipped cream a violent shake. I pretend to go back to my phone, but I'm keeping an eye on her until she puts the whipped cream down.

"Grow up," Amanda says, stomping to the island and grabbing a plate.

Jessie points the dispenser at her. "Says the woman who tackled me for an *X* in Scrabble."

She sticks her tongue out, but Jessie's quick with the whipped cream dispenser, and before Amanda can flinch away, Jessie fills her mouth.

Amanda runs to the sink to spit it out before turning on Jessie. "You're dead, J."

Jessie takes a step backward. Amanda takes one forward.

I know how this is going to end. Amanda's taller and more athletic. Jessie picked a fight she can't win.

Amanda lunges, and the dispenser clatters onto the island as Jessie loses her grip when she jumps back. Amanda snaps up a kitchen towel and Jessie curses, weaponless.

Celia and Evie break into cheers as the chase winds around the island twice. I sit on my barstool in the middle of it, pretending I'm engrossed by an email.

The whipped cream dispenser is right next to me and my fingers itch. Jessie and Amanda have reversed direction, slowing down, with Jessie walking backward, getting closer to me, her hand out like she's going to reach for it.

I should stay out of this.

"Now, Amanda," Jessie says as her sister twists the towel for a good snap. "Why don't we take this outside—"

My fingers close over the whipped cream dispenser. Given how hard Jessie shook it before, it should be good to go.

"—and settle this with a friendly snowball fight?"

Jessie is alongside me. It's too easy. I hold the dispenser out and press the nozzle. Whipped cream hits her on the cheek, splattering all over her face, and landing in her hair.

Jessie freezes, eyes wide, face striped with whipped cream.

Amanda doubles over, howling with laughter. Everyone's laughing, Evie jumping up and down, demanding a turn.

Jessie's not laughing. She turns on me, slowly. "You shot me in the face."

Her choice of words sends heat creeping up my neck. She wipes a handful of whipped cream off her cheek. I pick up my coffee and fight the urge to grin.

Jessie moves, but not toward the dispenser I've still got a death grip on. Nope, she wipes that handful of whipped cream all over the side of my face and into my hair. I jerk back, my too-hot coffee sloshing over my mug and into my lap. With a hiss, I leap to my feet, plucking my jeans away from my body.

"Sorry," Jessie says with a wince as Amanda hands me her kitchen towel.

"Are you all right, Nic?" Celia asks, concern knitting her brows. "I have an ice pack if you need it for your penis."

Celia saying *penis* like that makes me cringe.

Evie giggles. "If you need it for your D."

"I'm fine," I say through clenched teeth. My damp jeans are rapidly cooling and I lucked out with most of the hot coffee missing sensitive areas.

"That's lucky," Jessie says. "Every model in LA would go into mourning if you scalded your dick off."

I glare at her as whipped cream drips down my face, but I can't say she's wrong—not exactly. It's been months since I've had sex but before that...I slept with a lot of women and quite a few happened to be models. I'd like to think I'd get a few sympathy texts, but the sex was meaningless and I never slept with the same woman twice, so I doubt I would.

Celia sighs when her stern look goes unnoticed by Jessie, who's complaining about whipped cream in her hair. "Go clean up, you two. I'll keep your breakfast warm."

We've only got one shower and the moment our eyes meet, I see Jessie has realized it too.

Celia's startled laugh follows us as we race out of the kitchen. My longer legs put me in the lead and I take the stairs two at a time, Jessie hot on my heels.

We disappear into our respective rooms and meet again, bursting into the bathroom from our separate doors. Jessie's too winded to do anything more than point at me and shake her head. She's a fucking mess, whipped cream streaked in her hair, smeared on her face, her chest heaving from the race up the stairs.

I want her so badly I have to clench my hands at my sides. "What happened between us was a mistake," I tell her, pissed at myself all over again. We wouldn't be here like this if I hadn't had a lapse of judgment in the laundry room.

Jessie puts her hands on her hips, still trying to catch her breath. "Right. You tripped and fell face-first between my thighs. Total accident."

"I said a mistake, not an accident!" I scrape at the stubble on my jaw. My face is sticky from drying whipped cream.

"If you want to pretend things never happened, fine. If you hated every minute of it, that's your problem. I enjoyed myself." Jessie pulls her sweater off, tossing it onto the floor. The bra she's wearing today is covered in little red bows, a tiny one nestled between her tits. "The first shower is mine."

"You get the second shower." I reach back to pull my shirt off. Jessie watches me, her eyes narrowed but not so much that I can't see the simmer. My dick is already thickening, pressing against the cold wetness of my jeans.

Jessie doesn't say a word as she walks to the shower and yanks on the tap, but when she turns, her hands go to her leggings and she deliberately shimmies them over her hips.

Her panties have gingerbread cookies on them.

"Do you own normal underwear?" I ask, undoing my jeans and shoving them down.

"Do you *really* want to know about my underwear?" she asks in a husky voice. Then she gets tangled in her leggings and trips because her eyes are on my underwear as I kick my jeans aside.

"No." I lie. "I don't." I want to know everything about her underwear, but mostly I want to take them off her. "The first shower is mine."

Jessie shakes her head as she unhooks her bra. It probably falls to the floor, but I don't notice because her tits are gorgeous, her pink nipples hardening, begging to be sucked and tugged.

Shit. I shouldn't be here with her. I shouldn't be pushing down my jockey shorts. But I am pushing them down, and Jessie's taking off her gingerbread panties. Then we're naked. Staring at each other. This time when she looks at my dick, she doesn't look disappointed. She looks hungry.

Jessie steps into the shower, adjusting the heat before giving me a saucy little look. That's all the invitation I need to follow. When I touch her, her skin is warm and wet and she turns in my arms and I crush her into the tiled wall. The feel of her body, slick against mine, has me so damned hard. My hands are everywhere, touching her everywhere, drawing little whimpering sounds from her. Twenty years of pent-up lust unleashed just like that. The softness of her might kill me, but fuck. Worth it. I tangle one hand in her hair and cup her face with the other.

I don't give a damn if this is the biggest mistake of my life. I'm going to make it.

"We do this once." I warn her, brushing my thumb over her plump lower lip.

I want her lip between my teeth. The taste of her in my mouth. Jessie nips my thumb and I let my hand drop to rest in the notch of her collarbone. My fingers curl where her neck meets her shoulder. "We don't tell anyone."

Jessie nods, her eyes wide.

When I bend to kiss her, she stops me, her eyes wary. "I'm not interested in a pity fuck."

Is that what she thinks the laundry room was? I mean, I don't know what it was, but I know it wasn't that. "I don't fuck for charity."

"It probably won't be any good. For either of us." Her voice is breathy as I skate my lips over hers.

I'm not sure that's possible, but I agree with her anyway. "We won't want to do it again."

She gives me an almost gentle push. "Go get a condom. We do this once and go back to normal."

Normal would be good. I really, really need normal.

Chapter Thirteen

Jessie

Any second, Nic's going to come to his senses. He's going to stop searching his jeans for a condom, realize it's me, and walk out of this bathroom without a word. I know it in my bones.

God, my impulse control sucks. He's going to hurt me again.

I tip my head back, closing my eyes as warm water rinses the whipped cream from my hair. Anticipation thrums through me from head to toe. I'm trying to be okay with the fact that Nic's going to walk out, leaving me unsatisfied and humiliated and I'm going to have to spend the rest of the holiday pretending I don't care.

His hand slides over the wet skin of my waist, and I suck in a breath.

He didn't leave.

He doesn't press against me, not right away, but I can feel how close he is. My skin buzzes with the knowledge. His touch is light and teasing, trailing down my stomach and dipping lower, the only contact between us. A small moan escapes my lips as his fingers find my clit.

I need this so damn bad.

He kisses me, hot and wet, where my neck and shoulder meet, as he closes the gap between us. His body is hard at my back, his erection pressing against my ass. He slips a finger inside me, then another, his touch hitting just right.

"You're so wet for me." He mumbles into my shoulder, his teeth scraping my skin and making me shiver.

I rock my hips against him and gasp at the sensation that unfurls within me. "We're in the shower, dumbass."

He pulls his fingers free, his hand skimming up my body as he brings them to his mouth. "Definitely you." He uses that hand to turn my face to his for a surprisingly gentle kiss.

I break away from the softness of it and his lips go back to my neck. I don't want gentle. Not from him. This is the laundry room, part two, and I'm not going to lose sight of that.

My impatient noises bring a smile against my neck, his hand cupping the side of my ass as his lips peel away from my skin. "Impressive bruise. What happened?"

"Slipped on some ice." It doesn't hurt anymore—I have enough cushion, something his hand takes advantage of as he palms me. I press back into him, closing my eyes as he thrusts his dick against my slippery skin. I need it inside me. Five minutes ago. Why is he talking about my bruise? We need to fuck and we need to fuck now. I don't think anyone in my family will put waffles on hold to check in with either of us, but if we're gone too long..."I'm not here for your conversation, Nic."

His hand moves across my collarbone, drawing a shudder from me as he lightly covers my throat, his thumb under my chin tilting my head back so he can leave a trail of hot kisses from my temple to my jaw. "Got another use for my mouth, Jessie?" His other hand slips between my legs again as he thrusts against my ass.

"Kiss me," I tell him. I'll leave the where up to him.

Instead of kissing me or reaching for the condom he set on the soap, he turns me around. His lips rest against my forehead, his hands heavy on my shoulders. For a long moment, we stand still, the only sound the drumming of the shower.

This is it. He's changing his mind. Asking for a kiss made this too real, and he's remembering all the reasons this is a huge mistake.

I just want an orgasm, for fuck's sake. I want to break the tension between us and feel some goddamn relief after twenty years of suppressed lust.

"Nic—"

He shoves his hands into my wet, tangled hair, tilting my face up so his hazy eyes hold me, soothing away the tightness in my chest. "Shh. I'm only here for your moans."

Nothing could prepare me for the way he kisses me. Not the laundry room, not the snow fort, not that gentle kiss a minute ago. There's nothing soft, nothing slow. Nic cranks it straight to an eleven, his usual reserve gone, replaced by something greedy and consuming, wholly unexpected but so good. I feel it in my toes when his fingers tighten in my hair, in the pulse between my legs, the sweet sting of my scalp when he tugs my head back to deepen this kiss.

There's overpowering relief, too, as I give in to hunger, digging my nails into his back to pull him tight. I can't get close enough, our wet bodies slipping against each other. He's so hard and I want to touch every inch of him. Marvel in the grooves between muscles. Find out if he's ticklish. Watch his abs tense under my fingers as I dip them lower. His body is amazing and I want to explore it.

But that's not what this is. This is scratching an itch.

A sentiment he clearly doesn't share. He keeps one hand buried in my hair at the back of my neck, holding me to him, but his other hand claims every inch of skin he can reach, setting me alight.

It's strange how natural this feels, being with him. We fit and it's terrifying if I think about it. Luckily, the haze of pure hormones inspired by the feel of his body against mine makes it pretty damn hard to think about anything beyond one solid, very hard fact:

I'm finally getting my hands on that dick.

The sound that comes from his throat when I reach between us and wrap my fingers around his length is everything. He repeats it when I give him one long, slow stroke, his hips thrusting in time when I do it again and again.

Nic tugs my lower lip between his teeth as he breaks off the kiss. His smile is wicked as he slips from my grasp. I forget to be disappointed at losing my plaything when his tongue swirls around my nipple and he draws it into his mouth, setting off an echoing pulse between my legs. My fingers slide into his wet hair, my body arching into him as he works me until I'm moaning before kissing his way down my stomach.

I know what's coming when he kneels and hooks my left leg over his shoulder, but I still gasp, putting my hands against the wall when his mouth touches me, licking me and sucking me like a man starving, like he can't get enough. The idea that he wants me this badly makes me so damn wet.

"Fuck, Nic." My words have all the substance of the steam surrounding us. I lean forward into the wall, freeing one hand to wind my fingers through his wet hair.

His face grows slick against my thighs and my hips rock, seeking more. He slides a couple of fingers inside me, thrusting and curling, hitting the spot that makes my world come apart.

My legs give out as I come, the cry on my lips disappearing into a gasp. But Nic holds me up, driving me right up another peak. Or maybe it's the same peak, but higher? Or I'm going to come forever. Again and again, because Nic wants me to and my body is with him on this until I can't take anymore and beg him to stop. I'm not sure how I'm standing when he does. I rest my forehead against the cool tiles of the wall as I try to catch my breath. What the hell did he just do to me?

Can he do it again?

Is he going to walk away, like he did in the laundry room?

I turn toward him. "Nic, I—"

He holds his finger to my lips with a smile. "No conversation."

Jerk. I bite him.

He pulls his finger free from my teeth, smacking my ass before reaching for the condom. "I want you to come for me again. On my cock. What do you need for that?"

"I need a few minutes." I don't want to wait. I don't want to risk him changing his mind or deciding I'm not worth it again, but I'm still pulsing from my orgasm—the lightest touch will hurt like hell right now.

Nic puts the condom back and pulls me under the spray of the showerhead, kissing my forehead and banishing my fear. He touches me with careful but firm hands, tilting my head to trail kisses down my neck, pressing me closer, his hips moving ever so slightly, his dick rubbing against my stomach. His teeth sink with excruciating tenderness into the spot where my neck meets my shoulder. My moan brings his lips back to mine and after kissing me sweetly, he pulls back and stares into my eyes like he's searching for something.

I think I prefer overstimulation to this. Whatever *this* is. It feels like a bruise on my heart, and my heart has nothing to do with Nic. Maybe he isn't as bad as I thought, but there's no reason for soft eyes and a softer kiss to bring this ache to my chest.

I reach for the condom, stepping away from him. "Let's go." I need him to use me hard and fast so that when that tenderness is back on the shelf and out of reach, I won't remember it. Won't even miss it.

Chapter Fourteen

Nic

THE LAST HANDFUL OF seconds have been the longest of my life, but I'm pretty sure only thirty seconds have passed. "Are you ready?"

Jessie rips the condom open in response.

I'm not going to argue—she knows her body and what she needs, and right now I need her so damn bad I could cry.

She doesn't roll the condom over me right away. Instead, she traces her fingers around the head of my cock, down my length, her fingernails dragging feather-light from root back to the tip. When her hand closes around me, I push into her slippery grip.

Jessie rises onto her tippy-toes to nip at my lips as she rolls the condom over me. "I need you hard and fast."

Perfect. I don't want to hold back, not my one time with Jessie. I turn her, pressing her hands onto the shower glass, my fingers lacing with hers. "This okay?" Taking her from behind is less personal. Less intimate. Safer. I can't afford to see anything in her eyes that might make me want more.

"God yes." She gathers her wet hair over her shoulder, and I let my gaze follow the gentle bumps of her spine down to her perfect ass. Goddammit, she's beautiful like this, waiting for me. Wanting.

I press my lips between her shoulder blades.

"Do me already," she whispers.

"Getting to that," I reply, nudging her legs farther apart. She groans my name in frustration as I slide the tip of my cock through her folds, her slickness evident through the condom, until I'm shaking with need. I ease my tip into the entrance of her pussy and seat myself in one slow, steady thrust, and she takes me. Perfectly.

It's a struggle to catch my breath. She feels so damned good and I'm not even moving. Steam and the scent of sex fill the shower and I'm not sure how long I'm going to last.

Jessie rocks back, whining my name. I'm not giving her what she wants, so she's going to make me. I like that about her. I tighten my grip on her hips and my next thrust has me biting down on my lower lip. She shouldn't feel this good, or sound this good, or smell this good, or taste this good. This is all I get, and I already know I'm going to want more.

I find a rhythm. Not hard and fast, not yet, but not gentle either. It makes her moan, but won't end me prematurely.

When I glance up, though...

Oh, god.

It's Jessie's reflection in the mirror over the vanity, me behind her. Steam blurs our edges and her tits bounce as she takes each thrust, but it's the expression on her face. Pleasure painted over every feature.

I reach up, cupping her neck with both hands, my fingers under her jaw, tipping her head up. "Look."

Her eyes meet mine in the reflection and white-hot lust surges through my veins at her moan. Her hand drops between her legs, fingers circling her clit, but her eyes stay on the hazy reflection of us fucking.

I'm not sure I can outlast her, but I can't slow down, thrusting into her hard and fast. I'm watching her in the mirror and she's watching me and sex has never been this good. My release is already building, tightening my balls, tingling along my spine. Jessie comes and thank god. Her orgasm ripples around me, squeezing me tight as my muscles tense and I slam into her and then I'm coming, pulsing to the wild beat of my heart or her pleasure—there's no difference.

We're both wrecked, still gasping, when I have to stop. I have nothing left inside. Jessie's taken everything out of me. I wrap my arms around her and pull her to me, holding both of us up as my head tips back and I struggle to draw enough of the steamy air into my lungs.

Coming down from this high is going to take a while. That euphoric, limp feeling is more intense than anything I've experienced in ages. Or ever.

"Wow," Jessie murmurs. She tenses like she didn't mean to say that out loud.

I drop my gaze to hers in the mirror, catching the moment the smile falls from her lips.

Oh god.

Panic wallops me in the face. I release her and step back, my cock sliding out of her. This is Jessie. Someone I shouldn't fantasize about, let alone touch. God, if she tells anyone...if I slip and tell someone...

She watches me as I tie off the condom and drop it on the floor. Even when I close my eyes and step under the showerhead to make sure the whipped cream is gone from my hair, I can feel her stare.

If I see hurt there—or regret—

I shouldn't have touched her.

When I open my eyes, I pointedly look away, but she's still standing there, waiting for me to say something. I need to get out of here, away from the steam, away from her. Stepping out of the shower, I put the condom in the trash and reach for a towel.

I walk out before it's even tied around my waist.

With her amber eyes shut behind my door, I'm safe. Sad and lost and pathetic and screwed. But safe.

I dry off and dress, numb to everything but the sound of the shower still going. Regret, for leaving her, fucking her, everything that has ever happened between us since the day we met drags at me until I sink onto my bed, my head falling into my hands.

If Timothy finds out, or Celia, or anyone...

What the hell is wrong with me? Is this who I am? More worried about the repercussions than her feelings?

I'm fucking terrified of her feelings. Of her not having any, of her having too many. Of her disappointment.

My door flies open and Jessie stomps in, a towel wrapped around her, another around her hair. "What the hell, Nic?"

My hackles go up because they always do with her. "You wanted to fuck. We did. Was I supposed to stay and shampoo your hair?"

"I don't want *that* from you." Jessie stops when she's standing between my knees, jabbing my chest with her finger. "I wanted a check-in. A 'thank you.' A 'that was fun, maybe we could do it again sometime.'"

Does she want to do it again? The possibility seeps through my skin and I know for the rest of the time we're under the same roof, I'm going to want her. What a miserable way to spend the holiday. "We can't do it again."

Jessie shakes her head. "You walked off like I was some dirty tissue you'd ejaculated into. Why would I want to do that again?"

That hits me in the guts, taking away my ability to speak, to apologize. Her finger is gentle under my chin, but the effect is a jolt of electricity holding me in place as she tips my head up, forcing me to meet her eyes. Whiskey and fire. "Thanks for the fuck, Nic," she says flatly, turning and walking toward the door. "See? Easy."

"Jessie, I'm—"

She slams the door on my apology.

Chapter Fifteen

Nic

"Who's getting dick for Christmas?" Timothy asks with a yawn, a massive cookie arrangement in his hands as he walks into the kitchen.

Jessie's hand shoots up. "I am!"

About a dozen gingerbread dicks jut out of the arrangement, white icing dripping down their tips. It doesn't matter that this is about the cookies. Heat rises up my neck. Jessie's blushing a little, too, avoiding eye contact with me.

"They're from work," she adds when she realizes everyone—except the kids, who've finished breakfast and are already outside building snowmen—is staring at her.

This has already been the most awkward breakfast of my life, with Jessie eating waffles and ignoring me. Meanwhile, I can't stop looking at her. Studying the way her still-damp hair is piled on top of her head. Watching the way she holds her body, the way she eats her breakfast. The changing expression on her face as she makes small talk.

Everything is so normal on the outside that it hurts. Less than an hour ago, Jessie was moaning my name. Half an hour ago, she'd been ready to yank my balls off—rightly so, I was a jerk—and now she's laughing like nothing happened.

I am such an asshole. I should've said something to her in the shower. Not *thanks for the fuck* either. Maybe she needed to be asked if she was okay. If we were okay. A short conversation about what happens next between us. An offer of friendship. Some kind of aftercare.

Timothy's eyes land on me as he hands the cookies to Jessie. "S'up with your face?"

I can't remember how to act. How to keep my expression neutral. All words, excuses, anything. Gone. *I fucked your sister* blares through my head and I press my lips together.

"He's intimidated by my gingerbread dicks," Jessie says casually, slipping one free.

"Jessie." Celia warns as she inspects the cookies. *Be nice.* It's been said to her about me so many times it doesn't need to be spoken aloud. I don't want Jessie to be nice to me. I've done nothing to earn it.

"Oh, eat a dick, Mom," she says, rolling her eyes. Amanda sputters her coffee and Timothy's loud laugh is joined by Hazel's, but Celia just smacks Jessie's arm and helps herself to a gingerbread. Timothy steals one and points it at me before walking out.

I breathe a sigh of relief. For a minute, I'd thought he was on to me. If anyone in this house could look at me and *know*, it would be him.

How hasn't he figured it out yet? Maybe he's too distracted by Mina.

Celia aggressively bites the tip off her gingerbread dick and all laughter stops. William is standing in the doorway, coffee cup in hand, eyes wide. Without a word, he backs out slowly.

Celia, queen of TV cooking programs, swallows, draws herself up straight, and announces with dignity, "Not the worst dick I've had in my mouth."

Everyone loses it, but when Jessie's eyes meet mine for a second, my laugh shrivels.

My normal is broken—or I am. I can't find it in me to glare or carry on our usual performance antagonism. If it weren't for Timothy's wedding, I'd fake some excuse and catch the next flight to LA.

"Better put those gingerdicks somewhere the kids won't find." Celia suggests, and Jessie nods, getting up to hide the cookies.

The day drifts by at odds with the storm inside me. I should feel relaxed after sex. Curiosity satisfied. Instead, I feel lost. Like the world should've crashed down on me for my sins and it hasn't but I can't stop looking up and wondering why not.

Amanda and Hazel take the kids out for the day and Celia and William likewise disappear. The house is oddly quiet. Jessie and Mina take over the kitchen table with their bachelorette party preparations, and I find a dozen excuses to wander through, even though I'm supposed to be helping Timothy prepare for his party.

"Oh, hey, Nic's back," Mina says pointedly. "Again."

"Stocking the bar," I say, stepping into the butler's pantry. Shit. I can't keep doing this. I need to talk to Jessie. I lean against the door. "Hey, Jessie, can you show me what bottles we're allowed?"

She doesn't glance up from the tiara she's hot glue-gunning pink rhinestones penises on. "Ask Mina."

Mina laughs. "I don't remember. You show him. In the butler's pantry." She picks up the Tinsel Tits mug Jessie gave her this morning and takes a knowing drink.

Maybe Timothy's not the one I have to watch out for.

Jessie gives her a long look, but sets the glue gun aside and gets to her feet with a sigh. She walks right past me to the small selection of wine Celia keeps in the butler's pantry. The wine-cellar downstairs is off-limits to us.

When I get close to her, she freezes. "Can we talk?" I ask.

"I've said all I wanted to say." She pulls out a couple of bottles and hands them to me.

"I haven't."

She won't look at me. "Your actions said enough."

"Jessie—"

"We're good, Nic." She turns to give me another bottle, looking annoyed when I have to shift the two I'm holding to take the third. "We're back to normal. Like we both want."

I want that. Right? I don't know. "But—"

"Our normal is we hate each other. It's not hard." She adds another bottle to the ones I'm holding.

I don't hate her. I've never hated her. She gets under my skin and makes me uncomfortably aware of all my shortcomings and we've never managed to be near each other without fighting, but that's not hate. "I want—"

"What do you want, Nic?" Timothy asks from the doorway.

I nearly drop the bottles. Goddamn, he's sneaky. "Champagne?" My voice sounds weak, but it's the first thing my eyes land on.

"That's ours," Jessie says, crossing her arms.

"Nic wants champagne," Timothy says, mimicking her pose.

"Nic needs whiskey."

He looks at me. Really looks at me. "Good call, twinsie. You're not looking so good, Nic. What's up?"

"Yeah, Nic." Jessie smirks. "What's up?"

For a split second, I wonder what would happen if I said it. *I'm unbalanced because I fucked Jessie in the shower this morning and I know I shouldn't, but I want to do it again.* I'd love to see the look on Jessie's face if I said it.

I have no clue what Timothy would do—laugh, probably—but Jessie would kick my ass. I can't say it, though, because even if Timothy was cool with it, he can't keep his big mouth shut. Every Foley in the state would know about it before dinner. The whole thing would be blown out of proportion and when the dust settled, everything would be different. I can't lose this family. I can't lose my best friend.

"Nothing's up," I mutter.

Timothy finally takes pity on me. He snags four bottles of champagne and jerks his chin for me to follow him downstairs.

"We're not going to drink any of this," he tells me as he makes space in the bar fridge for the champagne.

I stow the bottles of red wine on a rack that probably ended up down here because Celia didn't like it. "Someone might want wine."

Timothy closes the fridge and pats his pockets. A slow smile spreads across his face. "Oh no. I left my phone in the kitchen. Go grab it for me?"

I give him a look to let him know I know what he's up to—even though I hope to god he's not up to anything—and head back upstairs.

Jessie doesn't look at me, but the whole-body sigh she does when I walk into the kitchen lets me know exactly what she thinks about seeing me again so soon.

Timothy's phone isn't on the island. Or any counter in the kitchen. "Have you seen Timothy's phone?" I ask.

"Over here," Mina says absently.

Of course, it is. Now I have to walk into striking range of Jessie's glue gun. If I'm not careful, she'll glue a pink rhinestone dick to my forehead, like the one she's gluing on…

I'm too late.

Timothy's leather phone case has half a completed pink rhinestone dick on it.

"I'll take this," I say, leaning over her, reaching for it.

She bats my hand away. "I'm not done."

Timothy won't be mad about a dick on his phone case—if anything, he'll love it—so I don't know why I grab Jessie's wrist. When she brings the glue gun toward me, I grab her other wrist. She bumps her chair back against my body, but I hold on. Her eyes when she looks up at me are smoldering and I forget all about Timothy's phone.

This spark between us isn't over yet, whatever it is.

"Aw," Mina says, leaning on the table, a goofy grin on her face. "This is like that scene in Ghost. Only with a glue gun and rhinestone dicks instead of clay."

I release Jessie and step back, hands in the air.

"No, no," Mina says, delight in her eyes. "Don't stop on account of me."

"Finish the phone case," I say to Jessie, crossing my arms.

Jessie goes back to work, but Mina's attention is fixed on me. Not good.

"What have you boys got planned for tonight?" she asks.

"Poker."

Jessie laughs. "Well, you're fucked."

So, so fucked.

"Here," Mina says, holding a piece of paper out to me. It's Mina's handwriting—neat and small, not Jessie's loops and flourishes. "Read it. Let's see if Jessie can guess what you are."

"A dick?" Jessie suggests.

"You have dicks on the brain," I say.

"Not where I like them." she admits.

I clear my throat because I'm thinking about giving her my dick again. Pretty sure that option flew out the window when I walked out of the bathroom. With nothing else to say, I read the slip of paper. "*I come in many sizes. It feels good when you blow me.*" I groan.

Jessie sets the glue gun down, getting to her feet. She hands me Timothy's freshly decorated phone and taps me on the nose. "Boop."

"Right! Nose." Mina laughs.

Jessie's eyebrows lift and she blinks innocently at me. "Want me to explain it to you?"

"I get it," I say, but she's standing too close. If we were alone in this kitchen, I'd throw her over my shoulder, haul her over to the mistletoe, and kiss the shit out of her. Then she could demonstrate exactly what this little riddle means by blowing me.

Which would be a mistake. A mistake I don't think I could stop myself from making—what is it about this woman that has me crossing lines and ignoring warning signs?

My head is full of her. The smell of her, the way she tastes, the sound of her laugh, and the softness of her skin. There isn't room for anything else.

My hormones have a lot to answer for.

Tonight will save me. I'll be locked in a poker game with Timothy and a bunch of his friends. With a little luck, I won't see Jessie until morning. I'll have my shit under control.

A couple of Timothy's old high school friends—the only ones he's more or less kept in contact with over the years—turn up after dinner. I never bothered to keep in touch, since they were more his friends than mine. And I loathed Scotty Bryant.

"How's your sister?" Scotty asks Timothy, and my grip tightens on my beer.

"Still off-limits," Timothy says. His tone is good-natured. His eyes are not.

I take a swig of beer and wonder if this applies to me.

"I forgot how much I don't like him," Timothy whispers to me later, jerking his chin toward Scotty.

A handful of stunt guys who flew in from LA for the wedding show up and I'm happy to see Danny among them. There's at least one other person here I can stand.

The night begins with pool and darts and moves on to poker. I move on to whiskey but I'm taking it slow.

Somewhere upstairs, Jessie's playing games in skinny jeans and a black shirt with an exposed midriff. Red, red pouty lips. I'd caught a glimpse of her earlier through a crack in the door of our shared bathroom. Pausing to watch her apply her lipstick felt illicit. The drag of the red stick over those lush lips was obscene. My desire to grab her chin and smear that color with my thumb was balanced only by my desire to not be murdered.

She caught me peeping. The smile she gave me was suggestive and cruel. My heart stopped when she walked up. I could already taste her kiss. Until she slammed the door in my face.

She's making me pay for it. Hopefully, she's still thinking about my hands on her, my kiss, the way my cock—

"You're up, man."

I don't look at my cards. "Check." Playing blind is my only shot at winning. Timothy knows all my tells. Except whatever will give away the fact that I fucked Jessie. If he knew, he wouldn't keep silent, therefore he doesn't know.

It was supposed to be one time. That's why I touched her like that. Kissed her like that. It could only be once, and I wanted to remember it. I wanted her to remember it.

I want to fuck her again.

Goddammit.

"Nic?"

I'm not going to throw myself at her feet, begging for more. No way. "All in."

I win on a pair of twos.

"Hey, the stripper's here!" Scotty's voice intrudes on my thoughts. I glance up at the faces around the table, all turned to a spot behind me as someone comes down the stairs.

Timothy looks up from his cards, scowling. "Gross. That's my sister, asshole."

I turn in time to see Jessie drop the middle finger she'd been giving to Scotty. What she's doing barely registers because of what she's wearing.

Her bikini is tight and black, the triangle scraps of cloth so low and so small a nip slip is inevitable and those pink buds are perfect. My throat tightens as though her invisible fingers wrap around it.

I reach for my whiskey, turning away.

"Heading out to the hot tub already?" Timothy asks, after an annoyed huff because no one is paying attention to the poker game anymore.

"Nope—got caught cheating at a drinking game and this is my punishment." She doesn't sound too happy about it.

I can't look away for long—I set the empty glass down, turning in time to see her bend over to dig around in the fridge.

Jesus Fucking Christ. Am I having some sort of medical event? My heart thumps. I can't breathe. Can't think. That fabric stretches tight, the cut is cheeky, and instantly I'm back in the shower, my fingers digging into her hips.

My cock is already hardening at the memory and I reach for my glass, knocking it over before I remember it's empty. The urge to pull her aside and pour my stupid heart out, begging for forgiveness for hurting her is as strong as the desire to kiss her, touch her, and fuck us both into oblivion.

When I look up, Timothy's watching me.

"Hey Jessie," he calls out, his eyes never once letting go of mine. "Can you grab a water for Mr. Fontana? He's looking *thirsty*."

Fuck. Fuckity fuck fuck this is not happening.

She shoots me a *What the hell is your problem* look, tosses a water bottle my way, and pulls two bottles of champagne out of the fridge.

The water bottle is cold in my hot hand. Did I catch it? It could've bounced off my head for all I noticed.

Timothy and Jessie talk, but I'm underwater, unable to understand their words so long as Jessie grips a bottle of champagne between her thighs. Her fingers circle the neck like she had my cock. Her other hand palms the cork, twisting, twisting—

It pops softly and I nearly jump out of my seat, but my world comes into focus as she sets the bottle on the bar. Until she grabs the other one.

Do I have to survive this a second time?

"Who's winning?" Again she clamps the bottle between her thighs. I want those thighs clamped around me. My hips, my head. Not sure which.

"Who do you think? Now go away." Timothy waves her off. "If you see any strippers, send them down!"

She laughs, the champagne pops, and she takes both bottles upstairs. Eyes follow, drinking in the spellbinding bounce of her ass.

She is not out of my system. She is my system.

"Guys." Timothy clears his throat, shuffling the cards. "That's my sister. You will be respectful of her and the other ladies in the house. Or you know where the door is."

That, I remind myself, includes me. I'm going to sit right here and respect that Jessie wants nothing more to do with me and lose some money and—

Nope. I'm going after her.

I mumble something about needing to take a piss and take the steps two at a time, but there's no sign of Jessie. I wander off in the direction she would've taken out to the hot tub. Just one minute alone with her, to apologize, to taste those lips...

"Shit, honey, are you okay?"

Celia's voice deflates my hopes. Jessie's gone, and I missed her. I backtrack into the kitchen, hoping I don't appear as dejected as I feel. Celia catches me in the doorway, giving me a perfunctory kiss on the cheek for the mistletoe before dragging me onto a barstool. "Sit. Eat." A plate of hors d'oeuvres is pushed at me. "I'll make you a cup of coffee."

Do I look drunk? Am I drunk on Jessie?

By the time Celia sets a cup of coffee in front of me, my mouth is stuffed and most of the plate is gone. She leans against the island, sipping a hot chocolate that's probably half Bailey's, watching me. When the plate is empty, she hands me a napkin. "Okay, honey. Talk."

Nope. I shake my head and take a long drink of coffee.

She reaches out, lightly touching my hand. "I'm always here for you. You know that. Now, have some stuffed mushrooms."

Celia keeps my cup full and talks about her new show, never requiring much of a response. I let my thoughts wander. What would it be like to accept her offer? To never do another movie again. To move back here, where the only family I have lives. I think I'd like that.

Jessie's in the city. Not far.

A door opens somewhere, and Jessie's voice rings out, shepherding a chorus of drunken giggles out to the hot tub.

"Makeovers, dress up, and a photo booth. In my room." Celia explains. "Mina got a hold of a bunch of costumes. William's putting Liam and Evie to bed, but I'm guessing he fell asleep in the chair upstairs."

Costumes. Christ.

How can I get my hands on those photos?

Celia pushes a plate of bruschetta my way. The guys walk into the kitchen, heaping shit on each other, as I'm eating the last one.

Timothy claps me on the shoulder. "There you are. Thought Jessie abducted you, not Mom."

Celia throws a potholder at him, hitting him square in the chest.

Everyone attacks the food, talking and laughing. I try to follow along, but I'm thinking about Jessie in the hot tub in that little black bikini.

When the plates are cleaned of everything but crumbs, Timothy pushes a low-alcohol beer into my hand and turns to the group. "All right, boys. Strip off as much as you're comfortable with and let's go outside. We're crashing the bachelorette party."

Chapter Sixteen

Jessie

Nic slides into the hot tub next to me with a short, casual nod. He looks delicious in a pair of black jockey shorts that are going to cling to his dick like an obsessed fangirl when he gets out. Not to mention all those muscles on display.

Life isn't fair. Sex with Nic was good. Incredibly good.

Throw-all-other-men-in-the-garbage good.

I could be seducing him for another round, but no. Nic's an asshole and assholes gotta asshole. I don't need that in my life. Even if the way he watched me when I interrupted their poker game had me thinking about dragging him away for a quickie.

The other guys file in from the patio, shivering in their underwear, laughing and shoving, climbing in. Timbo's tight cannonball into the middle leaves everyone not quick to turn away with a face full of water. The hot tub is massive, but twelve people make for a squeeze. When Scotty Bryant splashes down on my other side, I scoot closer to Nic.

A hand cups my ass, more protective than sexual. I lean back, turning my head and dropping my voice. "That better be you, Fontana."

His response is a gentle squeeze. Water bubbles from the jets, obscuring anything and everything happening underwater, so no one else knows when he hooks his thumb under the waistband of my bikini bottoms and gently strokes me.

Jesus Christ, Nic. Moving away means moving closer to Scotty; telling Nic to stop runs the risk of drawing attention.

Except I don't want him to stop. The pressure of the jet on my back takes on a more sensual feel with him touching me. The little hairs on the nape of my neck, dampened by steam and frozen in the cold night air are suddenly in sharp focus, the contrast from the heat of the water, stark. I shudder and out of the corner of my eye, I catch the briefest smile cross his lips.

Scotty turns my way, his eyes darting down to my tits as though a quick peek makes it less obvious. "Haven't seen you in years, Jessie. What've you been up to?"

Nic's hand tightens on my ass, but his attention is on the conversation on his other side. I'm on my own, so I give Scotty some bullshit generic response about working in marketing. No way am I volunteering I work for a sex toy company to any of Timbo's stupid-ass friends. When I turn the conversation to him, he chatters on, oblivious that I'm no longer listening.

I'm a magnet for assholes.

I scoop foam from the top of the water, watching it freeze in the cold night air before crunching it in my hand. My boredom is punctuated by Nic occasionally squeezing my ass, which is both arousing and annoying. I'd like to forget about him and he's making that impossible.

The hot tub is sheltered on three sides for privacy, easily overlooked during the day thanks to my father's gardening. It opens out to the small lake, the view stunning at dawn or dusk. Tonight, the stars above are obscured by steam, replaced by the twinkling of Christmas lights on the surrounding shrubbery and over the arch of the pergola. Everything beyond is a soul-sucking black.

Scotty touches my arm with the back of his hand as he makes a joke I didn't hear and I hiss. Nic leans around me to glare at him, his hand moving to the base of my neck. Where anyone could see.

"Oh, hey Nic. Didn't see you." Scotty hesitates, gives a weak smile, and turns toward Amanda on his other side. Nic doesn't move his hand. He's still staring at Scotty.

Fucking cavemen.

I push his hand away. It falls from my neck, only to return to my ass. I glare at him, he blinks frozen steam from his ridiculous lashes and stares back, all innocence. He's enjoying himself, the prick.

The uncomfortable tingle between my legs needs to die because I don't want to enjoy this. Reaching past him for my drink allows me to get close enough to whisper, "Off my ass too." While I take a long drink, Nic removes his hand, skating it up my spine. When it breaches the water, he rests his whole arm on the edge of the hot tub behind me, ensuring I can't lean back without tucking myself under it.

I down the rest of the fruity hell in a red solo cup and silently curse him.

What the hell is wrong with this man? He has no right to get all territorial and besides, I would never consider any of my brother's old friends as potential one-night stands. I went to high school with these losers too. The stunt guys I don't know but I assume they're all exactly like my brother. I'm not interested.

No, the only company I want tonight is the old, soft, squishy plush unicorn toy from my childhood. Roxy cuddles are the best cuddles—and Roxy never pushes me away, even when I leave her under a pile of laundry.

Nic's leg bumps against mine and stays.

For someone who did his damned best to make sure I knew I was nothing more than a quick lay, he's doing a hell of a lot to undermine that. Does he think he's getting another chance? Was that what he wanted to talk about in the butler's pantry?

Woof.

I am not jumping back on his dick because he's horny again, even if some parts of me want to give him multiple chances as long as parts of him give me multiple orgasms.

His thigh rubs against mine and I get a little lightheaded. All this not-so-innocent touching under the water is threatening to break my resolve.

The initial excitement the party crashers caused dies into normal conversation. Well, as normal as possible for a large hot tub crammed with drunks. The occasional awkward silence hangs in the steamy air as different conversations come to a natural end at the same time. It has a dampening effect. I stifle a yawn.

The booze, the heat of the water, the rollercoaster that is this situation with Nic, all of it makes for one hell of a day. I should go to bed and sleep it off.

"Round three!" Mina stands on her seat, stunning in her royal blue bikini as steam rises off her body, collecting into frost on her pink dick tiara. Timothy gazes at her, pure worship on his face as she holds a wire basket of Ping-Pong balls on high.

An Everything look. I want a man to look at me like I'm his entire world, not just his next five minutes. Is it too much to ask?

Next to me, Nic's head tips up to the dark sky, his mouth soundlessly forming the word *fuck*. I try not to laugh. He hates all the games forced upon him, yet he keeps coming back. Masochist.

"Don't let the Ping-Pong balls touch you!" Mina's voice fills the sheltered space, rising over the bubbling of jets. "If a white one touches you, you're rolling in the snow for ten seconds. A blue one means you slam your drink. A red one, now that we have you boys, means you kiss the nearest nonrelative. And a green one—I decide your fate. If you miss the basket when you toss your ball back in, you get another drink. Got it?"

Wait. Kiss? That wasn't a part of the game. Red is supposed to be truth and green is supposed to be dare. Crap. Mina's gone rogue.

She grins at me and plunges the basket upside down into the water, quickly getting out of the way as she releases the Ping-Pong balls to the excited screams of her friends. Blue and white make up the majority, with a few reds and one green floating around. Most people will be getting drunk and cold.

"Feet on the bottom!" Mina yells out as Danny, one of Timothy's stunt buddies, tries to splash a white Ping-Pong ball away with a massive foot.

I snatch the blue one that bobs into me. They're harder to see in the dark than the others, but definitely the best option. Downing my drink, I stand to take the shot at the basket. I miss by a good eight inches, drawing a shout from Mina. With a sigh, I turn around to refill my cup from one of the pitchers ringing the tub. Fruity bubbles slide across my tongue as I drain it.

She's trying to kill me. All day she's been watching me, especially anytime Nic's around. Making me go downstairs to get that champagne was a setup.

Did I use the opportunity to torture Nic a bit? Of course. I'm a petty bitch. But Mina's up to something.

Nic is watching me, gray eyes hazy. It must be the booze or a trick of the Christmas lights overhead. He should be staring at my tits, inches from his face in this ridiculous bikini, but his hungry gaze is locked on mine, feeling a lot more like an Everything look than a Five Minute look.

"Fontana!" Mina's up and pointing, startling us out of the moment. "Roll in the snow—ten seconds!"

Nic frowns at the white ball bobbing in the water against his chest. With a sigh, he gets to his feet. I sink up to my neck into the water to hide.

Mina nudges the basket. Nic's ball misses by an inch. "And a drink!"

He shoots her a glare and climbs out, his body steaming against the cold night air. I gape at the sight of black boxer briefs dragging low on his hips, the fabric sucked tight against an obvious semi. He ignores it, not a trace of embarrassment on his face as he walks with determination, sleek and dripping, stalking the snowbank.

I am jealous of a snowbank and that's a new personal low.

He rolls in the snow like a warrior while everyone counts down from ten. I watch, open-mouthed, oblivious to the danger of the other Ping-Pong balls or of anyone catching me ogling the man I can't stand. At zero he's on his feet, shaking his arms and jumping a few times before walking back to the hot tub, his usually pale complexion gone rosy from the snow. He pauses, still standing outside, to demolish his beer and grab another, and all the while I can't take my eyes off the thick outline of his dick. That semi is gone, but damn.

He reaches down to grip the edge of the hot tub and hops in with hardly a splash.

I want to slide onto his lap, to feel the cold of his body warm beneath mine, his dick awakening as I kiss warmth back into his icy lips.

How drunk am I?

Dammit. I need to stop staring, but I can't drag my eyes away once I meet his. It's like an understanding is passing between us. An acknowledgment that we're not through.

This is nuts. We're through and I'm drunk. I have to be.

"Hey, Jessie." Scotty's voice breaks through my lust fog.

"Hmm?"

"Behind you."

Shit. I move forward, toward Nic. It's no use. The red Ping-Pong ball follows in my wake. *No!* I surge to my feet, moving away from it, tangling myself on Nic's legs. It's too late. The red Ping-Pong ball touches me, and Mina sees.

"Lady's choice! Nic, or..." Mina pauses, frowning at Scotty. "I'm sorry, what was your name again?"

I snatch the ball, toss it at the basket, and miss. Whatever, I need some liquid courage. The sparkling fruity drink adds to the fluttering in my stomach. Nic wouldn't reject me again, would he? Because I don't want to kiss Scotty.

Under the water, Nic grabs my leg and I hope that means he's claiming this kiss. Setting the empty cup down, I sink onto his lap, carried by relief, the rush of booze, and the pulse of hormones. I can't look away from the heat in his eyes, can't stop my hands from sliding into his hair. It's damp, half frozen between my fingers.

A lifetime passes in a second or two as we stare at each other. My fingers tighten.

His mouth meets mine, tasting of snow and beer. His hands are late but they make up for lost time, one on the nape of my neck, the other sliding under the water to pull me down on his hips. I tug on his hair, claiming his mouth with my tongue, the force of my need shockingly strong. He's hardening underneath me, holding me tight so I can feel exactly what I'm doing to him.

I want him again. God. Dammit.

He pulls away, his eyes burning. Then—poof—the moment is gone. His cool gaze drifts away, his hands drop from my body.

Hoots and whistles break out around us, overwhelming the pounding of my heart. My face burns. That wasn't how two people who hate each other kiss in a drinking game.

I'm ready to drown myself. In his eyes, in my booze, in the goddamned hot tub itself.

Nic leans back, returning to manspreading. I stare at him until he bounces me on his knees.

Shit! I'm still straddling him. I slip off his lap, horrified, nearly falling onto Scotty before finding my seat.

"Oh. My. God." One of Mina's friends—Charlotte—fans herself.

Under the water, Nic nudges me with his leg—*are you okay?* I nudge him right back. *I'm fine, piss off.* He nudges me again, turning it into a mini-war until I pinch his inner thigh, making him yelp.

No one notices because they're all watching Timothy roll in the snow—or do gymnastics in the snow. Might be an interpretive dance. Who's to say?

No one gives us a hard time about the kiss. We're soon outdone by Danny and Charlotte. Others fall victim to white Ping-Pong balls and take the roll in the snow with a hell of a lot less dignity and a lot more noise than Nic had.

Nic pays no attention to the threat. He seems content to lean back, watch everyone around him act like idiots, and occasionally bump me with his knee. I ignore him.

He kisses me again five minutes later when a red Ping-Pong ball bumps into him. What the hell is drawing these bastards toward us? This time he merely turns toward me, his reasonably chaste kiss hotter for how exposed it feels with only our lips touching.

The green Ping-Pong ball floats right into Nic. He isn't looking—he's staring at the sky while I sit silently, leaning forward so I don't end up under his outstretched arm behind me.

"Strip, Fontana!" Mina calls out, winking at me when she catches my eye.

That's it. I'm out. If I see Nic naked again, I'm not going to be responsible for my decisions tonight.

I excuse myself, scrambling out of the hot tub. The blast of cold air on my skin brings some relief. Until those black boxer briefs hit the ground next to me. I ignore the squeals and giggles mostly—but not exclusively—coming from Mina's friends Lexi and Charlotte.

Nic's hand brushes my calf, jolting me. "You okay?"

Focusing on the Christmas lights that blur and dance against the velvet black of night, I nod. I can't risk seeing what might, or might not, be in Nic's eyes—or what I know is under the water. Heat rushes to my face. For a moment, I think I might pass out. I'm standing here stripped to the bone; anyone who looks can see right through me.

I hightail it to the warm shelter of the house.

Chapter Seventeen

Jessie

A long, warm shower doesn't help me feel better. Mostly because I spend the whole time with one eye on the door handle to Nic's room, half expecting him to walk in and finish what we started in the hot tub.

When he doesn't, I'm disappointed all over again. I don't like Nic and this is sharp enough to hurt. It shouldn't and I'm mad about it.

I slip into my softest pajamas, cast one last, pitiful look at the stubbornly closed door to Nic's room, and go into my bedroom.

My mother redecorated a few years ago in a style she thought might make this place a retreat for me, all luxurious shades of cream, soft gray, and pale pink. It's nice, but it's not mine anymore.

Mina's fruity drink isn't sitting well, so I head to the kitchen and make myself a cup of tea. It doesn't help. Neither does digging my Roxy unicorn out from under a pile of clothes and cuddling on my bed.

I need to brush my teeth, go to bed, and forget every single thing Nic can do to my body. He was fucking with me in the hot tub, payback for my little stunt with the champagne down in the man cave. It meant nothing or he'd be up here for more.

I fling open the bathroom door, a soft scream dying on my lips because there he is, standing in front of the mirror, toothbrush in hand.

"You scared me," I say, resting my hand on my chest. My heart is pounding.

From the fright. Obviously.

Liar.

I pluck my toothbrush from the holder as Nic leans forward to spit discreetly into his sink. "Seriously," I ask, applying toothpaste to my brush, "how long have you been staring at yourself? Did you get lost in your own eyes?"

He leans against the vanity and I try not to stare at his bare chest. Or the loose fit of the flannel pants he's wearing. I can smell his body wash. He must have showered while I was downstairs. Has he been in here the whole time, brushing his teeth, waiting for me?

Of course, he wasn't waiting for me. I need to get a grip.

"I shouldn't have walked out on you this morning," he says after a long pause. "Or the other day in the laundry room."

My toothbrush is in my mouth, saving me the difficulty of having to say something. Not that I have anything to say because he shouldn't have walked out on me like that.

"I was an asshole and you deserve better."

"I do," I mumble around my toothbrush because I do deserve better. I spit my toothpaste out as politely as I can and dump my brush back into the holder.

"I got scared," he says softly.

Making eye contact with Nic is a mistake—his usual cold gray eyes are so soft. I can still feel the ghost of his kiss from the hot tub and if I had half a working brain, I'd keep my distance. I wouldn't stand frozen as he closes the space between us.

"Of what?" I cross my arms over my chest, hugging myself tight. Do I really want to know?

"Of what would happen if anyone found out. Of you."

"Me?"

"I didn't want to disappoint you."

My bar has been set pretty low thanks to dating apps and men in general, but I keep that to myself. "The sex was good."

"Better than good." Nic reaches out to me, uncrossing my arms, his hands sliding down to my wrists. He takes my hands, his thumbs brushing over my skin. "We could do it again."

Oh, hell no. I yank my hands from his, horrified by the thrill running through my body. "You were right this morning. Everything we've done has been a mistake. Really, really good, but a big, big mistake." My stomach twists—goddamn that drink! I take two steps backward to the safety of my door.

A frown mars Nic's perfect face as he runs a hand through his damp hair. "I was wrong. Nothing we've done has been a mistake."

I stare at him while my brain screams *the nerve of this guy!*

"Admit it." A smug grin replaces his frown and my traitor body goes a little weak. "You want me. Again." He leans forward, his voice dropping. "We could spend the holiday finding out all the ways we could be good together."

"I have a suitcase full of sex toys that can give me *very* good without making me feel like shit. Nice try."

His eyes darken. "Bring them over to my room, and I'll make it up to you."

Christ. No. Absolutely not. I back to the door, groping for the handle. "Good night, Nic." I close the door on him and suppress the urge to let out a frustrated scream because I don't want him to know how he's getting to me. Diving into bed, I bury my face in my pillow and groan.

The arrogance of this guy. Like I'd want to subject myself to his rejection—again!—once he comes, his horny goggles fall off, and I go back to being his mistake.

Fool me once. Twice, in my case. Or is it three times? I'm too revved up to count and thinking about the laundry room and the shower is turning me into a mess of sexual frustration. Even the kiss in the snow fort gives me too much fuel for fantasies.

I throw my pillow onto the floor, rolling onto my back.

Is he in his bed, imagining the same, my name on his lips as he gets himself off? The image my brain conjures up has me clenching my thighs.

I do want him.

It's wrong and maybe that's the appeal. Nic's the forbidden fruit, my brother's best friend, and someone my family adores. He's the Sexiest Man in America and I don't have access to this caliber of hotness.

Whatever it is, I want to ride Dominic Fontana and I accept that about myself. I'll look into twelve-step programs later. Now I need to decide what I'm going to do about it.

If I'm forced to admit it, and I'll never admit it out loud, I have these feelings for him that are warm, nebulous, and confusing. They've always been there, waxing and waning depending on how big a dick he's being. Or how big a dick I'm being, since he's not holding up this feud on his own. If I do this, I'll have to leave those feelings at the door so I don't get hurt. Pretty sure I can do that.

My family can't find out, and this is the big problem. I'm not sure if they'd be happy about us hooking up or not, but things would be awkward. I'd be in deep shit if I hurt him, and if he hurt me...I doubt my family would turn their backs on him, but Nic might walk away from all of us, and we're the only family he's got.

But a week of good sex, no strings attached, and a whole year before I have to see him again?

I throw back the covers, swinging my feet out of bed. Good dick on tap is worth the risk. Besides, it's not like I'm in love with the prick or anything.

Knocking softly, I push his bedroom door open. It's dark and I swear to god if he turns me down because he wants to sleep, I'll smother him with a pillow. "Nic?"

Blankets rustle and I blink when he flicks on the bedside lamp. He sits up, wide awake and possibly naked, hopefully naked, looking smug as hell. Like he spoke sex into happening.

Dammit, he might have.

"I'm in," I say, because no way am I admitting I want him *to him*. The man's ego is big enough.

He scoots over, pulling the blankets back for me to climb in next to him. Not enough to tell me if he is naked. But he totally is.

"What is *this*?" I ask, sitting on his bed so we're thigh to hip instead, motioning between us.

Nic runs a hand through his hair as he thinks about it. "Friends with benefits?"

I'm already shaking my head. "We aren't friends. Enemies with benefits?"

"Are we enemies?" he asks softly.

I don't know how to answer that. "Fuck foes?"

With a laugh, he reaches for me, one hand sliding down to the small of my back, the other cupping my cheek. "I don't care what you call it. I want you."

Warmth spreads through me from his touch, but when he tries to draw me closer, I stop him with a hand on his chest. "This is just a holiday sex-capade, right?" I press. "It's over when we leave, but for the next week we have as much sex as we can?"

His thumb brushes over my cheek, his smile fading into something hungry. "Yeah. That okay?"

"It's perfect." My hands slide up his chest and back down and the feel of him, all hard muscle and smooth skin with a light dusting of hair is sexy as hell. "I'm not interested in a relationship with you."

"Ouch," he says sarcastically as he leans closer, ghosting a kiss over my lower lip that leaves me buzzing.

"You aren't interested in one with me either." I point out, but the kisses he's trailing toward my neck make me sound breathless and turn my statement into a question.

"I'm not." He agrees, scooching back against the headboard and hauling me onto his lap. Burying his hands in my hair, he eases my head back, exposing my neck to his lips.

Christ, I can feel him, hard, beneath the blankets. I rock my hips and he groans against my throat.

"I'm not done," I whisper.

"I don't fucking care," he whispers back. "I agree to everything."

One hand slips over my breast, his thumb dragging over my nipple again and again until it's hard as a rock and aching for his mouth. "This stays a secret," I tell him. He knows what's at stake if anyone in this house finds out and lord knows I don't want to end up in the tabloids as Nic's next fling.

He stops kissing my neck and his hand drops from my breast, but when he pulls back to look at me, I wonder if he even heard me. He grabs the hem of my camisole and pulls it slowly over my head, drinking me in. "Definitely our secret."

"We need to be up front with each other," I say as my skin pebbles at the way he's looking at me. "Expectations. When we're finished. What we need."

"What do you need right now, Jessie?" he asks my tits in his gravelly voice.

"Your mouth on my nipples." I'm not afraid to tell a man what I want in bed, never have been, and I think Nic likes it. His eyes flare and his knees draw up behind me. He pushes me back against them, bending forward, cupping me, kissing me, and finally sucking one tight bud into his mouth. I whimper.

Nic takes his time and I know I've made the right choice because he's so good with that mouth. "Why did you go down on me in the laundry room?" The question is out before I can stop myself. Frankly, I'm so turned on I don't know how I found the words. Or why I need to know.

He releases my nipple and looks up at me, his eyes dark and half-hooded.

"It was...random," I say when he stares at me.

"Nothing about it was random," he says, cupping my face. "I've wanted you since the moment you slammed into me under the mistletoe. When I walked into the laundry room and you were standing there almost naked, teasing me about mistletoe and kisses...I took a chance."

"I don't need cuddles and pillow talk from you after," I say softly. I don't need those things for a fling. "But I don't want to feel tossed aside and worthless either. That's important to me."

"I'm sorry. I won't do that again." There's such an open, earnest look in his eyes. He's always so guarded and closed off that for a moment I stare at him. But I believe him.

I pull him in for a kiss, and suddenly he's rising beneath me, lifting me. For a moment we hang balanced on a tipping point, then we tumble, his arms around me, down onto the bed. I laugh because being playful is also something I didn't expect from Nic. He's full of surprises, and I like it.

Also, he *is* naked. I knew it.

"Anything else?" he asks after kissing me breathless.

"I'm good." The feel of his hard cock sliding against my pajamas over my clit is divine. "You?"

"Oh, I have a question," he says with a sly grin as he works his way down my body. Instead of asking it, he circles one nipple with his tongue, giving it a soft suck that makes me moan. Then he's moving down, kissing my stomach, his mouth hot and damp, his fingers slipping beneath the waistband as he pulls my pants and panties off.

He takes a long moment to look at me before meeting my eyes. "Did you think I wouldn't notice my action figure banging Rudolph?"

I laugh. The kids were out of the house today, so I may have put his action figure in various suggestive poses. "You made that nose glow."

His hands slide up my thighs and press my legs wide open. "Or later, my action figure giving Santa a blow job?"

"Peppermint jizz. It's a scientific fact about Santa." I'd shoved a broken bit of a candy cane into Santa's opened pants to serve as his dick—Mina's suggestion. My soon-to-be sister-in-law is brilliant.

Nic touches me, tracing through my folds, dragging my wetness to my clit where he draws light and teasing circles. "The threesome with Mrs. Claus and the Elf on the Shelf might have been overkill. The reindeer watching was a nice touch though."

"It was jolly."

"You have the real thing now, no action figure." He shifts, lowering himself to his stomach and kissing my thigh.

Nic must enjoy mixing things up because this is nothing like the shower or the laundry room. He slowly and lazily kisses or licks every place he can reach before finally placing the softest kiss against my clit. Even after he slides his fingers in, the steady thrusts and slow way he tongues me have me squirming against him, desperate for more he's in no hurry to give.

And I enjoy every torturous minute of it. Especially when he shifts so he can stroke himself. It's a hell of a show.

Slow, it turns out, is good. I don't need to go off like a short-fused bottle rocket because this is Nic. With the longer fuse, I become one of those big, showy fireworks that crackle with golden sparks. When I come, I light up the whole goddamned sky.

CHAPTER EIGHTEEN

Nic

JESSIE TUGS ON MY hair after she comes, and I let her drag me up her body. I'm so lost in her soft warmth, the sweet smell of her, and the taste of her still on my tongue that only the insistent throb of my painfully hard cock keeps me tethered.

She wraps her arms around me, pulling me down to her neck, a contented sigh on her lips.

After all the shit we've put each other through—not just the last few days, but for decades—she's in my bed. It feels unreal and I'm terrified any moment it'll all come crashing down.

Jessie arches under me, rolling her hips. "Why aren't you in me yet?"

Instead of reaching for the condoms, I slip down her body, rolling the tight bead of her nipple in my lips and flicking my tongue across the top before lifting my head to meet her eyes. "Got somewhere you need to be?"

Her lips twitch toward a smile and end up pursed. "In the middle of orgasm number two."

"We've got all night." I pull that hard little bud back into my mouth, giving her a long, deep suck, watching lust haze her eyes.

She bites her lip and lifts an eyebrow. "Did I say number two was the finale?"

"You realize I'm not a superhero, right?" I mean it in jest, but my voice comes out sharp. So I drop my head to swirl my tongue around her nipple, hoping she didn't notice.

"Nic."

I ignore her, drawing her into my mouth.

"Nic, stop."

Shit.

I let her slip from my mouth, my body going cold and tight. I've messed it up already. This has to be a new world record. Maybe with Jessie, I'm meant to be stuck on a loop, endlessly screwing things up between us.

She rolls us, putting me on my back and straddling my thighs. Her amber eyes are soft, but her voice is firm. "I don't want a superhero or a celebrity. I want you. The Nic I know."

I swallow, warm relief overwhelming me at how badly I needed to hear that from someone. From Jessie, it means something.

Her hands graze my pecs and work their way down to my abs, her touch appreciative. She settles herself between my legs and Christ I want this woman. Her fingers skim my hips, little electric jolts zipping up my spine, and when she takes my cock in hand with a cheeky smile on her face, I can't stop grinning at her.

"Besides," she says as she lowers her head, her lips grazing the tip of my cock. "Warwick wouldn't be my first choice."

I open my mouth to protest, but her tongue is warm and wet as she laps the bead of precum before taking the head of my cock into her mouth, and whatever I planned to say flies out of my head.

Jessie, her auburn hair falling in waves around her as she sucks my cock, is even better than I've been imagining. There's a mischievous glint in her eyes that tells me how much she's enjoying herself. I gather her hair up, wrapping it around my fist so I can ease her off. My cock pops out of her mouth with a soft sound and she gives me an annoyed look.

"Who's your first choice?" I ask.

Jessie shoots me a look but crawls to the nightstand, treating me to a great view of her ass as she digs through the drawer for the condoms. There are always condoms in this house, in the bathrooms and drawers.

"Thor," she answers, then holds up the box. "Good thing I have you, I think I'd need a bigger size for the god of thunder."

I roll my eyes.

Jessie laughs, mollifying me with a kiss before tearing the packet open and sheathing me. "I want to be on top."

I nod because yeah I want that. I hold her hips as she positions herself, and she slides down my cock, hot and wet, and so damned tight I clench my jaw. This is not going to be over too soon. Not until she's done with me.

When she takes all of me, she stops, letting out a shaky breath. For a long moment, she sits still, letting her hands glide over my body, up to my shoulders.

"You okay?" I ask.

"Mmm," she murmurs, leaning forward until her tits graze my chest, her lips soft on mine.

"Glad you aren't fucking Thor?"

"Shut up, Nic."

The slow way she's riding me takes away my power of speech and maybe her own. I grip her ass, squeezing and rocking her on me as she picks up speed. She kisses me, our tongues tangling, and when she pulls back, her creamy skin is flushed pink.

I roll my hips and thrust up into her, wanting more, wanting to be deeper. Jessie leans back and the view of her, one hand braced on my pec, the other dropping to her clit, threatens my control. The bounce of her tits is glorious, but it's got nothing on the expression on her face. Her brows are drawn tight, and her lips are almost pursed. Her eyes—fuck. She's close.

Her head tips back, her eyes fluttering shut, my name a whimper on her lips just before she comes with a strangled gasp, grinding down hard on me. I grit my teeth and try to hang on. The moment I feel the ebb of her orgasm, I flip her underneath me, pulling her leg up my thigh to get deeper. She clenches around me, crying out as she comes again and I fuck into her, coming hard with a moan. Every pulse, every echoing beat of my heart, feels incredible, every thrust more intense than the last until I can't take it anymore.

I collapse onto that sweet spot on her neck.

We got a little loud there, but I doubt anyone heard us. The walls are thick in this house.

I kiss her sweat-dampened skin. "Just how many orgasms do you want?"

She laughs, squeezing me with her entire body. "One more, in a bit."

Sprawling naked in my bed and staring at the ceiling while we catch our breaths, it doesn't take too long for us to come together again. And again after that. I'm half-delirious as I wrap myself around her and pull the blankets over us, but I know one thing. This holiday fling is the best decision I've ever made.

"One more, before you go," I whisper into her warm neck. It's a lie—we're both too worn out and sated to chase after more orgasms, and Jessie has to know that. I'm exhausted enough to admit to myself that I just want the feel of her warm body next to mine as I sleep.

She yawns, snuggling into my pillow. "You might knock Thor off the top."

"Fuck yeah, I will." I murmur, fitting my body to hers, floating on a feeling of warm contentment as I fall asleep.

DECEMBER TWENTY-THIRD

There's a bang on my door and my heart leaps into my throat as a stray knee connects with my groin.

I hiss, cupping my abused balls. What the ever-loving hell is happening? I find myself face to face with Jessie's wide eyes and for a moment I stare at her, stunned that she's in my bed.

Last night comes flooding back to me. Everything we did. Jessie's thoughts are mirroring my own if the pink blooming on her cheeks is any indication.

"Nic!" Timothy bangs on the door again before rattling the doorknob. I suck in a breath.

The door is locked, thank god. Timothy pounds on it again. "You can't sleep all day on my wedding day! I need you to take my hag of a sister down the aisle."

I let out my breath as Jessie pulls the blankets over her head. Like he won't notice the Jessie-sized lump next to me when he manages to break in.

"Did you lock your bedroom door?" I hiss at her—because that's probably Timothy's next stop. Thank god he didn't climb onto the roof and come through the window.

The blankets fly off and Jessie leaps up, naked, and makes her exit through the bathroom door, closing it softly. I can hear the shower kick on.

"Nic!" Timothy bangs on the door again.

"I'm up, you ass," I say loud enough for him to hear as I swing my legs over the side of the bed.

A used condom is plastered to my thigh—guess we were too sex-drunk last night to put it in the trash—and I'm peeling it off and wincing at every leg hair I'm ripping out when my door flies open. I whip the blankets back over my lower half and send up a quick prayer that Timothy doesn't go near the small trash bin where the rest of the used condoms are.

Timothy has a huge grin on his face as he holds up a bobby pin and walks in. "Have a good night last night?"

I rub the back of my neck and mumble something about a hangover.

Timothy gives me a lopsided grin. "I counted your drinks. You were off your head, but it wasn't the alcohol."

"I'm not on anything, if that's what you're implying." I snap.

Timothy makes a noise and stops. Directly over Jessie's pajamas, lying on an otherwise clean floor. His grin gets impossibly huge as he rubs his hands together and bounces on his feet. "Why are my sister's pajamas in your room?"

I yawn to give myself time to come up with something. "She keeps leaving her shit all over the bathroom floor. Thought I'd hold them hostage until she agrees to clean up after herself."

Timothy's smile dims. "She'll starch your undies in retaliation. Is she up yet?"

"How would I know?" I ask, irritated. "What time is it?"

He glances at the door to the bathroom and frowns. "Ten."

Dammit. That doesn't leave much time for a coffee. "Shouldn't you be getting ready?"

Timothy glances down at his faded black Warwick T-shirt and torn jeans and shrugs. "I already look good. You look like you went a couple of rounds with—"

Celia shouts Timothy's name from somewhere downstairs and he sighs before yelling back that he'll be down in a minute. "We leave in thirty—tell Jessie to get her ass out of the shower."

"You tell her," I say with a yawn.

"I don't want to die on my wedding day."

"And I do?"

Timothy grins and jabs two fingers at his eyes, flicks them to me, then back to his eyes, but he walks out and I think our secret is safe. For now.

Chapter Nineteen

Jessie

THE BUTTERFLIES IN MY stomach, jolted into action by Timothy's rude wake-up, never settle. That was too close. I'm going to ignore Nic today. Might even be a little mean if I find either Timothy or Mina watching us.

The venue is a gorgeous villa none of us have time to notice as we scramble out of cars, a little more than fashionably late, in a flurry of garment bags, scarves, and shouted instructions as we split into three groups. I follow Mina down the elegant hall to the bridal suite, glancing over my shoulder to exchange a heated look with Nic before he's pulled into the groom's suite.

Mina is freaking out over her vows. Lexi and Charlotte tease her and soothe her in turn while my mom bustles about, possibly fueling Mina's panic with her nervous energy. Hazel comes in with Evie and someone pops the champagne. After a few glasses and some hilarious stories about Timothy, Mina calms down enough to have her hair and makeup done. Hopefully, she's realized the only way she could screw this up would be to not make it down the aisle.

One of my few skills is the ability to transform myself from a swamp hag to Instagram-worthy in a short time, so I'm ready before the others, without the help of the stylist.

I sneak out, hoping to catch Timothy before the ceremony. He shouldn't be in the chapel yet, but it's on my way to the groom's suite, so I stop and peek inside. It's a winter wonderland, with garlands, red roses, and little lights twinkling. It's cozy and elegant and maybe I don't paint anymore, but if I did, I'd try to capture the details. Red petals against pine needles. The drape of a satiny white ribbon. No Timothy, but already family and friends are seated inside. More people will come for the reception in the Crystal Ballroom but Timothy and Mina wanted this part to be more private.

I knock on the door to the groom's suite. Nic opens it and slips out, closing the door behind him just enough to shield the room from my view. He gives me a slow, appreciative once over, his smile growing. I might be gawking—he looks like a dream in his tailored three-piece charcoal gray suit. I think I smile back at him, but those butterflies flitting about my stomach all morning? They take flight and I forget I'm supposed to ignore him. I forget everything because this secret sex thing with Nic? It's exciting.

Nic glances over his shoulder. "I don't think I can sneak away."

"I don't want you," I whisper.

"Liar," he whispers back.

From somewhere in the room, Timothy calls out, "Tell my soon-to-be missus it's bad luck to see me before the wedding, no matter how badly she needs to jump on this—"

"It's Jessie." Thankfully, Nic interrupts him before I hear enough to make me lose my breakfast. Which consisted of cookies scarfed down in the car on the ride over.

"Oh. She can come in." Timothy calls back. "Danny's mostly decent."

Nic opens the door for me, leaning over to whisper, "Your brother is obnoxious today. Like a kid on a sugar high."

"Today? Try always," I say, walking into the room.

I don't look to see if this Danny person is dressed—Timothy's smiling this dopey smile at me and I rush straight to him, wrapping him in a hug. I guess my holiday plans of fixing my relationship with him will have to be extended into the foreseeable future. I've been distracted by Nic, he's been distracted by Mina. But it feels like we're in a better place already.

"I am so happy for you." I manage with a sniffle, batting my eyelashes to keep from crying and ruining my makeup before the wedding starts. He's had a shit year recovering from his injury and retiring from the job he loved. I want to tell him how proud I am that he didn't let it destroy him, how lucky he is to have Mina, and how scared I was that I'd lost him, but I can't force any of the words out. Not in anything more elucidating than a squeak, anyway.

"Thanks, J," he says softly, crushing me, understanding anyway because he's my twin, and something of the bond we used to have must still be there. "That means a lot."

I sniffle again. "Mina is great and you make each other so happy and I just—" can't or I'm going to be bawling and I need to walk down the aisle looking composed soon.

"Told you so," he says, pulling back and grinning at me. His eyes are all teary—he's going to cry during his wedding and I love that for this family. We'll roast him forever. "How's my wife doing?" he asks.

"About the same as you. Freaking out."

"What? I'm not freaking out. Guys, am I freaking out?"

There's a resounding "yes" and someone throws a little squishy basketball toy at him, bouncing it off his head.

Timothy digs around in his pocket, pulling out a tiny Tupperware. "Give these to Mina. Don't let her eat them all unless you want to hear some wild shit about jellyfish."

"Goddammit, Timothy, really?" I shake the container of edibles in front of his face.

He shrugs, but he's still grinning.

Nic opens the door for me, leaning in close to my ear. "You look beautiful."

"I want to rip your clothes off," I whisper back, pulling the Tupperware out of the way when he reaches for it.

"Fontana!" Timothy bellows and I run, my laugh ringing through the hall and turning a few heads in the chapel.

I burst into the bridal suite, handing the Tupperware to Mina. She takes one look inside and laughs. "No."

My mom homes in on it, plucking it from Mina's hands. "You kids need to get your own damn edibles. Stop stealing mine."

We laugh and talk and drink champagne until showtime when nervous energy takes over again as we file out of the room.

Mom, Amanda, and Hazel head down the aisle to find their seats. Timothy is already standing by the altar, looking far too jittery to have taken one of Mom's edibles.

I fluff about with Mina's dress, but honestly, it's perfect. She's perfect, smiling and glowing, joy radiating from her.

Soft music starts and Liam, adorable in his suit and holding the rings, goes first, Evie following and scattering red rose petals.

There's a brief panic next—we haven't rehearsed, and no one has a clue who's supposed to go next.

Lexi solves the problem, snagging the grumpy-looking groomsman whose name I don't know because he didn't make it to the bachelor party, and pulling him toward the aisle. Charlotte follows shortly after on Danny's arm.

Mina squeezes my hand and waves me off toward Nic.

I take his arm, my heart beating so loud that for a moment, I can't hear the music. He takes the first step and I stumble, a startled laugh ringing out of me as he steadies me.

"Please tell me you didn't have one of the edibles," he murmurs to me as he leads me down the aisle. "I can't take more Muppets discourse."

A girl gets stoned one time—ONE TIME—and tells anyone who would listen, in graphic detail, what sex position each cast member of The Muppets prefers and why, then spends the rest of the night convinced light switches are little penises, and suddenly everyone is like 'don't touch the edibles.' Sheesh.

"You wouldn't stop flicking the lights on and off," Nic says under his breath.

"I'm going to murder you later," I say with a smile, squeezing his arm. Everyone is watching us and I want to laugh. This is so absurd, but I'm having fun with him. I wish things could always be like this, with us.

"Looking forward to your attempt."

The way he says that sends tingles through my body.

We've reached the altar, so we separate. Timothy slaps Nic on the shoulder and leans close to whisper something in his ear. Nic's face goes red. When

Timothy jabs two fingers at his eyes and flicks them to me, I nonchalantly use my bouquet to hide my middle finger from the guests.

The music swells and everyone turns.

Mina steps into the room and Timothy's eyes go all starry, the smile on his face dopey as she makes her way to him. Because he's Timothy, he can't wait. He jogs to meet her halfway like he's pulled by a magnet to her. He whispers something in her ear that makes her laugh before escorting her the rest of the way to the altar.

Their vows are beautiful and funny and heartfelt and I spend half the ceremony blinking back tears. My mother has a tissue pressed to her nose, but I can see her smile and the way she leans against my dad.

I sneak as many looks at Nic as I think I can get away with and our eyes meet often enough I suspect he's doing the same. Honestly, I can't help it. He looks too damn good in that suit.

The officiant pronounces Timothy and Mina man and wife and the entire room cheers as he sweeps her into a kiss. They come back up with wide smiles and shining eyes, then Timothy grabs her hand and they run down the aisle laughing.

Nic offers me his arm. I take it, hoping he doesn't notice the tremble in my hand. He escorts me down the aisle and I smile brightly for the photographer and the guests, but all I can think about is Nic.

"Think anyone would notice if we disappeared for five minutes?" he whispers in my ear when we exit the chapel.

I slap his arm, but I'm looking around and wondering if we could get away with ten when the photographer corners us. As the guests head to the Crystal Ballroom and an open bar, we're ushered back into the chapel with the rest of the bridal party and family for photos.

Since Timothy and Mina have disappeared, the photographer takes extra photos of the rest of us and Nic uses the excuse of us being packed together like sardines to get handsy. I take every opportunity I can to innocently brush against his dick. By the time Timothy and Mina join us, I'm certain they'll notice the frenetic need-to-fuck energy between us. But they don't. They're happily disheveled and wrapped up in each other. Nic and I could make out on top of the altar and neither would see.

Everyone else would though. Something I'm reminded of when I catch my mother scrutinizing us. We're not in this picture, standing as far out of the way as we can, and Nic has his hand on my hip—hidden, I thought, by my bouquet.

I take a small step away from him and his hand drops. Sex will have to wait until the reception when sneaking away will be easy.

My mother's waiting for us outside the ballroom, a fake smile plastered on her face. I try not to let my impatience show when she calls Nic over, but I can't stop myself from following in hopes that this will be quick and we can sneak off after.

"Nic," my mother says without a glance my way, "This is Simone. Your date. She's a sous chef at Rodrigo's."

My jaw drops and I hastily clamp my mouth shut. Date?

Simone steps forward, offering her hand.

She's gorgeous. Her dusky pink dress is old school glamour, her golden blonde hair falling in sleek waves down the exposed back. She's petite, but otherwise, she looks a hell of a lot like Addison.

Nic glances over his shoulder at me, his lips barely moving in a quick 'sorry.' He takes Simone's hand and says something that makes her laugh, a little tinkling bell sound. They walk into the reception together.

I stand, staring after him while the butterflies in my stomach rampage in anger and humiliation.

My mother finally acknowledges me, sweeping me into a hug. "Your date's already at the bar."

"*My* date?"

"I told you." She huffs, taking my arm and leading me into the ballroom. "I believe you've already met him."

Oh yeah. Turns out we've met all right. Celebrity chef Colton Craig turns at our approach. The flirtatious smile I remember is somehow oily now.

Colton Craig is a regret. A poor decision made during the worst week of my life. When I needed the distraction of no-strings sex five years ago, I was disappointed to discover the arrogant prick who could fillet a steak a million ways couldn't find the clitoris to save his life.

I greet him because my mom's still standing there, but the moment she walks away, satisfied with her horrible matchmaking skills, and the moment Colton starts undressing me with his eyes, I order a drink.

Chapter Twenty

Jessie

I'm in hell.

There's no separate table for the bridal party. No seating chart at all. Everything is chaos because my twin is chaos and I guess Mina is along for that ride.

Colton sits beside me, critiquing the food. Aunt Kimberly is the only one listening, but only because she has a crush on him and watches his show every week. She can have him.

I have a clear view of Nic and Simone. His suit coat is draped over his chair and he's rolled the sleeves of his crisp white shirt up to his elbows, the slut, showing off the corded muscles of his forearms. Simone is eating it up.

It should be me eating him up, right now, back in the bridal suite or failing that, a supply closet.

Disappointed doesn't begin to cover how I feel.

He leans over to say something that makes her laugh, the little lines around his eyes crinkling as he smiles. She touches his arm and Nic picks that moment to turn and catch me glaring. Whatever it is he tries to communicate with me before he brings his attention back to his date goes over my head.

It's just sex, and we didn't agree to be exclusive. It's good we have dates—that'll keep my family from catching on and me from catching feelings. Last night and this morning, it was too easy and too comfortable with Nic. I could start to like the guy. This is the shot of reality I need.

Still…it shouldn't feel this shitty.

Simone seems lovely too. What if Nic falls for her? I don't want to lose my sex buddy.

Colton abruptly stops bitching about the salad dressing to tap his knife on my untouched chicken. "That's overcooked. Try my salmon." He shoves a forkful in my face.

Is this supposed to be sexy? I push his fork away before the urge to stab him with it can overpower me.

"Excuse me," I say, dropping my napkin onto my plate and heading to the bar.

The swanky ballroom is decked out in silver and gold, with pine boughs covered in red berries everywhere. Candles and white seed lights twinkle off the glass, casting warm shadows across thick white table cloths. It's breathtakingly romantic and I hate it.

Not as much as I hate Colton Craig. The man is as shallow as a baking sheet and as interesting as a ladle. He's a pretentious hipster foodie Karen. With nasty cologne. Who thinks he deserves sex because he has a handsome-ish face and a show on TV.

Nic has depth. I like that I can't tell what he's thinking. Everyone in my family wears everything on their sleeves, so Nic's reserve—even when it felt cold—has always been a reprieve. Plus, he smells nice, overall he's a decent human being, and he can fuck.

I order a drink and stare at the dark wood grain of the bar. I'm not eccentric like Timothy and Mom, organized and driven like Amanda, or smart like Dad. I'm not as pretty as Addison or Simone. I am average and unremarkable in every way, and I thought I was happy with that.

I'm not.

I want to paint. I want recognition for my work and for who I am. I want to be with Nic tonight. For once in my goddamn life, I just want to be the center of some positive attention from someone. Anyone.

I slam my drink as my cousin Lauren joins me.

"Men are awful." I proclaim, waving my empty glass about.

Lauren snorts and brushes her strawberry blonde hair away from her face. "Your date sure is. You were gone for thirty seconds and he made a pass at me."

I set my glass on the bar and cover my face. "Ugh, I can't believe I slept with him."

"What?" Her voice rings out. "Today? When? And—ew, *why*?"

"Five years ago," I say, dropping my hands and turning to signal the bartender. I'm going to need another drink.

It was at the Foley Folly—our Christmas Eve party. I'd already endured meeting Addison in my filthy cow onesie. I already heard her judgment of my art. I sat silently while Nic announced their engagement to everyone. Three days, having to watch Addison simper and cling to Nic while getting progressively colder toward the rest of us. I was half-drunk, flirting with Colton, when I saw Nic and Addison kissing in a quiet little corner. My heart was still broken from Camden and here was this perfect couple, engaged, happy, and awful, with all their glamour, sparkle, and style.

It hurt. I needed a distraction, some other feeling to push out all the heartbreak. I'd turned to Colton and asked if he wanted to go upstairs. He was too sweaty, and the sex was awful—poke-poke-poke-done awful. I felt worse after, so I got plastered and when that shockingly didn't help, I asked Timothy to drive me home. He did, without prying, which was a true Christmas miracle.

He would've spent the holiday with me, but I'd insisted he go home. Someone had to keep Mom from murdering Addison. That was the excuse I gave him, but really I wanted him to leave so I could spend the day drinking in my pajamas and binging reality TV and crying.

I didn't crawl out of that place for months.

It was Timothy who came to New York to pull me out of it. He introduced me to his ex-girlfriend Elle, who gave me a job. He helped me get my shit together, even though I resented the hell out of him for it back then. That's Timothy though. He'd do anything for the people he loves, even meddle when they just want to be left in broken, sharp pieces.

The bartender sets my drink down, and this needs to be my last one. If I get drunk enough to hook up with Colton Craig again, I'm Googling 'chastity belts that don't unlock without passing a breathalyzer.'

A group of relatives, including my sister and Hazel, are gathered at the other end of the bar, huddled over what I'm guessing is Amanda's phone. Since I slept in and spent my morning getting ready with Mina, I've missed out on the chance to place a bet.

Betting on big family gatherings—weddings, funerals, holidays—is a tradition. The cash isn't the biggest prize. Bragging rights are. There's also a fair amount of cheating and attempts at finding loopholes.

There's an eclectic mix of people tonight—a handful from LA, mostly stunt guys as far as I can tell, a handful from my mother's world, obligatory family, and anyone willing to give up a night this close to Christmas for an open bar. The place is packed and there's a lot of uncertainty as far as betting goes.

When Lauren points out that Colton appears to be looking for me, we decide the safest course of action is to hide with the cluster at the other end of the bar.

"Twenty bucks Timbo blows up the cake." It's a sure bet and something he's threatened to do for years if he ever got married.

Amanda, our family bookie, glances at me with a frown, but keys it in. "You're a bit late to the game. Twelve other people have placed the same bet."

I'm shrugging when I catch my name on the screen. I reach for her phone. "What's that?"

Amanda is a lot taller than me and merely holds her phone above my head. "Top secret."

It's not surprising I'm on there, given my track record. At Amanda and Hazel's wedding, I got trashed and hooked up with the DJ. The man played every single song I'd demanded all night—essentially nothing but Bananarama and some Bangles. I was going through a phase where I loved all the music Mom subjected me to as a child. It was awesome.

I jump but fall short. "What's the bet?"

Hazel snatches the phone from Amanda and scans the document. "Well, one of those is a sure thing."

One of those. I'm on there more than once.

"Tell me."

"Against the rules." Amanda drops her phone into her purse.

"There are no rules." Loopholes exist for everything. Negotiations over what constitutes a win could take days to resolve. "Tell me."

Hazel laughs. "Timothy has money on you punching out Colton Craig before the end of the night. I'm only telling you because I want to see you do it. Did you hear him abusing that waiter?"

I hadn't, but he is that asshole. If I thought for two seconds I wouldn't swing and miss, I might consider helping Timothy win some money.

"What else?" I demand.

The group goes silent, but the look on Lauren's face is pure guilt. Her freckles are in danger of disappearing under her blush. She knows. And she'll cave because she always does. I turn on her. "Tell me and I'll introduce you to that hot accountant at work." The one she's too shy to talk to but has spent a lot of time undressing with her eyes.

She hesitates. "There's a lot of money on you and Nic hooking up before midnight."

"Lauren." Amanda glares.

"Names," I demand, ignoring my sister.

"Oh, calm down, Jessie," Amanda says with a huff. "You and Nic hooking up has been bet on at every family event since you both turned eighteen. The odds are usually so low and only Timothy ever makes that bet, but..."

I gasp. "You bet on it, didn't you?"

Amanda winces.

Lauren laughs because she doesn't have siblings and therefore, doesn't understand my pain. "The whole family did," she says. "Except for your mom. And you and Nic, obviously."

My mom. Celia Foley is a fucking cockblocking shark. For a moment, I almost respect her game. She got us both dates, told no one, and she stands to rake it in tonight because I will not be hooking up with Nic.

"We saw that kiss in the hot tub," Hazel says, fanning herself.

Dammit! What the hell had I been thinking, kissing him like that? "I have a suitcase full of vibrators. I don't need Nic's massive dick." My eyes go painfully wide, my stomach leaping into my throat. "No, wait—"

Too late. Everyone is laughing at my slip.

Amanda pulls her phone back out, her eyes teasing. "Does this mean you've already hooked up? Was it today?"

"*He's* a massive dick." God, I sound whiny. "That's what I meant."

"Well, it's looking like we're losing that bet tonight," Hazel says, her voice sympathetic. "Unless you want us to distract the blonde so you can go hit that."

"I don't want to hit that," I say, crossing my arms and mostly meaning it. I do want to hit him, but more in the slapping sense of the word.

The conversation shifts to Timothy and Mina, who are making out after some asshole started that stupid tapping on a wineglass nonsense. They look so happy in a world of their own, eyes only for each other.

The cake is safe from fireworks and I'm out twenty bucks.

Nic and Simone are still at their table, chatting and laughing like old friends. He doesn't need to try so hard—she's interested. I think he might be too.

Dammit. I need another drink. I leave the safety of the pack and wave at the bartender.

"Hey." Mina slips in next to me, stealing my drink before it hits the surface of the bar. "You and I need to talk, and I need to pee. Come help me with this dress?"

Since that's the most important job for a maid of honor, I follow her to the ladies' room, slightly alarmed when she makes sure we're alone before locking the door.

"Why does Nic have a date?" she demands, slapping her hand on the vanity.

I jump at the sound, a little confused about why she cares. "My mom set him up."

"Your mom." Mina echoes, falling into a broody silence. "Why would she do that?" she finally asks.

"So she can cash in on us not hooking up?" I shrug. "Do you have to pee or not?"

Mina ignores that, instead stepping closer to me, dropping her voice. "You and Nic have been hooking up this whole time, haven't you?"

"Is this another bet?" I don't need to ask. It must be. "Because honestly, I don't want to talk about Nic."

Mina's face goes all sympathetic, and she nods, but says, "I'm sorry you're hurting."

"I'm—" I can't even deny it. I couldn't leave my emotions at the door. Nic could. He's moved on to the next woman while I'm barely holding it together in the ladies' room.

"I'll fix this," Mina says, determination settling over her expression as she pushes past me and unlocks the door.

"Don't you have to pee?" I call after her.

"Nah," she says over her shoulder, "Timothy helped me with that after we fu—excuse me," she interrupts herself politely as Great-Aunt Glenda shuffles in. With a little laugh, Mina disappears.

"To be young again," Glenda says with a gusty sigh, shaking her head.

I do not want to be cornered by Great-Aunt Glenda so I try to slip past her, but she grabs my arm. "Got any more of those pretty little flower stimulator thingies?"

Somehow, I've become the family sex toy dealer. The ninety-year-old accosted me at a Fourth of July barbeque and said if I was handing out sex toys, she deserved one too. I was not handing out sex toys at a family barbeque and whoever told Great-Aunt Glenda about my job deserves a smack to the back of the head, but I sent her a tulip-shaped clitoral stimulator, the most senior-safe product Sploosh! makes, and after that, orders from the retirement community rolled in.

Honestly, good for them. Not great for me every time someone forgets to charge their toy and Glenda gives them my number.

"Sorry," I say, slipping out of her bony grip and motioning to my lack of a handbag. "I don't."

I make it to the bar and order another drink. Music starts and Timothy sweeps Mina onto the floor for a slow, pretty Ed Sheeran song. Thirty seconds later it switches to a thumping medley of every filthy song released in the last ten years.

The DJ doesn't call the wedding party up. No parent dances either. Everyone is invited to the floor and I'm treated to the sight of Dominic Fontana twirling a petite carbon copy of his ex-wife on the dance floor.

It hurts. My insides feel like they're being turned inside out and an all-consuming dread pumps through me with every heartbeat.

It shouldn't hurt this much.

I knock half my drink back the moment the bartender sets it in front of me.

A hand wraps around my waist, the solid body suddenly behind me smelling like cheap cologne and sweat. Colton. I suppress the urge to gag.

"Let's dance." He says in what he must think is a sexy voice.

Another strike against continuing down the road of casual relationships—how much asshole behavior do I have to endure to be rewarded with the slim chance of an orgasm?

Far too many guys half-ass my pleasure if they even care at all.

Even when it was a one-off in the laundry room, Nic took the time to get me off first. He cared about my pleasure.

I need to stop thinking about Nic.

"One dance," I say, slamming my empty glass on the bar. We're on the dance floor before I realize the song is a slow one.

Worse, Nic and his date are gone. Off to some dark corner, no doubt. Something hot and sick twists in my stomach at the thought, everything roiling as Colton's hands slip over my waist.

"I have a room in the hotel across the street," he says, his hand drifting to my ass and squeezing.

"Not a chance," I say, striving not to gag as I try to pull away from him.

His hold on me tightens. "Don't be like that."

"Get off me." I snap. When he scoffs and doesn't let me go, I shove him as hard as I can. The people closest to us stop and stare.

Colton shakes his head. "Come on, Jessie," he says quietly, sounding disappointed in me. "We've had fun before."

The reminder of that night makes my skin crawl. I turn, racing through the crowd, back to the safety of the ladies' room, tears of anger burning my eyes.

I close myself in a stall and grab some toilet paper to dab at my eyes.

Fuck this guy. Colton, Nic, whoever. All of them. I'm over it.

Tonight, I will touch up my makeup, walk back out with my head high, hang around long enough for the cake, and go home. Alone.

I'll cry after I wash my makeup off. Like the goddamned pro I am.

Chapter Twenty-One

Nic

I see enough of what goes down on the dance floor to cut Simone off mid-sentence.

Jessie, who only hurts with her words, shoved her date hard enough that he nearly fell. This means the creep deserved a slap at minimum.

"Excuse me," I say to Simone, stepping back. My eyes are tracking Colton as he moves over toward the cake and I trip over Lexi, who winks at me before taking my place, introducing herself to Simone.

I catch Colton nibbling a cracker and some cheese from a nearby platter as he casts a critical eye over the five-tier wedding cake trailing white roses. I hate this man. Hate that I even know who he is. That he's been in my spot next to her all night. I hate that five years ago, I watched her walk upstairs with him when he doesn't deserve to touch her.

I grab his shoulder, roughly pulling him around. "You need to leave."

He sneers at me, setting his half-eaten cracker on the tablecloth, far too close to the cheese platters, and looks me over. "I'm not going anywhere."

"I didn't ask." I tug at my sleeves, but they're already rolled up. Colton's bigger than me, and the only fights I've been in have been carefully choreographed, but a hell of a lot of training goes into throwing a convincing punch.

Colton laughs. "I'll leave as soon as my date's ready."

That implication makes my fist clench. "She's not leaving with you."

He dismisses that with a shrug. "Go back to Simone, she'll spread her legs for you."

I grab his arm and push him toward the door, but he turns on me, shoving me hard. A round of gasps turns to silence as the DJ cuts the music. I collide into the table behind me, five tiers of cake rocking dangerously.

I grab the edge to steady it, my heart pounding from the shot of adrenaline.

"Seriously, Blue Steel," he says, his voice full of warning, "fuck off."

One step. Two more as I draw my arm back.

I hit him with everything I have.

The crunch under my knuckles is satisfying. The startled gasps of the crowd barely register as pain blooms across my hand. Colton staggers backward, cupping his nose, blood trickling through his fingers.

I shift my stance as I wait for him to come at me. God, I *want* him to.

His eyes telegraph his attack before he pulls his hand away from his nose. I'm gleeful. I get to hit him again.

Timothy steps in out of nowhere, clotheslining him across the throat when he charges me. Colton goes down on his back, hard.

When I take a step closer, Timothy holds out a warning hand.

A broken nose isn't enough, but I let it go, shaking out my fist as Timothy hauls Colton to his feet and with the help of Danny, manhandles him through the crowd to the door.

All the eyes in the mostly silent room drift back to me as I scan for Jessie.

She's at the back of the crowd, her face pale and bewildered.

I take a step toward her before I'm accosted by a flurry of white satin and lace, like some demonic swan.

"You asshole," Mina says in a low voice. I flinch, turning my head, but not fast enough to avoid the glancing blow of her fist. Momentum throws me back toward the table.

For half a second, I think I might catch myself before the collision.

That doesn't happen. Instead, the table and I go down with a bang. Along with five tiers of cake, buttercream, and fondant.

Shit.

I squeeze my eyes shut and take a deep breath. How the hell did I get here, to this moment? Sprawled on my back next to a smashed cake. Fighting at my best friend's wedding.

What if Jessie never talks to me again? Or any of the Foleys. I'm certain Timothy and Jessie took down the cake for one of Celia and William's milestone anniversaries, but they're family. I'm not.

A loud clap echoes in the silence. I open my eyes as Mina snaps a photo of me on her phone, her grin wide. Timothy comes our way, clapping loudly over his head, encouraging others to do the same. His drunk-ass high school friends and the handful of stunt crew who flew out for the wedding take the cue.

Hesitantly, a few other guests join in. Hazel lets a whistle rip, and the crowd breaks out in cheers.

The relief pulls the tension out of my body, leaving me sagging over the busted table. I'm not getting disowned. At least not for this. I'll still have to deal with the publicity nightmare, though Celia's no phone policy for the guests might limit that damage.

"What was that for?" I ask, rubbing my jaw as Mina stands over me. Thank god she pulled her punch. I've seen what this woman can do to a punching bag—if she wanted to hurt me, she would've.

Mina jabs a finger at me. "You aren't supposed to have a date."

I pull my hand back from my face. There's buttercream on my fingers. "No shit." I can't even say it's not my fault, because it is. I asked Celia to set me up. I should've told Simone up front I couldn't be her date tonight. "You hit me because I have a date?"

Mina raises an eyebrow and says in a low, threatening tone, "Vegas."

A laugh breaks out of my chest. I convinced her the best way to get Timothy back after they broke up was to jump off the Strat in Vegas when a phone call would've done the trick.

"You," Timothy says, hauling me to my feet, "cost me twenty bucks. My money was on Jessie breaking that prick's nose."

"He's a creep." The defensive growl in my voice has everything to do with the mention of Colton, even as Timothy pulls me into an embrace, clapping me hard on the back before letting me go.

"Hey, boys."

We turn at Mina's voice, but instead of the photo I expect her to snap, she smashes a handful of the vanilla cake into each of our faces, smearing it around for good measure. The sound that comes out of Timothy is half-animal as he grabs his bride, hauling her in for a messy tangle of mouths and buttercream. It sends the crowd into wild applause.

"Here." Amanda laughs as she hands me a wet wipe from her purse. I take it gratefully, wiping what must have been a buttercream rose off my face. Amanda looks at the cake and shakes her head. "Pretty sure no one had money on 'Jessie murders Nic for destroying the cake before she gets a piece.'"

My gaze jerks up to where I'd last seen her, but instead of barreling toward me, she's gone.

Amanda hands out wet wipes to Timothy and Mina when they come up for air, and when the venue manager appears and stares at the broken table in horror, Amanda nudges her brother, and the two of them move to intercept him.

"I'm sorry about the cake," I say to Mina.

She brushes a few crumbs off her shoulder. "I don't like cake." For a moment she scans the crowd—most are still keeping an eye on us. "I think I know where Jessie's gone. Come on."

I follow her through the crowd, but when she moves to open the door to the ladies' room, I grab her arm. "I can't go in there."

She looks at me like I'm trying her patience. "Jessie's in here."

"Maybe you should go in, make sure she's okay."

She rests her hands on her hips. "Or you can go in and explain why you're having such a good time with your date when up until now you and Jessie have been banging."

My body goes cold all over. "We haven't."

"But you want to."

Mina doesn't know. I shake my head, but she rolls her eyes, grabs my arm, and hauls me inside.

Jessie's standing in front of the mirror, lip gloss poised but forgotten as she turns toward us, eyes wide.

"Nic has something to say," Mina says, elbowing me right in the kidney.

I wince and cover my side with my hand. "I'm not sorry I broke your date's nose. That guy's a prick."

Jessie snorts and goes back to her reflection, swiping the rosy pink applicator over her lips.

"Not that," Mina says, but at least this time she doesn't elbow me.

I can't say what I need to in front of Mina, so I catch Jessie's eyes in the mirror. "Can we talk? Alone?"

She turns, glancing at Mina and back at me, uncertainty in her eyes.

"Please?"

"I think you should hear him out," Mina says as she takes a step toward the door.

Jessie puts her lip gloss in a hidden pocket in her skirt, her expression carefully blank. "Fine."

"I'll stand outside, make sure you have privacy," Mina says with a diabolical grin. "Can you get it done in two minutes?"

"Thirty seconds will be enough," Jessie says.

Shit. I'm going to have to make every second count.

Mina scoffs. "No way is he that good."

Jessie laughs and I silently thank Mina for the tension breaker.

The door shuts and I close the distance between us. It's hard to keep my hands to myself, but I manage, leaning forward to whisper in Jessie's ear—in case Mina's eavesdropping. "You're the only one I want."

Jessie shivers and I take that as a good sign, so I reach out to brush a loose curl from her face.

"I was in the room when your mom set you up," I say, tilting her chin so I can meet her eyes. "I asked her to set me up, too, because I didn't want to be alone when you were with someone. It's been hell tonight, watching you with him again."

"I've been miserable. You've been having fun," she says accusingly, brushing my hand away.

I shake my head. "I'm playing my part. You don't have your phone on you and I haven't been able to get you alone anywhere."

Jessie sighs and slips her arms around my waist, resting her head against my chest. "This sucks."

"It does." I hold her close. "I want to be with you tonight, and not just whatever scraps of time we can steal without anyone noticing." I kiss the top of her head. "I know what we have is temporary, but this is..." What is it? It's us—me and Jessie—after so many painful years. It feels bigger than anything else I've had with another woman, and maybe that's because I know her so well, or because of who she is to me.

I want to explore whatever this is. There's no time for anyone else. "This is exclusive. You and me. Okay?"

Jessie's eyes are wide and she nods, her arms going around my neck. She breathes my name in a tone so soft all I can do is hold her tighter. Then she's rising up on her toes, but instead of kissing me, she licks my cheek. I missed a bit of icing, apparently, because she moans. "I hate you. That cake was delicious."

Our two minutes are up. Jessie leaves first. I follow a minute later. Mina's not lurking outside the door. No idea if she was when Jessie came out, or how much Mina knows. Hopefully, Timothy will make his wife forget anything she's figured out.

A few people pause to give me shit about the cake, but no one says a word about Jessie. My eyes are immediately drawn to her and I track her movement around the room as she smiles and laughs.

I'm a bit unbalanced. I said more than I meant to and it feels like I've edged into deeper water. Everything I said was true though. Until this holiday ends and we go our separate ways, I want to spend every moment I can with her. Making her smile, making her moan my name. Just being in the same room as her and catching one of her flirty little looks has me feeling more alive than I've felt in years.

It's addictive and I want more.

The realization I don't want this thing with Jessie to end hits me like a bus and for a long moment I stand near the dance floor, blinking. What the hell is wrong with me? It can't last. For a hundred different reasons from *I can't lose the Foleys* to *Jessie lives in New York*. But also...she knows me. She's happy with the sex for now, but when that gets old, she'll drop me.

Amanda taps my arm, startling me. "Timothy put that creep in a cab. And Mom's pissed at him—she said she'd handle it. In the scary voice."

I've only heard that voice a couple of times and never directed at me. The memory is still enough to make me shudder. Also—and I don't understand this—Celia has some power. She's like the fucking Godfather and people who cross her end up changing careers. The only kitchen likely to welcome Colton Craig will be one with a drive-through and his TV career is toast.

"Mom's already on damage control," Amanda says. "I don't think what happened will get out. And"—she smiles—"your date left with Lexi."

Thank god.

Chapter Twenty-Two

Jessie

December Twenty-fourth

It turns out that acting like Nic and I aren't sleeping together is hard. It's weird pretending we still hate each other, but he's adamant my family can't find out, and I agree. Mostly. He's the family favorite and I'll be responsible for his heart—whether it's involved or not in what we have—and I don't want that on me.

The problem is, I want to lay my head in his lap while he sits on the couch and smack his ass when I walk by in the kitchen. I want him to kiss me under the mistletoe and for it not to be a big deal for everyone if he does.

To distract myself from wanting things I shouldn't, I finally opened the email from Elle sitting in my inbox. It's more information about the commission Gretchen Torres wants to offer me. I need some time to parse through this, not to mention a break from pretending I don't want to touch up on Nic, so I escape to the attic.

Dozens of my canvases are stacked against the walls, turned away, or covered at my request so I can't see them, should I come up here. Mom refused to take down the one from the great room—the one Addison snubbed—and the ones in Timothy's room and my room, but everything else is up here. Boxes full of watercolor paper, towers of watercolor journals...most are little studies of flowers from my mother's garden. Most embarrassingly, a lot of fan art from the shows and books I had short but deep love affairs with.

Those should've been burned.

A large canvas of the tire swing by the lake on a summer's day has been turned around and I stare at it for a moment, wondering if Mom's been up here lately and why she looked at that one. My fingers itch to turn it around so I can't see it, but I don't.

I find an old but mostly empty sketch pad and a couple of pencils—in case I want to doodle—and sit in the middle of the room on the threadbare rug. Light pours in from a small circular window, the dust motes I stirred up falling back like snow.

Gretchen wants what she's calling 'pieces of eroticism,' like my doodle of the woman's face as she comes. Something like a hand clenching sheets or lips parted on a head thrown back. Simple and clean. The mood should be light, but not quirky. More a statement than a suggestion. The email goes on, whittling away possibilities in maddeningly vague terms until the little creative spark I felt from 'pieces of eroticism' snuffs out.

With a sigh, I drop the sketch pad on the floor next to me.

Gretchen rejected my paintings when she was with Torres and Strauss. She told me, albeit kindly, my art didn't have the special something she was looking for. That was a decade ago and I haven't picked up a brush in five years. I doubt Gretchen would find anything compelling about the whimsical but impossible shafts I normally doodle, and quite frankly, that's all I'm good for these days.

The sound of the ladder being lowered in this quiet space makes me jump. Nic's head comes into view, the worried look on his face vanishing when his eyes meet mine. He takes another step and pauses.

"What are you doing up here?" he asks.

Spiraling.

"Just wanted some space," I say instead.

He ignores the hint and climbs the rest of the way up the ladder. He has to duck his head or risk getting clocked by the rafters, but he comes to sit beside me anyway, our knees touching.

"Are you sketching?" he picks up the sketch pad, frowning at the blank page.

I shake my head.

"Why did you stop painting?"

The look in his eyes tells me this time I won't get away with a flimsy excuse of being busy. I've never opened up to Nic about anything before. I didn't trust him, but mostly I didn't want him to see me weak. Thinking back on the two decades I've known him, I can't think of a time when he took an undeserved shot at me. He's snubbed me and rejected me, but he's never been cruel. Maybe I can trust him with the truth. I could try. It might feel good to talk about it.

"No one wanted my art." The words sink in and oh my god, it does not feel good to talk about this. My face is already hot, tears are already prickling my eyes. "Apparently," I say, bent on destruction, my tone turning acidic as I try to turn this beast around, "my art is *simplistic, boring, and tacky.*"

Nic sucks in a breath. When he reaches for me, I squirm away. I don't want him to touch me or look at me. I can't believe I repeated his ex-wife's words. Worse, I've let them define me. Gross.

After a few minutes, Nic speaks, his voice soft. "Remember the pictures of my house? Timothy shared them in the group chat, asking everyone to rate them on a scale of meh to purgatory."

I snicker, because yeah, I remember the pictures, though I never rated them. That house could've been beautiful.

"Addison thought she knew what was trendy, what would inspire envy, but she couldn't get a foot in the art world, even with help from her parents. She made that house into an empty, soulless statement piece."

"You told her she was right, she was the expert."

His eyes narrow. "That's not how I meant it and that's not how Addison took it, trust me."

The image of him pulling her close to say that quietly in her ear makes it hard to trust him. Nic must read the skepticism on my face.

"Addison fucked up a show at one of her parents' galleries a few months before," he says. "So she took it as the insult it was. We fought about it the rest of the holiday."

"Oh." I hadn't noticed them fighting. Maybe I was too drunk, too locked in my misery, too scared to look closely because I didn't want to see him in love.

"I'm sorry." His thumb slips over the corner of the sketchbook, the pages rustling softly. "Sorry I brought her here, sorry I asked her to marry me, sorry she made you feel bad, but mostly I'm sorry I made you feel bad. I like your paintings. I always have."

"Not always."

He knows what I'm talking about. He draws a deep breath into his lungs, holds it, and slowly releases it. "About that…"

"You weren't in a good place. I didn't mean to paint you—I didn't think I was—but I saw it after, how it looked like you, and I'm sorry."

"I still have it."

I whip my head around to look at him. "What?"

His brows knit together like he's not sure what to say. "I found it sitting by the trash and I brought it home. It's been wrapped up in my closet since. You can't have it back."

"Why would you do that?"

"You threw me in the trash!"

"It wasn't you!"

We stare at each other for a moment before his lips twitch up into a smile. Mine follow. Then we're laughing. I feel lighter, the heavy grudge I've been holding against him lifting. My hurt is healing.

Nic leans over and kisses me, a quick kiss that turns into a longer, sweeter, slightly desperate one before he pulls back. He grins at me. "Wait here a moment."

When he returns, he sets a laundry basket down and pulls the ladder up behind him, shutting us off from the rest of the house. I can't see what's in the basket until he brings it over and sets it down in front of me.

A beginner's watercolor set. Some plastic cups. Bottles of water. A small canvas.

"You don't have to help me," he says, unpacking everything. "But hang out with me?"

"Sure. Want an easel?"

He nods, so I get to my feet and dig around until I find one of my old ones in a corner. I set him up next to a small table, adjusting the angle so the colors won't run. So I can see him, but not the canvas from my spot on the floor.

"What are you going to paint?" I ask, watching him carefully pull the plastic off the set of beginner watercolors.

Nic shrugs. "I don't know. The lake? That can't be too hard."

"Oh, Nic. You sweet, innocent man."

He grins. "No one expects me to paint anything good. All I have to do is put some paint on a canvas and someone will buy it for the signature in the corner."

I sigh and stretch out on the rug, snatching the sketchbook again. The world is unfair. People are going to throw money at Nic—or this charity, more accurately—if all he does is paint a blob. But maybe it sucks that they don't want him, or care about his talent or lack thereof. They just want a slice of him to bring home.

My head is as blank as the sketchbook still, so I watch Nic as he carefully pours some water into a cup.

"I watched a few YouTube videos on how to paint with watercolors this morning," he says as he arranges everything on the little table next to him. He fusses over placement for a bit, then turns to the blank canvas on the easel and stares at it for a long minute.

"Go on," I say, failing at my attempt to not smile. "Show me what you've got."

"I'd rather show you what I've got than paint this picture." He mumbles under his breath. I laugh. He picks up a brush, dips it in water, and wets some of the paint in the tray.

My hand aches with how badly I want to do that, so I grab the pencil and tap it lightly on the sketchbook as Nic starts painting.

He might not have a clue what he's doing, but his body relaxes as he works, and the way he bites his lip and looks at the canvas like he's not sure what to do is adorable.

"Do you remember the day, down by the tire swing?" Nic lifts his chin toward the only painting turned out to face us. "Timothy was in detention. We were walking home from the bus stop. You weren't talking to me."

I snort. "That could've been any day. He was always in detention and we never talked."

Nic drops his paintbrush in the water, a grin on his face. "You wanted to stop and sketch some flowers to paint later. I stole your pencils and wouldn't give them back."

"That was a dick move."

"Why do you like *Summer Camp*?"

The abrupt subject change leaves me scrambling and I bite my lip to stop from saying something flippant about his dancing. There's genuine curiosity in his voice. He's open to the truth, and he deserves it, but this is hard. "You left. Suddenly, you were in these perfect photoshopped ads selling jeans or cologne or whatever. Timothy would talk about wild parties and women. You became this other person. I didn't like it."

Taking a deep breath, I let it out slowly before I continue. "*Summer Camp* came out, and my friends dragged me to it and I could see you in the character. Quiet, a little awkward, but real. I missed you and that movie gave me a piece of you I thought I'd lost."

Nic looks thoughtful as he picks up a different paintbrush and wets a new color. "You know that scene by the tire swing?"

His character shared a first kiss with his summer crush by an old tire swing, near the lake the summer camp was supposed to be situated on. I nod.

"It was supposed to take place on the dock, but there was a problem and they couldn't do it. I suggested the tire swing." He dabs some paint on his canvas, then looks up to meet my eyes. "That's your favorite scene, isn't it?"

My face goes hot. "No," I say petulantly. "The skinny dipping scene is my favorite."

Nic raises a brow. "Because of the vaguely blurry image of something that was not my cock?"

The scene that launched a hundred internet rumors about his dick. "In my fanfiction version, a snapping turtle bites it off."

That earns me a laugh.

I feel like I'm tap dancing, trying to distract him away from a place I'm not ready to go. "Then the snapping turtle drops it and a giant catfish noms it up."

Nic winces and falls silent for a few minutes as he focuses on his canvas. "That day by the tire swing, when I stole your pencils...I almost kissed you."

"I...know." For years I thought I'd daydreamed that moment between us, but it was real. I'd pretended I didn't care about the pencils, grabbing the tire swing like I intended to climb through it. Nic stood on the other side, holding my pencils just within reach. When I caved, he moved them higher. I threw the swing at him, but he caught it, pushed it aside, and in a heartbeat he had his free hand around my waist. We stared, wide-eyed, at each other for a solid thirty seconds. I don't think either of us breathed.

Then he'd stepped back, and it was over. I snatched my pencils from him and ran to the house, my heart a mess.

Nic glances back at my painting of the tire swing. "The date in the corner..."

He hasn't gotten close enough to read the date, so he must have been the one to turn it around. The whole time he was up here looking for Ping-Pong balls, he'd been looking through my paintings. It makes me feel all warm and fuzzy and a little nauseous if I'm honest.

I'd painted the tire swing the day after *Summer Camp* came out. Because the kiss in that movie could've been us and maybe I'd wanted to relive that moment a little. Maybe Nic wanted to, too, when he suggested moving the kiss to the tire swing.

"Why didn't you kiss me?" I ask. I didn't kiss him thanks to a healthy fear of rejection from someone who only ever showed me indifference.

"Seriously? You'd have removed my nuts."

If he'd kissed me that day, testicle removal would've been delayed a good 72 hours as I recovered from the shock. More than enough time for him to change his name and move out of state.

"And I don't think Timothy would've reacted well." He adds.

That makes me laugh. "Nope. He had a huge crush on you."

He nods and sighs a little. "He was my best friend. Couldn't risk it."

"He's still your best friend." I point out.

"He doesn't have a crush on me anymore." He dabs some paint on his canvas and frowns. "It kind of feels like he wants us to get together sometimes."

"Of course he does, he's been betting on us for years."

Nic's jaw drops, but he recovers quickly. "Actually, that makes sense."

"Timbo's gotta Timbo," I say, tapping the sketchbook. My face is already growing warm. Maybe it's something about this conversation and clearing the air, or maybe I'm starting to suffer from carbon monoxide poisoning shut up in the attic, but I can't stop myself from confessing, "I had a crush on you too."

CHAPTER TWENTY-THREE

Jessie

Nic's eyes drop back to his canvas as he concentrates on whatever he's painting, the tips of his ears going pink. "I was infatuated with you in high school," he says quietly. "Every class we had together I failed or came close to failing."

I laugh. "Seriously?"

He shrugs, stepping back to look at his canvas before plucking a different brush from the cup of water.

"That game of spin the bottle. You refused to kiss me because of Timothy?"

"I'd only known you both for a month. I thought he'd beat my ass."

"He didn't beat anyone else's ass." I point out.

"No one else kissed you the way I would've," he says, glancing up, his eyes dark and heated.

"Very good answer," I say, dropping my eyes to my sketch pad. The silence between us is comfortable as Nic paints and I think about how I'd paint little glimpses of an erotic moment. Not how Gretchen wants it, but how I feel it. My fingers are itching for a paintbrush.

There's a blank page in front of me, but I don't want to doodle.

"Can I sketch you?" I ask.

Nic glances up. "Sure, but..."

"But?" I prompt.

"Nothing mean. No snapping turtles biting my dick off."

I gasp. "I would never."

He raises an eyebrow.

"Okay, I would. But I won't. Promise."

Nic puts his brush down and walks around the easel. He pulls a beautifully wrapped gift out of the basket and hands it to me before sitting across from me, his knees touching mine.

I know what this is, the familiar weight and shape in my hands. Goose bumps break out over my skin, and my stomach twists painfully.

"It's not Christmas yet," I say stiffly.

"Open it early."

I could refuse. Tell him I don't want the paints, I'll never use them, but...

"Come on, Jessie," he says in a soft voice, his hands moving up my knees to my thighs and back down. "It's just the two of us. You can leave it all up here if you want. No one needs to know."

He's right. I don't have to do anything with whatever I paint. There's no pressure to get it right for Gretchen, no stress from submitting something to a gallery. This can be for me, if I choose to pick up a brush again.

I rip the paper like it's a Band-Aid and doing it faster will hurt less.

Oddly, it doesn't hurt at all.

The little palettes are expensive, the colors rich. Nic pulls other gifts from the laundry basket, and I rip open high-quality brushes, more paints, and a set of small canvases.

"Thank you," I say, leaning forward to kiss him. "I need to sketch a bit before I can start painting."

He nods. "I want you to paint something for me."

"Okay."

"Yourself."

"Why?"

He motions to the stacks of canvases. "All these paintings, and not one is a self-portrait. It's like you're not a participant in your own life."

That's incredibly rude and completely inaccurate, but so close to how I felt as a kid. I was lonely. I never felt like I belonged even in the place where I should belong, and I suppose I shouldn't be surprised Nic picked up on it. Despite having the full attention and love of my family, he still seemed lonely too. It was one of the things that drew me to him, despite what felt like his indifference.

"You have to promise to put it in your closet with the painting of Not You."

"It's going on my bedroom wall." He gets back to his feet. "Go ahead and sketch me while I finish this painting."

I don't sketch him, exactly. At least, not in a way anyone would be able to identify him. Instead, I do a quick series of little studies. His hand gripping his thigh as his body reclines naked in a chair, mostly off-page and deeply shadowed because I've drawn enough dicks to last a lifetime. Another sketch of his jawline, his parted lips just visible. Another of his legs, bare, kneeling on the floor.

Little pieces of eroticism, pulled from memory and fantasy. I could paint them. Maybe I will. But not today.

"I think I'm done." Nic announces with a disappointed sigh.

I get up to take a look, and sure enough, it's a lake. Or something blue that might be a lake, with something green that might be the shore. Birds the size of pterodactyls fly the skies, and there's a sailboat cruising across the horizon. A couple of grayish blobs for clouds. It's not bad for his first time painting.

"You did well," I tell him, going up on my tiptoes to kiss him.

He kisses me back and pulls the sketchbook from my hands while I'm distracted. "Wow. These are incredible."

"They're just—" They're not doodles. They're not pointless little sketches either. They're something. "A start."

He sets the sketchbook down and pulls me close, his lips skating my jaw, his kiss hot on my neck. "Do you have any idea how hard it's been, alone up here with you for the last hour, not kissing you or touching you or making you come? And you were sitting over there drawing *this*?"

I slip my hands under his shirt, his abs tightening at my touch as I go lower. "Do you know how hard it was to not drag you to the floor so I could ride you?"

He nips my earlobe. "Do it."

I grab him by the waistband and tug him to the rug in the middle of the room. Nic sits, pulling me onto his lap, pulling my sweater over my head. His hands go right to my breasts, freeing them from my bra's lacy cups, while we kiss. Something feels different this time. My heart is pounding a little harder, a little faster because of it.

"I don't have a condom," Nic murmurs against my lips.

"Me neither." I'm wearing leggings—no pockets—and I can feel him hard through our clothes. No way are we walking out of this attic unsatisfied.

"Sit on my face?"

Hell yeah. Nic helps me shimmy my leggings and panties down. I leave them wrapped around one ankle partially because I can't wait but also because there's no lock on the attic door. "I feel like a damn teenager," I mutter as Nic lies on his back.

He laughs. "Yeah. Hurry, before someone comes looking for us."

I'm giggling as I kneel over him. His large hands slide up the outside of my thighs to my hips and he pulls me down to his mouth. My giggle turns to a moan and I brace my hands on his chest because shit. Nic is really, really good at this.

I push my hands down his body to the hem of his shirt, then reverse direction, pulling the soft fabric up to reveal his flat stomach. When I toy with the thin trail of hair leading into his jeans, Nic gives my ass a light slap and reaches down to undo the buttons on his jeans. I take his dick out while he pushes his pants and boxer briefs down his hips.

The moment my lips touch his shaft, he moans, pulling me tight against his mouth. I want to tease him and make this last, but I'm not getting caught in a sixty-nine with Nic. The way I'm half-dressed to his fully dressed, combined with the danger of getting caught, only makes this hotter. So I suck him down, using my free hand to stroke him from the base to my lips. The slow, sensual way he's eating me out changes to something sloppy and desperate as his grip on my hips tightens.

Nic comes first, but I'm right behind him. After, he needs a washcloth for his face and I need a breath mint, but he helps me put my clothes back on and I do up his pants and we lie back down to cuddle on the rug. We've already said a lot, so we're quiet now, simply enjoying each other. His fingers draw circles on my arm, I do the same on his chest.

"Nic! Jessie!" Timothy's voice is muffled but he's close. Nic groans, kissing me quickly on the temple before getting to his feet.

By the time Timothy gets the ladder down, Nic is back at his canvas. All I had to do was roll over and grab my sketchbook and hope Timothy doesn't pick up on the thick scent of sex in the air.

He doesn't seem to. He climbs the ladder with a big ass grin on his face, going straight to Nic and looking at the canvas. "So this is what you two have been up to," he says.

Nic crosses his arms. "I painted this on my own."

That makes Timothy laugh. "No shit. What is it?"

"The lake, asshole."

I duck my head to hide my smile as Nic and my brother squabble over the merits of his painting and whether Gabriel Sinclair's entry will be better. My pencil quickly fills in my blank page with flowers and vines.

"Are you two ready for tonight?" Timothy asks.

I look up in time to see Nic give Timothy a deeply dubious look. "How can anyone ever be ready?"

He has a point. The Foley Christmas Eve party is unhinged.

Timothy shrugs. "I start planning five months ahead. Longer if I need to source firecrackers."

Nic gives Timothy a light shove. Once upon a time, their horseplay would've ranged across the attic, ultimately swallowing me by accident, until something broke or someone got hurt. Now Timothy gives Nic a dismissive swat to the back of the head and strolls over to see what I'm doing.

"Doodles?" he asks, nudging my sketchbook with his sock-clad toe.

"Sketches." I pull it closer—the last thing I want is for this dumbass to turn the page and see my 'pieces of eroticism.'

Timothy bends to pick up a palette of paints. "I see someone couldn't wait until Christmas to give you your gift."

"He just had to give it to me early," I say, blinking innocently at my twin.

Timothy freezes, shooting a look over his shoulder at Nic.

Somehow, Nic keeps a straight face. "I couldn't wait to give it to her."

Our eyes meet and there's nothing special in the moment, nothing in the way Nic's looking at me to warrant it, but something inside me shifts violently, realigns, and settles in a split second.

It's like taking a lightning bolt to the chest on a blue-sky day: I love him.

I love Nic.

I've *always* loved him.

Oh shit.

Oh no.

This can't be happening.

I toss my sketchbook into the laundry basket, along with all the paint supplies on the floor. I snatch the paints Timothy's holding, belatedly realizing his response to the innuendos Nic and I shot back and forth was a loud "gross."

I feel gross, but also...

Too many other things. Love, confusion, elation, fear, resentment, fear again—no wait, abject terror. Nausea, because how can I hide this from Nic? From my brother and the rest of my family?

I have to hide it and our little sex deal needs to stay a secret. My heart is going to break when Nic leaves and if anyone finds out, if they blame him...

I can't stomach the idea of Nic not coming back every Christmas.

"That went too far. I need to shower," I say darkly, heading toward the ladder. Timothy's watching me, his eyes trying to bore through me, trying to ascertain if we're joking or if something is going on.

"You started it," Nic says in a flat, uninterested tone, and I know he's acting, but he's a shitty actor. He doesn't feel the same. I'm the one who caught feelings—who caught them a long time ago.

What a fucking mess.

Chapter Twenty-Four

Jessie

My family's Christmas Eve party is the highlight of the season. When I was a child, it seemed like this glamorous event, full of pretty people drinking elegant cocktails, wearing sequins and suits. I dreamed of walking into the room in an over-the-top red ball gown, turning heads, and being swept into a kiss under the mistletoe by the most handsome man in the room.

Then, one year, Timothy scaled the massive Christmas tree in the great room, bringing the whole thing crashing down, and one of the guests declared it was folly for Celia Foley to throw a holiday bash with a son like Timothy. The Foley Folly was born. The guest list narrowed, growing more eclectic. The glitz gave way to a wild frivolity. Kid-me would've been disappointed, but adult-me loves it. Some nights have ended in drunken impromptu concerts by musician guests, others in one-handed cook-offs over crème brûlée. At some point, Timothy will do something ridiculous, but instead of turning up their noses, the guests will cheer.

And instead of gracefully descending the stairs in a knockout gown, I'm rushing to straighten my red and green tinsel cat ear headband before running out of my room, heels in hand so I don't trip down the steps.

My heart trips instead.

Nic's standing at the bottom of the stairs, toying with the garland wrapped around the banister and this feels like something out of my childish Christmas

Eve party fantasy. His dark gray pants hug his thighs and cup his butt with such loving devotion that I'm guessing his tailor views him as a muse. The midnight blue button-down shirt is striking on him, setting off his pale complexion and making his eyes appear darker.

A warm, fluttery feeling takes flight inside me when he looks up and my stomach simultaneously pinches tight. I love him and he's going to leave.

Goddammit. I thought I'd wisely used the last couple of hours to get my feelings under control. Guess I'm a dumbass for thinking a hot shower, a face mask, and a meditation podcast would make it all go away.

I can't let it show. I tilt my chin up, then step gracefully down the stairs, pretending I'm in the sparkly red gown of my childhood fantasies. Inside, I'm a wreck. Seriously, am I dying? Why do I feel like my chest is going to explode? This can't be normal.

He watches me, an amused smile on his face as I stop on the step above him.

I nailed it. This asshole has no idea I love him. Good job me.

Nic tugs on my skirt. "What the hell is this?"

My dress is classy. The black cap sleeve bodice is a soft velvet. The skirt is covered in kittens in Santa hats. "Christmas pussy," I say with a wink. Nic lifts me off the step, spinning me around and making my heart soar before he slides me down his body to set me back on my feet.

"It's hideous," he whispers, and his minty breath is warm on my lips.

Voices float out of the great room, but for the moment, we're alone. I slip a knee between his legs, pressing myself closer. "Choose your next words carefully, Mr. Fontana, or Mittens won't be responsible for what happens next."

"Oh, Mittens is not responsible for this," he mumbles, kissing the corner of my mouth, his lips light along my jaw, moving toward my neck as his hands slide up my ribs, his thumbs grazing side boob.

My lips brush his ear and suddenly his thigh is between my legs and I'm ready to hump him right here in the foyer where anyone could see, when the guest bedroom door flies open.

Nic flings me away as Timothy and Mina stumble out, laughing. That laughter dies abruptly when they see us.

Timothy's eyes are wide like Christmas morning. Mina, meanwhile, has a Cheshire cat smile on her face.

Shit.

I bend, using the excuse of putting my shoes on to hide my red face.

Nic is doing nothing to help our cause by standing there, rubbing the back of his neck in silence. So long as no one notices the outline of his hard-on in those too-tight slacks—

Goddammit. How could anyone not? I take charge, stomping up to Timothy and tugging his bright blue tie so I can inspect the print. "Dancing dicks wrapped in Christmas lights? You think you can win with that?" The coveted Best Dressed trophy is as good as his.

The trophy is a dildo mounted on a plank of wood, the whole thing spray-painted in glittery red and white stripes, like a candy cane. Two massive bells serve as balls. The winner each year scribbles their name on the plank. My name is on it twice. Timothy's is on it five times. Nic has never and will never win.

My brother eyes my dress, shaking his head sadly. "Kittens in Santa hats. I'm disappointed."

I yank his tie because I'm an ass. "Where did you get this?"

"I made it," Mina says. "I commissioned the art and had it printed onto the fabric."

Timothy looks over my head at Nic. "What were you two—" He coughs when I tighten his dick tie enough to let him know I will strangle him with it.

"Come on." Mina takes my arm and pulls me away.

"That's brilliant," I say, pointing to her shoes. The same material as Timothy's tie adorns her shoes in ridiculously large bows.

"Seriously, sell me some drawings and we can make whatever we want." Mina pauses. "Although it might be a good idea to limit the dicks."

She has a point. Unlimited dick is going to get me in trouble.

She guides me into the dining room with all the instincts needed to survive a Foley Folly—straight to the booze.

My mother's punch, topped with a splash of champagne, is responsible for plenty of hangovers and a lot of bad decisions. Loaded up, we loop around to the fire in the great room, a little apart from the handful of early arrivals chatting with Amanda and Hazel. Christmas music plays softly over the sound system, something remarkably tasteful by a string quartet. The raucous stuff will come later after the kids have been put to bed and the punch runs out.

Mina smiles when I take a sip of my drink. "Your lipstick is on Nic's ear, by the way."

Shit. Nic is still out by the door with Timothy and as big of a dumbass as my brother is, he's bound to notice the bright red shade.

"Don't worry." She laughs softly. "Timothy will tell him before anyone else sees. But tell me, honestly, when did you two start hooking up? And don't deny it, we know you are."

They know. That's it. Timothy has a big mouth. By the end of tonight, my whole family will know. Every single guest, and whoever they tell, on and on until someone publicly connects me to Nic. Then the entire world will know I'm another notch on his bedpost.

I take a step away from the fire, suddenly too hot.

Mina prods me.

"The day you arrived," I mumble.

"Yes!" she shouts, hands in the air. "I won!"

The room is silent for half a second before bursting into polite applause. Everyone goes back to their conversations because someone crying out that they won isn't unusual at a Folly.

I groan. "Another bet?"

Mina grins.

Fuck my life.

"It's not just a little bet." She concedes in a quiet voice. "Timothy came up with this surprise wedding to throw you two together and—"

I round on her. "I swear to god if the two of you faked your wedding—"

"We didn't fake anything." She assures me with a pat on the arm. "What I'm trying to say is you and Nic have obviously been dancing around this for years. It was inevitable."

Christ.

"The inevitable being a no-strings sex deal lasting until the holiday is over before we go our separate ways?" I raise an eyebrow. My brother, the evil genius.

Mina frowns. "But—"

"That's all it is." I down my drink and my stomach heaves in response, so I excuse myself, ducking into a bathroom. The velvet of my dress is itchy over my chest and back and I tug at the fabric.

Timothy put us under the same roof, with adjoining rooms. Like lighting a firecracker and tossing it into a pile of gasoline-soaked rags. I'm about to have my heart destroyed thanks to my goddamned twin.

It was easy to hate Nic because his indifference hurt me, to pick any little excuse to feed the grudge that kept my head above water. Forcing us into close proximity like my brother did wrecked that for me. Hell, I would've married Camden and clung to him like a life preserver, just to avoid acknowledging this.

I'm drowning now.

How could I be this stupid? I walked into a no-strings sex hell and gave Nic the key to lock me in. Sure, he's opened up to me, he's been surprisingly affectionate, and he *used to* have a crush on me, but he hasn't done or said anything to give me any indication this is more than sex for him. I am screwed and I don't know how to hide it.

The rest of the night, I stick to the edges of the party, slipping in and out of conversations I make no effort to contribute to. Everything becomes a blur of ugly Christmas apparel. Dinner passes. The night gets loud. Avoiding Timothy is easy if I stick to the quieter pockets. Nic catches my eyes a few times, but he doesn't approach me because we agreed we'd be careful.

Still, I miss his steadiness as I drift through the Folly.

My mother's excited voice cuts through my haze. "Jessie! Mistletoe!"

I'm standing in the doorway—the one place I've carefully avoided all night.

A young guy with dark hair and an ugly green Christmas sweater takes a tentative step forward.

Nic's fingers brush the back of my neck. I can't see him, but I know his touch through some internal bullshit where my heart aligns itself to seek him out as my true North. He tugs and my body complies, falling gracefully as he dips me low, his kiss lasting long enough for me to relax into him, for him to relax into me. Longer than can be excused as platonic or melodramatic.

He kisses me like it means something for a handful of glorious seconds before he rights me. When he walks away, my world follows, while I stand in the doorway, unable to move.

Chapter Twenty-Five

Nic

ALL NIGHT I'VE BEEN keeping tabs on Jessie. She's been quiet, disappearing into the background, and Jessie never disappears. She's always bold and bright, with that mega-watt smile and her expressive face, so something must be bothering her, but I can't ask.

I hate that I can't ask. That I can't wrap my arms around her and rub my fingers against the soft velvet of her dress. I want to walk her into the kitchen and out just so I can kiss her under the mistletoe again and again.

Shit. That's why she's mad. I kissed her in front of everyone when we are keeping this a secret. That's fair, but no way was some random guy kissing her.

It's impossible to follow any conversation while I'm scanning the room for her, so I give up and go looking. She's not in her room, or my room. Not in the attic or downstairs or outside. Her rental car is still in the driveway.

I'm standing alone in the kitchen—everyone else is in the great room being serenaded by a group of drunks wearing only mostly well-placed Santa hats or stockings—when I hear it. The scrape of fork tines on a plate.

Jessie jumps when I slide the door to the butler's pantry open, her wide eyes upbraiding me as she chews the bite of pear cake.

"Hiding?" I ask, relief rushing out on a sigh.

She nods, setting her fork on the plate. The light in the pantry is dimmed to be unnoticeable from the kitchen, so when I close the door, it takes my eyes a moment to adjust.

I force a smile to my face. "I'd be hiding too if I were wearing that dress."

She flips me off. I grab her hand and haul her close. Her lips taste like ginger and brown sugar. I can't get enough. I'm not sure I'll ever get enough and I've only got a week left.

Jessie hesitates, staring at the floor. "This thing with us...it's just sex, right?"

"Right," I say automatically, my mouth going dry. It can't be more. This is already complicated enough. We're already risking too much. I flaunted our no public touching rule with that kiss under the mistletoe. "I know it's supposed to be our secret, but stay away from the mistletoe. These lips"—I brush my lips against hers—"are mine."

She opens her mouth to protest, but I kiss her first.

It ignites something between us. Like we're both desperate to cling to this lie about what we are to each other. Within seconds, we're panting, trying to get as close as we can. I palm her breast, the velvet soft in my hand, and she moans. She presses her hips to mine and I hiss, then I'm lifting her, setting her on the small counter space, pulling up that ugly full skirt, and shoving aside her panties. Her hands are already reaching for my pants, undoing the button, and sliding down the zip. Her fork clatters to the floor and I shove the plate back to safety as my mouth continues to plunder hers. She wraps her hand around my cock and—

Voices. Moving closer.

Jessie pulls away from me, eyes wide in terror as she looks at the door. It stands open a couple of inches. I hadn't closed it all the way—what the fuck was I thinking?

I wasn't because I can't think around her.

Somehow I get my cock in my pants and my phone out, wedging myself into the doorway, blocking Jessie from view. I hold up my hand in acknowledgment when I'm noticed and pretend I'm in the middle of an important phone call, closing the door for privacy as more people drift into the kitchen.

Jessie slaps her hand over her forehead. "What are you doing?" she hisses.

"Any lipstick on my face?" I whisper, horrified I didn't think of that before going to the door.

She shakes her head, but reaches up and wipes at my ear.

"I'll get you out of here." I promise, giving her a quick kiss. "Be ready to sneak out."

I ease myself out of the pantry, making a big deal out of pocketing my phone as I nod to the nearest guests.

The kitchen is full, and no one looks like they're stopping in to top up a drink. Worse, Celia's in the room, the odds that she'll nip into the butler's pantry to grab something going up by the second.

Desperate times.

"Hey," I say in a quiet voice to Timothy. "I need a favor. No questions asked."

His light brown eyes flick from me to the closed door of the butler's pantry and he raises an eyebrow, the tiniest smile playing across his lips. "You were banging my sister in the pantry and need a distraction—caused by me, the master of distraction—so she can sneak out and you two can pretend we don't all know?"

"No." I answer way too fast, heat rising from my suddenly too-tight collar.

"Oh? Jessie's not in here—" He grins as he turns, taking a step toward the door.

I grab his arm, stopping him. "We were talking, okay?"

He brushes my hand off with a laugh. "Sure. Talking."

Shit, this is a mistake. I should've yelled 'fire.' "Will you help me or not?"

He smirks and claps his hands, his loud voice instantly quieting the room. "Listen up, everyone. This asshole—"

The look he shoots me steals the heat from my face. Timothy wouldn't drop me in it, would he?

"—thinks that, because he can do *some* of his own stunts, he can land a better backflip in the snow than me." Timothy's grin widens. "Off the porch roof."

Goddammit.

"Timothy." Mina is unamused. Not Celia-level yet, but close. It raises my hopes that she'll put an end to this. The entire room is silent, watching the unspoken exchange as Timothy gives her the biggest puppy dog eyes. It's so obvious I can practically hear them.

Timothy: Please, please, pretty please, can I backflip off the roof?

Mina: Are you serious with this shit?

*Timothy: Please, baby? It's 99.9 percent safe (for me) and I want
to make Nic do it.*

Mina glances at me, back to Timothy. She sighs. "We leave for our honeymoon in a few days. You better not break anything I'm going to need."

Timothy leaps onto a barstool, pointing at his wife. "Don't worry, baby—I could land dick first and still be ready for game day." He turns back to me, looking smug and satisfied as he rolls up his sleeves and loosens his tie. "Gauntlet thrown, Warwick. Come show me how a badass superhero does it. Unless there's some reason you might want to chicken out? Any *reputations* you might be concerned about?"

My glare feeds his grin.

"Outside, everyone!" His voice rings through the house. "We need judges for this epic match of...ego? Nope. Dick size. Definitely dick size." He grabs me by the shoulder, shoving me ahead. "Come on, asshole." I've given him an excuse to get on the roof, and he grins happily at me, squeezing my shoulder.

Celia's voice rises above the commotion as everyone filters out of the room behind us, sweeping us outside. "No trips to the ER, boys. Please."

I'm going to break my neck. The thought passes through my head again when I clamber onto the roof after Timothy. If I couldn't stop him from playing The Floor is Lava at the Warwick wrap party, there's no way I can stop him when he has Mina's permission and Celia is oddly chill about it.

I can try. "Should you be doing this?"

He shrugs. "The ground is covered in snow, I'll clear the roof. You going to be able to do this?"

That's a good question.

He rubs his hands together with glee. "You wanna call this off, you know what you have to do."

What I have to do, I strongly suspect, involves declaring my intentions toward Jessie from the rooftop.

I catch sight of her as she slips into the back of the crowd. Her eyes meet mine and her face pinches with worry.

"You know we all know, right?" Timothy's voice is low enough that only I can hear him. "Just make it official so you don't have to sneak around."

I blow out a deep breath. Everyone knows. Or Timothy's full of shit. Fifty-fifty odds.

He nudges me. "Thanks to your inability to keep your dick out of my sister for a few days, I lost a bet to my wife. You don't want to know what I owe her—actually, it's mostly sex, so thanks."

I meet Jessie's eyes. *Do they know?* I mouth.

Her eyebrows pinch and lips purse, but she nods.

Dammit. Whatever happens when the holidays end, I'm going to have to deal with it.

"Okay," I say. "I'll make it official."

He grins, clamping a hand on my shoulder. "I'm happy for you. Really. Best Christmas ever." He claps his hands twice and calls down. "Nic has something to say, so listen up."

It's not the idea of telling everyone that I'm afraid of. It's the consequences.

They already know. Just admit it and get off the fucking roof.

I clear my throat and stuff my hands into my pockets to warm them up. "Jessie and I are having a holiday fling."

Cheers and whistles fill the cold air. A few elbows nudge their neighbors. Jessie's eyes are saucer-wide, her lips parted in an *oh*.

"No shit!" Mina calls up.

"Um." What the hell am I supposed to do now? I'm still holding Jessie's gaze and smothering the delirious laugh that's fighting to escape. "Thank you."

"Jump!" Someone shouts from below.

Timothy laughs. "Fontana?"

"Shit no."

The crowd is silent, staring at Timothy as he climbs down the ladder. When he reaches the ground, he turns to everyone and takes a bow. They cheer him. For using a ladder.

Honestly, I'm impressed he didn't jump. But because he's Timothy, he does a backflip in the snow anyway.

I climb down next, and everything feels different. There's a warmth in my chest I'm not comfortable with and it's at odds with the feel of spinning out of control.

Celia gives me a quick hug, patting me on the chest. "We're happy for you, sweetie. It's about time." Then she's gone, heading with the crowd toward the warmth of the house.

Jessie waits for the guests to stream past her before stepping forward and nailing me in the chest with a snowball. "We could've denied it."

"Maybe, but now we don't have to sneak around." I brush the snow from my chest and frown. "Are you mad?"

"No, but…" Jessie bites her lip as she rubs her hands together for warmth. "What if they read too much into it?"

"We're adults. We can have our holiday fling, go our separate ways, and they'll move on." I bend and scoop up a handful of snow. "Just like you."

"And you," she says, wary as she watches me pack the snow into a loose ball.

I don't want to think about that, so I launch my attack. Jessie doesn't move fast enough. I'm on her in seconds, dumping my handful down the back of her dress. With a growl, she tackles me into the snow. The scramble to throw the cold stuff at each other ends with us laughing so hard we can only cling together.

The distant voices of the party are muffled by the front door shutting. Suddenly we're alone, the struggle of catching our breath the only sound in the cold night air.

Jessie shivers and I pull her to her feet. Her bare legs are red from the snow, her shoes destroyed, and her cats in Santa hats hanging limp on her damp skirt.

I crouch down. "Up on my back, Jessie. I want you out of that fugly dress and into a hot shower. And put that abomination in the bottom of the hamper so Mittens can't see what I'm going to do to you."

She laughs and smacks my arm, but climbs on my back.

The snow on our clothes melts between our bodies and she nestles against my shoulder. "I was afraid if they found out, you'd want to stop."

"I don't." I give her ass another squeeze before opening the door and carrying her up the stairs. I don't ever want to stop, but I'm not going to worry about the implications of that tonight.

CHAPTER TWENTY-SIX

Jessie

DECEMBER TWENTY-FIFTH

THE HOUSE IS DARK but verging on dawn when I wake tangled in Nic. We're in my bed for a change, my head on his bare shoulder, and I'm happy. I want to stay like this forever. There's a bittersweet edge to my happiness though. Every hour that passes brings us closer to an end.

I don't know how my family's going to take it. Nic was pretty clear on the roof last night that this is only a fling. Best-case scenario, everyone believes him and no one reads more into this. Life goes on as it always has.

Worst-case scenario, no one in my family believes this is just a fling. They see through to my feelings and turn a cold shoulder to Nic when he breaks my heart. Or, more likely, a cold shoulder to me when they impart feelings on him he doesn't have and decide I broke his heart.

Whatever happens next, I'm going to make the most out of not having to sneak around. It'll be nice to cuddle him on the couch and kiss him under the mistletoe.

Does he even want that? Do little public displays of affection have a place in a sex-only relationship? There's affection between us, but will it complicate things? Will it make it harder for me to let him go?

Maybe he won't break my heart. Maybe the week will end, but we won't. I have no idea how we'd make it work with me in New York and him in LA, but...maybe he'll want more. He had a crush on me in high school, maybe...

This, right here, is how my heart gets smashed into pieces. Why would Nic do a long-distance relationship with me? He can do better. Date someone more exciting, more interesting. Prettier, sexier, everything. Whatever. Boredom, horniness, and a long history of sexual tension brought us together, but that's it. His teenage crush doesn't mean anything now.

Nic's warm and naked, and I need to focus on living in this moment with him. I spend another five minutes listening to his heartbeat and the soft way he breathes, trying to soak up how it feels to lie next to him. To be unguarded with him. I love him so much I want to wake him and show him, but I have a job to do. A job I'm late for.

Carefully, I slip out of bed. Nic doesn't wake up, just rolls onto his side. My pajama pants are on the floor, but I can't find my shirt, so I put on Nic's and my cardigan, grab the big bag of presents out of my closet, and head downstairs.

Light filters in through the windows, the soft reflection of a dawn sky on a world of snow. The entire house feels muffled in the quiet expectations of a Christmas morning. Lights glow on the tree and holiday music plays softly over the sound system, setting the mood for yet another weird Foley family tradition.

When I was five, I heard my exasperated mother tell Timothy Santa wouldn't bring him anything if he didn't behave. I knew my brother—he wasn't going to get a goddamn thing. He was the best to me, always looking out for me, making me laugh, and drawing me out of myself. I loved him. So I searched the house for little treasures, anything he might like that didn't already have a clear owner and wrapped them up. In the middle of the night, I snuck downstairs to put them under the tree.

I'd scared the shit out of my father, who was in the middle of actual Santa duties, and his startled scream made me scream. We woke the whole house, and I spoiled Santa for myself and my brother. My mom threw her hands in the air, declared that we were all Santa—very Spartacus of her—and a new tradition was born.

Every year, we sneak down to the tree, sometime between midnight and 5 a.m., to leave our presents for each other. It has to be done in secret, so if anyone else comes in before we're finished, we have to hide. One year we all tried to get it done early and everyone ended up hiding behind couches and in the curtains. Another year, Timbo was a dick and hid behind the tree, scaring the ever-loving shit out of each of us with the never-expected honk of a kazoo. After that, I committed to being the last. Even Timothy couldn't stay awake behind a tree until 5 a.m. to scare me. At least, not with the amount he usually drinks at the Folly the night before. Since I'm always last, I arrange all the distinct piles left by everyone else until the whole thing looks cohesive, like something out of a magazine spread.

Plus, it allows me to snoop.

I'm surprised when I find two presents from Nic with my name on them since he already gave me paints. One's heavy, one's light. They're both about the same size, but the heavy one is slim. I shake the heavier one.

"Merry Christmas, honey."

I nearly drop the gift at the sound of my mother's sleepy voice.

"When you're finished snooping," she says with a yawn, "come have a coffee with me in the kitchen."

"Not snooping," I say quickly, placing the gift back on the pile. "Merry Christmas!" I call after her.

It takes me a few more minutes to integrate the last pile of presents into the whole, and when it's done, I wrap my cardigan tight around me and survey my work. It's the perfect Christmas morning.

Mom already has a cup of coffee waiting for me on the table. I sit and take a sip, surprised to find she's laced it with Bailey's before the sun is up. I'd have snuck some in when she wasn't looking anyway because it's Christmas Day.

My mom preheats the oven before dropping into the chair next to me. She's already wearing her Christmas morning outfit—a red and green murder robe and tinsel-topped kitten-heeled slippers. She looks like an unstable 1950s Mrs. Claus after a bender.

"So you and Nic," she says cheerfully.

I take a sip of my coffee and murmur.

"We're all happy you're finally together—"

"We aren't together."

My mom's brows draw down. "But you're..." she makes a circle with her thumb and forefinger, poking through it with the forefinger of her other hand in freakishly rapid succession.

"Jesus, Mom." I don't know if I should laugh or cry. "We aren't dating. We aren't going to date. It's just sex and only for the holiday."

"Just sex." She waves that off with a laugh. "There's a box of condoms on the top shelf in the bathroom if you run out."

There's always a box of condoms on that shelf. In the drawer of every bedside table in the house. Mom's been replenishing them since we were in high school. The importance of safe sex was drilled into us from an early age.

"Seriously. It's just a fling like Nic said." I don't want her to be mystified and hurt when nothing ever comes of this.

"Jessie." Her voice takes on a stern tone and she levels a look at me over the rim of her mug. "That boy's been through a lot. He's fragile. Be careful with him."

Fragile my ass. Nic will forget me and be neck-deep in pussy while I'm still crying my broken heart out with ice cream, booze, and shitty TV shows. Why can't she see I need to be handled with care too?

Honestly, it's like no one in my family knows me.

My mother sighs. "That divorce...she cheated on him."

I know. The whole world knows, and it pisses me off that my mother feels the need to remind me. Addison broke him and I'm the emotional rebound to complement the physical ones the tabloids have documented since the divorce. Because regardless of what we agreed to, this has never been simple transactional sex. We know each other too well for that. I'm the next step on his way to being whole again.

It doesn't mean he's fallen in love with me.

There's no point in arguing. My mother buries herself in cooking, refusing to see anything she doesn't want to see. And she wants to see us in love.

I can only doodle so many dicks.

She gets up to put the cinnamon rolls in the oven, humming to herself, satisfied she's done her best to ensure her precious favorite won't end up getting his heart broken. I finish my coffee in silence.

Nic doesn't wake up when I climb back into bed. I snuggle against his back, wrapping my arm around him. I like being the big spoon, curling my body around his perfect ass. Tracing my fingers down the little trail of hair on his stomach. I want to wrap my hand around his dick and stroke him until he makes a mess on my bed, but he's still asleep. So I kiss his shoulder instead. I have to shimmy up a little to kiss along his neck, but by the time I'm there, he's awake. Like he can read my mind, he grabs my hand, pulling it down to his dick, moaning when I wrap my fingers around it.

He turns his head, capturing my lips, and a few moments later, he has my feet over his shoulders and nothing else matters. Just this, right now, with him.

We aren't the last to make it downstairs—Timothy's missing—but we might as well be. Smirks and knowing looks all around greet us when we walk in together. Not holding hands or anything, just...together.

"Ahem." My mother clears her throat, pointing to the ceiling.

Nic and I both look up.

Timothy's standing on the second floor, fishing pole in hand, a bit of mistletoe hanging from the hook a few feet above us. He grins.

"Seriously, guys—" I start, but Nic's lips on mine cut me off. There are some cheers and claps and from the second floor, a whistle. Evie's little voice saying "aw" and Liam's "gross" filter through.

Nic keeps it family-friendly and pulls away.

"Happy?" he asks everyone, but he doesn't sound mad or annoyed about it. He just sounds like Nic.

"Yup," Timothy says on behalf of the family. He's about to swing his leg over to take his usual shortcut down to the great room, but Mina stops him with a stern "Timothy" and he changes his mind, disappearing as he heads toward the stairs.

"Can we start opening yet?" Liam asks. He and Evie are sitting in front of the tree, clearly itching to get into the massive pile of presents.

My mom gets up from the sofa. "Have at it kids."

Liam immediately snatches a present, reads the tag, and booms out, "Uncle Timothy!"

"Throw it here!" he calls from the doorway, and the smallish box is hurtled through the air.

Mina scoots over and pats the couch next to her. No one is watching us in the chaos of the kids handing out presents, but they could be, so I sit perfectly straight next to Nic, a couple of inches in between us.

"This is weird," Nic says, leaning into me.

I nod.

He wraps an arm around my shoulders, tucking me into his side. "Feet up, like normal. Better?"

I rest my head on his shoulder and draw my feet onto the couch, and yeah, this is better. "You?"

He kisses the top of my head. "Yeah."

Timothy, being the absolute dick that he is, makes Mina scoot over so he can sit next to me, where he immediately reaches over and pokes me in the arm. "Hey, twinsie."

"Fuck off, weirdo." I kick him in the thigh. He pokes me again.

Nic sighs, scooping me into his arm. He stands, dumps me in his spot, then takes my seat next to Timothy. When Timothy pokes him, Nic grabs a throw pillow and nails him in the groin.

"You passed the test, Fontana." Timothy wheezes, covering his junk.

I can't see the look Nic gives him, but I know which one it is. Incredulous and irritated, all rolled up into one.

"You didn't let me pick on Jessie," my brother says. "Camden failed."

Camden pretended to ignore Timothy's childish behavior.

"You don't have to test me." Nic grumbles at him.

Obviously. This is just a fling, and these two have known each other forever.

Nic turns his back on Timothy and wraps an arm around my shoulders, pulling me tight. "Your brother's a tool."

"I've been aware of this fact my whole life," I say, sliding my arm between his waist and the couch.

"Blame Nic when I can't get it up tonight," Timothy says to Mina. Whatever she whispers in response receives an unintelligible growl from him.

Evie hands Nic a box wrapped in neon Christmas tree paper. It's one from me, and now that I know there are two more gifts from him under the tree, plus my paints, I wish I'd gotten him more.

He hesitates, fingers already at the seam of the paper. "Anything you want to say before I open this?"

I nestle against his arm. "Nope."

"It's not a hand-knitted penis cozy?"

I push against him. "Open the present."

"I'm too scared."

"Fine," I say with a long-suffering sigh. "It's a handmade scrapbook of shirtless Chris Hemsworth photos."

He laughs, planting a quick kiss on my lips. "You're the worst."

I kiss him back, and apparently, my brain is too dick-addled to work, because I smile at him and say, "That's why you love me."

Panic stabs into my chest.

Nic stares back at me. Just stares, and I can't tell if he's horrified or shocked.

I don't know what to do, so I lightly punch his arm like it's all a joke.

Relief crosses his face, but his eyes look unsettled as he glances down at the gift. "Better open this." He unwraps it carefully instead of tearing it open, like his mind is a million miles away, probably stuck around my accidental confession of feelings.

Goddammit. Why did I say that? He doesn't feel the same—it was all over his face.

Finally, he lifts the lid and sees the black knit sweater with copulating polar bears and snowflakes across the front. He smiles, his whole body relaxing.

"You needed a new ugly Christmas sweater," I say quietly. He outgrew his last one, bulking up for Warwick, and it's a serious oversight that no one has gotten him a new one.

He pulls me into a kiss. "Thank you," he says softly, standing. When he puts his arms through, the hem of his shirt rides up and I find myself staring at the inch-wide band of skin on display.

I'm pathetic, falling for a man I can't keep but will have to continue to see every year.

Opening gifts cheers me up a little. The set of bubble baths from Amanda and Hazel smell divine, and Mom and Dad gave me a set of fancy drink mixers I'll be drowning my heartbreak in soon. Mina and Timbo's gift is a set of pajamas in the same Christmas dick print that won Timothy the Best Dressed glitter candy cane dildo award last night.

The Kouame bag from Nic is gorgeous. I spend a good five minutes touching the vegan leather's wide basket weave. It's a deep purple, and it's so beautiful I'm going to have to perform some mental gymnastics to divorce my association of this bag with Nic. It's too beautiful to die in my Fuck It Closet.

The framed photo of his magazine cover gets some laughs from everyone. Mom casually mentions that I could hang it next to the cologne ad under my hot firefighter calendar. My face flames and I can't look at Nic because that cologne ad is easily eight years old.

Soon it's over. Timothy and Dad start cleaning up all the wrapping paper, and because Timothy is Timothy, he sparks a fierce wrapping paper ball fight that draws everyone in and leaves him a bigger mess to pick up when the rest of us head to the kitchen for coffee and cinnamon rolls.

"Hey." Timothy nails me in the head with a ball of paper. "Come here a sec."

I grab the wad off the floor and stuff it into the bag he's holding. He pulls me into a hug.

"I'm ecstatic you two are together."

If I have to repeat myself for the next week, I'm going to go mad. "It's a fling, Timothy. With an end date."

He laughs. "No, it isn't."

"Yeah, it is."

"Twenty years you two have had a thing for each other, Jessie. This won't be over in two weeks, for either of you."

"It will."

"Wanna bet?"

"Yeah, actually." It's a sure thing, so what do I want from this? "When it's over next week, you have to let it go. And I want bourbon maple ice cream from that place in New Haven. At least a couple of pints." I want to ask for gallons, but I won't be able to fit it in my freezer. Maybe I should ask him to buy me one of those chest freezers and fill it up.

No, my apartment is too small.

Timothy's thinking, tapping a finger against his chin. "And if it isn't over, I officiate your wedding."

That's never happening, so I hold my hand out and we shake.

Chapter Twenty-Seven

Nic

Jessie's painting.

She set up a small easel near the dining room window and I've been watching her as I bake a pecan pie. There's a soft expression on her face that sometimes shifts into a faraway smile or a deep look of concentration. She's happy, and that makes me happy.

She's still wearing my shirt from this morning, along with a soft-looking gray cardigan, and it fills me with this warm, full-to-bursting feeling. Her messy waves are caught up in a twist. One determined strand keeps falling free, only for her to absently tuck it up again.

There's something about Jessie painting while I bake that feels like home. The gently falling snow outside and the warm aromas of Christmas dinner cooking away add to the domesticity. I want to push pause on today and live in this moment for a while.

That's why you love me.

Jessie was joking, but I wonder if maybe I do, or if I could love her one day.

I was so sure about Addison though—or I thought I was at the time—and I was so wrong. That was fast too. We were only together for a short time before I proposed. I wanted to settle down so badly that I couldn't see that we wanted different things. Neither of us would bend or compromise, and the bitterness that grew because of it isn't something I want to experience again. The hurt and shame of her betrayal. How public it all was.

Jessie's been a part of my life, one way or another, for a long time. I don't want to confuse the affection we've found for something deeper. I don't want Jessie to reach the same conclusions about me that Addison did.

No. I need to be certain, and right now, I'm not.

Liam edges into the kitchen, and without a word I grab the container full of Christmas cookies, peeling the lid off. He takes two, gives me a thumbs up, and leaves. I put the container back on a shelf—where Amanda put it an hour ago to keep the kids from ruining their appetites—and stick my pie in the oven.

I start cleaning up. Celia will be in here soon to put the finishing touches on Christmas dinner. When I'm finished, I walk over to stand behind Jessie, slipping my arms around her waist and nuzzling into her neck. She makes an annoyed little noise at the interruption but leans against me as we stare at the paper she's taped to the board. Leaves and flowers, shapes and scribbles.

"Practice," she says simply.

I have no idea if she's rusty and needs to practice or if she's just scared—Jessie has so much talent everything looks great to me. It's unfair she's gotten such little recognition for her skill when I've become a household name despite my lack of any.

I kiss her neck and breathe in the rich, sweet smell of her skin. "When I practice, I get worse."

Jessie laughs.

"Serious. I overthink. It comes across on film."

"No way," she says in a monotone.

I tickle her for that and she squeals, but when she settles in my arms with a happy sigh, I close my eyes. I started telling her, on the walk home from Bawdy Carols, about the problems waiting for me back in LA. We were interrupted by the snowball fight and to be honest, I haven't spent much time thinking about it. Jessie's taken up all the space in my head.

"I'm thinking about quitting," I say after a minute. "You asked the other day if I loved acting, and I didn't answer. I don't."

Jessie puts her paintbrush down and covers my hands with hers. "I'm sorry."

"I don't really hate it. Sometimes I like it. If there's a good vibe on set, it feels a bit like family. But it only lasts for a few months before filming wraps. And I'm lucky to be where I'm at. The Warwick fandom's been great. But I don't know if it's enough."

When Jessie *hmms* in response, I carry on. "The new script is challenging. I don't know the new director and they're talking acting coaches. My agent thinks they might break the contract to recast the role, so this might be a good time to change career focus. Different kinds of roles, or maybe something else."

"What do you want to do?"

"I don't know." I want this to be my life. What we have today. Maybe it's just because I've been lonely and I've missed this family and I'm not happy with my life or the shitshow that's been the last twelve months.

The idea of leaving it all behind and discovering a different flavor of loneliness somewhere on the East Coast makes my throat tighten. This is just a fling.

"What do you think?" I ask her. "What should I do with my life?"

Jessie hmms again, and for half a second, I imagine what life could be like with her in LA. We'd sell my monstrous house and buy something cozier. Her art would be on the walls and she'd paint while I cooked or baked something in the kitchen. Long, lazy mornings in bed. Trips to galleries around the world.

But that could only be between filming. Mostly, we wouldn't see each other. My filming schedules are grueling, especially with the roles I tend to get, which usually involve all-day workouts ahead of filming and 'vitamins' someone inevitably puts me on that are probably steroids. Red carpets and premieres and paparazzi hounding her.

Jessie would hate all that. It's pointless anyway since she'll never leave New York. She loves her job, and she loves the city. She doesn't do relationships and I have nothing to offer her that she might want.

"I think you have to decide for yourself what you want," she finally says.

I hide my disappointment by kissing her neck again. What did I expect? Jessie to say she wants me to come home so we can be together? She'd never ask me to leave my career and move across the country to be with her, even if she did love me. She won't nudge me in one direction or another, the way Timothy used to.

The way my parents tried to and Addison did. Jessie's not like that.

"What do you want?" I ask her.

Jessie turns, wrapping her arms around my neck. Her amber eyes search mine and I have no idea if she sees what she's looking for. Her normally open face is closed to me. "I want you to be happy," she says softly. "I want us to spend the rest of the holiday making each other happy."

I kiss her and her eyes flutter closed. I'm glad for the respite. I have no idea what she can read in my face, but I don't want her to see any trace of unhappiness.

We only have a week. She's not interested in more. At least we're on the same page. That simplifies my decision about acting, I guess.

"I'll make you very happy later tonight," I whisper against her lips. She kisses me back, rocking her hips against mine, just enough to make it clear she's interested in sex.

The sound of an oven door opening is the first indication we're no longer alone. Jessie and I break apart, reluctantly. She smiles at me before turning back to her painting.

"Want a hot chocolate?" I ask her.

"Extra whipped cream," she says, winking at me over her shoulder.

Great. Now I'm thinking about our first time in the shower and trying not to get a hard-on in front of her mom.

"Your pie looks good," Celia says, opening a drawer and thankfully not commenting on catching Jessie and me making out. "I'm going to put tinfoil over it—the crust is browning a little too fast."

I make Jessie a boozy hot chocolate and set it on the table. I manage to steal a kiss and duck the paintbrush she tries to touch to the tip of my nose.

Celia's not leaving. It's showtime for her. The roast and potatoes are in the oven, but she has vegetables to cook and salads to put the finishing touches on. She lets me help like she always does, and we fall into an easy rhythm.

"I talked to Monica last night," Celia says, dropping a potholder onto the counter and resting her hand against her hip.

I have no clue who Monica is, but I nod like I do.

"I called to wish her a Merry Christmas and to suss out what she thought of that video I sent. The two of us in the kitchen."

Okay, Monica must be one of the higher-ups at the Home Cooking Channel.

"She liked the video but wants a different angle. Sorry, honey."

"It's fine." It wasn't something I was considering. I love baking and cooking too, but I'm pretty sure I'd be awful at it on camera. Still, I'm disappointed.

Evie peeks around the corner, catching my eyes and giving me a hopeful look. Celia's looking for something in the fridge, so I grab the cookies and quickly hold them out to her. She takes three, smiles at me shyly, and darts away. Before I can put them back, Timothy strolls in and grabs the container.

Celia closes the fridge with her foot and carries two bowls of salad to the island. Timothy's not fast enough to hide the cookies from her.

"Dinner is almost ready," she says irritably.

"So?" Timothy says with a mouthful of cookie.

"So don't ruin your appetite."

"Timothy." Amanda's voice snaps like a whip as she steps into the room, Evie trailing behind her. "Stop giving the kids cookies right before dinner."

"I didn't!" He points at me. "It was Nic."

I raise both hands in the air. "I would never."

Timothy's expression turns faux-murderous. "Better sleep with one eye open tonight, Fontana."

"I'd rethink a midnight murder, Timbo," Jessie says. "You might see something you don't want to see."

Timothy gags. "Never mind."

"Timothy and Amanda, set the table," Celia calls out. "Jessie, clean up your corner. Evie, sweetie, you can put the napkins out. Nic, get the wine. Dinner's ready in twenty minutes."

It's closer to forty minutes before everyone is sitting around the table, since getting all the Foleys together in one place can be a bit like herding cats. Conversation flows, everyone laughing, eating, and giving each other a hard time, and I can't remember a better Christmas. Ever.

Jessie and I hold hands under the table, and every time she looks at me, I smile.

Some future Christmas, Jessie's going to bring another boyfriend home to meet the family. A husband. Their kids, if they have any. I'll have to sit at this table. Make small talk. Smile. But every time I catch Jessie's eyes, she's going to remember this Christmas with me. I'm going to make sure she never forgets.

Chapter Twenty-Eight

Jessie

Everyone goes to bed early. We're all exhausted from last night's Folly and a big Christmas dinner. Nic's already gone to bed, but I ignored his hint that I should join him. I want to stare at the tree for a little bit. Think about today.

Painting felt right, and it's taking all the self-control I have not to spend the night with a brush in my hand. I think I'm going to take a shot at that commission from Gretchen Torres. I'm going to paint her little 'pieces of eroticism' the way I'd like to paint them. And never show them to her, because even if I love what I create, I can't see myself putting my work under her critical eye. She'll crush my heart and make it that much harder when I pick up the brush next. This is too new, too fragile for rejection.

My phone chimes.

> Merry Xmas WHY DIDN'T YOU TELL ME YOU AND NIC OMG?!?!

Lauren

Honestly, I thought the news would spread faster through the extended family. Lauren spent Christmas Eve with her mother's family, so she missed the drama of the Folly, but still.

It's just a fling. Nothing to tell.

ME

Oh, no. Not buying it. Your flings have made it so much easier to do my job. There has to be something you can share.

LAUREN

Lauren is the resident sex-pert at Sploosh!, handling advice about sex and relationships as well as products in blogs, videos, and social media posts. I used to do that job, but as I moved more into marketing, Lauren took over. And there is no way I'm giving her anything that might end up online.

We'll catch up—off the record—when I'm back in the city. Get a package <eggplant emoji> for xmas?

ME

Nope. Struck out at Timothy's wedding too. Am collecting cats for impending spinsterhood.

LAUREN

Can I join you?

ME

Not if you're banging Nic.

LAUREN

F-L-I-N-G.

ME

Suuure

Lauren

My family is impossible. I toss my phone aside.

Timothy drops onto the couch next to me. "What are you still doing up?"

I raise my hot chocolate. "What about you?"

"Need some water. Got to stay hydrated."

"Gross."

He laughs, then falls silent for thirty seconds. "It's been a great Christmas," he says wistfully, staring at the tree.

This has been the best Christmas I've had in years. Maybe ever. There won't be another one like it—whatever the future holds—and I want to draw it out a little longer. Make it last. Maybe that's why I'm still sitting down here when Nic's already in my room.

"It has. Thank you for the new sister-in-law. Don't know why she puts up with you, but I'm glad she does."

He laughs. "Yeah, I'm not going to question my luck. And neither should you. Get your ass upstairs."

Timothy's right. At least for tonight, I need to shut off my brain. I need to enjoy the time I have with Nic.

He heads to his room with a couple of glasses of water, and I drop my mug in the sink before I head upstairs.

Nic's sitting on the end of my bed, wearing only a pair of red plaid pajama pants and staring at my suitcase and the toys scattered about.

Shit. I forgot I dumped everything on the floor looking for a clean pair of socks earlier today. I've already given away all the sex toys I brought for various family members, but I still have enough of my personal collection that my room looks like ground zero in a sex toy-powered orgy.

"I swear I have hobbies that don't involve orgasms," I tell Nic, although I can't think of a single one. Drinking counts, right? Chocolate brownie ice cream?

I don't know why I brought so many toys, except I didn't know what I'd be in the mood for, and let's face it, at this point, I'm a connoisseur.

"I want to watch you," he says, his voice low and gravelly.

I suck in a breath, my core clenching, all paranoid thoughts of what he thinks my life must look like blown away. "Why?"

Nic motions for me to come closer. I do. I only have so much willpower. None, basically.

When I'm standing in front of him, he brings my leg up next to his hip, guiding me until I'm straddling him. "I want to see how you touch yourself." He pushes my cardigan over my shoulders, letting it fall to the floor.

I'd rather touch him. His skin is warm and taut over muscle, and when I trail my hands over him, his eyes darken.

"Show me," he says into my skin as his lips drag across my neck and his hands push my shirt up. "Then I want to show you how closely I paid attention." He pulls my shirt—his shirt—over my head, tossing it aside.

A little moan escapes as he takes off my bra, replacing the cups with his hands. I've never brought any toys out with a partner before. Camden was pre-Sploosh! so I didn't have the arsenal or the knowledge or the comfort I have now, and there hasn't been anyone since that I trust enough. I don't even have any toys geared specifically for partner use—I give those away when they land in my office.

Nic fucking me with a vibrating cock ring...

My whimper that we won't get the chance turns into a soft scream when Nic, in one swift move, throws me onto the bed and lowers his body over mine.

"Put on a show for me," he murmurs into my ear, his words buzzing through my veins, settling with an aching pull between my legs.

I trust Nic, and I want this. "Sit in the chair."

He has to excavate the chair from my pile of clothes, but he sits while I dig through my options. Bullet vibes, finger vibes, little clitoral stimulators...all small enough that they're guaranteed not to give Nic a complex. I bypass them in favor of a G-spot vibrator the color of Merlot. It's my favorite, the most powerful of the ones I frequently use. The tip is a little squishy and the premium silicone is soft. It has two motors, one at the tip and one at the base. Five patterns and five intensities for each.

I hold it up, raising an eyebrow at Nic.

He doesn't look intimidated by the length. Only five inches are insertable, but the handle makes it look impressive and it has some serious girth on the tip. If anything, his gaze grows darker behind those hooded eyes. There's no hiding the erection in his pajama pants either. He nods, slow and deliberate, his hand scraping over the five o'clock shadow on his jaw.

I grab a small bottle of lube and throw a towel from the bathroom onto the end of my bed. Once my pants and panties are off, I sit on the towel facing Nic. The room is small enough our knees are only a few feet apart. It's intimate.

"I don't want to be the only one doing this," I say, dipping my chin toward his dick. "You need to jerk off too."

"I will," he says, but makes no move to get his dick out. He looks way too comfortable just as he is.

It's hot that I'm the only one naked, so for now, I'll allow it.

I flick the vibrator on, adjusting the pattern for each motor. Then the intensity because I like to start slow. Since I'm putting on a show, I hold the lube over the tip, pouring it out in a thin drizzle. More than I need, considering how wet I am already. After capping the lube, I toss it to Nic, who catches it but still makes no move to free his poor trapped dick, even when I wrap my hand around the vibrator and stroke it a few times to spread the lube.

His eyes hold mine as I spread my legs, drawing my knees up so my feet press against my bed. The air in here feels heavy, and I feel exposed, but in a way that still feels like he's holding me, even though we're not close enough to touch.

When I place the tip of the vibrator against my inner thigh, his gaze drops and my heart kicks up a beat. Slowly, I drag the tip closer to my clit. When it touches me, I make a little gasping sound. His Adam's apple bobs as he swallows, and my vision swims a bit as my eyes flutter at the sensation. I'm not going to close my eyes. Not when Nic's lounging in my chair, his hand finally drifting, closing around his shaft and squeezing through the fabric of his pajama pants.

This is going to be over embarrassingly fast for me, so I slide the vibe down, pushing the tip against my entrance before bringing it back to my clit, teasingly light this time. My free hand moves over my breast, plucking and pinching at my nipple.

Nic's not looking so relaxed all of a sudden. His hand, still on his dick, squeezes again, tighter.

After a minute or so, the need to have something—this toy, Nic—filling me is too great to ignore.

"Fuck," Nic whispers reverently as I slowly push the tip inside me only to pull it back out again. The moment I hit my G-spot for any length of time, this show is going to be over, so I go back to my clit, circle for a few seconds, then bring it back down and push it a little further inside my pussy.

Nic finally, blessedly, decides to join the party, pulling his dick out and squeezing the base as he fumbles for the lube with his other hand, his eyes never once looking away as I fuck myself with the toy, pausing to flick the intensity up a notch.

Okay, two notches.

I love watching his hand move, the slick sounds he makes after distractedly dumping too much lube over his cock. He alternates his strokes, long and short, his thumb and forefinger twisting along the crown.

"Did you think about me?" I ask, my voice tight because I'm so damn close, but I want to give him a chance to catch up. "That first night here?"

"I did." The corner of his mouth lifts in a rueful smile.

Oh. Oh, no. Asking was a bad choice if I'm letting him catch up—I rest the vibrator against my thigh and take a deep breath to slow myself down.

He slips out of the chair onto his knees, and Nic Fontana kneeling in front of me might be the most erotic thing I've ever seen and I will never get tired of it. He moves close enough that I can feel his breath on my thigh and he licks his lips as he watches me, pushing his pants down, his hand moving faster, rougher on his dick.

His voice is gravel when he speaks again. "I thought about how good your perfect mouth would feel wrapped around my cock. How much you'd like it."

His free hand skates up my leg to my thigh, pushing the vibrator back to my pussy. He grips me where my thigh meets my hip, and holds me tight. "You're so much better than my imagination."

So is he and the greedy way he watches me push the vibe back inside, the soft *fuck* on his ragged exhale...

I'm close, pleasure building inside me.

"Jessie, I—" Nic glances up at me with those bedroom eyes, but instead of continuing, he surges to his feet. The moment his lips ghost over mine, I lose it. My orgasm rips through me and I cry out at the strength of it, my entire body lighting up, my hips bucking and my feet slipping.

I fall back onto the bed, or Nic pushes me, my thighs clasping tight to hold the vibrator in place a little longer as waves of pleasure crash over me. Throughout, he's right there, above me, staring into my eyes. The expression on his face is soft, full of awe and warmth, and I wonder how he sees me right now. What he feels.

Nic gathers me into his arms and lifts me to the head of the bed, his body hard and warm against mine as he kisses my neck. "That was beautiful. Thank you."

"You?" I can't form the whole sentence, but I can feel his erection against my thigh, slippery from lube, so I point in the general direction. "Why not?"

"I want to play with you first," he says.

And he does. He holds me until I'm ready, then he retraces my every move with the toy, reading my body like a goddamn expert, edging me until I'm begging. He's gentle and careful when he fucks me with it, doing exactly what I tell him to do.

It's perfect.

He kisses me while I come, and I'm still shaking as he shifts, pumping his fist fast, painting my tits with his cum before collapsing next to me again, holding me tight, kissing me and telling me how much he loved that.

My brain latches onto the fact that he loves 'that,' not me, but I'm too tired to digest it.

Nic has to carry me to the shower. He helps me wash off, towel dries me after, and pulls another one of his shirts over my head. We crawl into bed and collapse in each other's arms.

I'm exhausted, my body so thoroughly satisfied, but I can't fall asleep. My brain is a snow globe, and I've been shaken.

I love Nic.

It's just sex.

I don't want him to leave.

All swirling around until I feel like I might explode.

Nic talks in his sleep. He slurs his words enough that I can't be certain, but I think he might be running through his lines from the last Warwick movie.

It's fucking endearing.

It hurts.

Every minute that passes, I love him more than the last and each one is a paper cut to my already-bruised heart. I'm not sure what will be left of me at the end. I need to be unaffected when he goes—no one can see this heartbreak because I want him to come back, I want him to be welcomed back—but I'm not sure I can do that anymore.

The smart thing would be to leave early. I don't need to stay the full two weeks just because it's a family tradition. I'm only a couple of hours away—it's not like I can't visit anytime. Except I want to spend more time with my twin, I'm enjoying getting to know Mina, and I never see Amanda, Hazel, and the kids as much as I want to. I should stay through New Year's, as planned.

It's going to be a shitty New Year once Nic is gone.

Chapter Twenty-Nine

Nic

December Twenty-sixth

Last night was intense, so I'm not surprised to wake up alone. A little space might be good for us.

Jessie's painting in the attic. I bring her a cup of coffee, but she barely acknowledges me. Maybe I need the reminder that this is just sex for her, even if it's something more for me. What that something more is, I have no clue.

After breakfast in the kitchen with Amanda, Hazel, and the kids, I play pool with Timothy. Mina and Liam join us for the second game.

Jessie's still painting.

Timothy breaks out some Nerf guns, and it's me and Liam versus him and Evie but it turns out we've all underestimated William, who pulls a blaster out from under a throw pillow and nails each of us while barely glancing up from his book. Liam and Evie dish out the payback while Timothy and I watch and laugh.

Jessie comes down for lunch, speaks to no one, and disappears back into the attic with a sandwich.

She used to get like this when she was deeply into her art, so I let it go, but I can't shake the feeling that something's wrong. An hour passes and I need to see her. Talk to her. Touch her.

I grab a plate and stick a few cookies on it, then head to the attic. Jessie's standing back, looking at her canvas, head slightly tilted. She smiles at me when I reach the top of the ladder.

"How's it going?" I ask.

"Almost got it," she says, slipping right into my arms after I set the plate down. I kiss her and she kisses me back. Some of the tension eases out of me at the soft press of her lips, but it's not the reassurance I need.

I don't know what I need from her.

We kiss for a few minutes and maybe that's enough, but when she murmurs she wants to finish her painting and hints I should go downstairs, I know it isn't.

This is maddening. I shouldn't feel this way about her. About anyone. I'm still a mess and—

My phone pings. My agent.

> Call me when you have time to talk.

Denise

That's ominous. I head into Jessie's room, close the door, and quickly dial Denise.

She cuts to the chase.

"It's just a rumor, some stuff overheard at various holiday parties, but it sounds likely they will want to recast the role. Fandom loves you and I think we can put some pressure on them not to, but we'd need to start right away. If that's what you want."

Shit. Is it? This could be an easy out since I haven't signed on to any other projects. But then what would I do? I don't want to move home if it means seeing Jessie after she's moved on. It hits me like a fist. I can't move home. Ever.

"Yeah," I say, swallowing because my throat's suddenly dry. "Okay, what do I need to do?"

"Wrap up your holiday early. I'll see who's available for coaching. I'll call Rose Dashcombe and we'll brainstorm a publicity campaign but I'm thinking we need to show you are completely devoted to the role and willing to work hard. If we feed the fans, it'll make the studio think twice about pissing them off. I'll feel around, see what other opportunities might be out there for you, as a backup, but maybe leverage too."

Denise talks for a few more minutes, her excitement at taking action clear. Mine is nonexistent, more like a growing sense of dread gnawing on me.

I'm not good enough and the whole world is going to see just how bad I am if they don't replace me. But what else can I do?

Denise ends the call to start working—even though it's still the holiday and I tell her she shouldn't, not on my account.

I find myself in the one place in this house that soothes me—the kitchen.

Celia takes one look at me, and without a word, she opens the fridge, pulls out a skirt steak, and tosses it on the counter. "It's for fajitas tomorrow. Tenderize it, season it, and stick it in the fridge." She hesitates, her fingers twisting. "Did something happen with Jessie?"

"No, my job. They want to replace me."

"Oh." She sounds relieved, and I try not to let it irritate me. My job is my life and Jessie is just a holiday from it.

Celia leaves the kitchen with a "have at it, then" and I pull out a wooden cutting board and a meat tenderizer.

I'm going back to LA to try to salvage my career and it feels like the wrong decision.

Why couldn't I have a hobby or a passion or something that I want so badly I have no choice but to go for it?

I bring the meat tenderizer onto the steak with a satisfying thwack.

I'm a directionless, ambitionless disappointment. My parents saw it. Addison too. I wasn't enough for her. It wasn't even the cheating, she didn't break my heart. Just my ability to believe in myself.

Thwack.

Thwack.

"Beating your meat to a pulp?" Timothy asks and I jump. Where the hell did he come from?

I can't think of a single goddamn thing to say that might get him to go away.

"What's up?" Timothy asks, pulling out a barstool and sitting across the island from me. "Jessie?"

"No." I lie, but she's part of the reason I'm pulverizing this steak. It feels like she's slipping away from me, closing doors, and I don't know what to do to stop her. If I should. Hell, this is just sex, and the sex continues to be mind-blowing, so I should leave it alone, right?

Except the thought of leaving makes me feel like my chest is caving in on itself.

"Mom said something about you being replaced," Timothy says, eyes on the steak.

I give the steak a good thwack in response.

Timothy sighs. "Talk to me, Nic. Tell me what you want and we can figure this out."

"I don't know what I want." Thwack. "I've never known what I want." *I don't deserve what I want.* Thwack. "I'm not like you. I don't have some big life goal."

Thwack. Thwack. Thwack.

Timothy taps his head. "Hey. Recent life crisis, remember?"

Like I can forget his accident. Just thinking about it makes me break out into a cold sweat. I thought he was a dead man walking that day, bleeding into his brain as he tried to get back on set.

I have to push the memories out of my head or I'll lose it.

His stunt career is over, but he's pursued his life with Mina with the same focus and drive, changing one goal for another.

I don't have that.

Timothy's talking again, and I've missed most of it. "...if you ask her."

"Ask who what?" I ask, irritated.

"Jessie. To move to LA."

"She'd never move to LA." I would never ask her to uproot her life and try to fit into mine. She'd be miserable, I'd be miserable. We'd make each other miserable. I wouldn't be enough for her and she'd leave. I can't upend her life for nothing.

Timothy waves it off. "Well, not to your ugly-ass house. Have you looked at any places in Malibu? I think she'd like it there."

My jaw locks and it takes me a minute to unlock it. "It's a fling."

He gives me a look that screams *bullshit*. "Not from where I'm sitting."

Pull your head out of your ass, I want to yell, but instead, I give the meat another thwack and press my lips tight.

"You've been in love with Jessie for years," Timothy says, pushing to his feet and walking over to the fridge to pull out a beer. "Almost as long as she's been in love with you. We all know it, we've all watched this play out for decades. You'll be walking down the aisle within the year."

What?

The meat tenderizer drops from my hands, clattering on the bench. Is this—does her whole family expect us to ride off into the sunset and live happily ever after?

"I have plans for your wedding"—Timothy continues, oblivious—"They involves goats, and that's all you need to know."

"I am not marrying her." Or anyone else, I want to add.

He laughs. "Sure, Jan."

Why can't I get this through his thick skull? "I don't love her. I don't want a relationship with her. We aren't even friends. This is nothing more than a convenient fuck for—"

"Hey." Timothy taps my shoulder and when I turn, he punches me right in the pec. Not hard, but not light either. "That's my sister."

I rub my chest. "—for both of us. It's what we agreed on."

"Yeah, well, you're both lying to yourselves and each other." Timothy grumbles before falling silent. It doesn't last. "If you hurt her—" He punches me again, harder this time.

"Ow, fucking *stop*. No one is getting hurt." I turn my back on him. The distance between Jessie and me today has to prove as much. She doesn't care about me beyond what I can do to her body. And my feelings...when have they ever mattered? I can shove it down deep. Forget her. "Jessie lives in New York, I'm going back to LA. She'll move on, I'll move on."

Timothy snorts. "You're pathetic. Just own up to your damn feelings and tell her you love her."

I grab the tenderizer and point it at him. "I care for her, but I don't love her. We have chemistry, but that's it."

Timothy keeps his big mouth shut, for once. I can feel his eyes on me as I go back to work, his gaze concerned. Seconds tick by. A minute. He's going to open his mouth and I'm going to lose my shit and we both know it's inevitable, even if neither of us wants to do this.

This was exactly the reason I never should have touched Jessie in the first place. I don't want to fight with Timothy.

Celia breezes into the kitchen. "Nic, honey, it's been so lovely having you back under this roof, and I was thinking, if you and Jessie aren't ready for you to move into her place, you're more than welcome to stay here—" she freezes, staring at the steak in horror. "Oh, no. What happened?"

It's fucking tartare.

"Mom," Timothy says, a slight warning in his voice as he shakes his head and attempts to subtly draw his hand across his throat.

Celia stares at him for a moment, then turns her confused look to me.

"I'm not moving home," I say through gritted teeth.

She frowns. "Jessie's moving to LA?"

Of course not and I have to take a deep breath before I say something I'll regret.

"That's it!" Timothy startles me as he slaps the counter. "I'm going to find Liam and we're going to build a ramp. We'll need some rope and someone to drive my truck—think Liam can reach the pedals yet? And I need my old snowboard. I'm jumping Jessie's tiny-ass rental car in twenty minutes."

He runs out of the kitchen like an excited toddler on a mission while Celia and I stare after him.

"Oh, hell no," she says, following, shouting for Mina.

The entire house erupts into absolute chaos, and if I weren't a wreck on the inside, I'd laugh at whatever the hell makes Timothy think *this* is the way to save me from a conversation I don't want to have with his mom.

Instead, reality sets in. This fling has raised expectations in Timothy and

Celia, probably in the whole family. It was one thing, before it happened, to say they'll get over it when it ends. It's another thing to patiently explain over and over again that Jessie and I don't have a future.

To have to tell them it's over.

At least I won't be breaking Jessie's heart. If I did, I'd never be able to come back—the guilt would eat me alive. The Foleys are the only family I have and losing them would leave me alone in the world.

Except I want her to be heartbroken. I want her to hate me and curse me when she sees me in the tabloids with other women. Because there will be other women, even though I'll never marry one of them. The thought of causing her pain makes my chest hurt, but the idea of her indifference is worse. I want what we have to mean something and god this is fucked up. I should want her to be happy, to meet someone and settle down with him, and—I don't.

Could Timothy be right?

I have feelings for her. Strong ones. When we're together, she fills every corner of my being. Since the first time we hooked up, I've craved her with an unexpected, inexplicable intensity. I don't want this to end, but I don't see a way forward. We don't fit into each other's lives and trying to force it could cost me everyone important to me. It has to end, and keeping those feelings out of it is the only way to end it cleanly.

Do I love her?

Does it matter?

I'm glaring at the meat like it can give me some goddamn answers when Timothy slips back into the kitchen. "Jessie's leaving."

Chapter Thirty

Jessie

ALL I NEED TO do is make it to the front door. To my coat and boots, my handbag with the keys to my rental car tucked inside. Out the door.

"I don't love her. I don't want a relationship with her. We aren't even friends. This is nothing more than a convenient fuck for—"

"Hey. That's my sister."

"—for both of us. It's what we agreed on."

It was what we agreed upon, but something inside me broke when I overheard Nic's words. He didn't see me back out of the doorway. Didn't know I ran to my room and frantically packed my suitcase.

I can't be with him while loving him, knowing that even after last night, all I am to him is a convenient place to stick his dick.

My face burns and my eyes fill with tears. I knew it would hurt, but this is a living thing, teeth sinking into my already raw heart and there is nothing I can do to stop it.

I take a deep breath and hurry to the steps, as fast as my still-heavy suitcase will allow. At the top, I pause. There's a lot of noise, but it's coming from the great room. Maybe my parents' room. I don't know what is going on, but I take advantage of the chaos to haul my suitcase down the stairs as quietly as possible.

I'll stop on the road to tell Mom I've gone home. I'll come up with an excuse once I'm safely out of the house.

My coat is on and I'm zipping my second boot when Timothy bursts into the foyer, my mom hot on his heels. Mina trails behind, looking bewildered and potentially dangerous.

"Timothy, I swear to god—" My mom sees me first, stopping short, her hand flying to her mouth.

"There are only so many places you can hide a snowboard, I will find..." A frown mars his face and his voice fades away when his eyes land on my suitcase. "Jessie?"

Mina knows the score immediately. Her lips press together, but there's sympathy in her eyes.

"Why, Jessie?" My mom's pained whisper breaks the silence.

I zip the boot and stand tall. My mouth opens, but I can't come up with an emergency that might take me back to New York the day after Christmas. "I can't do this." My voice breaks, and I bite my lip. I'm not going to cry. Not until I reach my car.

"Why not?" my mom demands, hands on her hips.

"I don't want to," I say, reaching for the door. I need to get out. I can't face Nic and if he walks out of the kitchen, if he sees how much I care... "We were just sleeping together. Now we're done. I'll see you at Evie's birthday party next month."

My mom's hands go to her hips. "No. Jessica Jane Foley, do not open that door. You set that goddamn suitcase down and go talk to that boy."

"Let her go," Mina says quietly.

The look my mom gives Mina is sharp enough to cut, but Mina doesn't back down. "She just needs some space first. Then they can talk it out."

Mina is wrong. There's nothing to talk out.

"She needs to talk to her boyfriend." My mom insists.

Timothy wraps his arm around his wife, giving her his support. I could use a bit of that support. The pain is gnashing at my ribs, wanting out. Wanting to make someone else, anyone else, hurt.

I need to leave.

"He's not my boyfriend." Stepping outside, the cold sucks all the air out of my lungs.

My mom rushes to stuff her feet into Dad's winter boots, but I'm already out the door, hauling my suitcase down the porch steps. I need to join a gym and start some weight training. Maybe cardio. Escaping should be easier—I'm nearly gasping and I'm hardly a quarter down the driveway.

"What the hell is wrong with you?" My mom's voice rings out as she hurries after me. "You've pined after this boy for years, and now that you have him, you're throwing him away?"

I spin around to face her. "It was just sex and I have *never* pined for him."

"Anyone who sees you two together knows that's not true." She crosses her arms and glares.

I want to scream back that anyone who can see me would know how much this is costing me, how much it hurts, but I bite my tongue.

"God! I knew this would happen, that you'd do something like this. You're so goddamn flighty, running away at the first sign that something might not be easy for you. Relationships aren't easy, Jessie. They aren't supposed to be."

"Nic doesn't want me, Mom. He's fine. Let it go." I want to scream at her I'm not fine, I love him, but she wouldn't believe me. Nic is her precious angel and I'm the daughter no one likes all that much.

"I can't deal with you right now," she finally says, throwing her arms in the air as she turns back to the house. "Text when you get home, so I know you made it."

I take a deep breath. Another. Filling my lungs with bitterly cold air steadies me a little. I'll be fine. I just need to make it to New York, and when I get to my place, I can let it all out.

My hand tightens around the handle of my suitcase and I drag it after me, toward my car. Every step takes me away from Nic while my stupid half-dead heart tries to yank me back.

"Jessie."

My stomach plummets as his voice settles over me, low and deep. There's hurt in the way he says my name and I'm glad. I want him to feel some sliver of the pain inside me.

I should run for it, but I stop in front of the patch of ice because I'm a fool. Because a small part of me wants to believe he'll pour his heart out if I give him time. That my mother and brother are right and he loves me, and maybe always has.

Nic catches up with me, skidding to a stop. He brushes my arm, tentative, his face falling when I pull away. "Where are you going?"

"Home." It catches in my throat and I cough.

"Why?" The harsh word hangs in the air between us.

Because I can't stop this from hurting. Because I love you, and you don't love me. Maybe those words are in my eyes, or on my face, but Nic isn't reading them—his face remains impassive. I could tell him, but I can't stand here and listen to him try to find a polite way to tell me everything I overheard. He's not in love with me. He doesn't even like me as a friend.

He can never know I love him.

"I'm done." I manage. I don't sound like myself and my skin is prickling with sweat, despite the cold.

"Done." He echoes, crossing his arms. "Why?"

My shoulders lift in a helpless shrug. It's taking all my effort to keep from crying.

His voice rises, startling a bird out of the bare branches of the maple overhead. "If you're done, have the courage to tell me you're done instead of sneaking off."

I can't look at him, so I stare at my boot as I toe at the patch of ice on the driveway. A different girl fell on her ass a week ago, but how different was she? I'm still a coward. "I don't want to fuck you anymore. Can I go now?"

"Christ, Jessie. I don't want to date you. There's nothing to run from."

The broken pieces inside me slice through my heart, and it hurts so much more to hear him say it to me. *I don't want you.* He's waiting for a response and the cold indifference that's settled over his face is a sharp twist to my pain.

I have to hit him back hard. Protect what's left of my heart. "We've had fun, but you can't give me anything more than my sex toys can give me and it gets boring after a while, okay?"

He recoils. Another cut to my heart. I need to get out of here.

"So that's it?" His laugh is loud, cold. "I'm a lump of fucking plastic to you too?"

"Silicone." I correct him, tightening my hand on my suitcase handle as I step carefully onto the ice. "We agreed to casual holiday sex, Nic. That's all we've been to each other. Living, breathing sex toys."

"Jessie, wait—" His hand brushes my elbow, but I keep going.

Out of the corner of my eye, I see him lose his footing on the ice.

Chapter Thirty-One

Jessie

THE AMBULANCE TAKES NIC away and someone—Mina, I think—stuffs me into Timothy's truck and buckles me into my seat. She holds my hand in the hospital waiting room, but it doesn't help. Timothy's openly glaring at me. Amanda too. My mother's looks are softer, but she blames me. Hell, I blame myself.

And every time I close my eyes, I hear the crack of his head on the ice. I think of Timothy's accident—he hit his head and nearly died.

Nic said he was fine. He got back to his feet and walked into the house and he was *fine* but Mom called the ambulance anyway. Probably a concussion, the paramedics said. What if they're wrong? What if he's bleeding in his brain? Just like Timothy.

It's not just the sound of his head smacking into the ground that I hear either. It's every horrible thing I said to him. Every word he said to me, the way he looked at me, all the warmth gone. The pain in my chest is cowering in fear now that it's lashed out and hurt someone I love.

The doctor comes in. Nic has a mild concussion and—because my mother insists—they'll keep him overnight for observation. He needs rest and quiet, no stress. He'll have headaches, but no long-term damage. No apparent memory loss, but he's tired and irritable. The chances for a full recovery look good. Yes, we can see him once he's settled in his room, but we need to keep quiet so he can rest, and go in twos...yes, my mother could stay the night, but it's unnecessary, he's receiving excellent care, the nurses—

Relief pushes me to my feet and carries me out of the waiting room. He's going to be okay.

The click of my heeled boots on the hospital floor is oddly soothing, and after a few minutes of aimless walking, I find myself in the hospital gift shop.

I buy a small teddy bear with a canary yellow cape and mask and go back to the waiting room. I'm going to tell him I'm sorry and ask for his friendship.

Mina's sitting by Timothy now, so I sit alone, toying with the teddy bear's cape and refusing to take part in the silent conversation Timothy's trying to have with me. The character of Warwick doesn't wear a cape, but I think Nic will appreciate this little superhero.

"You couldn't be happy, could you?" Timothy finally grumbles.

I've been expecting it from him, but it startles me anyway, and I drop the bear, bending quickly to pick it up.

My brother is still scowling. "Do you have any idea how hard it was for him to take a chance on you in the first place? After the year he's had?"

Something in me snaps, my hands strangling the poor teddy bear to keep me from strangling my twin. "You should've stayed out of it and stopped trying to push us together."

"He loves you, dumbass."

Tears are close and I want to shout at him, to scream that he doesn't know what he's talking about. Instead, I draw a deep breath, my thumbnail dragging over the stitching on the cape. "He doesn't—he was bored and horny, and I was there."

Timothy gets to his feet. "If you think that—"

"Timothy. Jessica." Mom's voice is mild in tone, but loaded with threats we ignore.

"It was never going to work between us, numbnuts, and you know it." I push at the tears falling down my face, pissed off that I'm crying in front of him and not caring when my voice rises. "I hope this was fun for you because it sure as hell hasn't been for me."

"*You* were leaving *him*, Jessie, you don't get to be the goddamned victim!" Timothy ignores the tug on his arm from Mina, his shout silencing the waiting room.

"No, I'm always the bad guy, aren't I?" My voice can't sustain a shout, not with choking sobs threatening. "Aren't I, Timothy?"

"You could try another way to get attention."

From my twin, that hurts. Timothy should know me better than anyone, and *this* is what he thinks of me. If there's anything left of my heart, some particles of dust somewhere, they blow away. All I have is rage and fear and a mind-numbing sadness.

Our mother rises to her feet, her voice cracking like thunder. "Outside, both of you. NOW."

"Stay out of my life." I snap at Timothy.

"You can ruin it on your own."

I storm off first—I only know one way to get outside and I'm not going to awkwardly walk down the hall with that asshole. Pushing through the doors, I keep going in case he's behind me.

It's cold. The sun's gone down in a blaze of faded tangerine and rose, the day ending.

Everything is fucking ending.

Pulling deep breaths of the frigid air into my lungs does nothing to calm my racing pulse. I'm on the outside. Again. At odds with my brother.

Again.

I'm alone when I most need someone to pull me into a hug and tell me everything will be all right, that I'll get through this.

There is no getting through this, but I'd take any lie right now.

A sob escapes and I hold on to the cold metal of a streetlight, the teddy clutched tight to my chest with my other hand as I cry, tears freezing on my cheeks.

I want Nic. I want to wrap my arms around him and tell him I'm sorry, that I didn't mean any of the hurtful things I said to him. I should tell him I love him and let him reject me, and maybe he'll understand.

Except he's injured. He doesn't need me unloading my feelings on him. He doesn't owe me an attempt to make me feel better.

It's fully dark when I go inside. Mina's hanging out in the lobby. She pulls me into a hug and shoves her coffee into my hands to warm my numb fingers.

"We'll talk when you're ready," she says quietly as she leads me through the corridors to Nic's room.

We won't because I'll never be ready to talk about this, but I say nothing. She took my side today. Stood up against my mother. She's here when she should be with my brother.

Mina leaves me at the door and disappears down the hall.

Nic's lying in an upright position in the bed, his dark lashes fanned over his cheekbones. His sheets are pulled up to his waist, his hands clasped together over his stomach. He looks a little pale, but strong. God, things could have been so much worse, he could have...

A sob escapes my throat and my mother, sitting in the chair next to his bed, looks up. Her face softens. "Are you okay, sweetie?" she whispers, loud enough to carry her voice across the room.

Nic's long eyelashes flutter open and I want to throw myself on him and tell him how sorry I am, how scared I am. How much I love him.

But his lips tighten, his stare going cold. I did this to him. Made him look at me like this. It's awful.

I stop at his bedside, reaching for his hand.

He crosses his arms.

"Nic." I need the touch he denied like my next breath. Something little, the brush of our fingers. Anything. I am breaking all over again and I need him to tell me we're okay.

Shaking, I hold the teddy bear out to him. "I got you something."

His eyes flick to the stuffed animal and up to me. "I don't want it."

Right. I look down at the bear's cheery yellow cape. It was stupid to think he'd want a teddy bear.

Silence lies thick between us, and in that space, the need to tell him everything bubbles up. Overcoming my self-preservation, I reach for him again. My voice, when I speak, breaks under the weight of the sobs it's holding back. "I'm sorry—"

"Go home, Jessie." His voice is cold. Flat. The inches that separate us are miles.

My face burns, and my vision blurs again. I nod. Stuff everything back down. Lie to myself that I'm walking out of the room for him. He doesn't want me. He's done. I need to be done too.

I leave the bear at the nurses' station.

My father's waiting for me in the lobby this time, and we drive home in silence. My suitcase is still in the driveway, so I put it in my rental and drive to New York.

My East Village apartment belonged to my parents, before Timothy and I were born and they moved out to Connecticut. My mom kept it, though, for when she needed to be in the city. Amanda lived here while she went to college, and I followed in her shoes. Only I didn't leave. I'm too comfortable here. Too set in my ways. The rent I pay my parents is reasonable and I've never had to touch my trust fund.

The air inside is stale and I drop the suitcase inside the front door. It can live there, for all I care. I have more clothes in my closet, and unless I need a vibrator for work, I don't want to touch one ever again. So instead of putting things away, I kick off my shoes and walk directly into the kitchen. I grab a small carton of vanilla ice cream from the freezer and a bottle of Kahlúa from the cupboard.

There's an art to healing a broken heart. I pour the liqueur onto the ice cream and drop onto the couch. Right on schedule, the tears come back, streaming down my face until I give up on my ice cream.

Five years ago, Camden broke my heart. I drowned my sorrows in booze. Got fired for not showing up at work. The worst part is, my heartbreak over Camden was a lie. I couldn't see it at the time, but it was Nic marrying Addison that broke me.

It was hell, and I needed Timothy to help pick me back up. This time, I'm doing it alone. From my couch, with my boozy ice cream melting, it seems impossible. I'm drinking it straight from the carton between sniffles.

The scrape of a lock and the sound of my door opening and closing bring me to my feet. I barely have time to blink back the tears before Timothy crashes into me, crushing me into his jacket. I'm a snotty mess, but he holds me in a bear hug, murmuring nonsense at me like I've skinned my knee and I've never been more grateful to see my big-by-a-dozen-minutes-that-shouldn't-count brother.

"I'm sorry, J," he says tightly. "Seeing Nic like that, after my accident—I wasn't thinking. Didn't think about how you'd be feeling. I messed up, but I'm here now."

He's here. For me. He could be with Nic, or with Mina, but my dumbass brother drove all the way to the city. It turns me into a sobbing wreck all over again.

When I dry out enough, he sits me on the couch and goes in search of tissues, taking my boozy ice cream with him. He brings back tacos in the plain brown paper bag of my favorite Mexican joint, though, so I forgive him. We eat in silence, staring at the blank screen of my TV. When the tacos are gone, the whiskey comes out.

Timothy takes a swig straight from the bottle and passes it to me. "You love him."

My head drops, my hair obscuring my face as I clutch the bottle like a lifeline. I can't deny it. "He doesn't love me. You owe me ice cream, by the way."

"It's not over yet—I'll be officiating at your wedding because he loves you. He's just a self-destructive asshole under a lot of pressure. Give him a few days to regret it, and go to him. Tell him how you feel."

No way. I shake my head and take a drink from the bottle, handing it back to my brother, who happens to be a liar.

"It doesn't have to be this way, Jessie."

"It does."

"But you love him."

I do, but I'm shaking my head. "I overheard you talking in the kitchen. I'm a convenient fuck. Not even a friend."

My brother makes a distressed little noise. "He lied. I shouldn't have pushed him, but he shouldn't have said that. Trust me, it's not true."

"He told me to leave," I say flatly. "It's over. You need to get over it."

"He's scared." Timothy insists.

I want to scream, but I'm afraid I'll never stop. "Why is it none of you ever listen to me? Gimme that." I snatch the bottle back from him.

Timothy shakes his head at me, staring at my closed curtains long enough I suspect he's fallen asleep with his eyes open.

"Nic loves you."

I jump.

Timothy continues with certainty in his voice. "You know how after his divorce he screwed around a lot?"

Oh my god. The laugh that rips out of me is unexpected and it hurts. Or maybe the pain is because Nic will be back to screwing around soon. My insignificance shoved in my face with every single tabloid.

"Surprisingly, Timothy, this is not helping." I take a big swig of whiskey, coughing at the burn as I set it on the coffee table.

"Do you wanna know why he stopped?"

"Chafing?"

He laughs. "Hey, welcome back, humor. Glad to see Sad Sack Jessie hasn't completely smothered you with her bullshit."

I don't want to think about Nic sleeping with other women. Before or after me. "The door is right over there."

Timothy ignores my pointed remark. "He lived with me during the divorce, so I saw a lot. Heard a lot, actually."

I groan, putting down the bottle so I can place my hands over my ears—not that it's enough to block out his voice. "I don't need to hear this."

"You do. Because when you called on our birthday, he was there. I put you on speaker. You should've seen his face. It was like a bomb went off. After that, he stopped."

My hands drop away. I remember almost nothing about that conversation, except when Timothy answered the phone, I sang him an insulting version of Happy Birthday. "Correlation does not equal causation."

"Don't throw your big words at me." Timothy elbows me and grabs the bottle. "You weren't there, you didn't see his face. Ask Mina—that phone call made her a believer."

I'm crying now. Or laughing. It's a twisted combination of both and my throat feels raw, but I can't stop. "Why is it so important to you that Nic and I get together? Can't you just...leave us alone?"

"Because I made sure he'd never leave me for you."

I grab the nearest throw pillow and smack him with it. He easily blocks it with his arm.

"You're a dumbass," I say, dropping the pillow onto the floor.

He nods. "Yeah. But so are you."

I have nothing to say to that.

Timothy always has something to say though. "We both had a crush on him, but he had feelings for you. So I kept you two apart. Stirred shit between you. Made it impossible for him to ever ask you out."

I want to hit him with the pillow again, but I can't make myself reach for it. "Nic needed a friend. He was always going to choose you. I just wanted my best friend back." I smack his arm. "That's you, so you know."

Timothy slings an arm around me and pulls me in for a side hug. "I'm a dumbass."

I sigh. "Me too."

"Maybe because we're twins."

"Mom's fault." I agree.

"One hundred percent." He releases me. "I never tried to fix things between you and Nic. I had dozens of excuses—you two were adults and could figure it out yourselves, or it wasn't my fault because I was young, or it didn't matter because we were in LA and you were in New York. After Camden and Addison, I realized my selfishness messed up your lives. Then I nearly died and fixing things between you became something I needed to do. If I didn't believe with all my heart that you two are perfect for each other, I'd have let it go. But I ruined something that could have made you both happy."

"So," I say when he falls into silence. "You forced him to come home for your wedding."

He nods.

This time I make the effort to grab the pillow and I hit him full in the face. "We got together without your interference."

That makes him smile. "Maybe. Or maybe I'm just that good."

"You're not."

His head drops. "I'm not. But I do know he loves you and has for years. Hell, he broke you and Camden up."

"And turned around and proposed to Addison." It should piss me off, but the booze and all the crying have worn me out. "He doesn't love me."

"What did he say to you, that Thanksgiving?"

I rub my aching eyes. "He told me not to marry Camden."

"Jessie"—he grabs my arm, a smile on his face—"he told you that."

"He married Addison."

Timothy's excited now, latched onto this alternative universe he's creating in his head. "He wouldn't tell me what he told Camden, so I emailed him and—"

My jaw drops. "You emailed my ex?"

"Yeah. And Camden told me—"

"Timothy! You can't email my ex out of the blue and ask him stuff like that! What the hell is wrong with you?"

"Jessie, you aren't listening. Nic told Camden that he loved you, that he'd never stop loving you, and that he would end your marriage—"

"Yeah, that's what you do when you love someone. You ruin their life." Sarcasm drips from my voice.

"Did it ruin your life?"

"No." Not the point.

"What happened the morning after Thanksgiving?" Timothy asks abruptly. "Before you and Camden left."

He was a hungover wreck, thanks to Nic and Timothy. "He was sick, and I looked after him."

"You were curled together on the couch when I woke up. Nic saw the same thing I did and assumed you'd made your choice. He went home and proposed to Addison, figuring Camden would propose to you, and he needed to move on with his life."

"That's ridiculous, but you should look into becoming a screenwriter for a soap opera."

Timothy makes a soft snorting sound. "Camden was pissed, by the way. Said after he heard about Nic's engagement, he tried to call you a few times."

That much is true. I ignored the first few calls, and when he kept calling... "I blocked his number."

Timothy shakes his head. "He wasn't good enough for you."

"Nope." I pop the *p*.

"Nic is, even if he doesn't believe it. You should talk to him. He's too torn up from the past year, but if he knows how you feel, he'll open up. Promise."

I don't bother pointing out that he can't promise that. "What about me?"

Timothy's brows furrow. "What do you mean?"

"I can't face any more rejection, not from him." It sounds petulant, but I don't care. I'm halfway drunk and all out of fucks. Oh, and Nic said out loud to my dumbass brother that he doesn't want a relationship with me. He said it again to my face. I don't need to make him repeat himself a third time.

Timothy looks stumped. Finally, he laughs bitterly and rubs the back of his neck. "You two are impossible. Still got that sofa bed in the office?"

"No."

"I'm not leaving you alone tonight. Nic's my best friend and I love him, but you're my sister. I love you too. We all do. I think right now you need to hear it."

He might be wrong about everything else, but he's so right about that. "I don't want Nic to lose you guys. No matter what."

Neither of us speaks for a long time, but we continue to pass the bottle back and forth. I'm well and truly drunk when Timothy clears his throat. "He loves you."

Does he think repeating this to me enough times is going to make it true? Timothy and I are going to fight about this until we're both old and in a nursing home. "I got rid of the sofa bed. You can take my bed." He can't drive after the amount of whiskey he's downed.

He eyes me critically. "You're going to pass out hard on the couch?"

I nod. I'm smaller than he is and haven't put my body through the shit he has, so one night on the couch won't kill me. "Sheets are clean."

"Am I going to wake up with a dildo up my ass?"

Like I leave vibrators under my pillows and lose them under my blankets. "Only if you put one there. In which case, you can keep it."

He laughs, getting up and heading for the bedroom. "Good night, weirdo."

"Hey, Timothy."

He turns, leaning on the wall. He relived his accident today. It's a shadowy fear in his light brown eyes, and I understand why he blew up at me.

"He's going to be okay," I say softly. "And so are you."

My brother takes a shuddering breath. "Today scared the shit out of me." He pushes himself off the wall. "You're going to be okay, too, sis. This is all going to work out between you and Nic. I promise."

I nod. I don't believe him, but I can't bring myself to take that away from him. "Leave the bottle."

He laughs. "Not a chance."

Chapter Thirty-Two

Nic

December Twenty-seventh

A lump of fucking plastic wouldn't hurt this much, but that's all I was to her. Jessie. Addison. Probably every woman I've dated or slept with.

It's just sex.

Hadn't I told myself that? I told Timothy that's all it was, but hearing Jessie say it? Wrecked me.

It's just sex because I'm not worth anything more.

I want to go home.

"Nic?"

Celia nudges my arm and I finally open my eyes.

Jessie's bear is tucked under my arm—Celia must have brought it back. I hand it to her and she pushes it against me.

"I don't want it," I mutter. My head hurts, but it's a dull pain. I'm a little groggy still, my thoughts half-formed shadows in a fog that won't clear, but I know what happened.

Jessie was leaving me.

"You'll take this bear, Dominic Oliver Fontana or so help me god—"

In all the years I've known her, Celia has never full-named me. I snatch the bear and set it on the bedside table.

Celia sighs. "My daughter gave you that."

"Why are you still here?" It can't be much later than seven. She must have spent the night in that chair instead of going home like I told her to.

"Sweetie, you're hurt."

"I'm fine."

She snorts.

I'm not fine. Physically, I will be. The concussion is mild and in a few weeks, the headaches should be gone. I could have gone home if Celia would've let me.

Being in this hospital is making my skin crawl, but I haven't lost it like I did after Timothy's accident. I'm starting to think that my panic that day had more to do with the sheer terror of potentially losing him than with actually setting foot in a hospital for the first time since my parents' deaths.

Regardless, the urge to get up and walk out is only kept in check by the strong likelihood the Celia will physically fight me to keep me here.

An hour or two after breakfast, the doctors discharge me, advising me to rest.

Because my agent would want me to, I sign autographs for the staff on duty and a few patients too. Someone asks me to make an unofficial visit to the children's ward, so I do that. I'm delaying, building some distance and a protective layer over my heart because when I get home, Jessie will be there. I'll have to talk to her.

The bear with the little yellow cape is in my coat pocket as I climb into the back seat of William's car. Celia's quiet and William doesn't turn on the radio. Timothy's had a few concussions, so they know the routine. They're keeping things quiet for me.

Evie and Liam give me hugs when we arrive. Amanda and Hazel too. Everyone's quiet and subdued, and I don't know if it's out of concern for my headache or because of my fight with Jessie.

Jessie doesn't come to the door. She doesn't make an appearance after I'm ensconced in a chair by the fire in the great room. Celia sets me up with blankets, pillows, and a tray of cookies and coffee before leaving me alone.

Not alone, I guess. I still have the bear. Celia stuck him on the tray and Evie named him Captain Bearington. I stare at him. He stares back, black eyes shining and empty.

I love Jessie. Might have been nice to realize that before she broke my heart, but maybe that was the only way I was ever going to know. Wish she'd come down so we could talk about this. Maybe she's waiting for me to come to her.

Angry voices rise from the kitchen—Timothy and Celia.

"Pull your head out of your ass—she's hurting!" Timothy exclaims.

"She left him!"

"Because he—" Timothy's voice drops abruptly and I can't hear what he says, but I don't need to. They're talking about what happened between me and Jessie.

"No." Celia's voice is incredulous.

"Nic hurt her and you took his side—" Timothy's voice drops again.

Fuck. This is all my fault. I don't want to cause conflict between any of the Foleys. I know I hurt Jessie last night. She hurt me first. But that hurt should've ended with us and it didn't. I've made such a mess of things.

There's no way I can sit here. I get up and walk quietly upstairs to my room. After a moment's indecision, I go through the bathroom and knock softly on the door to Jessie's bedroom.

There's no answer.

I push open the door. Her room is exactly how we left it, but her suitcase is gone. She's gone back to New York.

It's over. Jessie told me what she wanted and now I should go too. I can't stay here and cause more problems for the Foleys. Maybe we just need a little time and space, all of us. I book a flight to LA. A car to and from each airport. By the time I finish packing, my head is pounding. I want to crawl under the blankets on Jessie's bed and sleep for a week.

There's a knock on my bedroom door. Timothy doesn't wait before walking in. His eyes land on my suitcase, sitting open on my bed. "Really?" he says in a flat voice. "You're running away too?"

"I'm going home."

Timothy drops onto the bed with a sigh, falling onto his back and rubbing his eyes. "I'm pissed at you right now."

I fucked up, and now I have to face the consequences. I take a deep breath and brace myself. "My ride will be here in twenty minutes. Say what you need to say."

"Jessie overheard you calling her a convenient fuck."

I shrug. "She called me a sentient sex toy."

Timothy groans. "The hell is wrong with you two?"

A lot, I suspect.

He stops rubbing his eyes, resting his hand on his chest as he stares at the ceiling. "You tell her boyfriend you love her, you tell her not to marry him, then you run off and marry the worst woman on the planet, and when you're finally free and you have a shot at something with Jessie, you trample her feelings then leave when she lashes out at you."

It's not that simple. Nothing ever is.

He sighs. "For once in your goddamn life, you need to make a decision. No more playing around with her feelings. Either you love her, or you let her go."

I close my suitcase and wheel it over to the door.

"Nic," Timothy says my name in warning, sitting up. The look on his face is one I've never seen before. It's dark. Angry. "Do you love Jessie?"

My stomach flips and I lie. "No."

Timothy pushes to his feet. "Camden walked away at the first hurdle too. Looks like neither of you deserves her."

I agree, so I say nothing.

"And another thing," he says, joining me in the door. He stares at me for a minute, like he's struggling with something. "I love you like a brother, but—" he kicks me in the shin. Even though he's not wearing shoes it hurts enough that I hop onto my other foot, which makes my head scream.

He stomps off. I give him sixty seconds, then follow.

Mina's waiting for her turn at me at the bottom of the stairs. If she wants to knock my head off my shoulders, I don't care.

"You helped me work things out with Timothy," she says in a quiet voice. "I can help you. But you have to stay. Give Jessie a little space, then go talk to her—you don't even have to jump off a building to impress her."

"No."

Mina takes a tiny step toward me and reaches out. "Nic—"

"I don't love her!"

My voice echoes and for a moment there's nothing but the pounding of my pulse in my skull and I wince, raising my hand to my head.

"Oh, honey."

There's pity in Celia's tone as she walks into the foyer. Amanda is with her. William too. But their expressions are closed.

"If you're going to lie to yourself," Celia says, "you should go."

I glance at Amanda, but she looks away. When I turn to William, he nods and puts a hand on Celia's shoulder.

"No," Mina says, stepping between me and everyone. "We can fix this, they just need to talk—"

"Let it go, baby," Timothy says, pushing past his parents and older sister. "Nic needs to decide for himself what he wants, and there's no place like the Fortress of Purgatory to reflect on all your fuckups."

I can read it in his eyes. I'm not welcome here anymore. There's no redemption for the hurt I've caused.

"It is an ugly house," Mina mutters.

"Hideous." Amanda agrees.

Celia makes a sound that might be a suppressed snicker, but it could be a sob. "We love you, honey, but go sort your shit."

I go.

At the airport, I open the family group chat. I've been a part of it since the day Amanda formed it. I've seldom contributed, but it's been there when I've been lonely. Amanda and Hazel posting pictures of the kids doing various sports, Celia filling the chat with recipes and memes, Timothy lobbing chaos, and William's occasional dry remark. Jessie's snark.

I type what I should've said when I walked out the door.

Take care of her.

ME

Then I leave the chat.

CHAPTER THIRTY-THREE

Jessie

I'm heartbroken and hungover. Timothy made me breakfast before he went back home, but other than that, I haven't left the nest I've built on the couch. But I have my phone and I've been texting with Lauren. I filled her in on everything. She's been supportive, even offering to come back to the city early to keep me company. I turned her down. For now, I'd rather be alone.

> Let's FaceTime and watch Love on the Line and talk shit about it. It's the perfect distraction.

LAUREN

I could use a distraction, and our cousin Ashley is this season's villain on the popular reality TV show.

> Let's do it.

ME

I venture from my nest long enough to secure popcorn and a cup of tea. Lauren video calls me as I'm settling back in.

"I haven't seen Ashley in at least ten years," I say as I cue up the first episode. "You?"

On my phone screen, Lauren shrugs. "The odd funeral or wedding?"

My parents and Ashley's parents hate each other. My dad never liked his younger brother, and after Uncle Jonathan sold my parents out to the tabloids back when I was a teenager, they stopped speaking.

Ashley is five years younger than me, but I remember her as a child following Timothy and Nic around. The hearts in her eyes whenever Nic glanced her way. The wheedling and pouting she'd pull to get her way—mostly with my parents.

After the tabloid thing, Ashley still came around, off and on, for the odd big family holiday party, but we never really spoke beyond a little small talk.

Lauren and I watch a couple of episodes, but snarking back and forth about the show doesn't distract me from the ache in my chest and I bail halfway through the third episode. It's impossible to appreciate Ashley's full embrace of villainy when my thoughts keep drifting back to Nic. Is he home from the hospital by now? Will he go back to LA or finish out his stay at my parents' house? Is there a small chance in hell he's changed his mind and he'll come here?

I know the answer to that one and it's no.

Honestly, I need to wallow in self-pity by myself. This hurts so much more than anything else ever has. But this time, when I go full broken-hearted-stereotype like the basic bitch I am, I'm going to do a better job with personal hygiene. Not a great job. Just better. Flossing? Don't know her. Makeup? Who's that? But deodorant? We've met. Shampoo? Besties. I'm going to eat vegetables too. I will drown them in cheese sauce but I will eat them.

I'm going to survive this. I have to because Nic's always going to be in the picture. So instead of doing what I want to do, I drag my hungover ass to the shower, put on real clothes, and stand in front of my Fuck It Closet, ready to confront my past. Sort of.

I left my paints at my parents' house, but I have more stuffed in this closet. As much as I don't want to dig through all the crap I've tried to forget about, I want to paint.

At least I found my way back to that again, thanks to Nic.

I open the door and the universe shits on me, everything spilling out, burying me in an avalanche of art supplies, old clothes, and god knows what else.

Well, if this isn't a metaphor for the mess that is my life. Except I can clean this up in half an hour. Fixing my life...

It feels impossible.

Like a masochist, instead of putting the old Christmas gifts from Nic back in the closet, I line them up.

The How To Paint book.

The jelly bra inserts.

A bottle of jellybeans labeled Bitch Pills. The jellybeans are long gone, victims of my lack of willpower when I needed a sugar hit.

Warwick's leather pants from the first movie—I'd put rubber gloves on before pulling them out of the box, complaining I didn't want anything his sweaty balls had touched.

The year after that, he was modeling underwear and signed a pair of white briefs for me and I'd threatened if he ever gave me something like that again, I'd make him eat them. After I got Timothy to wear them.

The very first gift I ever got from him is inside the Bitch Pills bottle. I'd tucked it in there when I'd moved into this apartment. It's a silver necklace, simple with a little infinity symbol. I've never been big on jewelry, but looking back...it's sweet for a fourteen-year-old boy.

I pick up a still-wrapped Christmas present in shiny gold paper.

The year Nic brought Addison home, I'd left before we opened presents. Timothy had brought all mine over later. I'd stuffed this one from Nic into the closet without opening it.

I should stick it back in the closet. There's no point in this little depressing journey of Christmases past. But I'm feeling emo so I might as well add to my pain. I rip it open.

It's a notebook. The paper is thick, made for watercolors, but instead of the plain black cover, like all my others, this one is a rich, buttery leather in a deep coral shade. I flip through it, and a small inscription on the inside of the front cover catches my eye.

I'm sorry. -N

He was sorry about Camden, I suppose.

I'm sorry I didn't turn Nic down in the laundry room.

That's not true. Even though it hurts, I'm not sorry about the time we had together. Only how it ended.

The presents go back into the closet—everything except the notebook—and I break out my old paints. Some of the tubes have dried out, but most of the pans are still good.

My work stuff is shunted into a corner as I turn half my home office back into the art studio it used to be.

Armed with a coffee and a sandwich, I sit down, grabbing a sheet of watercolor paper. I try to sink my pain and let it flow through the brush, but there's too much. I paint anyway.

After a while, I grow sick of practicing shapes and techniques. I grab the notebook, open it to the first page, and paint a green glass bottle, turned on its side.

I'm so engrossed in the light playing over the bottle that I don't hear them knock. Or maybe they didn't knock at all. Knowing my family, that's most likely.

I pause, paintbrush suspended midair. I'm not in the mood for another lecture about hurting Nic's feelings, but the voices coming closer sound cheery. It's forced—I can hear the strain under their words, practically feel the desperation to stick to a happy topic. But why are they here?

Timothy pops in first. "You painting?"

Mina pulls him out of the doorway, giving him a push down the hall. "Go make the drinks. Sorry," she says to me. "This was supposed to be only us girls, but his FOMO wore out your mom and she caved."

"What's going on?" I ask, turning back to my painting. I can hear Mina take a few steps into the room, but she stops before she reaches me.

"We're here for you," she says simply, then pauses. "Finish your painting, then join us."

Mina leaves the room, and I put my brush down. My hand is shaking. I can hear my mom's voice, and Hazel's. Amanda too. Timothy clattering around in my kitchen. They're here for me.

My apartment's not big enough for everyone, and as I listen in, I can't hear Evie or Liam, or my dad, so I'm guessing they've been left at home.

Where's Nic?

Could he be here too? I run a hand through my hair, paint crunching in my tangled curls. Mina would've given me a heads-up, right? I'm not ready to see him again, not like this, but I want to. So bad.

I'm halfway to my feet when my door opens again and my mom walks in, carefully carrying a very full strawberry daiquiri. Her attention is riveted to the glass until she sets it on my desk. She wraps me in a hug. "I am so sorry," she says, sniffling into my hair.

It crushes me. He's not here, he doesn't want to talk, and he's not about to walk in and tell me he was wrong. But Mom's hug is warm and comforting, the familiar scent of her perfume eternal, and for once she sees my pain. She's here and I'm not alone.

I'm crying again because I needed this hug almost as much as I needed her to see me.

"I didn't realize," she says. "He's wrong and he loves you, but I should've realized you were hurting. You're not flighty, and I shouldn't have implied you couldn't work through the hard stuff. I'm sorry, sweetie."

I untangle myself from the hug and carefully lift the glass to my lips, taking a big drink, hangover be damned. I set it back down almost immediately because goddamn Timothy mixes a strong drink.

"You love him, don't you?" she asks softly.

I sigh and shrug.

My mom twists her fingers, looking upset. "He's gone back to LA."

Oh.

So it really is over. The last few shreds of hope I've been clinging to fall to pieces.

My mom stares at the wall for a long minute. "We kind of told him to sort his shit."

My fingers are trembling as they cover my mouth. Dammit. This isn't what I wanted. I never wanted him to lose my family. I only wanted them to see me too. To make me as big a priority as him. "He's all alone?"

"He needs to be," Timothy says from the doorway, his voice soft. "He needs to decide what he wants out of life and to figure that out, he needs to be alone."

I hope Timothy's right, but there's an easier option right in front of Nic. Go back to his normal—fucking beautiful women and badly delivering lines in movies.

"And you," Timothy says, "need to put yourself out there and try harder."

"Excuse me?" I narrow my eyes at him.

"You give up too easily. Fight for something for once."

I turn an exasperated look toward my mother, but she shrugs. "He has a point, sweetie. Look at your art, for example."

"I busted my ass for years trying to get somewhere. No one wanted my paintings. I didn't give up—I had nothing left to give."

"Maybe." She concedes. "If it stopped bringing you joy, then quitting is good. But it would be a shame if you let fear of rejection hold you back from something you loved."

"Or someone." Timothy adds.

I ignore that from Timothy.

It was more than a handful of galleries and they weren't all in New York, but she's close enough I have to concede the point. Maybe I burned out a little and lost my desire to create, but mostly, I've been avoiding having my feelings hurt.

"Come on," Timothy says, maybe sensing that they're pushing me too far. "Grab that drink. Let's get trashed and play cards." Maybe our twin language is back, a little different because we're different.

It's nice to have almost everyone here, to get sloppy drunk on cocktails. We play spoons and scrap over cards and talk. I tell them about the commission opportunity and they're encouraging, but they don't push me hard like they used to. We talk about family but instead of swapping the usual stories about Amanda coming to the rescue or Timothy's shenanigans or my mother's wild stories, they talk about me. The time I tested Timothy's homemade zip line and landed on Nic. The time Mom tried to set me up three times at the same Christmas Eve Folly so I turned it into a game show.

Mom's edibles and Muppet sex positions come up. Now that I'm older and wiser, I have a few amendments to my theories.

But over the evening, as we order too much take out and laugh over silly things because we're a bunch of ridiculous drunks, I feel like I belong. Maybe they're only here because Timothy spoke up on my behalf, but the fact that my twin saw that I needed this and made it happen when I couldn't means the world to me.

I should've spoken up for myself years ago—maybe I wouldn't have felt like such an outsider in my own family—but hindsight and all that.

They want me to come back with them and finish out the holiday, but I don't want to sleep in my bed when it smells like Nic and all I want to do is paint, so I pass.

Before they leave, I hear Amanda whisper to Timothy. "Did you see the family group chat?"

He pulls his phone from his pocket, checks it, and sighs. "I'll take care of it."

After they go, I hunt down my phone. Nic's left the family chat after telling everyone to look after me. Only Amanda and Timothy have seen it.

I want to text Nic, but I don't know what to say. I don't think he wants to hear from me. Instead, I open his notebook and fill it with little studies of our history together.

As little scenes from our past take shape on the pages, I can't hide the fact that Nic is it for me. I love him and maybe he doesn't feel the same, but if I never tell him how I feel, he'll never know. He deserves to know he was never a fling to me, and I need to face my fears and put myself out there.

It's terrifying, but the more I think about it, the more I realize I have to do this.

I book a flight to LA in ten days. I need the time to fill the notebook, collect my thoughts, and gather my courage.

Chapter Thirty-Four

Nic

December Twenty-ninth

A knock on my bedroom door startles me out of my sleep. "You'd better be dead, Fontana," a deep voice calls out as the door swings open. "You're fifteen minutes late."

Jax. My personal trainer.

I groan. "I have a concussion. Go away." I'd forgotten about Denise's plan. As far as Denise knows, I got in last night, not the day before. Jax and I are supposed to post one of the hellish workouts he puts me through to bulk me up for Warwick on social media, thus showing how committed and excited I am for this next movie while also feeding fandom. After that, we're meeting acting coaches.

"You're going to need a doctor's note," Jax says in that desert-dry tone of his. "Got one?"

"My phone is in my pants. Don't—" He turns on the light before I can ask him not to, and pain slices through my head.

"You look like shit." He comments, stepping into the room and rummaging through the pockets of the pair of pants on the floor. "A hangover won't get you out of leg day. A hangover—"

Gets me burpees. I know from experience. "I have a fucking concussion you monster." He finds my phone and hands it to me. I unlock it, pull up the email with the discharge instructions, and hand it back to him, rolling onto my stomach so I can bury my face in my pillow.

"You have a concussion." Jax announces in a monotone.

"No shit," I mumble.

"Need anything?"

Only Jessie. "Dark. Quiet." Despite Jax's best efforts at being the surliest bastard on the planet, he knows a lot of people in the business, including my agent. "Call Denise, tell her I'm not up to meeting with her later?"

"Okay." The lights flick off and the door closes softly.

I miss Jessie. I'd give anything to rewind the clock three days. Do it all differently because I keep messing up, over and over, every time I have to make a choice. The last time I saw her in the hospital, when her lip trembled, her eyes filled with tears, and I told her to go home. Out on the driveway, when we'd argued, and I'd lied. Before that, when she overheard me say to Timothy she was only a convenient fuck.

I'm almost asleep when it hits me. If she was bored, like she'd claimed, she'd have told me without feeling the need to sneak back to New York. If what we had was just sex, my saying as much wouldn't hurt her—she'd simply agree. If all she wanted was friendship, she might have lashed out at me for being a dick, but she was leaving, and she'd only leave like that if it hurt to stay.

I ball up my fist and punch my pillow. She has—had—feelings for me and I blew it.

The realization doesn't matter. Even if she still wanted me, I'll never be good enough for her. She deserves more than a burned-out no-talent mess. She deserves someone who knows from the start how lucky he is to get an ounce of her attention. Someone who will take the smallest chance she feels something in return and hand over his heart with no fear of messing it up.

I want to be that man for her. For me too. I want to do something to make me happy, to bring me closer to the people I love. Jessie's a big part of that, but her feelings toward me aren't something I can control. The rest of my life, though...

Last night when I couldn't sleep, I'd gotten up, walked to the guest bedroom, and pulled Jessie's painting of me out of the closet. I'd brought it back to my room, set it against the wall, and stared at it until my head throbbed.

I shift around until I can stare at it again.

Jessie's done so well for herself. Even if she didn't end up where she wanted to, the job she has utilizes her creativity and she seems to love it.

The only thing I love to do is bake. I'm not sure turning my hobby and coping mechanism into a job is the right thing to do—it might suck the fun out of it and I'll have nothing.

It's shit like this that causes me to freeze up. If I make a mistake, if I try my hand at this and fail—well, I'm famous so everyone will witness my failure. But doing nothing keeps me in a rut.

My head aches, so I nap for a bit. When I wake up, I feel better. Over reheated enchiladas—Angie's filled my fridge with food cooked by some chef according to my dietary requirements set by Jax, so in this case, enchiladas are heavy on meat, low on carbs, and all but missing the cheese—I grab a pen and a piece of paper and start a list. Ideas that would put me in a kitchen instead of in movies.

A number of options get crossed off immediately. I'm never going to work in a restaurant or catering—it's too fast-paced, demanding, and the hours suck.

I'm not sure about hosting a competition or doing a celebrity version.

Being on camera, like Celia...I don't know. I enjoyed making that demo pitch with her. Maybe with the right show, one where my purpose isn't to be eye candy...

So what kind of show would I want to be a part of?

I jot down a bunch of ideas, anything that comes to me, then reheat another serving of enchiladas. Sadly, there's no cheese in my fridge. No sour cream.

Dinner Rescues, I write. Then beneath it, *Dinner Fails*, when the natural yogurt and hot sauce I slather over my food fails to improve it in any way.

At least I have ideas. They might not be any good, but it doesn't hurt to pitch them at a place like the Home Cooking Channel or better yet, some streaming services.

Flipping the page, I make a quick to-do list.

Quit job/work out new ideas with Denise.

Sell house/move home.

Jessie.

December Thirtieth

I wake to the smell of bacon.

Seriously, too many people have the access code to my house. I roll onto my stomach—which is now grumbling—and vow to call the security company and have it changed. Who the hell is making bacon?

Something brushes my leg and I yelp, scrambling to sit up.

"Morning, sunshine," Timothy says casually, kicking me this time. He's leaning against my headboard, legs under my blankets, phone in hand.

My heart is hammering in my chest. "The hell are you doing here?" I ask, squinting in the morning light. Timothy has the codes for everything and comes and goes without ever feeling the need to explain anything as basic as why the fuck he is in my bed. That's not what I'm asking. I don't understand why he's here after everything that happened.

"You were talking in your sleep," he says, ignoring my question.

"Didn't bother your sister," I mutter without thinking. The pain hits half a second after the last word leaves my mouth, a heavy weight settling on my chest.

I miss her.

He glances at me over the top of his phone. "Pretty sure she'd like to hear the shit you were just talking about. Made me a little uncomfortable though."

I fall back onto my pillow with a groan.

"You love her." He says it in a quiet, confident tone.

I'm done denying it, done pretending I don't. "Yeah." I exhale slowly. "Why are you here?"

"You're my best friend," he says, sounding wounded. "You left the group chat and didn't return anyone's calls. We wanted you to go get your shit together, not ghost us."

"That's not what it sounded like." I dig the heel of my hands into my eyes. I know I'm being a dick. I was leaving them—they just agreed I should go.

"You aren't going to lose me or my family if things don't work out with you and Jessie. We sided with her because you were a jackass, but that doesn't mean we don't love you too."

"How is she?"

"Why don't you call her or fly home and see for yourself?"

I throw the blankets off and climb out of bed, pulling on yesterday's sweatpants and T-shirt. "I have some shit to sort out first."

"Good." He doesn't ask for specifics or give his opinions, and I don't need them. I'm going to make my own choices, unrelated to how anyone else feels about them. I'll probably mess up, but I seem to do that anyway. And it looks like I won't be alone. I still have the Foleys.

Everything wells up inside, threatening to burst out, but I'm done crying. It's time to sort my shit, not wallow in my misery. Been doing too much of that the last year.

Timothy gets out of my bed and comes to stand next to me, clapping a hand over my shoulder. "Hey. One other thing. I kept you and Jessie apart back in high school. Sorry about that."

I laugh and head for the kitchen. Does he think I didn't notice at the time? Timothy's never been great at subtlety. He wasn't willing to risk our friendship for his teenage crush on me. I wasn't willing to risk it for what I thought was a passing crush on his sister.

"She was off-limits because she's your sister," I finally say, because he seems to be looking for some response.

Timothy smacks my arm. "She's still my sister."

"Yeah," I say as we walk into the kitchen, "but now I don't care."

Celia drops the spatula on the counter, hurrying over to hug me. "How's your head? We love you, honey, we weren't kicking you out for good, we just wanted you to figure things out on your own, which it looks like you are." She zips back to the stove before I can answer, scooping up the spatula and deftly flipping a pancake. "I had a look at your ideas for a show," she says, nodding toward the notebook I left in the kitchen. "They're good. Do you need some help with any of them?"

Of course, she looked at it. At least her reading the list saves me from having to explain everything.

It might be good to get her input on my ideas since she knows this corner of the industry like the back of her hand, but I'm still not sure which to pursue or what sort of role I envision myself in—on camera or off.

"Not yet," I tell her.

"Oh, you left your charity painting at home, so we brought it, and—" Timothy picks something up from the bench and whips it at me. "How dare you abandon Captain Bearington?"

I catch the little stuffed bear on reflex when it slams into my chest. Guilt tightens my throat and I drop onto a barstool, setting the bear in front of me. I wouldn't blame Jessie if she didn't want to hear my apology. I don't know how to fix this mess I've made.

And I'm late getting my painting to that auction too. Shit.

The bear's cape is a little crooked, so I tug it back into place.

Timothy sets a cup of coffee in front of me and hovers near his mother.

I've thought about what I'll say to Jessie nonstop and nothing feels adequate. She'll slam the door on me and I'll deserve it. It's the right decision though. I'm done hiding from my feelings.

The smack of a spatula on skin breaks me out of my thoughts.

"Ow! Calm down, woman, I'm after some orange juice." Timothy protests, hands in the air as Celia holds him at a distance with her spatula.

"Like hell you are," she says, jabbing it at him. "If you so much as touch this bacon—and don't call your mother 'woman'!"

Slowly he steps closer, reaching for the cupboard where the glasses are. Of course, he's after the bacon. The moment Celia turns her attention away from him, he snags a piece off the plate and hustles to the fridge before she can whack him.

Celia flips a pancake onto a plate, cursing him under her breath while he pulls the orange juice out of the fridge and eats his bacon with a grin.

I shake my head, but I've missed this. I'm glad I haven't lost them. I can only hope I haven't lost Jessie too.

Chapter Thirty-Five

Jessie

January Seventh

I'm a nervous wreck on my flight. I'm shaking when my rideshare stops in front of Nic's gate in the hills and by the time she drives off, I'm nearly crying. Clutching my watercolor notebook for dear life, I take a deep breath. The late evening air is thick with the scent of unfamiliar flowers and trees and it's a hell of a lot warmer than New York. I tug at the collar of my sweater and press the button.

Nothing happens.

Either Nic isn't home, or he sees me through the security camera and doesn't want to talk to me.

"Shit," I murmur, pulling my phone out of my bag and calling Timothy.

Maybe I'm too late. It was a bad idea to wait so long just so I could paint through my feelings. I left three paintings for Gretchen with my boss, inspiration pulled from some of my sketches of Nic from the attic, from the scenes I painted of our lives. The figures on the canvases aren't recognizably us. They're not simply 'pieces of eroticism' either. There's something warm and glowing, tender and loving, in them. She might hate my paintings, but I'm putting myself out there again.

I painted a fourth, for Nic. It's in my suitcase.

My brother answers on the third ring.

"Nic's not home," I tell him, trying to keep the panic out of my voice.

There's a long pause. "Are you...in LA?"

"Yes, I'm in LA, outside his house, and he's not answering. I came out here to talk to him—what do I do?" It's Friday, a bit early, but maybe Nic has gone out. I've been watching the tabloids, and he hasn't been in them, but that doesn't mean he hasn't moved on. My stomach lurches at the thought. "Do you think he's—?"

Timothy laughs. "No. Stay there, give me a couple of minutes."

He ends the call and I have nothing to do but stand outside a celebrity's house looking every bit like a stalker.

This is not off to a good start.

Timothy calls back a minute later. "He has a meeting with his agent, then he's going straight to this charity auction. For now, I need you to go inside." Timothy gives me the code to the gate and I punch it in. Next, he gives me the code to the house. "Good luck making yourself at home," he says, and I can see why.

The foyer is cold, containing only gleaming white marble and a hideous chandelier.

"On second thought," Timothy says, "It's cruel to make you wait in that house. I'm sending someone over. Follow the instructions of every person who comes to Nic's house, unless you're unlucky enough to come face to face with a crazed fan, in which case, turn on the lights and every shiny surface in that ugly house will daze them enough for you to escape."

"Maybe I should wait—"

Timothy hangs up on me.

I spend a few minutes looking around the place. It's big and expensive, but everything about it is cold and imposing. One of those tricks of the uber-rich to let you know how powerful they are. The effect is sad and uncomfortable.

I don't peek into any bedrooms—if the door is shut, I assume whatever is behind it is private—and before long I end up in the kitchen. There's a single photo on the fridge of Amanda, Hazel, and the kids in their Christmas T-rex costumes, along with at least one hundred magnets, all different. Most tacky.

The doorbell rings, so I walk back through the house to answer it.

A tall Asian man pushes a garment bag at me and I take it reflexively. "I'm David," he says in a clipped tone. "And this is Meg."

I hadn't noticed the blonde woman behind him. She smiles and waves and we both follow David as he storms through the house.

A couple of times I catch the cringe on his face as he glances at the art on the wall or the hard lines of furniture not meant to be used.

"Did my brother send you?" I ask when David stops in the living room.

"I don't know your brother," he says, glancing at his watch. "My boss sent me, and Mr. Sinclair needs you ready to go in twenty-eight minutes. Meg?"

"Is there a guest room we could use?" she asks.

I don't know, but I lead the way. I hope Timothy is behind this and David isn't ruffling through Nic's underwear while Meg distracts me with her massive bag of—oh. She's a stylist and I'm about to get a glow up.

Twenty-five minutes later, I'm rocking a hell of a smoky eye, my hair has been brought back to life after being flattened on my flight, and I'm wearing a little black dress by an Australian designer I haven't heard of. And Louboutins.

I'm the daughter of a famous TV chef and I have a sizable amount of money in my bank account because of it. Everything I'm wearing I could afford to buy myself—I just don't. I get my clothes from thrift stores or quirky shops, and I like them to be comfortable. This isn't me, and I'm about to say so when Meg interrupts.

"This isn't about impressing a man," she says quickly. "There will be photographers outside, and this is about looking like you belong so no one will question what you're doing there."

"Doing where?" I whisper.

"The Hollywood Art Show and Auction," she says with a smile, pushing a clutch into my hands. "Put your phone in here, whatever you need. We'd better go."

David knocks on the door. "Car is here in two minutes."

I slip my phone into the clutch. At David's sharp warning, I hustle. Meg swipes everything into her bag and follows us out.

I arm the security system. As we walk out, a town car pulls up. The rear door opens and *Gabriel Sinclair* steps out, looking immaculate in a black suit.

"You must be Jessie," he says with a smile, extending a hand.

I've met a lot of famous people through my mother and I've never been fazed, but Gabriel Sinclair is dazzling. He has this golden aura about him that feels so...perfect. Nic's beautiful, but I knew him when he was a pimply teenager with barely any muscle. Gabriel Sinclair looks like he's never suffered through a pimple in his life. Like he was born from sea-foam, already formed and perfect.

It has to be fake.

I shake his hand and he ushers me into the car. I barely remember to turn and thank Meg and David, who are climbing into a separate car.

As the car winds through LA traffic, Gabriel explains that Timothy put him up to this. He had an extra ticket because his agent always gets two. He attempts to make small talk, but I'm too bewildered to manage beyond one or two-word responses.

I can't imagine my life like this. Trapped in Spanx under a dress that feels fragile, wearing shoes that are going to shred my feet, and traveling to some event where I'll be photographed.

If Nic wants me back, this could be my life. I'd do it for him. Take my job remote, or find a new one if I had to. Move to LA.

Gabriel is still trying to talk to me, more out of a sense of obligation, I sense, than any actual desire to chat, and I try to focus, but I can't. I'm on my way to Nic. My nerves are back to eating me alive.

Eventually, the car slows, then stops. Someone opens the door, and Gabriel climbs out first, offering me a hand.

"Follow my lead," he says, and holy shit. This event is a lot bigger than I imagined. There's a red carpet and photographers. Nothing like an awards show, but for a charity art auction?

Gabriel offers me his arm and I'm not sure if I should take it or not, but he did say to follow his lead and this is his world, not mine.

I wonder if Nic's here already. I'm anxious to go in, but Gabe stops in front of someone with a camera, answering his question with a smile directed at me.

"Oh, no. This is Jessica Foley—she's an art expert, and she's here to advise me tonight."

I'm not an expert. Barely more than a hobbyist, but I don't think I'm supposed to correct him. I don't know what I'm supposed to do. This wasn't a part of my plan.

My plan is Nic, nothing else matters. So I smile for the cameras trained on us and nod when Gabriel tells them I'm the sister of a friend. We go way back and I did not help him with his submission but he wishes he'd thought to ask me.

Did Nic stop and answer questions? I can't see him doing this. I've seen him on the red carpet when he attends award shows and premiers and he never looked uncomfortable, but he'd hate this. He's such an introvert.

Once inside, Gabriel releases my arm. "This is important, okay?" he says, making sure he has my full attention before continuing. "I made a point of the fact that we aren't romantically involved, but there might still be some speculation. It's best if you leave with Nic, but if things don't go the way you hope, you can find me and David will take you wherever you want—a hotel, the airport, wherever. Don't go rushing out the way we came in, especially if you're upset, because you will be connected to me, not to Nic, by the press. Okay? It's to protect us both," he adds.

I nod. Christ, I should've waited at Nic's place. Why am I doing this in public?

"Nic's at the bar," Gabriel says, motioning with his chin. "He hasn't seen us yet. Good luck."

For a moment I want to stay here, with Gabriel Sinclair, where it's safe and my heart is safe. Broken, but safe. That's old me though. Hiding from rejection by not trying. So I thank Gabriel and make my way to the bar. By the time I get through the crowd, Nic's gone.

Goddammit.

I snag a flute of champagne off a passing server and follow the flow of people through the crowded room into a glittering ballroom. No one pays me any attention and I ignore the pretty famous people.

Various paintings are displayed on tables along one wall, a form in front of each for the silent auction. I spot Nic's almost immediately and my heart swells even before I see how many people are bidding on it. Gabriel Sinclair's pencil sketch of a car isn't half bad, but Nic's painting has color and a certain moodiness. I look at each in turn. Some of the celebrities have more artistic talent than others, but every single one makes me smile.

The crowd moves into another room, adjacent to the ballroom. It's smaller and set up like a gallery. The paintings on the wall are by pros, and as far as I can tell, they're ones on loan from various celebrities and rich people. A few belong in museums, but a number appear to be commissioned art, and each one is a unique little look into people I know without ever really knowing.

Suddenly, I'm standing in front of a painting I recognize because it's mine. The little plaque next to it says *'Untitled by Jessica Foley, on loan from Dominic Fontana'* and the last time I saw it was when I tossed it on top of the trash.

Tears fill my eyes and I don't know what to feel. Upset I didn't know, crushed that I ever captured this vulnerable moment in the first place, stunned that Nic would show it to the world.

People around me comment on it as they move by. How moving it is, how they feel the sadness. One person remarks on the strength and how brilliant it was to leave it unfinished because grief is unfinished. Others remark that it looks like a young Dominic Fontana, or murmur approvingly. A few people walk by after barely glancing at it, and that's fine. Art is like that—not every piece is for everyone. But no one questions whether it belongs on this wall.

I need to find Nic. I spin around and run smack into someone.

Hands go to my waist, steadying me. It's Nic. I don't need to look up at his face to know it's him. My breath catches, all my hopes rising and lodging in my throat. I have to force my eyes up to meet his.

"Are you really here?" he asks softly. "Or am I daydreaming?"

His gray eyes are soft, his expression relaxed but in a practiced way that he's never quite mastered. There's an undercurrent of tension, a tiny furrow between his eyebrows. I step back to take him in, his arms dropping away as I do. He's so handsome, dressed in a black suit like Gabriel, but Nic makes it look like sin. "I'm here. I—" I wave my hand at my painting.

"Is it okay? I know it was a long time ago, and you never finished it."

"It's okay." It's more than okay. I doubt this will make or break me as an artist, but something I created is on this wall and people are looking. But I'm not here for this. "Is there some place we can talk?"

Nic leads me out of the room, back into the ballroom, and out via a different door. We exit onto a balcony overlooking the glittering lights of the city under an electric orange sky. We're not alone, but it's not crowded. I set my champagne glass on a nearby table. I've barely touched it. My stomach is already full of bubbles.

This is it. Now or never.

"I love you." I blurt out.

What the fuck, brain? This is not how I'd planned to start. I'm scrambling to remember what else I needed to say, what should've come first. I have no clue. Nic staring at me, his eyes wide and unblinking, isn't helping.

I open my mouth, and everything tumbles out. "I didn't realize until we were together, painting in the attic, but I think I've loved you for a long time. My feelings for you were always confusing and complicated, and I didn't like how that made me feel, I hated being the only one in my whole family you didn't like, so I made a point of disliking you but I never really did. I love you."

I have to pause to take a breath, but Nic doesn't fill the silence. Tears prick my eyes because he hasn't rushed in to say he feels the same, so probably he doesn't. This is going to end in rejection and humiliation, but I'm going to finish this anyway, and at least I'll know I tried. "I should've told you all this, as soon as I realized I was in over my head, but I was scared of what would happen if you didn't feel the same. When I overheard you and Timothy, it hurt. I had to leave before you or anyone else could see, but when you hit your head—" I sniffle, trying to hold back the tears. I don't want to remember this part. "I was scared I'd lose you for good, and I wanted to apologize and ask if we can be friends, and that's what I want."

Nic opens his mouth but I realize what I've just said and shake my head, quickly saying, "No, that's not what I want. That's what I'll settle for if you don't feel the same. What I want is you and I don't know what that looks like for us or how it works, but I want to try." There. I've said it. I take a deep breath and blow it out in a rush.

He's still staring at me.

I blink my eyes rapidly, trying to stave off the tears so I don't wreck my makeup. If I do, I'll have to escape over the balcony lest I accidentally embarrass Gabriel Sinclair.

Nic still hasn't said anything.

I'll have to force him to say something to put me out of my misery. "What do you want?"

He takes a step closer, his eyes locked on mine. Another step and he brushes his fingertips over my cheek. His next step backs me against the balcony railing and his lips press light to mine as one hand grabs a handful of my hair and the other slides over the small of my back, holding me close.

This might not be what I want, but it's not a rejection and all the tension that's been driving me falls away and I go limp in his arms. His kiss goes from gentle to demanding in a breath and I rest my hands on his chest. His heart is racing.

He breaks away to growl my name, but when he moves to kiss me again, I place my fingertips against his lips.

"I need to know how you feel," I whisper, trying to ignore the tremble in my voice.

Nic's hand falls from my hair to my waist, his head dropping until his forehead presses against mine. "I'm leaving Hollywood," he says softly. "I'm working on some ideas for what's next, but I want to be closer to home. I don't want to skate through life anymore, just letting things happen to me. I want to do the things that make me happy."

I nod and a tear finally breaks free, rolling down my cheek because maybe this is a rejection and that kiss was goodbye.

"Hey," Nic says, and suddenly he's cupping my face, tilting my head up so I have to look at the way twilight has softened his eyes. He brushes the tear away with his thumb. "I want to spend the rest of my life making you as happy as you make me."

The noise that bursts out of my chest is a messy sob-like creature, born of pure relief.

"I love you, Jessie." His thumbs wipe more tears away. "I always have, even when I didn't know it, when I took any excuse to fool myself into thinking what I felt was purely physical. I was afraid of what it meant for my place in your family. That I would disappoint you, and them. That I'd have to make choices I wasn't ready to make. I'm ready for that now. I want a life with you, back in New York. I want you with me as I figure out the rest."

"Nic," I move to kiss him, but he turns my head and my lips graze his cheek.

"Let's go," Nic says softly.

Chapter Thirty-Six

Nic

January Eighth

"I was a mess," I say, tapping the page with the painting of me curled around Jessie's stuffed unicorn.

Jessie takes a sip of her coffee and nods. She's wearing a blanket, sitting on my bed. We've only left my room to cook breakfast, and the discarded plates are stacked on the floor. I'm sprawled on my stomach, naked, flipping through the watercolor notebook I gave her five years ago. Every page is a memory of us—some happy, all complicated. Knowing Jessie loves me takes the edge off the harder memories.

"I was going to tell you how I felt when I came up to your room. I thought I had, that you understood me. But when I woke up alone and found you and Camden on the couch, I thought you'd made your choice. I'd lost my chance, and it was time for me to move on."

Jessie sets her coffee on the bedside table and lies next to me, draping the blanket over us both. "I didn't understand. Even if you'd told me you loved me, I don't think I would have believed you."

"I don't think I could have said those words. I loved you, but I'd lied to myself for so long. But I couldn't let you marry him. I'm sorry I caused you pain."

Jessie flips the page. The next painting is a bunch of mistletoe, and she holds the notebook over my head, leaning in to kiss me. "Our past is a mess," she says softly, "but our future is looking up."

With a little growl, I roll her onto her back and climb over her, kissing her neck, kissing her collarbone and her breasts, down her stomach. I don't come out of the blanket until I've brought her to orgasm twice. I have to crawl up to the bedside table to get a condom, and when I sink into her, she sighs happily and wraps her arms around me.

"Is that how you see me?" I ask, flicking my chin to the new painting hanging on my bedroom wall. It's the self-portrait I asked for, but her face is relaxed in a post-orgasmic glow and I'm there, in the reflection in her eyes. Staring back at her like she's everything. And she is. My past, present, and future.

Jessie's head tilts so she can look at it. "You're all I see."

I kiss her neck, working my way up to her ear. "I love you."

Her legs tighten around my hips and she pulls me tight against her. "I love you too."

We take our time, long and slow and sweet.

The rest of the day passes just like the morning, talking and making love. Jessie tells me about the paintings she sent to an art dealer. I tell her about my ideas for a cooking show. We talk about where we'll live—her apartment is too small—and future holidays with her family.

In the evening, she re-invites me to the family group chat, and from my phone, we send a picture of the two of us standing in the kitchen, my arm around her as she leans up to kiss me on the cheek. My face hurts from smiling. I've never been this happy.

My phone dings almost immediately.

> CAN'T WAIT TO OFFICIATE THE WEDDING

Timothy

My smile is gone. "Um...what?"

Jessie's eyes are adorably wide as I show her the message. "It was a bet. A stupid, stupid bet I shouldn't have made, but I didn't think you could love me. We don't have to get married—I'd understand if you didn't want to, considering..."

I kiss her on the forehead. "It's okay."

More responses flood in like everyone has been waiting for this. We read them together, huddled over my phone.

> We're happy for you two. Cute pic.

CELIA

> IT'S GOING TO BE EPIC

TIMOTHY

Mina sends twenty fire emojis and Amanda sends the same in hearts.

> PAY UP BEACHES—I CALLED METHOD AND TIMING OF ANNOUNCEMENT SO YOU ALL OWE ME.

> goddamn autocorrect. BITCHES.

HAZEL

> GOATS.

TIMOTHY

"Oh no." Jessie covers her mouth but laughs.

"He's made that threat before," I say with a wince.

> NO GOATS TIMOTHY

CELIA

<gif of a fainting goat>

Timothy

no goats.

Celia

<gif of a llama> ?

Timothy

"Christ, I'd rather deal with goats than llamas." I pull Jessie tight and kiss her temple. "Your brother is a menace."

"He'll bring a whole petting zoo." Jessie grumbles.

Mina, control your husband.

Celia

Yeah, come put me in time out. I've been a bad boy.

Timothy

Timothy, this is a FAMILY chat, not your personal space to sext your wife. Log off.

Amanda

"Okay, that's enough for tonight," I say, turning the notifications off and dropping my phone onto the counter. "I love your family, but they are unhinged."

"Yup," Jessie says, popping the *p*. "We're going to need to Timbo-proof our life."

I laugh. "Impossible. Now grab a seat. I'll make dinner."

Now that I no longer need to be Warwick-fit, my kitchen is stocked with a variety of food. Still, I want to make something fast. I settle for Tuscan chicken pasta because it's one of Jessie's favorites.

Instead of sitting down, Jessie hovers by the fridge, looking at my collection of magnets. Rearranging them. I have every kind of magnet on there, from letters of the alphabet to destinations to humorous little sayings. If I came across it when searching magnets and it wasn't something offensive, I bought it. I'm curious what she's doing with them. Sorting them, turning them into art.

Dinner is nearly ready before I stop what I'm doing to have a closer look at what she's been up to.

A large space has been cleared away, with a simple question spelled out with the alphabet magnets:

Nic

will you marry me one day

Her face is pink, her eyes shimmering. Her hands are clasped together, but that's not stopping them from shaking.

"I've been thinking," she says, taking a deep breath. "One day, when you're ready, if you're ready, I want to get married. I know I said we don't have to—and I mean it, we don't, I'll be happy so long as we're together—but I'd like to make you an official Foley. If you want." She winces and adds, "You don't have to take my last name."

I stare at her, still not understanding, but a warmth unfurls in my chest, spreading out. Her amber eyes are so open, so hopeful, and so full of emotion that I can't look away.

Jessie wants a future with me. One where we'll stand up in front of family and friends and vow to love each other through it all.

I swore off relationships and the idea of marriage after my divorce but it only takes a handful of refrigerator magnets to knock down all the bullshit excuses I put up in the name of self-preservation. It only takes a second of looking into her wide, beautiful eyes to know that I want to take her down the aisle and call her my wife and start a family with her, whatever that ends up looking like for us.

The whole thing leaves me floored, in the best possible way. It feels so right. I want it more than I've ever wanted anything. I want to make a home with Jessie and yeah, we don't need to get married to do that, but...I want goats at our wedding. I want our day to go down in Foley family lore. I don't give a fuck if her brother brings the whole circus. I want everything.

"It's too soon," she says in a rush. "Forget it."

I close the distance between us, taking her hands in mine. "We've known each other for twenty years. It's not too soon."

Her lips tip up into a hesitant smile. "It's not?"

"No." I sink on one knee. "Jessie, I'm ready. I love you, and asking you like this wasn't a part of the plan, but I'm all in. Will you marry me one day *soon*?"

"Yes." She pulls me to my feet and into her arms. I kiss her and she melts into me, and this, right here with her, is worth striving for. I will never take for granted all the little things that finally brought us here, to this moment. One perfect Christmas, and the promise of so many more to come.

"Sass and mistletoe," I murmur.

Jessie blinks at me, looking a little dazed but happier than I've ever seen her.

"That's what you were wearing in the laundry room." I remind her. "I'm going to need to know what other holidays you commemorate with themed panties." I pause to kiss her again. "Presidents' Day? Valentine's Day? Earth Day?"

She laughs. "Guess you'll have to wait and see."

I smile at her. "I can't wait."

Epilogue: Early Next December

Jessie

I can't sing with a candy cane sticking out of my mouth, so I hum along to the generic Christmas song playing in the background. I'm too nervous to paint and I'm caught up on work stuff, so I'm decorating the tree in the living room of the Upper West Side brownstone Nic and I moved into last spring.

All that's left is my vintage glass star tree topper, and I am woefully too short. Or our tree is too tall.

Gradually I bring my second foot up to the top step of the stepladder, wobbling for a second before I gain my balance. Even more carefully, I release my death grip on the handle and straighten. The stepladder is still sturdy beneath me, so I reach up, extending the glass star toward the apex of the tree.

Dammit. So close. But not enough.

I stop humming along to the music as I stretch onto my tiptoes. Almost there...

The front door opens and my heart shoots into my throat, but I only wobble a second.

"What are you—?" Nic's voice rises in alarm. "Jessie, get down before you fall."

No way. Victory is mine. I am so close. I shoot an *I know what I'm doing* glare at my husband.

Husband. It still makes me feel light-headed and bubbly to think of Nic that way.

There's a candy cane in my mouth, so I hum around it in what I hope he'll interpret as "I've got this." Except I'm not sure I do. My arm shakes and I cannot stretch any further and my balance on this stepladder is precarious at best and—

Nic's cold hands slide over my legging-clad hips, steadying me. My inward sigh of relief is cut short by the *mph* sound I make around the candy cane as he lifts me into the fucking air and I grab onto his head—it's the first thing I find with my free hand—to steady myself.

He grunts a curse that sounds distinctly directed at me.

There's no telling how long he can hold me like this, so I pop that topper on the tippy-top and thankfully it stays. If it's a little crooked—no it's not. I tap him on the head and make a noise around the candy cane that probably sounds like a soprano walrus in heat. For some reason this startles Nic, which is the only reason I can think of that he'd drop his wife.

Because I'm sensible, I'd tossed half a dozen throw pillows on the floor when I set up the step ladder, so it doesn't hurt when I land on my ass. I don't even lose my candy cane.

I give him an indignant look for dropping me anyway.

He laughs at me and I grab a throw pillow and whack his thigh with it, but drop it when he hauls me to my feet and into his arms. There's a dusting of snow on his wool coat and he smells like winter.

He pulls back to give me a stern look. "You couldn't wait for me to get home?"

I blink innocently and shake my head.

He wraps his fingers around my candy cane, pulling it until I bite down. His gaze heats, locked on my lips as he attempts and fails to gently pull the candy cane from my mouth.

"Jessie."

I love it when he says my name like that. Like he's about to lose control. I melt enough that he manages to yank the candy cane out, tossing it clear across the room, and before I can lecture him about our one-hundred-plus-year-old wood floors, his lips crash against mine and I forget everything that isn't him. The slide of his tongue and the way he grabs my ass sets off a deep pull between my legs. That warm, contented feeling of kissing my husband next to the glowing lights of our Christmas tree, in the home we've made together, fills me with happiness.

"You taste like Christmas," he says when he breaks free to shrug out of his coat.

"You taste like home," I reply, reaching for his pants and tugging his zipper down, dodging as he tries to nip my lips.

"We're not missing tonight," he says, stepping back after a moment.

My art.

In a gallery. A real gallery, not a Hollywood art auction. It's just one piece, but Gretchen Torres fell in love with the paintings I did for her, and it gave me the confidence I needed to send my work to a small gallery specializing in feminist art.

I'm terrified and trying very hard not to worry about the things I can't control. Like if anyone likes it or they all think I'm a hack who can't paint.

"We've got time." I insist. Two whole hours before we need to leave the house plus I need this right now, so I purse my lips in a pout and give him sad eyes.

Nic doesn't say anything as he glances at his phone to check the time and I hold my breath. But then he sets his phone on the coffee table and reaches for the thick blanket on the couch, shaking it open and letting it fall to the floor with all my throw pillows.

I keep my celebratory cheer respectable—my happy dance is more a shoulder shimmy.

"We aren't missing tonight." Nic repeats himself and I nod because I don't want to miss tonight, either.

"Come here." I pull him back to me with a big smile that makes it damn hard to kiss him. He moves to my neck anyway, hitting the exact right spot, and somehow, even though we don't separate for a second, he guides us down to the blanket on the floor, lowering his body to mine. I love the weight of him, the feel of his hips cradled in mine, the way we move together like our clothes don't exist.

Except they do exist, which is really annoying at the moment.

He leans back to help me out of my sweater and I help him with the buttons on his shirt as his lips find mine again. It takes a minute of fumbling, but together we get his shirt and my bra off. Then he's back on top of me, his skin warm against mine, his lips moving down my chin, my neck, my chest while my hands slide up his back and twine in his dark hair. He takes his time, leaving hot, wet kisses down my body to my stomach, until I'm aching, shaking with need. As badly as I want him, I'm not going to hurry him. I release his hair to adjust the pillow under my head and close my eyes, ready to enjoy every delicious second.

He hooks his fingers in the waistband of my leggings, pulling them down with a torturously slow speed I barely notice thanks to the almost-ticklish feel of his tongue. And then he stops.

Cool air rushes in where his mouth had been hot against my skin, and he laughs.

I lift my head and open my eyes, a smile already on my face.

"You're still hopeful," he says, brushing his fingers over the little mistletoe I drew on my skin with a sharpie, just below the waistband of my Christmas cookie underwear.

"About you?" I ask innocently, raising an eyebrow, my smile growing. "I'm certain."

He laughs then tugs my leggings and underwear off before pushing my thighs wide. "Are you saying I'm a sure thing?" His gaze sweeps down my body, stopping at my pussy. He licks his lips and my entire body goes hot and tingly.

"Yeah." My voice comes out breathy. "That's exactly what I'm saying."

He shakes his head, but lowers himself onto his elbows, grabbing a throw pillow and making me lift my ass so he can stuff it under.

"I am hopeful," I say as his warm breath caresses my inner thigh. He bites me, lightly, at the top of my thigh, the side of his face brushing my pussy and I hiss out a needy curse. "What we have is so" —he flicks his tongue slowly over my clit and I whimper— "fucking good, Nic, god—"

And then I can't say anything else, just his name, murmured like a prayer growing more and more desperate as he slowly brings me higher and higher. I cry out when I come, and again when he pushes inside me, filling me so perfectly.

He kisses me, tasting like me and maybe a little like that candy cane, and I think fucking under the Christmas tree might be my new favorite thing.

His body is softer now than when he was acting and I can't stop touching him, exploring him, like every time is the first time because I will never stop being fascinated by this man.

He grabs my ass, holding me tight while he fucks into me and I hold him tight right back, locking my fingers behind his neck and staring into those beautiful eyes. I can read every emotion that plays across his gorgeous face—devotion, desire, love, and a little bit of something that will probably always be bewilderment that somehow, we managed to get over all our bullshit to get here.

"I love you," he whispers, and as I whisper it back, I come again, taking him with me.

We lie on the blanket, wrapped in the afterglow and each other, admiring the Christmas tree from the point of view of a present too big to fit under.

"How did your meeting go?" I ask with a contented sigh.

"Good. We start filming in the spring."

Nic's pitch for a cooking show was picked up by a streaming service. It pits teams of students from various universities, each led by a celebrity chef, against one another in a cooking challenge to win prizes. The focus is on teaching easy, cheap, healthy meals using basic techniques that can be applied to a range of foods and cooked in a dormitory kitchen. Nic didn't want to be in front of the camera much, so he passed on hosting. He'll be among the celebrities on the rotating panel of judges, in addition to co-producing the show.

"How are you feeling?" I ask.

"Terrified, but I think it will be good."

"I think so too." And if it's not and he's unhappy, he can walk away. Whatever he wants to do, I've got his back.

"Oh, I got you something," he says like he's just remembered, reaching for his discarded coat and patting at it until he locates a pocket. He pulls out a small-ish box. "For the tree."

The box isn't wrapped, just held together by a thin gold ribbon, so it only takes a few seconds to open. Inside, cushioned on a bed of cotton, is a beautiful mistletoe ornament, a single pearl dangling from the top of the inverted wing-shaped stained glass leaves. It looks decidedly like something else.

"My first Christmas pussy," I say in a soft voice, holding it up so the lights of the tree twinkle through the glass.

"*Our* first Christmas pussy." He squeezes me tightly.

"The first of many Christmases to come," I say, kissing him. "I love you so damn much."

"I love you too." He kisses me back, nuzzling into my hair with a contented little sigh.

"Want to hang it on the tree? I'm sorry I didn't leave any ornaments for you to do."

He kisses me again and takes the ornament, standing up and looking over the tree for the perfect place—and giving me a hell of a good view of his naked body.

He finds a spot and hangs the ornament, turning to smile at me, happiness etched on his face.

I try to suppress the sudden giggle as I nod with approval, staring at his hips instead of the tree. "Well-hung, Nic. Well-hung."

He laughs, helps me to my feet, and together we head upstairs to get ready for tonight. Eventually.

The End

Sneak Peek! The Villain Edit

Want a peek at the third and final book in the Over the Top Love series?

Ashley Foley is the bad girl everyone loves to hate—a role she embraced long before a series of betrayals branded her as one of reality TV's all-time greatest villains. But now she's too toxic to get work and worse, she just watched the man she loves walk down the aisle with the wrong woman—again.

What's a bad girl to do?

Seduce the groom at the reception, of course.

But when the wrong man walks into the room, her plans blow up in her face.

Hollywood Golden Boy Gabriel Sinclair should have left that room the moment he sensed the trap. But getting caught with TV's bad girl might give him the edge he needs to hold onto his gritty superhero role in the face of a fandom that sees him as too much of a do-gooder to play their beloved morally-gray superhero. And Ashley's reputation could use his shine.

But fake dating means bringing Ashley on his cross-country road trip. She's a temptation he can't afford, especially once he realizes she might not be that bad after all. Because Gabriel Sinclair isn't the good boy he's been pretending to be.

THE VILLAIN EDIT is the third and final book in the Over the Top Love series and can be read as a standalone. This fake dating, road trip, celebrity romance features a starchy hero who isn't what he seems and an unlikable heroine on a reluctant path to redemption finding their Happily Ever After. It also contains explicit sex scenes and strong language.

Keep reading for a look at Chapter One of The Villain Edit!

The Villain Edit Chapter One

ASHLEY

I'M THE VILLAIN OF several stories, but mostly my own.

Maybe other people tell themselves they're the heroes of theirs, but there's power in embracing the truth. I'm at my best, truest self when I'm at my worst.

Take tonight. My cousin invited me to her wedding and I'm here to steal her man.

Any minute Dominic Fontana will walk into this boudoir-styled dressing room and see me draped seductively on a chaise in lingerie that reveals everything. I hope he'll see me, sweep me into his arms, and take me on this chaise, but I don't expect him to. I don't need him to. He only needs to be in this room with me for a few minutes.

He might not be happy, at first, but he'll come to see how much better we are together. I'm doing him a favor, showing him now so he won't discover it down the line.

We've had this connection since childhood, but our timing is off. I can't wait one year, or two or more, for this inevitable divorce. Something in my life has to change, and I'm afraid if I don't take this opportunity, the universe might not give me another chance.

I have nothing to lose. My career is effectively over after my season on the reality TV show *Love on the Line* and my extended family...well, they don't like me anyway.

Footsteps come down the hallway and stop at the door.

This is it.

There's a mirror on the dressing table, and I turn my head for reassurance. My platinum blonde hair is perfectly tousled, my lips are the perfect shade of *fuck me* red, matching the delicate lace of my lingerie. It was a bitch to put on, ribbons crisscrossing my body. Uncomfortable under my black dress.

Yes, I wore black to this sham of a wedding.

I don't look too closely at my reflection. If I don't see the slim shadow of fear in my eyes or the uncertain tremble on my lips, they don't exist. All I see is what Nic will see when he opens the door.

Me.

Hot as hell. Ready to commit a sin or two.

The door opens and I say a quick prayer that the tits I gave myself for my twenty-third birthday will keep him in the room long enough for this to work.

The lighting is dim, but the man moving through the shadows of the short hallway has a natural panther-like grace. Nic, for how incredibly hot he is, doesn't move like this. I don't think his shoulders are this broad either.

I sit up straighter, peering into the darkness. Something's wrong.

This isn't Nic.

Oh fuck.

The man steps into the light and sees me, his jaw dropping.

My eyes are burning with tears I don't dare shed. I am going to murder my assistant Lea so dead it will be like she never existed. *How could she mix them up?*

Gabriel Sinclair, Hollywood's golden boy, is staring at me like someone dropped a whole live squid on his plate and he's not sure if it's a prank.

Gabriel and I have never met, but everyone knows him. He rescues kittens from trees (twice) and helps old ladies with their shopping. *Literally.* It was on the damn news. He's an obnoxious do-gooder who manages to pull off the *I'm so much better than you* without opening his damn mouth.

He clears his throat as he tugs at the cuff of his suit, and it sounds like the universe slamming another door shut on my path to Nic.

No. I refuse to accept it. This still could work. They look a little alike—a *very* little. Enough that Gabriel Sinclair was cast as Nic's replacement in the Warwick superhero franchise. They're both white, but Gabriel's skin has a golden hue compared to Nic's porcelain. Gabriel's hair isn't as dark, his eyes are dark brown not gray, and he's a smidge bigger, his features a little stronger.

Gabriel Sinclair is also the kind of guy who needs six months of dating and a diamond ring before he'll take a woman to bed, only to fuck her in missionary. Once. With the lights off.

Nic would fuck a woman against the wall in a club without needing to know her name.

"I'm sorry." Gabriel's voice is deep. Plush. "I must have the wrong room. I'll—"

He starts to say *go* but stops.

He doesn't go. Of course, he doesn't. I'm the fantasy and he's the fly in my web. The wrong fly, but seriously, I think this might work.

"Stay," I say in a breathy whisper, sliding my hand over the soft velvet of the chaise next to me.

He's frowning, his eyes maddeningly stuck on my face when the rest of me is right here on display. Instead of sitting by me, he pulls a chair over and sits. He's at ease in his Tom Ford suit, leaning back, crossing his legs so one black leather wingtip shoe rests on a knee, looking for all the world like he's in control of the situation.

He's not and I want to break him. Mess him up. Leave him looking on the outside how I feel on the inside.

"What's this?" he asks, sounding tired. Worn. The perfect place for me to pick and pull until every thread holding him together is in a tangle on the floor.

Instead of answering, I take my time rising to my feet.

His gaze stays on my face. "Some woman claiming to be my assistant told me Gabriel Sinclair wanted a word with me in this room."

The seductive smile I've been holding in place falters and I catch it before it can break into a scowl. Lea is fucking *dead*. How did she not recognize him?

"But the thing is," the insufferable man continues, "*I'm* Gabriel Sinclair, and my PA is a man who went back to his hotel room two hours ago." For the first time, a bit of a smile crosses his lips. It's not a happy one. It's vaguely threatening, even. It's surprising on him and I like it. I'll tell him the truth. A version of it, anyway.

"I'm waiting for a man," I say. I still have my heels on and they make my legs look endless. I sway my hips as I move closer, but he still won't glance at my body. It's insulting.

"Me?" He sounds annoyed by the idea.

Same, asshole.

"No." I stop in front of him. He hasn't sat up any straighter, hasn't dropped his gaze down my body. Either this man has superhuman willpower, or he isn't sexually attracted to women. The tabloids have photographed him with women outside the industry, but those women could be paid decoys.

"So the woman who told me I wanted a word with myself—?" One thick eyebrow arcs up.

"Had nothing to do with me," I say with an innocent little shrug that bounces my tits—not that he looks.

His frown deepens as his eyes flicker over my face. "Have we met?"

I bend forward, placing my hands on his thighs and my lips inches from his, putting my tits on full display. The muscles under my hands tense and goddammit I don't need the little flicker of desire that inspires. They're just thighs. Thick and hard but not Nic's.

His eyes though. Now that I'm closer, I can see the lighter shades of brown dancing in the dark like flames around his dilating pupils. He has the kind of eyes I could drown in.

"We haven't met." I focus on his lips and unfortunately, he has a mouth made for all manner of sinful, despicable things. Not that he would ever do sinful, despicable things. "But I wouldn't mind becoming better...*acquainted*."

He laughs.

And then he moves.

His massive hands take mine, pulling them off his legs as he stands.

The man towers over me. I'm not frightened—Gabriel Sinclair wouldn't hurt a bug—but I am intimidated. This is going to be hard if he isn't going to play along.

"Lady," he says in that deep, serious voice, releasing my hands, "you need to examine your life choices."

He turns away, but I snatch his sleeve and pull him back. He tries to shake me off, but I hold tight.

"I'm not interested in whatever scam you're—"

I grab his tie, yank him down, and shut him up with my lips.

He's not Nic.

But he looks enough like Nic, and in this dim light, through the open window to the balcony across the courtyard where the photographer is hiding, the whole world will think I'm kissing Nic. My cousin Jessie will think I'm kissing Nic.

I'm getting my chance if I have to burn down the world for it. Gabriel Sinclair is collateral damage.

He grabs my arms, but he doesn't push me away. He doesn't pull me in or kiss me back. He makes a surprised noise and freezes, hopefully giving the photographer a few extra shots.

Ideally, Gabriel would take me over the chaise. I could close my eyes and pretend he was Nic for the two minutes it would take. Photos and grainy videos of that would have Jessie running for a divorce. But this is Gabriel Sinclair, so *of course* he won't even kiss me back.

When I pull away, he's looking at me like I've lost my mind. He's wearing more of my lipstick than I am. I've managed to muss his hair up, not to mention nearly strangle him with his tie.

I hum, satisfied.

It's done. We'll be trending on social media before we step out of this room, although I guess technically Gabriel Sinclair won't be. Not that he'll want to correct them.

He stays perfectly still as I walk around the chaise to retrieve my dress off the hook on the door. Maybe I've broken him.

That was too easy, no fun at all, really.

"What's your name?" he asks gruffly.

"Ashley Foley."

He blinks. Swears. A mild *dammit.*

I feign offense at the obscenity, clutching at my chest with a gasp. His eyes narrow. But yay! He knows who I am. It finally clicked in his empty head.

"Zip me." I turn my back to him and pull my blonde hair aside.

He ignores me, looking upset as he paces his side of the room in short bursts. "How close are you to the bride?"

Ugh. "We're cousins. Why?"

His hands are in his thick hair, making more of a mess than I did. He's talking more to himself than to me, so I let him ramble on as I do my zip as high as I can. Maybe it would be better if I came out half-zipped, looking freshly fucked anyway. I turn to the mirror to transform the mess I've made of my carefully chosen lipstick into something artful.

I only look at my lips.

"I shouldn't have come to this wedding." Gabriel is still having his boring existential crisis, muttering to himself. "How am I going to explain to Nic I'm taking a restraining order out on his cousin-in-law?"

I stop. "Restraining order?" That would ruin everything. "That's not necessary—"

He shoots me a filthy look. Not the fun kind. This kind says I am worse than a shoe-ruining pile of dog shit. "I appreciate my fans, but you just crossed all sorts of lines."

A wild laugh rips out of me, pushed by the surge of anger because I never wanted him in this room. I stomp up to him, but already his hands are up in the air. "I am not a fan of yours."

His look suggests he doesn't believe me but might play along in case I turn dangerous and honestly, I am *this* close.

I lean in and to his credit, he doesn't back away. "I despise you."

His glare intensifies. "Two minutes ago you were trying to suck my face off."

"I didn't enjoy it." I push past him for the door. My half-zipped dress is already slipping down, exposing the top of my lingerie. "If you'll excuse me, I have a party to—"

I open the door to a camera flash. A dozen camera flashes.

And I freeze. My heart pounds in my ears and I'm going to be sick. This wasn't the plan. Where did they come from?

The first volley of flashes stops and a second of shocked silence falls.

"Gabriel Sinclair?"

Stunned voices. Stunned voices saying his name, turning hungry. Rushing toward me, cameras flashing.

I'm yanked back into the room, the door is slammed shut and locked.

I stumble to the chaise and drop onto it.

Fuck.

Gabriel Sinclair, golden boy, says it out loud.

Acknowledgements

I started this book in early 2020 with a simple premise: a brother's best friend where the brother wants them to get together but they hate each other. I made the rest up as I went and it was the most fun I'd had writing, even if that first draft was lacking, well, a plot. It was so fun that I wrote most of it in something like eight weeks. It went through a few rounds of feedback with critique partners and beta readers before I tossed it into Pitch Wars—a contest where un-agented writers submit to traditionally published authors for a short-term mentorship before a showcase where agents can request your revised manuscript. Tricia Lynne (who writes amazing badass heroines and spice that will melt your face off so go read her books) chose my book, taught me how to give the book a plot, the characters an arc, and how to edit to a tight schedule. I wouldn't be here right now if it hadn't been for her. So Tricia—thank you for making me a better writer, for seeing something in that rough manuscript, and helping make it shine.

While this book went on to get an agent, it didn't sell on submission. It happens to a lot of books, but I didn't want to shelve this book and I wanted to tell Timothy's story (which had to be book one) and I was very excited about an idea I'd come up with for book three. So I decided to take some time off to pursue self-publishing, which meant rewriting this book again! And then another time because I messed it up. So extra thanks to my CPs, Maggie North and Alexandra Kiley for helping me iron out all my changes, for letting me bounce ideas around, and for letting me drape myself across that chat. You two are the best and I am forever grateful you put up with my nonsense and my messy first drafts.

Speaking of messy first drafts, Ingrid Pierce had a huge influence on this one, not only in helping me learn to write better steamy scenes, but also in countless DMs as we pantsed the hell out of our respective drafts. Thank you for the laughs, the feedback, and the encouragement.

I was lucky enough to snag some amazing beta readers for this book. Mae Bennett, Shannon Bright, Laya Brusi, Michelle Cruz, L.E. Foley, Chrissy Hopewell, Kara Kentley, Michelle Merritt, Nicole Poulson, and Kathryn Ferrer all took the time to read and provide thoughtful feedback. I appreciate each and every one of you for helping make this book better. Thank you!

I couldn't do any of this without the support of the amazing writing community. In particular, Kathryn Ferrer for all her moral support (that warm yogurt manifesting magic), Laya Brusi for all her help with self-publishing, and my RomDom Pitch Wars alums Regina Black, Courtney Kae, Maggie North, Nikki Payne, and Ella Sinclair. Thank you to everyone in the #FridayKiss community, as well. The weekly #FridayKiss prompt is always a highlight of my week.

Thank you to my family. Self-publishing isn't cheap and it's certainly time consuming and I appreciate all the sacrifices you've made so I can make this dream come true. I love you so much.

And last but not least, thank you to all the readers who've taken a chance on this book, who've read the first book in this series, or who've left reviews. You're the best and I hope you stick around for Gabriel Sinclair and Ashley Foley!

About the Author

Sarah Brenton (she/her) writes steamy, sex positive romance with strong characters getting dropkicked by love. She lives in New Zealand with her husband and kids and wishes she had enough time to write all the stories in her head.

Want to know more? Visit www.sarahbrenton.com, sign-up for my newsletter, and follow me on Instagram!

Also By Sarah Brenton

<u>Over The Top Love</u>
Love and Other Risky Business (book one)
Holiday Vibes (book two)
The Villain Edit (book three)